Circle at Center

"Douglas Niles is a master at creating strange and unique fantasy realms that make readers believe in the unbelievable. *Circle at Center* is a special work with strong appeal to fantasy lovers."
—*Midwest Book Review*

World Fall

"In this second installment . . . Douglas Niles so eloquently describes each circle readers will have a vivid visual image of each land. Fans of Tolkien and Brooks will love this epic fantasy and eagerly await the next book in the series."
—*Midwest Book Review*

"Niles has again conceived a fantasy setting of great richness and scope. His fans are sure to enjoy this sprightly tale."
—*Publishers Weekly*

Praise for the Watershed Trilogy:

"Douglas Niles and I worked on *Dragonlance* together. This book captures all the adventure and romance of *Dragonlance*."
—Margaret Weis

"The landscapes are sweeping and complete, and the various races are believable . . . new and exciting. The detailed pantheon of gods gives the readers a deeper and richer understanding and appreciation of the motivations of the characters. Any reader will come away from this book fully satisfied."
—R. A. Salvatore, bestselling author of
The Demon Awakens

"Douglas Niles . . . writes so well that his characters come to life after only a few lines. . . . This middle book . . . keeps the trilogy moving."
—*Starlog*

WORLD FALL

Book Two of the Seven Circles Trilogy

Douglas Niles

ACE BOOKS, NEW YORK

WORLD FALL

An Ace Book / published by arrangement with the author

PRINTING HISTORY
Ace trade paperback edition / September 2001
Ace mass-market edition / December 2002

Copyright © 2001 by Douglas Niles.
Cover art by Jean Pierre Targete.
Cover design by Rita Frangie.

Visit our website at
www.penguinputnam.com
Check out the ACE Science Fiction & Fantasy newsletter!

ISBN: 0-441-00998-0

ACE®
Ace Books are published by The Berkley Publishing Group, a division of Penguin Putnam Inc., 375 Hudson Street, New York, New York 10014.
ACE and the "A" design are trademarks belonging to Penguin Putnam Inc.

PRINTED IN THE UNITED STATES OF AMERICA

10 9 8 7 6 5 4 3 2 1

To Allison and David,

who have been more inspiration
than they'll ever know

Warrior's tear
on mother's breast,
Mother's fear
Of battle next;

Weapon's tale
on battered flesh,
Final nail,
To lasting rest.

From the Tapestry of the Worldweaver
Chronicles of a Circle Called Earth

Prologue

Nothing lives long
Only the earth and the mountains

Cheyenne Death Song

The infant was a week old, and still she hadn't cried. In all other respects she was a normal baby, suckling her mother's breast, eating and sleeping and waking in a steady cycle of new life. Hers was an existence of warmth and comfort, peace and security.

Sometimes she would open her eyes and look at the world through irises of deep violet. Then her mother, Spotted Fawn, would take her out of the smoky tepee so that she could see the sky, the plains, the horses, the creek, and the People.

"There goes Black Kettle," the mother whispered when he walked past, and the baby watched the great chief with an expression of bemused curiosity. He was a dignified old man, wearing a woolen robe and canvas slacks for, unlike the northern Cheyenne, who still dressed in furs and buffalo robes, the southern branch of the tribe had accepted many goods in trade with the whites who were becoming so prevalent in all the lands between the Arkansas and Platte Rivers.

"The white men gave Black Kettle a banner," Spotted Fawn sang, dancing a gentle shuffle as she carried her child about the large camp. "Stripes of red and white . . . the blue of the twilight sky, covered all over with stars . . ."

She sang to reassure herself as much as to entertain her child, although deep down she knew that she should believe that she had no cause to be afraid. Certainly her husband, Limping Wolf, felt certain that the tribe was safe in the camp on the sandy creek. He was gone now, buffalo hunting to the east with most of the braves, but he had reassured her before he left.

"We have moved the village here at the white man's invitation. There are People making war against them on the plains, but they are far to the north, or east in Kansas. Here, with the fort so close, we are safe. They have traded blankets and food with us and pledged peace to Black Kettle. You and the baby will be safe, and soon I will return with meat and buffalo hides, cause for celebration." He offered further assurances: the invitation to hunt had been extended by the army commander at Fort Lyons, who had reported a great concentration of buffalo in the east. And most of the whites were north, in the valley of the Platte River, or northwest, in the great city called Denver.

So Spotted Fawn fed her baby and tended her tepee and her fire, and waited through the chill days of the Moon of Rutting Deer. Still, she did not sleep well during these long, cold nights, and her disquiet was caused by more than the baby periodically stirring at her side. Often, during their three years together, she had spent nights away from Limping Wolf, but now she felt as though his absence created a chilly void, that the fifty miles of plains separating them might as well have been a vast gulf of time and space.

So it was that on this cold evening the baby fed, and burped, and then looked around with those curious eyes. Spotted Fawn wrapped her child in a deerskin blanket of the same dappled fur as her namesake. With a woolen shawl over her own head, she held the baby before her, ducked through the flap of her tepee, and went for a walk about the bustling village. Fires smoked and flared in the early darkness, and she heard boys shouting among the ponies gathered on the other side of the creek. Her own breath frosted into vapor, but the baby, cloaked and held against her, remained snug and warm.

She came to a fire where three women, the Walking Moon sisters, were seated, and they invited her to join them. Spotted Fawn seated herself and let the welcome heat from the coals caress her face and hands.

"I will dream tonight of White Feather," said Red Moon, the youngest of the sisters, speaking of her new husband. "And tomorrow he will slay the chief of the buffalo, and bring me his tongue!"

"Is it just the *buffalo* tongue that you miss?" White Moon asked bawdily.

Spotted Fawn and Crescent Moon giggled as Red Moon swung a careless slap at her older sibling before she, too, convulsed with laughter.

"Truthfully, these nights are too cold while the hunters are away," the new mother suggested. "Even a small tepee seems too large for just the child and myself."

"Has her infant name come to you yet?" asked White Moon.

Spotted Fawn shook her head, unconcerned. There would be plenty of time for a sign, some revelation to show her what this infant should be called during her childhood, for the thirteen years before she was granted her true life name as an adult woman of the People.

The baby wiggled and fussed, but though her movements were strong, the sounds of her voice remained soft and muted. She opened her eyes again and looked at Spotted Fawn with an expression both mystical and wondering. A flare of firelight reflected in those eyes, deep and multifarious, as if it possessed the wisdom of many generations.

"Agate . . . your eyes are like the purple stone that fires with sunlight," whispered the young mother. "But your eyes spark in the firelight, in the night."

And that revelation had come. "I will call you Agate-in-the-Night," she whispered, nuzzling her nose to the little girl's face. She looked to the sky and saw the flash of a shooting star. Clearly the name was right.

Later, as she was making her way home, she came to a big fire, where several men were gathered in conversation. One of these Spotted Fawn recognized as Gray Blanket Smith, the trader who had come out from the fort a few days before. He had set up his wagon on the fringe of the village, and though he spoke the People's language only crudely, he was welcomed by the Cheyenne throughout the camp.

Three warriors, among the few who remained with the tribe while the rest went hunting, were seated around the fire with Gray Blanket. She recognized one, Buffalo Roars, and remembered that he had broken his hand a few weeks earlier; he would not be hunting again until spring. Several older boys were also near the fire, and a few other people watched and listened from the nearby shadows.

Spotted Fawn checked the baby, saw that Agate slept soundly. What could it hurt to linger here for a bit? News was scarce, and she was curious as to what the thick-tongued trader was saying.

"Yes . . . it's a good thing you're here, near the fort," Gray Blanket Smith declared. "There's a new soldier, Chivington, up in Denver. He's raised an army of volunteers, plans to make war against the bad Indians. And he's a fierce one. Black Kettle is a wise chief to stay here."

"What about the knives?" asked Buffalo Roars. "You said you would bring them when next you came to us."

"Ah, and I will," the trader answered breezily. "Shiny steel, sharp enough to split hairs. My boy will bring them out here any day now, so long as you all stay put."

"Why does it take so long?" asked another brave.

Gray Blanket shrugged. "You gotta know, this big war back east, that's taking most of the country's attention. Out here in Colorado, we're real low on the list, so to speak."

There was more, though Spotted Fawn couldn't really understand many of the words. Still, it was enough to know that the trader was still here, that he planned to stay for a while. It made her feel a little ashamed to know that her husband's soothing words had not been enough to calm her fears, but she had been worried. An uneasy voice of concern had been whispering in her ears since before the baby had been born. She didn't trust the whites, but neither did she believe they would send a trader if they weren't interested in peace.

Back in her own tepee, she still found it difficult to relax. As the baby slept, she lay in the dark, snug and warm but still anxious, even frightened. Sleep, with a stealthy approach and a patient, relentless attack, finally took her, but then the fear rose within her dreams. In those dreams she was running, but she couldn't escape the nameless, terrifying thing that pursued her.

Agate-in-the-Sun opened her mouth and uttered a single, piercing cry, a wail that split through the predawn silence and brought Spotted Fawn flying out of her bedroll to kneel, trembling and frightened, in the dark tepee. The evening's fire was a mound of pale ash, barely enough lingering warmth to keep her breath from frosting. She held the child close, felt the baby's stiffness as if it was her own pain.

Sitting, she offered a breast, but the infant fussed and turned away. So again she wrapped her in that deerskin and took her outside for an easy walk through the dark, silent village. Agate fussed and fidgeted, so Spotted Fawn walked away from the tepees full of sleeping People, made her way to the bank just above the great bend of the shallow creek.

The sky had paled now, soft blue stretching upward from the east. Spotted Fawn could see that the creek had frozen over, at least on the surface, though she could hear water still chuckling along under the sheet of ice. The cold air, clear and clean, tickled her nose with frost.

She heard something else, then . . . a distant drumming. The noise grew into the thudding rumble of many hooves on the sand flats, like a great herd of buffalo or horses. The sounds swelled quickly, and she was certain the galloping herd approached the camp.

Then she heard the jingling of metal spurs, the hoarse

shouts and barked commands of men, cursing and whooping whites. Their sounds formed a dull gurgle of sound, an encompassing background. Now a dog barked, and then dozens of the tribe's hounds came to life, a howling, yammering chorus of alarm.

Voices shouted from tepees, questioning, calling. The thundering swelled into a deafening cadence, drawing some disheveled Cheyenne out of their homes. Dim shapes moved through the shadowy brush, then burst into view, riders charging toward the village! Spotted Fawn saw the beards and hats, the huge horses, and she knew these were white men.

Finally, all these sounds vanished under a sudden, rippling crack that was too harsh to be thunder, too foreign to be anything but gunfire. The young mother saw a ragged line of cavalry coming from the right, horses lumbering right in among the tepees of the village. Someone came out of a door, a big boy bouncing eagerly to his feet, and a soldier hit him with a sword. The child fell, head half dangling off of his body.

Spotted Fawn felt the rumbling of the ground underfoot, vibrations caused by those monstrous animals, and only then did she think to drop down, lying among the brush at the crest of the riverbank, then slipping down the bank so that only her eyes were above, horrified but compelled to watch. The baby was utterly still, perfectly silent in her mother's arms.

People were screaming, coming out of their tepees all through the village. Everywhere were those soldiers on their giant horses, looming in the breaking daylight, shooting down any Cheyenne who came into sight. Gunfire crackled everywhere, a cloud of smoke lingering from a volley down beside the pony herds on the other side of the creek. Deeper pounding shook the ground, explosions of smoke and fire belching from the fringe of the camp. These were the great, wheeled guns, ripping into the village with lethal blasts.

A warrior came out of a tepee with his spear, turning it to thrust into the flank of a horse and rider charging past. The mount shrieked and twisted, while the soldier took a clumsy shot with his pistol, the Cheyenne ducking below the blazing muzzle. With a rush, the brave knocked the rider from his saddle, though the kicking horse gave the white man momentary protection from the heavy spear. Then the animal bolted, and the warrior raised the spear, but a volley of bullets cut him down before he could deliver the blow.

The horse, struck by a stray bullet, also thrashed and went down. The rider climbed groggily to his knees. His eyes fastened upon the face of the dead warrior, and he let out a whoop. Drawing a big knife, he pulled the Cheyenne's hair upward, hacked away at the crown of his head, and pulled away the scalp.

Spotted Fawn caught a glimpse of color in the growing light, red and white stripes. She saw the great flag, the banner the white men had given to Black Kettle. The chief was raising it on the pole before his tepee! Another pennant flew there, a flag of white, and Black Kettle was calling to his people to come to him, to gather under the protection of the flag.

A dozen horsemen pulled their mounts to a halt before this display. Spotted Fawn saw Black Kettle raise his hands, imploring. Rifles and pistols popped, and a woman beside the chief fell. More of the People were dying then, though somehow the bullets all missed Black Kettle. But the flag was clearly no protection, and the Cheyenne scattered away from the chief's tepee, seeking the shelter that did not exist in the tortured village.

More soldiers came through the camp, charging from the other side. The white men whooped and shouted, leveling rifles awkwardly in their saddles, shooting wildly. The first volley from this new wave rippled high over the heads of the fleeing Cheyenne. Near Spotted Fawn, a soldier was knocked from the saddle, head shattered by a bullet fired by his own comrades.

Everywhere terrified People raced through the village, ducking away from the deadly riders. Some of the Cheyenne ran toward the creek, to a bank upstream of Spotted Fawn's position. A line of horsemen galloped to bar the route, but a leaping warrior seized the bridle of a horse, jerking the animal's head around, pivoting the steed into the path of its fellows so that the formation broke into a chaotic tumble. She recognized Buffalo Roars, saw his one strong hand hooked onto the mount's reins, reaching up to grasp a handful of mane. The warrior sang a wild death song as he clung to the bucking horse, his body bleeding from cuts, until he was finally knocked down and trampled.

But many People escaped in the confusion, mothers clutching babes or pulling toddlers along, grandfathers scuttling along with remembered sprightliness, older brothers protectively herding their siblings past the curtain of swords. Some fell, cruelly slashed, but many others scrambled down the protective stream bank. The soldiers lunged this way and that, wild and confused and angry, and the Cheyenne took advantage of this confusion to race into the creek, crossing toward the high bank on the other side. Another brave lunged into the press of horsemen, and he fell, but not before dragging a rider from his saddle, using the man as a shield against the brutal attacks of his comrades.

Spotted Fawn gasped in horror as she saw the Walking Moon sisters, all three of them. Half dressed, they fled toward the river, while five horsemen cheered lustily as they rode behind, waving pistols. Two of the women were shot and left for dead, but the men leaped from their saddles and bore pretty Red Moon to the ground. They tore away her clothes, and Spotted Fawn thought she knew what would come next. Instead, she could only shrink back and sob as they slashed at Red Moon with knives, pulling away pieces of her flesh, until all the beauty of her womanhood was gone and her killers stood like beasts, holding their gory trophies overhead and howling into the light of the rising day.

More soldiers came closer, riding along the edge of the stream now, looking down the embankment to search for the Cheyenne who fled from the camp in a terrified flood. From somewhere upstream, she heard cracks of gunfire, a few shots whistling around the heads of the nearby horsemen, scattering them out of their saddles to sprawl defensively on the ground. They shot wildly back.

She guessed that some of the warriors were fighting there, shooting from shallow pits on the far side of the creek. Many of the People, those who survived, made their way toward those positions. With a glance up the creek, Spotted Fawn ducked low and crept along, holding the silent baby, trying to escape notice as she ran toward the bend of the channel.

But more horsemen were there before her, finally riding down onto the very shore of the frozen water. One pointed at Spotted Fawn and shouted something. His mouth looked like a big black hole within a sea of red whiskers. She saw the trader, Gray Blanket, standing beside the soldier, looking at her and laughing.

She darted away from the bank, breaking through the ice into cold water that swirled as high as her knees. Still she ran, kicking through the brittle crust of frozen water, toward the first dry sandbar rising from the creek bed. Finally she broke free, sprinting now on hard-packed ground. Not daring to look back, she could only pray that the horsemen would find someone else to attack, some other direction to go.

The bullet that struck between her shoulders ripped through her heart and her lung and her baby's innocent body. Spotted Fawn fell, and even then, she clung to her slain and bloody child. She saw ice and water rising, as if to embrace her in frost.

Instead, against her flesh she sensed a burst of pleasant warmth, and then she tumbled into a hole of soft, warm light.

1

Center

In the Center stands the fulcrum,
Seven Circles stay.
When the dragon came to pull some
Worlds they fell away.

Elven Nursery Rhyme

He hesitated before he fastened the shutters across the large window, reluctant to cast the great room into darkness. He hated to bar the daylight and the fresh air, but he was going to be gone for a very long time, and he was even more unwilling to allow the ravages of weather, nature, and time to affect the villa. This was a holy place to him, as holy a place as there was in all the Seven Circles.

Here, he and Miradel had lived. They had cooked and gardened on this pastoral hilltop. She had taught him about this world and many others, and he had learned so much from her. At this same splendid window they had looked together upon Circle at Center. Strange, that . . . she had been gone for three centuries, and he still thought of this as a view they had shared.

Finally, he pulled the wooden boards over the large opening and fastened them into place. Making his way through the house, he found that the kitchen and pantry were already cold as well as dark. Chill seeped from the slate flagstones. Absently, or with unconscious purpose, he wandered down the corridor, stopped in the door to the room at the end of the hall, and the coolness was replaced by a sense of lingering warmth. This room, this part of the house, could never be cold.

Still, he remembered, as if it had been this morning, her magic reaching out to him, pulling him at the moment of his death from the Seventh Circle to the Fourth. He saw the three glowing wicks, lanterns arranged in a precise triangle around her, casting their magical light. Each time the picture came into his mind, the thought of her beauty took his breath away. For one night, a night that would linger in his mind for all eternity, they had made love, a physical and spiritual melding that had been nothing less than a rebirth for him and a mortal sentence for her. She brought him, alive and young and whole, to this world, and never in that wondrous night had he suspected the price that she, in all willingness, would pay.

That lay far in his past, now. Even the twenty-five years he and Miradel had shared, the years after she had cast her spell, were a blur of ancient time, three centuries old. When he tried to remember her gray hair, the wrinkles that had creased her face, the age that had weakened her flesh, all he could recall was the image of those pure, violet eyes . . . the eyes that had never clouded, never grown dim with age.

As for the rest of her, it was only that image of radiance, of love, that he could recall. He smelled the air in this room, with its fur pallet, the niches in the walls holding lamps and candles. There was still a touch of her perfume, and the fragrance of the red flower she had worn in her hair, lingering here. The man closed his eyes and drew in that smell, cherished and held it. Then he turned and left the villa and started down the steep hill toward the completion of his life's work.

THE old dog huffed and lifted his head as Natac reached the landing at the foot of the hill. With another grunt of effort, Ulf rolled himself onto his belly and stood, wobbling on his four frail, rickety legs. "I'm sorry I couldn't make the climb with you," he said, panting out the words in a series of shallow breaths.

"No need to worry. . . . In truth, I was grateful for an hour of solitude. I hope you enjoyed a little nap in the sun," Natac said fondly, setting down the backpack and satchel he had carried down from the villa.

Ulf sighed and turned his head sideways, a dark, watery eye inspecting the sky. "It is bright, sure enough . . . but somehow, it doesn't seem to warm these old bones as it did before."

"I'm glad you decided to come across the lake with me."

Ulf snorted again and laid his head on his outstretched paws. "I don't get out so much anymore . . . but this has always been one of my favorite places." The dog sighed heavily. "A bittersweet favorite, to be sure."

"You couldn't have saved her. . . . You know that. The Delvers would have killed you, too, if you'd been here."

"Still, it is a regret that has lingered."

"I grieve that Miradel was killed by violence," Natac said softly. "But you know, I truly believe she was ready to die."

"Yes. I am beginning to understand what that means," replied the old dog. The man looked down sharply, but Ulf merely wagged his tail in good-natured affection.

Sitting on the edge of the landing, Natac patted the dog's head and looked across the cove. Circle at Center was out of sight around the point, but he savored the sight of the silvery lake, so broad that the far shore was but a thread of green. "Any sign of our ride?" he asked.

"Roland said he was going to do some fishing, but Sirien is with him. She'll make sure that he's back by midday."

No sooner had the dog spoken than Natac spotted the angular golden sail and sleek hull as Roland Boatwright steered the *Osprey V* into view. The druid, master sailor and one of Natac's oldest friends, worked the wind skillfully. His bride, a golden-haired elfmaid, held the tiller. She made a graceful turn and guided the sailboat through the mouth of the cove. Roland eased back on his windcasting so that *Osprey* slipped gently up to the stone wharf. Natac rose, shrugged into his pack, and lifted up the satchel.

"A ride, sir . . . over waves or wind? You have but to name the medium, and I shall take you!" proclaimed the druid with a flourish.

Natac laughed and, despite his encumbrance, leaped easily onto the deck. He took the hand of the beautiful elfwoman who stood beside the mast and kissed her on both cheeks.

"I just wanted to hold your hand," the warrior said with a grin. "It's not that I was going to lose my balance."

Sirien laughed, too, her voice like music as Natac set his traveling gear on the deck. Meanwhile, Ulf hesitantly stepped onto the gunwale with his forepaws, and the elfmaid helped him onto the deck. From the stern, Roland Boatwright smiled a cheerful hello. His neat black hair and the short whiskers framing his chin in a sharp line seemed like shadows in the bright daylight.

Ulf curled through several circles and then plopped down on the deck before the mast. Roland didn't alter the spell-casting of his hands. One arm was wrapped around a large wooden bowl, while the other spun a small paddle around inside the container, much as if he was stirring invisible soup. But in reality, he was stirring the wind, guiding it with magic and skill.

Sirien again took the tiller. A gust swirled from the shore, filled the limp sails of the *Osprey V,* and nudged her away from the dock with insistent force. Soon the boat sliced a creamy gash in the emerald waters of the cove, picking up speed. Natac went forward, but his eyes looked past the stern, up the steep hill for a last look at the lofty villa that had served as his home for so long.

By the time the boat came around the point of the cove, he was looking forward. Across the lake spread the dazzling vista that was Circle at Center, the great silver spire of the Worldweaver's Loom marking the heart of the great city, surrounded by verdant hills and the many fabulous manors and marbled palaces of that enchanted place. But Natac ignored those wonders and focused immediately on the airship.

The massive, colorful shape of silk and webbing hung in the air. The flotation spheres were fully inflated now, seven of them strung into a long cigar shape. The vessel strained against anchor lines, visibly anxious to fly.

"She's ready," he called back to Roland, his gaze never leaving *Skyreaver*.

"Socrates and his alchemists finished inflation yesterday," the druid confirmed. "Right on schedule."

Natac inspected the craft with a critical eye. Alchemists from the College had been generating helium for days, pumping the light gas into the great vessel. The flotation "tube" was actually seven huge, spherical sacks, suspended in a row within the webbing of a feather-light net. Each of the bright silk bags, in the colors of the rainbow spectrum, had been inflated to the same size as all the others. This would be the biggest airship ever to set sail in Nayvian skies, and the warrior could barely contain his excitement at the awareness that the magnificent vessel had been made and was being launched at *his* instigation.

"Are you ready to go?" Natac asked, looking at Sirien with a smile.

She nodded, her almond-shaped eyes wide and serious. "I'm glad you decided to take me."

Natac laughed. "I don't think Roland would be speaking to me if I wasn't . . . but that aside, you'll be a valuable member of the crew."

She threw her head back in a very humanlike gesture, letting the lake wind whiff through her golden hair. "I remember it like it was yesterday, the two of you, riding into Hyac without a care in the world. You were rather surprised when my father had you arrested, if you recall."

"Indeed," Roland said wryly. "The khan seemed as willing to burn us as to speak with us. Very unusual, for Nayve."

"We Hyac are unusual elves, as you learned. For one thing, we spend all our lives at the edge of Riven Deep. . . . It makes you think when you have all that nothingness off to the side."

"Yes . . . the chasm," Natac mused. "Back then, it brought

our explorations to an end. My maps show nothing of what lies beyond, because it was impossible to cross."

"But now . . ." Roland said with a meaningful glance at the great airship.

"Now, we'll have the chance to see," the warrior agreed. Again he looked at Sirien. "You know, it would be possible to plot a course that took us far to one side of Shahkamon or the other. We do not have to fly over your home."

"I know . . . but I want to. There's no need to divert from the straight course, just because my father might be carrying a hundred-year-old grudge. No, I think I am ready to see him again . . . even to ask for his forgiveness."

"You have nothing to be ashamed of!" Roland objected. "You were a grown elf, and you made the decision to leave your home and see the world. Think of all you've seen, and done, over the last hundred years!"

"I know," Sirien said. She pulled the druid close and kissed him warmly, an unabashed display of affection that caused Natac to turn his eyes to the lake again, politely studying the glittering water. "And I wouldn't trade a minute of it. But perhaps this is the time when I can go home again."

Within two hours, they had pulled into the crowded Mahogany Harbor, one of the great ports that had grown up around Circle at Center in the past centuries. Roland maintained his shipyard here, where the finest boats in Nayve were built, but for now he steered toward the private berth where *Osprey V* would be moored.

"I'll miss this old boat," the boatbuilder said wistfully, as he, Sirien, and Natac prepared to disembark. A dozen bustling gnomes collected their baggage and gathered their belongings on the dock. Natac gently woke Ulf and carried the dog off the boat. Then his eyes turned toward the airship, still clearly in view beyond a nearby hilltop, as Roland continued. "But I wouldn't miss the chance to man *that* tiller, not for all the fair winds in all the Seven Circles!"

"Let's go," Natac agreed heartily. "We'll stow the provisions tonight. The plan is for a ceremony just after tomorrow's Lighten—and then we're off."

Owen huffed. "Another chance for those senators to boast about how useful they are and how they would be going instead of you, if only they had the chance."

The warrior laughed. "You might be a trifle unkind, but true enough, nonetheless." In fact, the Senate that was ostensibly in charge of the affairs of Nayve had had nothing to do with the preparations for the expedition. The airship had been constructed through the efforts of alchemists, druids, and a few adventure-minded elves such as their Belynda Wysterian and Tamarwind Trak. Supplies had been purchased from contributed funds, and a team of gnomes had volunteered to sew the great flotation bags.

By consulting the Tapestry of the Worldweaver, for centuries druids had been following technological developments on the Seventh Circle, which was now in its nineteenth century A.D. Nayvian expertise and magic had allowed the druids and others to improve upon the balloons of Earth, generating helium instead of hydrogen, for example, and creating enchanted provisions light enough for aerial transport.

On the dock they hired a centaur cart to haul their possessions to the airship, and the team of gnomish stevedores immediately started to load their bags. "Do you want to go back to Belynda's or come to the Willowfield?" Natac asked Ulf, who had limped off the dock to accompany them to the lakeside avenue, where their cart had pulled aside from a heavy traffic of pedestrians, horses and centaurs, chariots, wagons, and sailing cars.

"I wouldn't miss your departure," the dog replied. "Perhaps I could ride to the field?"

"Of course." Natac arranged a suitable bed atop their belongings and settled the dog into the cart. "Nice and easy," he told the centaur. "No need for hurry."

"As you wish, Lord Natac," replied the steed with a sweeping bow of his human torso and head. His tail swished with a jaunty air, and the centaur started off at a pleasant walk, leaving Roland, Natac, and Sirien to amble along on foot.

"What about Owen and Juliay?" asked the elfmaid.

"They're already there. Juliay was storing the food supplies, and Owen was seeing to our weapons."

"Do you really think there'll be danger?" asked Roland breezily. "This is Nayve we're exploring, not some wilderness of Earth."

"I know," Natac said. "But remember, we're going in the direction that is neither metal nor wood, farther than anyone has ever gone before. If I've learned anything in three centuries of exploring, it's that it pays to be prepared."

It really *had* been three hundred years ago, he found himself thinking. Sometimes he had traveled alone, at others with good companions such as Roland Boatwright or Owen the Viking. He had seen so much of this world, already mapping more than two-thirds of Nayve's surface, crossing the coast from one shore of the Worldsea to the other. Only where the great chasm yawned had his explorations been blocked. And now, at last, he had the means to cross that barrier.

Three hundred years. He still couldn't grasp the idea; the very notion inevitably filled him with a sense of disbelief. For three centuries he'd been working on this task . . . and for three centuries he had lived without her, without his druid. If this voyage turned out as successfully as he hoped, the former would be complete.

As to the latter, he couldn't even make himself think about it.

His wife's first kick, to his ribs, awakened him. Her second, to his head, got his attention. Awfulbark rolled out of bed only because he wanted to avoid the third of Roodcleaver's blows, the stomp that would undoubtedly have been aimed at the sensitive juncture of his long, scaly legs.

"All right!" he snarled, pounding a gnarled fist on the wooden floor. "I'm up!"

"It's half through afternoon!" screeched Roodcleaver.
"And the food bin is empty these past two days. Now, you go
get me some food, or I'll be lopping off your foot for soup!"

Awfulbark cringed, for although his wife's threat was extreme, it was not unthinkable; trolls had been known to make
do with even gamier fare. So he rose to his feet, limbs creak-
ing like wooden tree trunks bending in the wind. Indeed,
those gangly arms and legs bore more than passing resemblance to branches of rough-barked oak. His trollish skin was
a stiff and protective shell, while his broad face—and the face
of his wife, as well—resembled nothing so much as a round
burl on the side of a thick, gnarled bole.

Right now that roughly spherical head was filled with
enough pain to kill any two lesser beings. In retrospect, perhaps he should have stopped drinking before Breakwind
opened that last cask of whiskey, but he had been having such
a grand time. He remembered something else: His gambling
had been going well, too! Then they had dipped into that third
keg. . . .

The memories were vague after that, but a look at his
empty gold sack confirmed the developments of the rest of
the night, or morning, as it had turned out. No big matter, the
loss of a dozen gold coins—at least, no more than the absence
of food. After all, as king of Udderthud, Awfulbark merely
needed to walk around the town until he found someone who
had money or food, whichever he sought at the time. The king
would simply threaten the citizen with dismemberment,
and the loyal subject would inevitably pass over a tribute
sufficient to spare himself the beating. Still, such paucity
was an irritation now, as he realized that Roodcleaver was
staring angrily at him. He raised his knotted hands to ward her
off.

"I go," he croaked, twisting the dry stalk of his tongue
around in a mouth that seemed unusually fetid. "I return with
food for your cupboard."

"Then you could stay and eat with me," Roodcleaver said,
her shrill voice a little more conciliatory. "Just . . . just bring

me something!" With that, she raised her own twisted hands to her fibrous face, turned, and ran from the room.

She didn't run far; two steps took her to the stairway through the floor, leading down toward the base of the great oak tree wherein they made their home. This luxurious upper chamber, devoted only to sleeping and the storing of treasure—on those occasions when Awfulbark had some treasure—was the envy of Udderthud. Most trolls were forced to eat and sleep, copulate and collect, in one ground-level room within the bole of a mighty forest giant. Some nobles had houses with two levels, but only the king had this grand abode of three full rooms stacked one upon the next.

Awfulbark followed his wife down the steps more slowly, through the smoke room on the second floor, down to the tiny kitchen where she fussed with the stove. He emerged into such daylight as seeped down to the town streets through the vast canopy of limbs and foliage overhead. Even with that filtering, it was strangely bright here on Crowned Knoll, and the troll blinked a few times. He saw many of his neighbors outside their own trees, all of them looking up nervously at his appearance. Stretching his stiff muscles, he turned and ducked through the narrow doorway to reenter his home.

"What you want I should bring?" he asked.

"Anything!" Roodcleaver snapped, then sniffed, a sound like a whirlpool draining down a gutter. "Venison would be nice . . . and milk, if you can find it."

"I'll do what I can," the king of the forest trolls retorted, before once more going forth from his den.

Not surprisingly, the trolls that had been busily going about their business a moment earlier had all disappeared. He grimaced. He never should have let them know that he was awake. Of course, he would probably have roamed farther afield anyway, but now he would need to make two stops, since the chance of finding a single contributor with both deer flesh and milk was virtually nonexistent.

He was in a bad mood as he plodded down the steep trail from Crowned Knoll to the main street of Udderthud, a dirt track pocked by frequent kettles of gooey mud. Avoiding these low spots, he took long strides, his broad feet smacking into the ground. As usual, he bypassed the trollish domiciles in the immediate vicinity of his own home. There were his most loyal supporters, and a key component of that loyalty was that he left them free to accumulate a few possessions of their own. So he would go to a different neighborhood, if necessary climbing to the top of one of the other knolls to make his wishes known.

He sighed. It probably *would* be necessary, unless he was lucky enough to find a target on the street. That was always preferable to breaking down someone's door. Even when he succeeded in forcing entry—which was far from a guaranteed outcome—he inevitably caused himself considerable pain in the process. But now, as so often seemed to happen, the trolls on the street scattered out of sight well before the king drew close. And though Awfulbark was the biggest and strongest troll of Udderthud, he was far from the fastest and knew better than to waste his energy in fruitless chasing.

Sauntering along, Awfulbark came around the base of one of the rocky knolls that gave Udderthud its shape. The oaks where the trolls lived grew tall and sprawling on the crests of these steep-sided outcrops, while the narrow and twisting ravines between created the routes through the town and out into the forest beyond.

It was the work of many lesser trolls to go into that forest and return with deer, fish, berries, apples, greens, firewood, and other necessities. It was the work of noble trolls to collect a portion of these possessions, mainly in return for protecting the lesser trolls from the avarice of other nobles. And it was King Awfulbark's prerogative to visit any troll, lesser or noble, and demand from him such items as were required to make the royal existence more comfortable.

All in all, it was a very good thing to be king, Awfulbark understood. But why was it still so difficult to keep food in his cupboard and treasures in his chamber? Winding along the trail, deep in the gorge, the troll found himself sinking deeper and deeper into gloom. There were times when he'd *had* treasure, lots of it, but the other trolls always took it away when the king was drunk and gambling. Last night, it had been Breakwind, the big, pale-barked noble, who was one of Awfulbark's most loyal subject lords, who had insisted on dicing even after the king wanted to go home. And then he had produced that third keg, an irresistible allure.

That memory made his current decision easy. He splashed through a narrow stream near the bridge that had fallen down a hundred years ago and started up the steep trail toward Breakwind's hilltop.

He found the noble troll with several henchman gathered around a fire that crackled high in the midst of the oak tree neighborhood. It so happened that the trolls had a young deer speared through with a massive skewer and were taking turns holding the log in the flames. One troll held each end, and every minute or two they would give it a quarter turn. Already, Awfulbark could see that the two holders were smoking, the woody skin of their knees, hands, and forearms scorched black from the hot fire. But they held on until the heat grew so intense that one of the trolls was forced to drop his end of the skewer. The charred cook danced, howling, away from the fire.

Another stepped in to take his place, helping to lift the carcass, now ash-covered and flaming, out of the fire. Breakwind himself poured a bucket of water over the blackened meat, and then two fresh holders took a turn at hoisting it back over the heat. The original pair, still charred and smoking, hurried down the hill to leap into the stream.

"Ah, Breakwind," Awfulbark said casually, coming up to clap the noble on the shoulder. Breakwind was clearly less than overjoyed to see his king, but he was respectful enough not to run away.

"What do you want?" he asked suspiciously.

It was then that Awfulbark noticed a drinking sack being passed between two nearby trolls. The one passing the sack had a telltale mustache of creamy white on his woody lip.

"This milk!" said the king, clocking the second troll over the head and intercepting the flask. "And I will settle for one haunch of that deer."

"One haunch?" Breakwind was no doubt at least a little relieved that Awfulbark wasn't going to take the whole deer. "Very well. But it won't be cooked until the Hour of Darken."

"I will wait," said the king, pleased with the way this day was turning out. "And perhaps share some of your whiskey."

"Of course!" cried Breakwind, signaling for a cask. "Even so, the time is long. Shall we hurry it along with a bit of gaming?"

The king scowled. "How can I game, when you took all my gold last night! How do I wager?"

"Well," shrugged Breakwind. "It doesn't have to be gold. I see you've got some milk."

THE Willowfield was the largest open space on the huge but crowded island that was Circle at Center. Located near the shore of the lake, just to the metal side of the direction of wood, it was a grassy meadow nearly a mile square, surrounded by a fringe of mingled evergreens and hardwoods. The field had been used as a drilling ground when Natac first trained an army here, though in the centuries since it had primarily served as a gathering place for picnics and festivals.

Now the massive airship loomed over the flat like some kind of giant blossom, the spectrum of seven colors—red at the bow, violet at the stern—was bright and surreal, spanning far to the right and left over the grassy mead. The gondola, supported like the hull of a small boat beneath the massive flotation spheres, was tethered tightly to the ground. As the sun descended toward Lighten, the explorers stood on the foredeck of that gondola, a wide platform some twelve feet above the ground. Natac looked outward with a sense of awe and destiny, mingled with that loneliness that never entirely went away.

Much of the Center's population had come to witness the

departure. Elves and giants, gnomes and goblins and druids, faeries and centaurs, all of them brought food and drinks, banners, kites, and quilts, and spread themselves across the field in a panoply of celebration. The aromas of elven sweet-cakes and icewafers thickened the morning air. Sweet wine and cider, flasks of cold milk and warm beer, all bobbed through the crowd, seeking and finding thirsty lips.

Minstrels of all the races danced through the crowd, giants blowing their silver horns, elves strumming lutes, druids playing flutes, goblins rhythmically pounding their large, skin-covered drums. All through the pre-Lighten hours peo-ple had come from throughout the city until, by an hour after full daylight, the field was so packed that even elves and gnomes had difficulty moving through the throng.

Nevertheless, a giant figure came striding quickly closer, his beaming face fixed upon the skyship, seemingly oblivious to the placement of his big, heavy boots among the crowd. Yet somehow Rawknuckle Barefist didn't crush so much as a loaf of elven bread. Behind him came a pair of elfwomen, golden haired and serene in their long gowns even as they hurried to keep up with the giant.

Natac, followed by his four crewmates, descended the steep ladder leading down from the foredeck to the midship platform, the largest open deck space on the gondola. Leaning over the rail, he took one of Rawknuckle's big hands in both of his own.

"Farewell, my friend," said the warrior. "It is good of you to see us off."

The giant's bearded face darkened into a scowl, a thunder-cloud passing across that beaming sun. "Would that I could go with you," he said mournfully.

Natac nodded. "The curse of exploring by air. My only re-gret is that I have been forced to leave you behind, stalwart companion."

"Ah, yes. Do you remember when we mapped the Karton Valley, beyond Granitehome?" Rawknuckle hefted a sloshing drinking flask, a sack made from the skin of a whole hog. He took a long pull, then obligingly hoisted it so that Natac, Roland, Sirien, Juliay, and Owen could all partake. Natac and most of his companions took polite sips of the biting amethyst ale, only the Viking gulping down a great draught, smacking his lips in satisfaction.

"It seems the Senate wants to send us off with some pomp," Natac said, noting that Cannystryius, one of the co-speakers of that illustrious body, was standing before the ship and addressing the crowd. Fortunately, the pudgy aristocrat was facing directly away from them and could not be heard.

"I'm all for pomp," Owen chuckled. "Especially if that means there's beer." Cheerfully, he accepted another long drink from the giant, and then his blond-bearded face creased into a frown. "You don't think we'd be able to hoist a few more kegs along, do you?"

Natac laughed good-naturedly. "In some ways you don't change, my friend," he said affectionately. "But no, I've allotted space for one, and you'll have to make it last."

"It's not like the other voyages, going in the direction of metal, or wood, when we could count on a few civilized lands below us. Gnomish brews, or this fine giant draught. Even elven beer, though it might be piss-thin, is still beer," retorted the Viking.

"I know . . . I know," Natac, who had never developed a taste for fermented spirits, agreed.

"Now we go looking in the third direction, and I reckon a fat lot of wilderness is all we're likely to find, at least beyond this canyon, this Riven Deep that you and Roland discovered."

"Hardly discovered; after all, Sirien's people have lived there, in Hyac, for thousands of years." Natac remembered his last excursion in the direction that was neither metal nor wood, an exploration by horseback a century earlier. "But as to the deep, it's far too wide to cross . . . much too steep to enter. Only now will we really be able to see what's on the other side."

"I guess that chance is worth going thirsty for a few

months," the Viking allowed, then looked down with an affectionate smile as a young-looking woman, with golden red hair and a pretty face dotted with freckles, emerged from one of the ship's small cabins.

"It's not big," Juliay admitted with a wave, shutting the feathery light door that closed off her and Owen's small cabin. "But I wouldn't miss this trip if I had to ride in a teacup."

"We can always leave Owen's beer keg behind to save room," Natac suggested, to the outraged protests of the Viking.

Underneath the banter, the warrior felt the tension familiar from his previous aerial journeys. He had checked and rechecked the supply list. They had plenty of rations, enough of the light but nourishing elven cakes called *hedras* to last them a year, even if Owen would run out of beer long before then. They had axes and adzes, saws and hammers and bolts and chisels and planes, every conceivable tool necessary to repair the airship. There were spare canisters of helium lashed to the outside of the gondola, which itself had a boatlike shape with a distinct fore and aft. Great sheaves of silk were folded and placed in the hold, enough material to replace two or more of the seven spheres supporting the airship.

Natac went to the afterdeck now, which was the highest part of the hull. He stood atop the small platform, the roof of his cabin. From here, rope ladders led upward, one each to starboard and port, swaying through the air, offering passage up either side of the great flotation tube. The larger cabins, one for Roland and Sirien as well as Owen and Juliay's, were amidships and lower down. In the bow was the largest compartment, the hold where they stored their food, tools, and spare equipment.

"Just one sword?" Owen asked, cocking an eyebrow as he held a pair of keen-edged weapons. One was a bastard sword nearly as long as he was, with a gleaming diamond in the hilt, while the other was a more slender longsword. Finally, the Viking sighed and shook his head. "I can't decide—in this I

will take them both." He girded himself with the smaller
sword and took his great weapon toward the supply cabin.

Natac checked his own weapons. He had the sword that
Darryn Forgemaster had made for him during the war, still as
sharp and strong as ever. Each of them had a double-curved
bow as well as a powerful, dwarf-made crossbow, and they
carried hundreds of arrows and an even greater number of
spare arrowheads in storage. Stowed within their own cabins
were the special objects belonging to each of them: his own
compass and mapping tools, laid on a wide drawing table in
his cabin, numerous windcasting bowls of various shapes and
sizes for the druids Juliay and Roland, Sirien's small harp and
ivory flute, and Owen's cask of beer.

He heard a cheer from the crowd and saw that the last of
the speeches had concluded. Cannystrius was just now stepping down from the podium, as the eyes of the assemblage
turned in unison toward the great airship. The rest of the crew
came onto the afterdeck, which was crowded by the five of
them but gave each a vantage over the crowd.

They saw a wizened old elf coming toward them, hobbling
with the aid of a cane while the crowd respectfully parted to
let him pass. This was Socrates, the senior alchemist of the
College. He had been given that name since he had been born
to an enlightened family at the time the human teacher of that
name was enjoying vitality and some degree of prominence
upon the Seventh Circle. The vitality of the Earthen Socrates
hadn't lasted, but his prominence in the following centuries
had only grown. His counterpart here on Nayve had continued to study, to learn, and to teach.

"I'm glad you could come," Natac said, as the frail old elf
squinted up at him.

"Well, she's a beauty, and I had to see her fly, didn't I?"
Socrates retorted crossly. "That is, *if* she gets off the ground."

"Oh, she will," the warrior replied with a laugh. "She was
designed by the wisest fellow in all the Seven Circles!"

"Are you ready?" asked Cillia, the druid elder. She and a
full hundred of her order were gathered on the ground at the

stern of the airship. Each druid was seated and had a wind-casting bowl in his or her lap.

"Ready!" Natac signaled back.

Immediately, the elves arrayed around the hull released the ropes that had held *Skyreaver* securely against the ground, and at the same time, the druids began a synchronized casting. The vessel lifted free from the ground with an eager hop, then rose more gradually. Natac watched the crowd slowly fall away. The gathered citizens of Nayve watched in silent awe as the magical wind took the great ship in a gentle embrace, lifted her, turned her across the field, and then started *Skyreaver* on her way.

At first they moved slowly. Still rising, the ship was carried along faster and faster as the druid-cast wind heightened. All the city was below them now, and Natac was once again stunned by the beauty of this place, the pools and gardens and grottos that only came into focus from the air. Streams and ponds, waterfalls and fountains dazzled like jewels. Hillsides of marble façades, columns, arches faced them, while curving stairways and winding avenues of smooth stone linked the city in a web of passageways. And all of this stone was almost overshadowed by verdant trees and shrubs, by carpets of blossoms in every color of the rainbow and many more.

Soon the silver spire of the Worldweaver's Loom was the only thing higher than the ship. They could see the grand façade of the Senate, the sprawling, ivy-encloaked campus of the College, and the towering oaken expanse of the Grove, all three ringing the marble temple and the silver spire rising so straight and tall above. The wind pushed on, and the gas spheres held firm. The Willowfield diminished so that the people, hundreds of thousands of them, merged into one huge canvas of color. They coursed over the shore, and the blue waters of the lake dazzled below them.

Natac turned forward. The lake was a blue so deep that it suggested purple or violet . . . and for a piercing moment he remembered her eyes. The Ringhills were in view, a tumbling and rocky horizon beyond the pristine water. Beyond that barrier, which was but scenery from this airship, they would cross plains and woodlands and come to the edge of the canyon called Riven Deep. What lay past that canyon, no one knew.

And still they climbed, so high that even the World-weaver's Loom was below them, as the airship made stately progression in the direction that was neither metal nor wood.

MIRADEL.

Her name was *Miradel.*

She was here again, in a place that she had not been for a very long time. She felt a warm embrace, comfort soothing what little pain lingered in her body. Her hand went to her chest, to the place between her breasts where she had been wounded . . . slain, actually . . . only then she had had no breasts . . . not even awareness of much at all.

The memories were strangely vague . . . of warmth and food and a loving mother, of a stark, terrified moment . . . and then that white light that had taken her in, brought her to this place.

"Goddess . . . Goddess Worldweaver . . . I am dream-ing. . . ."

She had been gone for a long time. Now the memories came pouring back, a flood of history that had carried her through three centuries, lives lived here and there, each sepa-rate from the others. When she had wallowed in despair, forced to walk the Trail of Tears in the great Cherokee exo-dus, she had not recalled life as an Algonquin along the shores of the great lake, Mich-I-gon. Now she remembered greeting the fur traders, the bearded men who spoke the language called French. And then she recalled, in a terrifying flash, an-other instant: She was an Iroquois maiden, yet unwed, and there were muskets blazing and bearded, white-faced men moving through the village, always killing.

Of her last sojourn on the Seventh Circle, her final days upon the world of Earth, she could recall only that warmth and comfort, the life-giving embrace of a mother. "I was a new baby, wasn't I?" she murmured into the warm space. "I don't know what happened. . . ."

That is mercy . . . alas, it is the only mercy you have known in seven lives.

"Mother . . . Goddess . . ."

Miradel was filled with reverence; it was the rarest of blessings for a druid to hear the voice of the Worldweaver! Only then did the rest of the truth envelop her, grow real in her mind.

She had returned to Nayve. Once more, the goddess had summoned her from the chaos and violence of the Seventh Circle, had rewarded her with the mantle of druidhood.

And then the rest of those memories assailed her: the starving boy nursing at her shriveled breast as she lay dying, consumed by the smallpox that swept up the valley of the Missouri River . . . the rattle of gunfire ripping through a sleeping village, again and again—she was Seminole when that attack came, or Iroquois, or some other tribe—always terrified, watching children scream and die, fearing the flesh and the steel of the bearded white men who came first for the land but ended up claiming the freedom and, eventually, the lives of her people.

In the Seventh Circle she had lived each life once, and in the awareness of that solitary existence there had been some comfort; in the ignorance of her isolation there was at least room for hope. But now she saw it all, peoples of a whole continent succumbing like a beach to a tide, in a pattern of ruthless violence ever repeated.

At last that warm light was a balm on her skin. Hers was a body enclosed in flesh, and she opened her eyes. She lay in a bower of godswood, dewy blossoms dangling from heavy limbs. Water splashed in a pool nearby, the sound gentle and musical, the force of the liquid controlled and contained.

She looked into a long space, a vision of silver light, and recognized intuitively that she lay directly beneath the Loom of the Goddess Worldweaver. She was filled with roiling emotions: lingering terror tinged with grief, a sense of loss coupled with astonished revelation. This was Nayve, and the goddess had brought her home.

And then, in a flash of joy so piercing that it reduced all the rest of her awareness to nothing, she remembered Natac.

2

First Circle

In the darkness
Evil breeds.
Through the blindness,
Evil feeds.
With the hatchet
Evil needs
To shatter all in sight.

From *Song of the Delvers,* Seer Dwarf Chant

"All 'em down there, right," Hiyram reported, the goblin's big eyes narrowed to an approximation of a shrewd squint. "We gonna thump 'em, right?"

"Right," Karkald agreed. "I only wish Zystyl was with them."

The goblin shrugged. "Delvers is Delvers. Kill 'em when we can, right? This time, no arcane there—makes it that much easier to kill 'em."

The dwarf agreed in principle with this sentiment, but at the same time he felt growing frustration. He had been warring against the Blind Ones for centuries, and it seemed as though the pattern of the war never changed. His own Seer Dwarves and their goblin allies had won many victories, paid for those victories with treasured lives, and never seemed to gain any real headway against their sightless but implacable foes.

"The charge is set," reported Jordon, his demolitions expert and second-in-command. "The blast will close off the back tunnel, so they'll be trapped. The fuse will start when you set off the coolfyre."

"Did you get a last count of the Blind Ones?"

"Couldn't see," Jordon replied. "But it sounded like at least a hundred, give or take."

"All right." There was no point in further delay; any moment, one of the Delvers might smell the dynamite and spark a general retreat. "Let's move out. Attack as soon as I set off the coolfyre. Everybody good with the plan?"

Hiyram and Jordon nodded. The goblin and dwarven infantry companies nearby stood at ease, waiting for their commander's orders. The warriors of the two races were about the same height, but the goblins' sticklike limbs, potbellies, flapping ears, and wide, watery eyes were distinctly different from the bearded, solid dwarves planted firmly on their short, bowed legs. These two companies were the elite of Karkald's regiment, each warrior a veteran of at least two centuries of campaigning. They would do their jobs well, he knew.

Karkald himself went back to join the Rockriders, the two dozen Seer Dwarf cavalry who would support the attack. Each was mounted upon a restive ferr'ell, the furred, slender-bodied steeds that had been domesticated by the Seers in the last few centuries. With their wicked teeth and long, whiskered snouts, the ferr'ells looked dangerous—*were* dangerous—but in the hands of a stern and capable rider, they had proved to be reliable beyond all expectations. Karkald wasted no time in climbing into his own saddle. Bloodeater danced beneath him, eager to run, but the dwarf took one more minute to consider his deployments, visualize the attack.

They were in a vast cavern, one of many such passages bored through the rock surrounding the great underground vault that was the First Circle, Underworld. The Delvers were a mile away along this same cavern. This was apparently a work party, for the Blind Ones had been hauling large equipment deeper into this hitherto undiscovered network of caves. Even so, at least half of the enemy dwarves would be warriors, fully armed and ready to fight. Jordon's explosion would cut off their retreat, and the goblin and dwarven infantry would advance side by side. The Rockriders, their slinky mounts clinging to the cavern sides with sharp claws, would ride above.

Karkald placed a tiny pinch of flamestone on the tip of his sword, then rubbed his callused thumb sharply across the powder. Immediately, it began to glow with a soft light, barely enough to illuminate their surroundings. He saw the grimy faces of the infantry, each warrior masking his tension with a façade of bored indifference. Overhead, he could see the pointed tips of many long stalactites, though their bases on the lofty ceiling were still lost in shadow. But that was fine; he touched off this initial light only so that his troops could see enough to advance with a modicum of silence. Indeed, other spots of gentle illumination also came into being now, as each platoon sergeant similarly ignited a tiny bit of powdered stone.

Like creatures of one mind, they moved out together, dwarves and goblins advancing across the rough cavern floor, somehow maintaining a solid line as some of the troops scrambled through deep trenches, climbed across boulders, or moved around the stalagmites that rose so frequently in their path.

The Rockriders, meanwhile, split into two groups. Karkald rode with the group that climbed the right-side wall. His leather saddle had stiff supports extending nearly to his armpits and collar, and his weight rested easily in this slinglike support as Bloodeater climbed the nearly vertical wall and then turned to advance in time with the marching foot soldiers. The other 'riders came abreast, some above and some below their leader. On the other side of the cavern, the second platoon of mounted dwarves paced them.

For many minutes, the attackers moved through the gloomy passage in a measured, deliberate pace that created

little risk of an untoward noise. Soon they heard sounds
ahead. First it was the dull rumble of large wheels, as the
Delvers' great digging machine lumbered through the cave. A
sharp burst of hammering echoed quickly, the work done in
moments, and Karkald knew that the Blind Ones had
smashed another cave formation, smoothing out the floor into
an approximation of a roadway for their great digging tool.

Then the attackers were close enough to hear Delvers
barking and hissing and snapping at each other. They spoke
the same language as the Seers, but somehow the words
emerging from the Blind Ones' mouths sounded harsher,
more crude and guttural, than the same sounds made by
Karkald's people.

The goblins and Seer Dwarves came around a great bend
in the cavern, and now the sounds were direct, originating
only a hundred paces away. Karkald waved his sword, the
sign for the infantry to halt. He and the other Rockriders continued ahead, the long, sinuous ferr'ells gripping the irregular
wall with their sharp claws. Noses and whiskers twitched, but
the excited mounts were well disciplined and made no telltale
sounds.

Finally, the noises indicated that the vanguard of the
Delver party was right below him. Now Karkald reached into
his saddlebag and drew forth a glass sphere. Within, he felt
the weight of flamestone and the small, brittle vial of gold
dust. There was no longer time for delay; at any moment, one
of the Delvers would be sure to detect the attackers by smell
or sound.

The dwarf pitched his globe, waiting as it tumbled through
the air, hearing the crash of breaking glass as it landed on the
stone floor. Immediately, bright light flared everywhere, high-
lighting the Blind Ones as they were caught in the midst of
their march.

"We are lighted!" shrieked a Delver. "Stand and fight!"

Shouts of alarm echoed, and the enemy dwarves immediately rushed here and there, a maneuver that had the look of
chaos but quickly moved the warriors into a line protectively

surrounding the miners. At least a hundred Delvers were down there, many carrying picks, shovels, and other tools. Dozens, however, were armed with the deadly multibladed knives favored by their kind, and these instantly formed a barrier of steel around the workers.

More globes shattered and started to glow, and almost immediately the whole vast cavern was brilliantly lit. The goblins and Seer Dwarves surged forward now, no longer concerned with total silence as their boots clattered across the floor. But neither did they raise any battle cries or make unnecessary noise that would reveal positions and movements.

Karkald spotted the leader of the Unmirrored, saw the plain black faceplate of his metal helmet, and knew for certain that this party wasn't commanded by an arcane. Of course, he had already been fairly certain that none of the supersensing Blind Ones accompanied this group—the Seer advance would surely have been detected, if that was the case—but he felt the familiar mixture of relief and disappointment at the knowledge that this party was captained by an ordinary Delver.

The infantry companies came into view, charging with soft footfalls into the wash of light. The Seer Dwarves formed a solid line, rushing shoulder to shoulder, holding small shields in left hands and keen short swords in the right. Beside them, the goblins made a looser formation but attacked just as swiftly. Each of the long-legged warriors carried a short javelin, and the front of the company was a bristly mass of razor-sharp spearheads.

Somehow, the Delvers sensed the direction of attack. Some of the guards, those armored Blind Ones armed with triple-bladed daggers, hurled themselves into the path of the advancing companies. Several were impaled on spearheads, but others pushed through the bristling mass, tearing into the lightly armored goblins with wild, swirling blows. Still more Delvers stood in the path of the Seers, blades clanging against metal shields, blows that were potentially lethal notwithstanding the fighters' blindness. The disciplined Seers parried these thrusts with their swords, each man guarding the flanks of those beside him. Abruptly, a frantically whirling Unmirrored dwarf thrust between two shields, knife tearing into a pair of dwarves at once, until a third Seer cut him down with a stab to the throat. The Axial warriors quickly enveloped each of the enemy fighters, some dwarves using their shields for protection, others lunging when they saw an opening for a stab.

A thunderous blast tore through the cavern as the fuse, ignited moments earlier by the flash of coolfyre, touched off the explosive charge. Bloodeater flinched but clung tightly to the cavern wall, as did the other ferr'ells of the Rockriders. Below, the Delvers were scattering in mad panic as the goblins swept around the great digging machine. This monstrous tool was the size of a big house, supported by wheels twice the height of a tall dwarf. A metal superstructure capped a great frame of wood, while the pointed, threaded bit of a massive auger jutted from the front of the thing.

The Seer Dwarves punched through the other side of the enemy column, cutting down any of the Unmirrored who stumbled into range of a sword. One Delver warrior lowered his head and barked a command. Immediately, a dozen of his fellows rallied to him, all of them armed and armored, forming a dense wedge with the commander at the point. Somehow, the blind dwarves aligned themselves precisely in the same direction, facing the gap between the two Axial companies. They advanced in a rush, blades slashing like sickles to both sides as the small group burst between the Seers and goblins. Still in tight formation, the Unmirrored raced into the darkness, seeking escape in the lightless maze of the cavern.

"After them!" shouted Karkald, whose Rockriders had remained in reserve in case of something like this.

Bloodeater sprang away from the wall. By the time the ferr'ell landed on the floor, he was already running, streaking along in a series of prodigious leaps. Karkald hung on to his saddle, allowing his mount free chase. With another wild bound, Bloodeater landed on the back of a fleeing Delver, bearing the hapless dwarf to the ground with a bone-jarring thud. The fellow lay there, moaning, as the animal sprang after a second victim. This one fell to Karkald's sword, the dwarf stabbing as his ferr'ell dashed past.

The rest of the Rockriders had rallied in the pursuit as well, and all of the Delvers who had broken past the infantry were quickly brought down and killed. By the time the mounted dwarves trotted back to the battle, the few surviving Delvers were being put to the sword. Even the workers fought to the last. As it had ever been in this war, neither side was interested in taking prisoners.

"How many?" Karkald asked, as Hiyram came up to him in his flap-footed gait.

"I had three killed, five cut up pretty bad. Four of them should make it back to the city. . . . One, he's cut in the belly. Seems we got about a hunnert thirty Delvers. Good bag."

Karkald nodded grimly. Even in a lopsided victory such as this, the casualties among his own troops seemed like a monstrous crime, a tragedy for which he, himself, had to bear some of the blame. He went to get the word from Jordon, found the dwarf captain standing atop one of the great wheels of the digging machine. He looked down at Karkald and shrugged.

"Lost Barton when the bastard Delver cut through the shield wall. Otherwise, just some nicks and cuts. Good lessons to the lads to be more careful next time."

"Barton. Damn." That dwarf had been a veteran of the Great Nayve War, three hundred years ago. He was one of the few survivors of that long-ago strife who had still continued to campaign for the crown. Dour and serious to a fault, he had nevertheless been a fixture of the company since before Karkald had been given command. Now they would carry him back to Axial, of course, and the king himself would no doubt say a few words of praise, but Karkald could only feel again that painful stab of guilt.

"Look at this thing," Jordon was saying. "This is like no auger I've ever seen before."

Karkald slipped out of his saddle and dismounted, then climbed up onto the digging machine by the metal rungs that were hammered into the great timbers of its frame. Once atop the thing, he saw what his companion meant.

"It's a fairly standard drilling bore," he remarked. "But what are all those springs for, underneath? And that framing . . . it looks as though they could crank the bit upward."

"*Way* up," Jordon agreed. "There's enough frame there that, if you unfold it, you could drill into a surface fifty feet up the side wall, or even through the cave roof overhead."

"Over here, Captain," called Hiyram. He stood with several goblins at the side of the cavern, pointing upward.

Karkald saw a seam of darkness in the rock of the wall and ceiling. Already, several of the Rockriders had ridden over there to check, their ferr'ells creeping easily up the steep wall. One by one, they disappeared into the entrance. In a few moments, one of them, a youngster named Rallakar—a recruit of barely a hundred years' campaigning experience—came racing back.

"They've broken through the wall," he reported excitedly. "There's a new passage up there, wide enough for an army. They've done some preliminary work, getting it ready for transport."

"Which direction?" Karkald asked, trying to grasp the strategic implications of this new avenue through the First Circle.

"It starts toward the Center," reported the scout. "And looks like it goes for a long way."

"They've found a new route to Axial!" Karkald declared, the very notion sending a tremor of alarm down his spine. "Jordon, Hiyram, get the companies back to the city and report directly to General Paternak and the king himself, if you can."

"And where do you go?" asked the goblin calmly.

"I'm taking the Rockriders. We're going into that cave!"

WHERE *is* he?" muttered Darann, restlessly clumping around her dressing chamber. Coolfyre lamps cast the room in gentle brightness, the light softly reflecting from the brass rails of the bed, the golden combs on her marble buffet, and the silver that framed so much of the walls and the ceiling.

But the opulence might as well have been tarnished tin for all the pleasure the dwarfwoman drew from it today.

"Now, my daughter," said Rufus Houseguard, his gray beard curling with a sympathetic frown. "Karkald is doing something important; we all know that."

"Well, why can't he do it *here,* in time for the Festival of Fyre?" Even as she asked the question, she was appalled by the whining tone of her voice. She drew a deep breath and fixed her father with a determined glare. "His best uniform is twenty years old, and he's going to lead his whole regiment past the king at the festival. Doesn't he know it takes time to get measured, to find the materials, even if all he gets is a new tunic?"

"It's my impression that Kark hasn't added a pound of weight in the last twenty years. Why not give the tailor his old uniform and let him make a new one of the same size? Then it might be ready when he comes back."

Darann grimaced. Her father's suggestion was practical, which is what annoyed her. After all, it wasn't *just* for his tailoring measurements that she wanted to see her husband again. She missed him, she worried about him, and she wanted him to be here for her and to be visible to the dwarves of the city before this great celebration on the tenth centennial of the discovery of coolfyre.

"Now, Dary," Rufus said, coming forward to offer a sympathetic embrace from which she stomped away. "I know how important this is to you.... Finally Karkald gets the recognition you and I know he deserves. But surely you realize that such recognition is *not* terribly important to your husband? Isn't that one of the things that you like about him?"

"Oh, don't be so dark-cursed *reasonable*," snapped the dwarfmaid. "I'm not in the mood to hear how lucky I am!"

"Well, you'll hear it anyway!" groused Rufus, stalking to the door but turning back to address his daughter. "You're married to the hero of the Nayve War, but Karkald has never forgiven himself for letting that arcane, Zystyl, escape. He won't be able to rest until that little matter is resolved!"

"I know Zystyl!" snapped Darann. "He almost killed me. Remember? But that was three hundred years ago! For all we know, he's already dead!"

"You think that, if you want," the dwarven lord declared. "As for me, I'm glad we've got men like Karkald keeping their eyes open."

With that, he exited and was none too gentle about closing the door behind him. Darann sat on a chair, then bounced up to pace around her dressing chamber. "Men!" she growled, before stopping in front of the mirror and frowning at her image. "Why do they have to be so *stubborn*?"

She scowled back from the looking glass, and the expression did not make her feel any better about herself. Her cheeks were round and, now, flushed with displeasure. Her whole face seemed like a big circle, in fact, and as she dropped her eyes, she groaned at the realization that her body seemed to grow more round each year. Damn Karkald again. How could he remain as trim and wiry as he had been when they married, more than three centuries ago? And he could eat and drink prodigiously!

Appraisingly, she hefted her large breasts, and now she missed Karkald with a poignant ache that went much deeper than her spiteful petulance. If only he was here! She wouldn't care that he didn't have a new uniform, might not be the best dancer or the most effervescent conversationalist. She only wanted to hold him, kiss him, make love to him. *Then* they could see about getting him some new clothes.

Feeling a little better about things, she dressed to do some shopping, donning a blue cotton frock that seemed to fill out nicely where she wanted to swell and to conceal the places she wanted to hide. The material was soft and luxuriant, an import from Nayve, and she liked the thought that she would draw some eyes in Axial's thriving market. She tied her hair back with a blue silk ribbon, then changed her mind and pulled the ribbon more loosely behind her ears and over the top of her head. Her blond hair spilled out the back in a sheer cascade, halfway down to her waist, flouncing playfully when she tossed her head. She slipped her feet, which were small for a dwarfmaid, into sandals of black leather with an inlaid pattern of golden wire. She had a matching bag into which she dropped a few coins of gold and silver, then carried it with her as she left the apartment to face the world—at least, the part of the world that lay at the center of the First Circle.

At the balcony, she paused to take in the view of Axial, the great city of metal and stone sprawling below, cleanly etched in the glare of a hundred coolfyre beacons. The apartment, one of the most splendid locales in the city, was located high in one of the Six Towers. These were natural pillars of stone rising from the bedrock of the Underworld, massive and irregular, expanding above to merge with the stone surface of the Midrock, more than a thousand feet above the floor.

She and Karkald lived in a splendid set of rooms about halfway up one of the central towers. This was prime real estate indeed, but Karkald's status as the hero of the Nayvian War had earned him the place for a fraction of the housegeld that any other dwarf would have to pay.

Leaning on the stone parapet, she looked across the brilliant façade of the Royal Tower, the central pillar in all the great city. The entire face of what had once been bare cliff was now shaped into columned porticos, walled balconies, many exterior stairways and walks, and lovely gardens where greenery, and often trilling water, spilled over the edges to add color and texture to the splendid expanse.

The king of Axial lived there with his wife and many of his royal guards, and Darann sighed with the memory that she, too, could once have moved there. After the war, the king had offered Karkald a posting with the palace guard, but her husband—damn his stubborn ways!—had respectfully declined, saying that he would prefer to remain with the scouts and watchmen, those Seer Dwarves entrusted with keeping the city's environs free of the pernicious Delvers.

She had been prepared to put her foot down about the specifics of his assignment. There was no way in all the Seven Circles that she intended to be marooned on a remote watch station again! But the king had solved the problem for her, commanding Karkald to investigate the domestication of the wild ferr'ells that stalked through remote parts of the First Circle. These beasts were known to be fast, strong, and smart. Related to the deadly wyslets, they were larger than those carrion-eating brutes, and at least potentially trainable. Kark had taken to the task with enthusiasm, and Darann admitted to a sense of real pride whenever he and the rest of his mounted company paraded past on their wild, red-eyed steeds.

Below, the great plaza of Axial, a mile-wide ring between several of the great stone pillars, was bustling in the throes of a market gathering, the great orgy of buying and selling that arose once every ten cycles, taking on a life of its own as it possessed the center of the great city, drawing the attentions of very many of Axial's citizens.

A lot of those dwarves were already there. As she looked down, Darann could see festive tents, small stalls, roofless inns, taverns, and cookhouses set up haphazardly. Several great wagons, some so large they were hauled by two dark-bulls, rumbled along the crowded avenues and pathways across the market. The music of a hundred drummers resonated through the air, while horns and fifes added melody and vivacity to the songs. Throngs of people moved across the stone ground, though the dwarfmaid could still see the paving stones in many places. By the time the market reached its climax, in twelve or fifteen hours, the place would be so packed that a viewer above would only see the teeming mass of dwarves.

Darann made her way to the lift, pulling the lever that would bring the metal cage, riding smoothly in the midst of three oiled rails, up to her. Steam hissed as the platform came to a halt before her, and she stepped inside with a thrill of anticipation. She never got over enjoying the ride.

"Wait! Wait!" A voice attracted her attention to the far side of the balcony, and she politely held the door as a dwarf, dapper in high leather boots, a red silk jacket, and golden epaulets, hurried to join her. "Thank you," he panted, as the gate slid shut and the lift began to sink swiftly downward.

"I am Marshal Nayfal," said the other dwarf, clicking his heels together and bowing stiffly. "And of course I recognize Darann Houseguard, heroine of the Nayve War."

"Well, thank you," she said, self-conscious as ever when someone brought up the past. She had heard of the marshal, knew he was a highly regarded member of the king's court, and a key adviser to the commander of the royal army, General Paternak. "That was a long time ago, of course," she said dismissively.

"Ah, but your climb to Nayve has made a great difference to our daily lives," said Nayfal. "Do you ever reflect that this lift, like so many things in the First Circle, from that lovely cotton dress to the new types of ale being brewed all through the city, are products that resulted from the great ascent you and your husband made during the war?"

She looked at him, strangely unsettled by his praise. "Why, these are the products of the traders who make the regular caravans to the Fourth Circle."

"Yes, but you were the trailblazers, the ones who marked the pathway that brought an entire army of Seers up to the Fourth Circle."

She could do little but acknowledge the truth of his words. Indeed, though the dwarves of that great army had quickly retired to their sunless domain, they had seen enough of Nayve that many industrious traders had recognized the possibilities for commerce. Now scarcely an interval went by that did not include some expedition returning to Axial from the Fourth Circle, offering exotic foods and materials, the delicate works

of elven artisans, and—perhaps most significant of all—
information gained from druids who spent so much time observing the humans of the Seventh Circle.

The use of the steam power moving this lift, for example,
was inspired by human developments on the world called
Earth. Although the elves disdained such technology, the
dwarves, with their vast troves of ore and coal, and their skill
at metalworking, had embellished their civilization with
steam power in many ways. Not only had the city of Axial
expanded along a web of rail lines extending to outlying valleys, but the dwarven capital had risen upward because of in-
novations such as this lift and pumps that could propel water
six or seven hundred feet above the level of the city floor. Under their protective canopy of coolfyre, the illumination that
held the sunless darkness of their world at bay, the Seer
Dwarves were prospering as never before.

"Of course, not everything changes," the marshal noted.
"We must be alert, as ever, to the Delver threat."

"Yes, I understand. We need to find new ways of fighting
them, always," Darann agreed.

"New ways, yes. Such as taking the ferr'ells? In fact, I
have learned to ride myself. . . . It is a quaint pleasure, though
I do not think useful, overall, for real fighting. It is as General
Paternak says: We should stick to the proven tactics, those
that have brought us success for centuries."

"Oh?" Darann replied coolly, relieved that they were nearing the bottom. "I wouldn't know."

"It has been a pleasure," said the marshal, bowing again as
the lift reached the bottom.

"Thank you. I will tell my husband of your kind words."
Darann was startled to see a shadow cross Nayfal's face, as if
the mention of Karkald caused him a momentary irritation.
She told herself to be certain to mention the conversation, for
just that reason, as soon as Karkald returned.

She wasted no time in making her farewells, choosing a
roundabout way toward the bustling plaza in order to make

sure that the splendidly dressed nobleman would take a different course. For some reason, he had begun to make her uncomfortable.

Darann passed a stall where a smith was selling fine blades, from daggers to swords, and stopped to watch a glassblower who rendered colorful ornaments and beautiful bottles from globes of colored, heated sand. A goblin peddler was offering tiny sips from the juice of a citrus fruit, carried in at great difficulty from Nayve, and she parted with a gold piece for a taste, enjoying on her tongue the sensation of liquid that was both tart and sweet at the same time.

She was skirting a band of five drummers and one horn player, skipping along in unconscious cadence with the beat, when she was hailed by a familiar voice.

"Hey—it's my sister! The dwarfmaid warrior from the sky!"

Borand, her elder brother, was there, wearing his scarlet tunic, shiny boots, and golden helmet: full ceremonial garb for his rank as captain in the Royal Guard. He came up to her and gave her a hug. She playfully pushed him away after pecking him on his bearded cheek. "You know how I hate it when you call me that!" she chided. "I'm no more a warrior than you are a dancer."

"Ooh, that cuts deeply," chuckled Borand, dancing a little jig that had nothing at all to do with the rhythm of the music clattering so loudly beside them. "But I was just trying to impress my new lieutenant with my excellent pedigree."

For the first time, Darann noticed the young dwarf standing awkwardly just behind Borand. He had a splendid black beard, oiled and neatly combed, and wore a dazzling uniform lacking just a few of the epaulettes that made her brother look so dashing. His helm was silver, polished to a mirror's clarity.

"Allow me to present Konnor, of House Coalguard," Borand said, stepping to the side.

The lieutenant made a sweeping bow—clearly, this one *did* have some abilities as a dancer—and took Darann's outstretched hand in both of his own.

"This is indeed an honor," said Konnor. "There is not a dwarf in all of Axial who has not heard and celebrated the exploits of Darann and Karkald, the heroes of the Nayvian War!"

"Better stop that," Borand said, poking his elbow into his mate's ribs. "She doesn't like to be reminded of that."

"Don't pay any attention to him," Darann said with a laugh. "It's kind of you to say so. Just remember, that was a very long time ago!"

"May we give you an escort around the market?" Borand asked, extending his arm. "Looking like that, you never know what kind of ruffians you're going to attract."

"I seem to have captured two of them already," the dwarfmaid replied in delight, taking an arm from each of the officers and walking between them.

"You do look, er, utterly splendid," said Konnor, a blush pleasantly coloring the pale skin of his face where it showed above his beard.

"Konnor is just in from the Woodreach," Borand said dismissively. "He hasn't seen a female in two years."

"What?" The lieutenant's flush turned crimson, until he grimaced with the realization he was being teased. "Of course I have . . . and even if I hadn't, why, you'd look splendid. I mean, even if I *had*—no, I *have*. . . ." He spluttered awkwardly, stumbling over words, finally clamping his mouth shut with a glower at Borand.

"*I* think he's perfectly charming," Darann said. "And you'd better leave him alone, or it will be you who gets sent to the Woodreach!"

"Perish that thought and bite your tongue!" her brother retorted. "I'm not like that husband of yours. I *like* it here, under the lights of the city, surrounded by people, music, life."

"Where is the legendary Karkald?" asked Konnor, as they moved on through the crowd, which suddenly thickened, dwarves clustering around to gawk at something. "I should like to meet him."

"I daresay you will," Borand said offhandedly, as the trio

broke through the ring to see a filthy, disheveled dwarf striding toward them. Mud matted his hair and beard and plastered
across his face to give his eyes a wild, staring quality. His
gaze was fixed upon the edifice of the Royal Tower, which
was clearly his destination.

"Karkald!" squeaked Darann, surprised. She was happy to
see him—and dismayed by his grimy appearance. "You're
back!"

Her husband stopped, those wild eyes finding her in the
crowd of faces. He cracked a smile, though he glanced toward
the king's palace, as if frustrated by the distraction of seeing
her. Only then did she realize that she still had her hands
through the arms of the two officers. She held them there, not
wanting to make the guilty gesture of pulling them away.

"Yes!" he said, nodding as if she'd just announced a splendid revelation, coming up to her. "I came through the
Midrock with news for the king!"

"What is it?" Borand said, all business. "We'll take you up
there right away!"

"Thanks," Karkald said absently, as Darann disentangled
her arms to grip her husband's hands in her own. "It's news
about the Delvers." For the first time, he seemed to realize his
disheveled appearance. He stepped back and rubbed his
hands over the muddy cloak of his field dress.

"I came through the Midrock—that's why I look like
this—following a tunnel they're excavating."

"Here?" asked Konnor in shock.

"Yes. If I'm guessing right, they're planning a new attack.
And they'll be coming at Axial from above!"

HIS mistress was dead, but that was a matter of little importance. In fact, he had grown bored with her over the last interval, so he would not lament her loss. And, too, her dying
had been an experience of exquisite pleasure, stretched out
for two full cycles. Sounds and tastes, touches and odors, all
had tickled his senses with an aura of penetrating delight.

Most wonderful of all had been her *thoughts,* as his arcane
senses had sampled them: the terror that had dawned when
she had first realized that this lovemaking was to be their last,
the pain that had seared through her flesh and became, somehow, transformed into the rarest of delight when those burning sensations had made their way into Zystyl's mind.

For that experience alone, he had worked to keep her alive,
longed to relish her dying through a third, even a fourth cycle.
He had tied her down and worked with patience and care, using only the tip of his dagger or slight nips of his metal-coated
teeth. But in the end, her flesh was as weak as her spirit, and
she had expired even before he reached the second climax of
his own pleasure.

Still, there would be others. . . . There were always others.
He would not let the loss dismay him.

Instead, he rose from the pallet and went immediately to
the stone, the cherished gem he called the Hurtrock, his
prized possession over the last two hundred years. He allowed his fingers to play with the numerous facets on the
gem, and as always, he could feel the colors seeping through
his skin, registering as beautiful patterns in his mind. "You
are blessed, my stone," he whispered, bringing the gem to his
metal lips. He kissed it and then tucked it safely under his tunic, where he would wear it just over his heart.

"Clean this up!" he barked, turning from the gory mess
that had become of his sleeping mat, calling to his servants,
who would not be far away. He heard two of them enter and
felt the awe welling from each as they were confronted with
the stink of blood and death. "And bring me a new mattress,"
he added curtly.

It was with a sense of refreshed vigor that he dressed in a
clean tunic and lifted a helmet of copper, which he placed on
his bald scalp. Unlike the helmets of the typical Delver, the
arcane's helm lacked the plain visor, which concealed the
face from the nose upward. Zystyl's nostrils were exposed
with purpose, for those moist, bloody apertures were a keen
part of his powers. He could smell the mixing of metals a

hundred yards away, or the slaughtering of a prisoner any-where within a mile. By the acrid stench of Delver sweat, he could tell his compatriots apart, sense the moods, desires, even intentions of his people.

Zystyl's mouth creaked into a grimace of pleasure. Those jaws were another mark of his status as an arcane, for they were lined with steel, a smooth and shiny patina that had af-fixed to his flesh when, as a young initiate, he had plunged his face into a vat of molten metal. The skin of his chin and lips had burned away, to be replaced with steel, while the flesh of his nose had been seared off, leaving his nostrils as the wide, gaping holes that now sampled the air of his palace chambers. For such was the creation of an arcane. Nearly all initiates perished from the damage they suffered during the burning, and most of the rest went quickly mad. But those few pre-cious leaders who had the strength and the will to survive and the inventiveness to open their senses to all the sensations of the world . . . those were the ones who went on to become the leaders among the Delvers, the masters of their people and—eventually, inevitably—would be the conquerors of the First Circle.

Now the arcane made his way down the wide steps leading from his apartments into the large, circular chamber in which he held court. Although nominally there was no king among the Delvers, only a few dozen arcanes competing for influ-ence and power among the teeming masses of their people here in Vicieristn, there was none so powerful as Zystyl. As a consquence, he attracted more followers, and his plans were given more serious consideration than the proposals made by any other.

It was in curiosity regarding one of those plans that Zystyl now strode into his hall. He heard the shifting of his atten-dants, smelled the clean metal of their weapons and armor as they genuflected while he passed. Though none of them could see him, the arcane broadcast his presence as a telepathic wave, insuring that all knew he was here, and knew to fear him.

But before he took his seat, he passed through the chamber and descended a long stairway into the furnace rooms that lay beneath his palace. The heat of coal fires welled through the vertical passage, and he smelled the keen odors of fire and ash, smoke and molten metal.

In the lowest of the working rooms, he found Jarristal, the female arcane he had appointed as mistress of this project. She detected his arrival immediately—her senses were almost as keen as his own—and she turned to him with the heat of excitement and pride emanating from every pore.

"How fares the golem?" asked Zystyl, from her reaction anticipating good news.

"It is almost complete, Master Zystyl," she replied eagerly. "Within the next three or four cycles, it will be ready to walk."

"Splendid," declared the Delver lord. "Your work is pleasing to me."

Her gratitude was another palpable wave of emotion, and as he started back up the long stairway, he reflected. He required a new mistress, and it had been a long time since he had physically relished an arcane. Of course, there were disadvantages to pairing with one who might, someday, entertain thoughts of equality, but experience had shown him that there were rare pleasures to be obtained from conjoinment with a lover who could sense his wishes and desires even before he expressed them.

Indeed, Jarristal would require some more thought.

Finally he was seated in the great chair of gold, the throne that had been molded exactly to fit the contours of his body. He drew a deep breath, a moist sucking into his broad nostrils, and confirmed that many of his loyal warriors, perhaps half a hundred, had gathered to partake of his wisdom. He could hear one of these breathing with some urgency and sent out a tendril of thought, probing the dwarf's mind. Indeed, this was a messenger with news.

"Speak," said Zystyl, and all present understood he addressed only this message bearer.

"My lord, there is news from the great tunnel," began the

Delver. "A massacre . . . all the workers slain, their machine taken by the Seers. Our enemies have set up a watch post in the cavern, and it will be very difficult to resume our excavations."

"Good," Zystyl said, sinking backward into his chair and chuckling. "Good," he reported.

"Lord?" said the messenger hesitantly. "I fear my miserable tongue did not make the facts clear. . . . There has been a disaster."

"Disaster?" The arcane was in a good mood and did not rebuke or punish the speaker for attempting to clarify. "Hardly. You said the Seers found the digging party, correct?"

"Indeed, Lord. And killed them all."

"And I said good—for that is precisely what I hoped would happen."

3

Oldest of the Old Ones

A world of clouds,
A land of mist,
A vap'rous shroud,
A sea of bliss.

A crown of height,
Corona gold,
Serene in sight,
Sky's ramparts bold.

From *A World of Clouds*
by Draco Minstrel

He had been sleeping for a very long time, so long that the very act of his awakening covered a span of better than two years. First came a flexing of massive blue nostrils, a single exhalation over many days. Air, musty with age and mildew, seeped from ancient lungs into the great cavern. Next came an indrawn breath, and for a full interval, those long-dormant lungs swelled with fresh air. The next time, his breath escaped more quickly, rushing with an audible hiss, stirring up wisps of cloud from the cave floor, and within a few hours, the Old One was again inhaling.

In the space of time it took him to unfurl one massive wing, the walls of his shelter shifted through another year of gradual change. By the time he opened both of his great eyes, turned the slitted pupils outward, and focused on the dim light emanating from the cavern walls, his breathing had steadied into a regular two-minute cycle, his heart was pumping with steady pressure, and his mind had begun to glimmer with awareness.

First he remembered his name: Regillix Avatar. Next came knowledge of his surroundings: He was in a cavern of fibrous cloud, high on a mountain peak near the center of the Overworld, Arcati. Beyond his shelter lay the Sixth Circle, with a vast reach of cloudy summits gathered around his own mountain.

Still thinking very slowly but propelled now by those memories, Regillix drew himself around the winding passages leading outward from his great chamber. His taloned feet sank easily into the misty floor, gripping comfortably as tendrils of that surface whirled and rose to tickle his scaly belly. Farther and farther he went, until at last he came around the final curve, and the cavern ended in a mountainside ledge.

Looking out over the towering landscapes of his world, the Old One saw that the cloud-mountains had changed so much that he barely recognized the place where he had gone to sleep a century earlier. His own summit was still the loftiest in view, but a great knife-edged ridge had formed across the canyon from him, and a nearby range, a line of purpled, sawtooth peaks, had grown noticeably taller and steeper in the interval of his rest.

He blinked and cleared his throat and, over the course of a full day, carefully studied his surroundings. At the height of its course, the sun blazed brightly from below, filtered rays beaming upward through the valleys between the great cloud mountains. The sky was blue as it fringed the horizon, but that color deepened to a deep, mystical shade of indigo directly overhead. As a master of cosmology, Regillix knew that, with the sun at its brightest in his own world, the Fourth Circle far below lay cloaked in the darkness of night. Eventually, the sun again began its steady descent, throwing darkening shadows between the great summits. As Nayve again welcomed the Lighten Hour, Arcati was plunged into the serene darkness of night.

By the next day, Regillix had regained enough alertness that he began to ponder what it was that had pulled him from a slumber that should, naturally, have extended at least for another dozen years. Looking around, he determined that there was no obvious geographical danger developing. In a shifting realm such as the Sixth Circle, it was not impossible for caves to gradually be enclosed by semisolid vapor, or a dangerous overhang to develop, threatening a cloudslide of thunderous power, with the potential for catastrophic destruction. But the slope of this mighty summit maintained its incline at an angle that showed no threat of collapse. And his cave was still wide, with no indication that the walls would soon close in and pinch off his egress.

Sinking his mighty talons into the ledge below him, Regillix extended his long neck, peering into the depths below. Now, once again exposed to the full light of the sun, the twisting valley at the base of the cloud peak was a line of brightness, shimmering yellow, so intense that he closed the thin and shaded membranes that covered the outer surface of his great eyes, shielding his gaze from the brilliance.

Down there he could see creatures flying back and forth, griffons probably, no doubt feeding on the cloudfish that swarmed into activity when the sun was at its brightest. There was no sign of alarm there; this was the pattern of hunting and hunted that had occurred since time immemorial, throughout the nearly one hundred centuries of Regillix Avatar's life.

But something, undeniably, had disturbed him, brought him from his rest, and the fact that this cause remained unknown he found deeply, profoundly concerning. This awareness caused him to extend his great wings, shaking free the dust of three decades rest. The vast membranes creaked and stretched until they stood straight and smooth, a proud symbol of the great dragon's utter dominance of all things in this world and every other.

For an hour, Regillix Avatar held that pose, allowing his

wings to grow strong and confident, to remember the ancient commands that had guided him so surely through the air. His tail uncurled over this same time, and he lashed it experimentally, pleased to discover that it remained supple and nimble, for it was a tool that was crucial to steering through the skies. His great legs, each as big around as an ancient oak, pressed and lifted, and his serpentine belly came free from the shifting, misty surface of his mountainside ledge.

At last he pressed all of those muscles into service, spreading the vast pinions, stroking downward, leaping into space. He felt the familiar dizzying thrill of flight as his wings bit through the air and pressed, just slightly, to give him lift and steerage.

He was not immediately interested in climbing. He always made a lair for himself in a lofty vantage of mountaintop summit, so that his first flight upon awakening could be a graceful glide, with a vast gulf of space below, room for him to remember all the intricacies of aerial movement and to plunge downward with the growing speed that, finally, brought his senses into full acuity, provoked the rapid beating of his heart that sent blood pulsing through his huge body and vitality returning to his limbs.

Mountains soared past in a stately march. One lofty summit of ominous black shouldered its way between peaks of pure white. Thunder crackled from the dark cloud, and sparks of lightning rippled across the surface, occasionally stabbing outward with crackling fingers. Regillix banked away, between two gateposts of cloudy peak, to glide over a skyscape of fluffy hills, clouds tinged with blue in a vast, irregular blanket. Here and there, new summits puffed into view right before his eyes, and he watched another misty hillock roll sideways with stately majesty and vanish beneath the encroaching slopes of two neighboring elevations.

This was the living sky, and it covered the great swath that lay at the center of the Overworld. These clouds were intensely warmed by the sun, and as a result remained unstable, the surface treacherous, devoid of game or secure landing places. Regillix didn't fly here any longer than was necessary to see that all was as it should be. Tilting his great wings, the massive serpent banked around and again made for the rising summits of the mountains.

He passed into a cloud canyon, between a pair of massive summits, and felt the power of the sun warming his belly. The light was intense here, pouring through the narrow gorge at the base of the canyon, reflecting dazzlingly from the cloudy walls to either side. Now, when he looked upward, it seemed to Regillix that the lofty tops were cast in shadow, that they glowered down upon him with threats of lightning and thunder.

Keening shrieks rose from below, and he saw more griffons screeching a warning to each other and diving toward the shelter of the countless side valleys that worked their way sinuously off the main canyon. He decided against pursuing them, since the chase would require a lot of effort, and the notoriously stupid griffons probably wouldn't know anything, anyway. Snorting disdainfully, Regillix glided past, ignoring the hawk-faced creatures who now clustered on ledges to caw and cry insults at the mighty dragon. Whether rising on their leonine hindquarters or flexing feathered wings and slashing with eagle-taloned forefeet, the griffons were careful to maintain ready escape routes in case the target of their jeering decided to chase after all.

Regillix did start to climb now, scooping the air with powerful downbeats of his broad wings, but he was well past the griffons, intent on finding somebody else to interrogate. A flock of harpies burst from cover on a mountainside, where their gray white feathers had almost perfectly blended in to the steep and irregular slope. The dragon tilted in their direction, enjoying the spectacle as the hag-headed vultures, grotesque arms trailing limply beside their wings, wheeled and dove in mortal fear. Two of the hideous scavengers collided, and in a chaos of feathers, talons, and curses, they tumbled into the canyon and vanished into the white heat of the sun. The others dove and dodged, vanishing around a shoulder of cloudy mountainside.

For a moment, Regillix was tempted to go after them. Harpies were the most hateful denizens of his world, and he hunted and slew them whenever he could. But he quickly realized he wasn't lively enough for such a chase, not yet. Furthermore, memories of the harpies' vexing combat habit—typically they hurled flaming spit at anyone they weren't trying to eat—convinced him to delay such satisfaction until later.

Again he banked, gracefully curling around another vast curve in the canyon's course. Now he came into view of the Cloudsea. Moments later, he emerged from the enclosure of the canyon and flew across a shoreline of rippling rainbow, as if the colors of the spectrum had been rendered into a band and stretched across the ground, forming an encircling beach around the dazzling swath of sea.

The Cloudsea itself was a mass of rippling purple vapor, shimmering and bright with the powerful glow of the sun shining upward through the mist. Regillix knew that surface could turn black and stormy under an onslaught of wind and rain, but now it was as pastoral and soothing a sight as he could remember. Gliding again, he soared just over the sea, feeling the cooling moistness of the purpled cloud as it passed below his belly.

A short distance away, the Cloudsea heaved and a sky-whale broke free from the surface, the rippling black body shining slick and wet. The whale's great maw opened, and a gout of fire erupted, searing away a patch of sea, leaving a streak of mist hanging in the air as the creature plunged downward again to vanish beneath the now roiling surface. The dragon touched that top with his wingtips, twirling twin circles of cloud in homage to the beast that was as much a master of its domain as Regillix was in his own.

But beautiful as the Cloudsea was, the wyrm knew that he would not find the answers to his questions here. He made a shallow turn, his low wingtip cutting a sparkling wake through the misty surface, and took a bearing toward the nearest shore. A series of gentle, rolling hills domed above the rainbow shore, with the lordly mountains visible in the far distance.

When he saw the colors of the beach strand, he tilted his wings, braking his speed sharply, dropping his tail and rear legs gently downward. The tail was the first to touch, the terminus splashing into the half-liquid sea, while most of the sinuous member slapped onto the red and orange stripes of the shore. His rear legs cushioned much of the impact of his weight as they came to rest on the yellow strand, while his belly straddled over blue and his forelegs settled onto indigo. His neck arched across the violet strip at the edge of the beach as he dug his claws in and, though he pitched forward, stopped short of hitting the first of the hills.

He heard a startled whinny and saw a pegasus rearing on the nearest hilltop, hooves pawing the air while its broad wings fluttered in agitation. Others of the flying horses had been grazing upon skygrass beyond, and they, too, rose in alarm at the sudden appearance of the dragon.

"Peace!" Regillix uttered the Word of Bonding, hoping that it would be enough to keep the pegasi from taking wing.

After another rearing and a buck, the stallion settled down and regarded Regillix with cool appraisal. The animal was a magnificent black, with wing feathers of pure white and a body sleek with muscle and gleaming hair. Finally, the proud head nodded, nostrils flaring in a snorted message to calm the herd.

"Peace," the stallion replied finally. "I will trust your bond. And you do not smell hungry."

"Thank you," Regillix returned. "Know that my bond is my life."

"You have been gone from the Overworld long, now," observed the pegasus. "Many of our foals have become full grown because of this."

"I am glad," said the dragon. If the stallion was being sarcastic, he didn't take note of the fact. "I was awakened by a premonition, a warning that summoned me from my sleep. Can you tell me: Have you seen a threat, anything of danger that may threaten disruption and change to our world?"

"Nay," said the stallion, shaking that great black head. But then his brow furrowed and he nickered thoughtfully. "But wait. . . . Do you know of the great storm, the Hillswallower?"

"Hillswallower?" Regillix Avatar felt a tremor of alarm ripple through his long, serpentine body. He had never heard that word before, but in the sound of it he heard deadly danger, and in the taste of it he found poison—so much so that he could not force himself to repeat it. "What is . . . what have you seen?"

"We used to forage on the White Hills, across the sea from here." The pegasus tossed his nose in the direction that was neither metal nor wood. "But in the Year of the Three Foals, the skygrass began to wither, and we were forced to fly far afield to fill our bellies. And then the next year, the Year of Falling Wingfeathers that was, some of the hills rolled down and vanished. A great storm took their place, bursting up from below and sweeping away all that came within its clutches. Our herd lost three, and we saw harpies and griffons get pulled into the storm. All that enters is gone."

"I thank you for your trust," Regillix said, fully alarmed. "Good forage to you."

"And good hunting to you—but somewhere else!" retorted the pegasus, rearing and fluttering his wings so that he rose from the ground in an elegant leap.

Regillix didn't have room to take off from the beach, so he folded his wings and trotted along the shore toward a lofty hill that rose not too far away. He was propelled by growing urgency, understanding beyond doubt that this Hillswallower storm was a great wrong, a violation of the Sixth Circle and possibly the order of all things. Soon he was climbing the steep slope, his talons sinking into the cloudy surface, gripping solidly as he pulled himself toward the crest. There he turned so that he was facing the Cloudsea, still dappled and purple below. He saw that the pegasi had gone back to their grazing, except for the stallion, who stood alert, wings poised, bright eyes fixed upon the mighty dragon.

With a single spring, the wyrm threw himself from the crest, instantly catching the air beneath his wings, stroking powerfully as he coursed out across the surface of the sea. Now he worked hard to gain altitude, and at the same time he banked so that he flew parallel to the shore toward the direction of metal.

Soon enough he would cross the sea and inspect this frightening storm for himself. But he had found the pegasus's warnings deep and fundamentally disturbing. He wanted to get more advice before he flew into the midst of something this unprecedented, this frightening.

So first, he would fly to the mountaintop and visit the angel, Gabriel.

HE had lain still in his bed for five days, with only the feeble breathing that fluttered his rib cage indicating that he still lived. Not once in that time did he open his eyes and turn that warm, wise gaze toward Belynda. Neither did he drink nor eat. He was dying, and she didn't know what to do.

So she sat beside him as much as she could, for hours at a time. She stroked the soft fur, caressed the long, white-tufted ears, even leaned to kiss the black nose that was moist but disturbingly warm. His cushion was as fluffy as any mattress in Nayve, and she would have covered him in silken blankets if she sensed chill. But the weather remained as perfect as ever, so she mostly just sat beside him in the garden plaza outside of her apartments, touching him often, speaking to him softly when her mind drifted over shared memories.

"I remember the first time you chased a goose—and caught it," she said in a whisper that was half chuckle, half sob. "Then it was the goose who did the chasing. I had to swat it away with a stick because you were hiding under my skirt."

The black nostrils puffed air, an exhalation of amusement, she was sure.

"And how you've been there, always, with your tail wagging, ready for whatever we were going to do." She sighed. "You know, I wish we had done more. . . . How did the time go by like that? Did you know that we've been together for five hundred seventy-one years? We have; I counted them just yesterday."

Again Ulfgang huffed, and one eye cracked open. "Not a bad age, for a dog," he whispered, making a visible effort to smile.

"Not a bad age at all," Belynda said, then gasped involuntarily as a quiet knock came from the door to her apartment.

She knew the meaning of that signal, for there was only one person who would be coming to her, one person who would get past the vigilant gnome Nistel, who stood guard outside her chambers. One person with one purpose, and she had been magically summoned to that purpose by Ulfgang himself.

The dog's eyes were closed again, and he whimpered, kicked one feeble leg as Belynda rose and went to greet her visitor. The sage-enchantress Quilene entered softly, nodded in response to Belynda's mute hello. The two elves crossed the large but sparsely furnished chamber and emerged into the garden.

The sun was receding overhead, though the day's warmth still surrounded them. Songbirds, bright flecks of orange, red, blue, yellow, and white, sat restless but silent on the branches of bushes and hedge. Ulfgang, in his bed beneath a shady magnolia tree, again twitched and made soft noises of distress.

"His wishes came to me this morning," Quilene said, laying a slender hand on Belynda's shoulder. "He is in very much pain."

"I know," the sage-ambassador said numbly. She knelt and once again touched that white head. "I understand, old friend. . . . My tears are from my own self-pity, that I am losing your companionship, your love."

Quilene knelt. "It will be a sleep of peace," she said. "And he will be free of pain."

Belynda nodded, held that soft old head in both hands. Quilene put a hand to Ulfgang's throat. Two rings, stones of blue and red, winked upon her fingers; magic arced in a gentle whisper of light. "Sleep, old dog," she said. "Be at rest."

The frail rib cage relaxed, and the nostrils puffed outward once more. This time, Ulfgang did not draw another breath.

FROM the log of the *Skyreaver*:

> *We passed from view of the great lake before the first Darken of our voyage, with a fine view of the Casting of the Threads. The spire of the Loom sparkled as if outlined in fire, and then tendrils of brightness, like gentled lightning, broke free to float upward and vanish into the sun. Thus does the Goddess Worldweaver cleanse Nayve of unclean impulses.*

> *I remember that Miradel taught me that those impulses are cast away to the "wasteland," to Earth. I wonder if that is true. Certainly, there has been enough violence worked on my native world in the past century. It is not impossible to believe that at least some of that villainy has been worked as a result of the castaway tendencies from this pastoral world.*

> *Ah, but that is a question for wiser minds than mine. To the voyage:*

> *The wind, raised by all the druids of the College, bore us steadily through the night and across the next Lighten.*

> *For two days we drifted above the Ringhills, their familiar crags and contours a comforting farewell as we move closer and closer to the unknown. The wind-*

stream from the center remained strong. Toward
Darken on the second day, Roland and Juliay spun us
a sidewind, and we drifted a dozen miles in the direction of metal. I had promised King Fedlater that we
would try to pass above the Dernwood Downs, and he,
in turn, had promised to celebrate our voyage in grand
style.

True to his word, the gnomish monarch had arranged
a display to welcome us. Before we reached his palace,
Skyreaver glided over the wide, terraced slopes of
Dernwood's fertile fields. Sheep dotted the green hillsides, like tufts of cotton on plush velvet. The prancing
ponies trotting toward the barns, the little burrows and
grand earthern mounds of that gnomish realm were a
pastoral balm to our eyes.

The palace of the gnome king is, to my mind, the
grandest wonder of the Ringhills. It occupies not one,
but seven hilltops, six encircling the central, loftiest
summit, all looming tall over a valley of immaculate
perfection. Bridges connect each of the hills with the
next and form a full circle around the vale. (Indeed, it
sometimes appears as though the gnomes would rather
build a bridge to connect two places than they would
walk a level path along the ground!)

King Fedlater and his entire court were gathered in
the courtyard just below the crest of the highest hill as
we approached. The airship rode a wind that had gentled with the approach of Darken. I could see him in his
golden robe, white-bearded and immensely dignified,
standing slightly ahead of his court. We exchanged a
wave, and then a chorus of trumpets brayed.

Immediately, skyrockets ascended from all the ramparts of the palace, a spectacular display of green and
red, gold and blue flames erupting around us. Misfires
were fortunately few; one massive rocket tipped sideways and shot across the royal courtyard, scattering

the king and his courtiers. Another ruptured our second flotation sphere. Sirien climbed the rope ladder under starlight and was able to effect a repair before we lost much helium.

But no one can launch a pyrotechnic display like the gnomes of Dernwood Downs. The fireworks continued to light the sky as we drifted on, and I confess to a certain melancholy as I watched with my shipmates from the stern. It seemed a last salute from civilization, for though we will still cross above the Hyac lands and their capital, Shahkamon, it may be a long time before we see a city with such splendor as Dernwood.

The following morning revealed us to be passing the Ringhills, with two hundred miles of scrublands, scored by numerous streams, extended below. For three days we crossed this belt, and now we are searching forward, eager for sight of the vast canyon that has hitherto blocked all exploration in the direction that is neither metal nor wood. The belt of grassy steppes, where the Hyaccan elves breed their great cattle, will be our sign that the chasm draws near.

Interestingly, the wind from the Center still bears us. No doubt the druids are maintaining their casting with devotion and energy, but I am still surprised that the effect has carried us this far. Roland laughingly says he enjoys the chance to loaf; as to Juliay, I wonder if, perhaps, she wouldn't be just as happy doing the windspinning herself. It seems to me as if she bears some secret unhappiness that is best buried in work. I spoke to Owen about it, and he claimed that I was imagining things.

I hope it is so. When I witness the affection he feels for her . . . when I see the love shared by Roland and Sirien . . . I feel as if they have found some place of contentment, some reason for living, regardless of a life's work.

For me, there is this voyage, these maps. . . .

Natac sighed and leaned back in his chair. How often did this happen? He began writing a detached account of his voyage, the discoveries and observations he made along the way. But inevitably his thoughts would turn inward, and the words on the paper would follow. He looked at the shelf of maps above his desk and felt a sense of deep satisfaction. These were copies of his real maps, of course—the originals were safely stored in the College—but they nevertheless represented a nearly complete atlas of the world of Nayve.

Three hundred years of exploration . . . Could it really be condensed into words and maps? Of course not. The wealth of those years came from the memories, the memories that he had acquired almost as a protective shield to insulate him from the one memory he dared not remember, the loneliness that was never far below the surface.

Natac's explorations had commenced immediately following the end of the war. Restless, he found that, since Miradel had died, there was nothing rooting him to Circle at Center. He had embarked on a simple trip to see some of the elven lands, especially Argentian. Traveling with Ulf, Tamarwind Trak, and Owen, he had kept a journal and drawn simple sketches of the route. When he returned to the Center some six years later, Belynda and other elves had found those sketches fascinating, and he realized that no one had thought of doing that before.

From that reaction, he developed an ambitious plan, a challenge that no elf, druid, or giant would ever have thought to undertake. He resolved to create a map of the Fourth Circle. He set out on one trip after another, sometimes with his original companions or else accompanied by the giant Rawknuckle Barefist, the centaur Galluper, and a host of others. He trod the pathways of Nayve on foot and on horseback. He sailed the waterways of his world by canoe and galleon, ships designed, built, and captained by Roland Boatwright. On those he marked the shore of the Worldsea, as it flanked Nayve in the directions of wood and metal. And, lately, his explorations had been conducted by balloon.

Sirien came in, bringing him a cup of tea. He thanked her, then sensed that she had some other reason for seeking him. "What is it?"

"It's . . . well, soon we'll reach the borders of Hyac."

"Right. Have you changed your mind about seeing your home again?"

"Oh, no . . . not at all. It's just that I wonder . . . Am I bringing you and Roland and Owen and Juliay all into danger, just so that I can see my father and my sister, share a feast with my people, again?"

"Your father is a proud man, and fierce. But I don't think he will be blinded by his resentments. I feel quite certain that he will welcome you, and us, as well as we could wish. Perhaps he'll even be intrigued by our mission."

"You're right," Sirien said with relief. "We're going to see things that no one has ever seen before." She touched Natac's shoulder in an expression of tenderness. "I am glad to be a part of this adventure."

She left, and he pondered the past and future of those adventures. Over the centuries, he had explored all of the major civilized realms, lands of elves and giants, gnomes and goblins. He had crossed lakes and seas enchanted by sprites and naiads, skirted the coastline of Nayve in the shallows of the Worldsea. Early on, he had mapped out the area around Circle at Center. Because the route in the direction that was neither metal nor wood was blocked by the vast canyon of Riven Deep, his voyages had naturally expanded along the other two poles of Nayve's compass, until he had traveled throughout the directions of metal and wood.

Lately, however, he had begun to fully appreciate the advantages that flight gave to him. Most significantly, that vast chasm would no longer be an obstacle.

Skyreaver was the fourth airship to be created for Natac's use. In the construction of these craft he had been aided extensively by Socrates and his alchemists, as well as by the druids Roland and Juliay, and many others of their order. They spent days, weeks, even years in the temple of the Goddess Worldweaver, watching the Tapestry take shape, following the creative genius of the great minds on the Seventh Circle, the world called Earth. Amid the wars and conquests, the sweeping panoply of wealth and destruction that was the eternal lot of humankind, they had taken note of scientific developments and technological advances.

Natac followed these developments closely. He knew that the earthen calendar had advanced to a year much of that world numbered 1865 A.D. In many respects, especially those requiring great quanties of iron and steel, Earth's technology remained far more sophisticated than Nayve's. Here in the Fourth Circle no one had bothered to build a steam engine for any practical purpose, so the railways that were beginning to crisscross the face of the human world had never appeared on Nayve. Nor was there any wish to clutter the great lake or the world's pure seas with any belching, smoking steamship. At the same time, the druids had watched humans create vessels that were lighter than air, had seen these balloons take to the skies in acts of derring-do and discovery.

And in this area, the druids of Nayve were more accomplished than their human cousins. Where earthen balloons must be filled with hot air or flammable hydrogen, Socrates had discovered how to generate plentiful supplies of helium. Even more significantly, a balloon in the skies of Earth was utterly subject to the power of the wind: it must either be tethered or go exactly where the wind took it and nowhere else. But the druids of Nayve had long ago harnessed the mastery of the wind, and it was this power that made the balloon such a splendid vessel for exploration: a druid such as Roland could cause the airship to float precisely where he wanted it to go.

A knock on the door of his cabin broke his reverie. "Yes?"

Juliay poked her head into the room. "We've spotted the Hyac steppe," she said. "It's a welcome bit of green. No sign of the canyon yet, though."

"It won't be long," Natac said. "We'll set down on the rim and take on fresh water. The khan will know we're here; *Sky-*

reaver is kind of hard to miss. The next move will be up to him."

"Yes . . . good." The druidess said, though the look in her eyes struck Natac as somber.

"Is something wrong?" he asked.

She suddenly smiled and laughed, the sound almost shrill in the small cabin. "No! Don't be silly," she chided him, and in her eyes he saw real affection and enthusiasm.

"I'm glad. Would you tell Owen to ready the release valves? I'd like to be sure we set down quickly when we spot the canyon edge and the Hyac."

"All right," she said, withdrawing and closing the door. Natac frowned, reflecting. For some reason, her eyes had clouded again, and it had been when he mentioned Owen.

MIRADEL walked slowly around the moist, verdant garden, her mind moving much faster than her feet. This was real, she convinced herself. There was the Worldweaver's Loom, the silver spire rising high overhead, right from the roof of the temple. And there, on the encircling ridge, she saw the familiar façades of the Senate and the College, just as she remembered them. And the lofty Grove of the druids, the great vault of huge trees and mossy bower, closed off the third part of the ring around the Center of Everything.

Finally, she asked the question of the great space around her, knowing the goddess could hear and, if she wanted, answer.

"How did I come here?"

She started to pace again, then halted when she heard something rustle through the leaves and whirled to see a woman approaching. Suspiciously, Miradel scrutinized the newcomer, whose graying hair, the tiny lines etched around eyes and lips, suggested an elder, perhaps a grandmother. Yet she was tall and sturdy and moved with the grace of a strong young woman, with a presence that demanded attention, possessed some mystical attraction. The woman wore a long robe of white silk. Her cheeks were plump and rosy, and her face abruptly softened into a tender smile. She was large, much taller than Miradel, with hips and breasts that swelled vibrantly outward against the rippling material of her gown. Despite her impressive girth, her appearance projected strength, not obesity. Indeed, somehow she projected a sense of inherent *fertility*.

"I thought this would make it easier for us to talk," said the matron, touching Miradel on the cheek, then seating herself gracefully on the bench. After a moment's hesitation, the druid sat, too, staring, wondering, slowly comprehending. Yet the last leap of awareness was too broad, unprecedented.

"Goddess . . . Worldweaver? You come to me now in flesh?"

"Do you like?" said the woman, in a very human fashion twisting slightly to look down her shoulder at her body and her legs. "I think I made my hips too big."

"No . . . it's . . ." Miradel found herself utterly flustered. "Why am I here? Did you bring me back? I remember seven lives on the Seventh Circle . . . lives filled with suffering and blood. . . . What did they mean?"

The matronly figure sighed and took one of the druid's small hands in both of hers. Her skin was soft, pleasantly cool against Miradel's flesh. "Seven lives . . . you needed at least that many before I could bring you back . . . that's the bare minimum, in fact. I gave your soul back to Earth as an innocent babe, and you lived and died . . . and when next you lived, you had no memory of the time before.

"But each time some kernel of your soul grew, increasing in understanding. You know, most souls never attain enlightenment at all. It is a tragic cycle. And for those few who do, those from the Seventh Circle that I summon here to druidhood in the Center, for them it can take a dozen lives . . . twenty . . . a hundred, before they are capable of understanding.

"For you, it was seven lives. You suffered much, and your soul learned quickly." The goddess leaned forward, elbows propped on her knees in a gesture that struck Miradel as manly.

"If learning requires suffering, I had excellent teachers," Miradel said bitterly.

The Worldweaver's expression grew stern. "You should know, child and woman and mother yourself, that I did not put you through any of those lives. When you perished here, in Nayve, your soul returned to the world called Earth. That, after all, was your original home . . . yours, and all the other humans in the seven circles, whether they have come to Nayve as druids or warriors or remain in their world of origin."

"But you called me here . . . again! Why?"

"Because you earned it, and because I need you, and Nayve needs you. Yours is a tremendously valuable soul, Miradel, and I brought you back as soon as I could."

"What makes my soul so wonderful?" demanded the druid. Her throat tightened as she remembered the young son, burning with fever, who had died in her arms. She knew she'd had a mother in her last life, a woman of the plains who had perished under the attack of the white soldiers, and it seemed monstrously unjust that they were merely cycling through pointless lives on Earth while she was brought here, feted by the goddess herself. "I don't want to hear about my valuable soul," she declared bitterly.

"Perhaps not, but you will. Your anger I can understand, but not your stubbornness. You rebel against the suffering, yet such was called for not by me but by the humans of your own world. You insist that you have no special value, yet it was you who brought the warrior Natac to Circle at Center. You summoned him from Earth at the cost of your youth, your immortality, in the end your very life . . . and he saved our world from the evil that would have consumed us all."

Miradel drew a deep breath and forced herself to be calm. She had a great understanding now of the differences between the two worlds. Even though, as she had lived her lives upon Earth, she had had no memories of her earlier sojourn in the

Fourth Circle, now that she was here, all of her recollections returned.

"Growing old . . . I did that several times. With the memories as vivid as they are, I don't know that I should have the courage to cast the spell again."

"I don't want you to do that . . . nor will you. But at the same time, that is why I need you."

Miradel felt a sense of purpose and realization settle over her. The agitation that had possessed her slowly dissipated. "What do you want me to do?"

The goddess sighed, and for an instant she looked like a tired mother, exhausted and worried over the fate of her children. "Nayve—indeed, all the Seven Circles—face a threat beyond any that has menaced us before. You know that, in the Time Before, the Worldsea dried up, and we faced invasion from Lignia, from Loamar and Dissona?"

"Yes . . . that was when you called the first druids here, was it not?"

Nodding, the goddess continued. "The Seventh Circle was much younger then, but in places such as Babylon and China, Egypt and Palestine, there were humans of advancing culture. People were learning many things, and during the course of lifetimes, several souls had sparked a sense of growth that allowed them to be brought here."

"Cillia was the first of these, was she not?"

"Cillia . . . yes, she has been here for more than four thousand years. It was she who learned how to harness the power of the wind, she who counseled me on others. There was the man the humans called the Buddha. . . . He used his learning to help the people of earth, and upon his seventh dying, I brought him here."

"Yes, I remember. In the Seventh Circle there is an entire religion founded upon his teachings."

"He was a good teacher. The same holds with the man they called Christ; he, too, came to me after the end of his life upon earth."

"His word was taught by the French who came to us on the

shore of Mich-I-gan," Miradel remembered. "He is the prophet of the white race in that land. A prophet of peace, they claim, though I never found them to be supremely peaceful people."

The goddess sighed and shook her head. "Do not blame the failures of the students on the teacher," she counseled.

"No," Miradel agreed. "But again, why me? What is it I can do for Nayve?"

"You brought the warrior Natac when we needed him."

"And is Natac yet here? Is he . . . well?" She was possessed of a sudden fear. Surely in the past three centuries he had taken a woman, found a willing druid to be his companion, his lover. The thought provoked an almost unbearable stab of pain.

"He is well enough," the goddess said. "Though I fear he is terribly lonesome."

Miradel's heart leaped. "I . . . I must find him, see him."

"Soon enough . . . but he is gone from the center, now. He floats through the skies of Nayve, making a map of the world."

"A map?"

The Goddess Worldweaver chuckled, a deep and musical sound. "No one else ever thought of that. But he has been working on it since the war . . . since you passed back to the Seventh Circle."

"And you say that he's . . . lonely?"

With a squeeze of her hand, the goddess showed Miradel she understood. "He has been chaste, pining for you all these centuries, almost as if he knew you would be returning. There will be time for you and him, I hope, when he returns to the Center. But there is time, now, for you to do my work."

"What is it you need?"

"First, we will have to learn. I sense great danger to the Center, to all the Seven Circles. There is a dire imbalance taking shape among the worlds."

"Where does it come from?"

"This much I know: The trouble lies in the direction that is neither metal nor wood. Loamar, the world of the dead, lies that way, across the Worldsea. I fear a grave disturbance there, as if the lord of that land grows restless, angry, as he did four thousand years ago. As to the nature of the danger, I cannot say. You will have to consult the Tapestry and learn what you can."

"I will do as you wish. But what is the nature of the threat . . . do you know?"

The goddess shook her head. "I first began weaving the Tapestry four thousand years ago. Did you know that? Before the first druids came, but after the war of the Time Before. Do you know why?"

"As a record, I thought, for all time, of all the worlds."

"It is more than that. It is a protection, a barrier, in fact. The Tapestry does not just record the lives of all who live, it *protects* those lives."

"Protects from what?" Miradel asked.

"From anyone who would think to claim souls for his own," replied the Worldweaver. "And that is enough for you to know, now."

"Where do you think this will lead?"

"It may be necessary for us to bring more warriors here, many more, if we are to have a hope of surviving the threats looming against the Fourth Circle. You are one of the few druids who worked the Spell of Summoning . . . and well you know, the cost of that spell is too great for it to be used with anything other than the utmost rarity."

"But warriors from Earth . . . How will you bring them here?"

"I don't know," the goddess said seriously. Her eyes, blue and deep and full of unimaginable tenderness, met Miradel's with an expression of profound fear. "But I am hoping that you will find a way."

4

Compass

Fire ravenous,
Devouring
Dancing ever toward wood.

Iron eternal,
Ferrous,
Called to metal.

Null and entropy,
Decay;
Destiny and death.

Fire and iron
Sire heat and steel,
Fueling the fullness of worlds.

Only wasting,
In the direction
Neither metal nor wood

From the Tapestry of the Worldweaver
Compass of the Cosmos

She had been a druid in Nayve for more than nine centuries, since they burned her as a witch on the Seventh Circle, in her small town in Provence during the Christian year 923 A.D. She couldn't remember, anymore, why they had burned her.

At the time it had seemed unjust, terrifying, brutally painful, but she had long ago accepted that Earthly death as the rite of passage that had brought her here to the Fourth Circle, into the service of the Goddess Worldweaver. For nine hundred years she had studied and mastered powerful magic, inhabiting a world of peace and beauty. She had shared her life with great friends, known wonderful men as lovers.

Now, as she put her arms around the waist of her man, her human warrior, and watched the world float past underneath the hull of the great airship, she told herself that she should be content, even happy.

"Eh, Juli," Owen said, his own burly arm going around her shoulders, pulling her tight. "Past the Darken Hour now . . . I think we should go to bed. We'll be setting down in Shahkamon at Lighten, you know."

Juliay nodded and kissed him on his muscular shoulder. "You go first. I want to see if Natac needs anything, but I'll be there in a few minutes."

"Don't be long," he said with an affectionate and suggestive slide of his hand down the round curve of her hip.

She felt his desire and knew what he wanted to hear. She whispered up to his ear, "I won't."

Owen ducked into their small cabin, and she looked around the little deck in the middle of the skyship, feeling helpless and guilty. In fact, she was halfway hoping that Natac would need her help with something, give her an excuse to stay out here at least until the Viking had gone to sleep.

The Tlaxcalan was up there on the forward deck, watching the landscape, occasionally making a note on the draft of his map. Even as she climbed the ladder, she felt her guilt grow into shame. For hundreds of years she had been Owen's lover, his companion, his teacher. She knew that he loved her with all the fullness of his heart. But she didn't want to go into that cabin, that bed.

The Viking was a good man, she knew. He had changed because of her, renouncing his days of carousing and wenching in the hopes of wooing her. He had succeeded, and he was kind to her, and generous, and humorous. At least, she used to think he was funny. Now, too often, she found his buffoonery tiresome, even embarrassing.

The Tlaxcalan warrior, general of Nayve, and the greatest explorer the Fourth Circle had ever known, gave her a shy smile as she joined him.

"How much longer until we reach the canyon?" she asked.

"It all depends on the wind. I think it's forty or fifty miles, at least, so we'll need the rest of the night, I expect, to get there. You know, it's odd; when we're going fast, I feel anxious because of all the detail we must be missing, and when we're slow, I fret because I'm eager to see what's ahead of us."

The druid chuckled, but beneath her humor was the awareness that she had nothing, no passion in her life, that could inspire her such as this man's curiosity drove him. His life was full, here on Nayve, and he had come from another, if much shorter, life of fullness upon Earth. Always he found his passion, whether it be war or Miradel or, now, his maps. Whatever its nature, it seemed to Juliay that passion itself was a driver of life.

"I came to see if there was something you needed. I could spin some wind, hurry us along," she suggested hopefully.

"Thanks," he said, looking at her in a way that suddenly made her feel uncovered, vulnerable. "But I think we'll make it by Lighten. And it would be good to have some daylight when we drop anchor at Hyactown. Sirien is worried, but I expect she will be welcomed with joy. We'll probably spend a day with the khan. He's quite a hospitable elf, behind his fierce exterior, and I don't doubt that he will make us welcome. So I think we'll have about a twenty-four hour stop there, even with the wind we have."

"Oh. All right," she said, looking over the rail at the expanse of starlit steppe, flat and lush as a velvet carpet.

"Good night," Natac said, turning back to his map.

She knew he wasn't sending her away, just assumed that

she'd want to be going. Nevertheless, she felt dismissed.
"'Night," she said softly.

Juliay went down the ladder quietly and opened the door
to her cabin. Owen was waiting for her, naked in the fur-lined
nest that was their bed. In moments, her gown had fallen to
the deck, and she joined him. His hands went to her breasts,
and she lay beside him and went through all the proper movements, mouth, hands going to him. They touched, and she felt
his urgency as they reached, came together.

But minutes later, as Owen swelled inside of her and she
met his movements with responses that had become practiced
and precise, her mind was far away. She thought of the warrior on the deck, alone, still staring into the night. She thought
of the world of her birth, and she wondered about things that
Owen would never understand.

Still later she remained awake. Ignoring the man's soft,
rhythmic snores, she rose and went to her small lockbox, her
most cherished possession. She opened the lid and saw the
candles, the small mirror, and underneath, the vial containing
her precious threads . . . her sample from the Wool of Time.

She felt a glimmer of disloyalty as she took up a tuft of that
wool, but she ignored her reservations. This tiny scrap, drawn
from the Tapestry of the Worldweaver, was her connection to
the life of another man, a man she had been observing for
years. He was distant from her, beyond the reach even of her
world, but at the same time he needed comfort . . . needed *her*
far more than Owen ever could.

When at last she slept, in her fingers she clutched the tuft
of wool, a few strands from the scrap that she kept in her box.
These threads were not the current sample of the man's life, for
they had been drawn from a time a year and a half earlier. But
she was learning his story and wanted to follow his experience in the proper order. She felt the great weight and presence of Owen beside her, knew that he was a good man who
had worked to be a better man because he cherished her affection.

But she was so, so tired of that affection, the effort to do

things that had once been effortless. And so she had her wool,
and her secret knowledge, the life she had been following
when she had the chance to study the Worldweaver's Tapestry, the story of the man named Jubal Caughlin. It was a truth
in her heart, but one that she dared share with no one else.
Still, she had her thoughts . . . and her dreams. She knew
what she had seen, and her heart, her whole being, cried out
to comfort one who knew nothing of druids, or the goddess,
or Nayve.

Her breathing steadied, and her eyes remained closed. Unconsciously, she clutched the shred of wool, the woven tale of
a man's life, and in her sleep, she cried.

*They arrived in Gettysburg when the battle was already
two days old. General Pickett had promised action and glory
for his boys, though, and by Abe Lincoln's hairy arse the men
of Jubal Caughlin's division were going to make a difference
in this fight.*

*He saw the rest of the army watching them on the morning
of the third day as Pickett's division and his own men marched
into position for the grand assault. Tens of thousands of the
Confederacy's proudest men arrayed themselves on Seminary
Ridge, with that vast, grassy swath of field and vale before
them. The men who had been fighting for two days, who would
watch this great attack from the relative safety of the rebel
lines, seemed tired and disinterested, though he knew they
were praying for success.*

*And he, like every other general officer of the army, un-
derstood the value of success. If Robert E. Lee could throw
his great army at the enemy, and break that enemy, then the
road to Washington—the road to a victorious outcome of this
hateful war—would lay wide before them. All they had to do
was break that Union Army in two.*

*Across the way, on their own height of Cemetery Ridge, the
Yankees were waiting. Hundreds of guns were focused on
those smooth fields. Tens of thousands of reserves waited behind the line, ready to reinforce or counterattack. But Jubal*

knew that his men were the finest troops in the world, and that their army was commanded by the greatest general in the world. If General Lee was willing to send his men to the attack, then it was known that the attack had a very good chance of success.

The order to advance came, and those three divisions moved forward with martial splendor. Unit flags and pennants, and that grand banner of stars and bars, sparkled in the air. Drums marked the cadence of the march, and fifes trilled an accompaniment. The first ranks broke from the trees, flags and pennants waving, lines trimmed and measured.

And then the Union guns added a thrumming basso.

For a full mile, the rebel divisions marched, and those awful cannons fired. Shells exploded on the ground and in the air. Bits of lethal metal hurled past his ears, one tearing the sleeve of his tunic. His men fell to the left and right, but the rest kept marching, lines trimmed and filled to mask the gaps torn by the guns. Through the vale, across the pike, and up the slope of Cemetery Ridge they advanced, picking up the pace of their march, shuffling, then jogging into a trot.

The enemy infantry fired now, and the cannons hurled grapeshot at close range, cut swaths of gory death through the Confederate formations. Men fell everywhere. A funereal mist of smoke and blood drifted through the air. He saw Ketchins, the sergeant who had been with him since Manassas—the first one—lurch backward and fall, his stomach a mass of blood. The brave man waved his general on, lifting himself up onto his elbows so that he could watch the attack for the few minutes of life remaining to him.

Now they were running wildly, bayonets extended, every voice shouting the rebel yell. He, too, was screaming as he raised his sword in his right hand, his pistol in his left. They were scrambling over the wall, bluebellies lying dead all around. More of the Yankees were running as the attack surged forward with a kind of hysterical elation. They were breaking the enemy! This huge force, the Army of the Po-

tomac, was gashed, split, dying, as more brave Southerners poured into the gap, crested the top of the hill.

His gun was empty, his sword covered with blood. Everywhere he saw men dying. Somehow they had reached this madhouse of killing, somehow survived the charnel house of the valley, but now the Yankees were everywhere. They pressed from the center in great, blue-clad legions. Guns roared from the flanks, and the bravest men in the world were torn to pieces by uncaring lead.

Finally they were falling back, running down the hill. Tears marked his face, ran in his beard. He had no right to be alive, to survive when so many of his men had fallen. He turned, shouted curses at the Yankees, waved his sword in the air until two privates took his arms and pulled him along.

Weeping, bleeding, defeated, the remnants of three divisions crept back through the bloody vale to collapse in the midst of their fellows. The army was defeated. The general had failed.

And yet the war would go on.

". . . and in conclusion, I move that the Senate approve the resolution, and commission the Statue of the Lost for immediate sculpting." *Finally,* Belynda added to herself, masking her feelings behind the cool façade she was presenting to the gathered senators.

She had a hard time breathing as she looked across the gnomes and faeries, the elves and giants, goblins and centaurs, and all the rest who made up the august governing body of Nayve. The huge chamber was full today, and for that she was grateful. But as she watched the cospeaker, Praxian, advance to the podium in that familiar, deliberately slow gait, she couldn't help but feel the weight of her seemingly eternal frustrations.

In truth, this vote should have been taken—by the goddess, the statue should have been *raised*—hundreds of years ago. She had first proposed the motion three years after the war. Though nothing happened quickly in Nayve, she had assumed that the idea of building a statue to commemorate some of the heroes who had given their lives in that war would have taken no more than a decade, maybe two, to ease its way through the bureaucratic tangle of Nayvian government.

Instead, it had taken nearly a hundred years just to identify the slain heroes who would be depicted by the sculpture. Some had been obvious: Fionn, the human warrior from the Seventh Circle, the isle called Ireland, had been a unanimous selection. But the elves couldn't agree on one representative, and for decades the debate had been tabled because each specific elven nation demanded the right for a representative. Naturally, the thought of a dozen elves depicted on the statue was unacceptable to the giants, gnomes, and the rest, and Belynda had made dozens of journeys to Barantha and Argentian, Honorrell and Kaerrili, and every other domain of her race. Patiently discussing, carrying counterproposals back and forth, she had finally gotten the elves to accept Deltan Columbine, the writer, poet, and warrior from her own Argentian. Since Deltan's epics of the war, written before his death in the last battle, had become a cherished part of all elven lore, the sylvan people had finally accepted her decision.

But so it had been with many of the rest. If it wasn't the identity of a particular hero, it was the placement. Initial sketches had depicted the giant, Galewn, looming over all the others, and this relative portrayal had proven completely intolerable to the gnomes.

Again the sage-ambassador had worked patiently, negotiating, compromising, often merely soothing hurt feelings and balming ancient resentments. Finally, it had seemed as though all the hurdles had been spanned; they had a sketch and a plan for a monument of which they could all be proud, and the druids had cleared a space within the vale of the Worldweaver's Loom, the place of highest honor in all Nayve.

That had been forty years ago. Since then, the Senate had been engaged in the portentous decision as to which direction the statue should face. Again, every delegate had his or her own view, and it had taken Belynda's best efforts to at last bring these opinions into synchronicity, as it had finally been agreed that the statue be oriented toward the Loom, the Center of Everything.

It was with a sense of fatigue rather than delight, that she heard the gnome, Nistel, move for approval. One of the goblins seconded, and when Praxian called for a voice vote, the *yeas* proved to be unanimous. Afterward, the senators gathered around Belynda, and she accepted their congratulations with as much grace as she could muster. She thanked Nistel for the motion, then gratefully backed away as the gnome started on a long recollection of his dramatic pause before asking for the vote.

Belynda found herself passing through the great doors unnoticed, standing in the balmy afternoon, and looking toward the College, toward her garden and apartment, with a sense of dislocation. For so long she had been working toward this. What should she do now? She had the irrational desire to tell Ulfgang, then a sense of real disorientation as she reminded herself that he was dead. Such a strange and final reality, was death. . . . Since the war had ended, she had almost forgotten what it was like. Now, she remembered, and thought of the terrible toll of those years of violence. What wonderful epics would the bard Deltan Columbine have written, had he lived? And her friend, the druid Miradel . . . despite the toll of the Spell of Summoning, she might have lived many more years if not for the brutal attackers who had seen in her an enemy to be killed.

The trees of the Grove rose across the vale of the Loom, and her feet turned in that direction. Since Miradel's death, she had not counted any close friends among the druids, but it seemed now as though the company of humans might prove refreshing after the tension and acrimony that seemed so characteristic of the peoples of Nayve.

The farther she got from the columned edifice of the Senate, the lofty halls and great portico, chambers that, no matter how breezy the day, always felt stuffy, the better she felt. The day really *was* beautiful, as were so many days in the Center. How many of those had she missed in the past centuries? She thought again of Ulfgang; in so many ways, the dog had been wiser than she herself. He had known to take the time for a run and had felt nothing wrong with a long nap in the afternoon sun.

She missed him, now, as she followed the flowered walk that skirted around the great temple. Hedges and blossoms surrounded her. Smells of flowers sweetened the air, and a pair of swans glided across a still pool in stately majesty. The Loom rose nearby, a towering spire of glimmering silver, reflected in the still pool in the garden. Someone moved there, and the elfwoman hesitated, halting under a memory that abruptly froze her in her tracks.

The person was a human, a druid with bronzed skin, long black hair, and a face of pure, sublime beauty. She remembered that face, had last seen it years before Miradel's death, before the druid had sacrificed her youth by casting the spell of summoning. Now she recognized that the woman was looking back at her with the same sense of recognition that was reeling Belynda's mind.

"Miradel?" she asked, her voice a whisper. "Is it you?"

"Hello, Belynda," said her long-dead friend, very much alive.

"But how . . . when . . . ?"

Miradel smiled, and it was the same beautiful smile that Belynda remembered, perhaps flavored with a tinge of sadness. "I am here. The Goddess Worldweaver, in her wisdom, has brought me back to Nayve."

"I see the warrior Natac, and the druid Roland Boatwright," Khan Lazzutha declared, haughty before the anchored hull of *Skyreaver,* on the plain above Riven Deep. He stood straight and tall, his long, golden white hair combed straight back. He spoke with immense dignity. "I see another human man, and a human woman. But I do not see an elf."

Sirien, standing with her four companions, gasped slightly and pressed a hand to her lips. "Father . . ." she whispered.

Abruptly, the khan's façade of dignity cracked, and he broke into a wide smile. "I see a daughter who has returned home after far too long an absence." The elven ruler held out his hands. "Welcome home, Siri," he said.

"Oh, father," she cried, throwing herself into his arms. "But why . . . ?"

For a moment, the elder elf looked sad. "Perhaps you will know a trace of the sorrow I felt when you left me . . . and I did not know if I would ever see you again."

Roland cleared his throat awkwardly. "My lord, I must beg your forgiveness for that. It was I who proposed to your daughter that she join the exploration of Nayve. You should know that she has become a fabled traveler, and the songs she composes are sung from the Metal Coast to the Wood."

"And you do not need to beg my forgiveness. Though you took me by surprise, I will state. Never did I think my daughter would leave me for a young man, and even in that never, there was no thought of a human even in the back of my mind.

"But know this, Druid of the Grove. I have had reports from the Center, and I know that you have been a good husband for Sirien. And I know, too, that she followed a path of her own choosing—ever it was so. I am now, in my dotage, simply joyful that her path has brought her again, at least for a night, to the doorway of her own home."

The khan and his Hyaccan elves proved to be every bit the hosts that Natac remembered from a hundred years earlier. The town, Shahkamon, stood on the very brink of the Deep, in places jutting out to hang suspended above the vast, misty gulf of space. The elven lord was a widower, but his daughter Janitha served as his hostess, and the two of them prepared a feast the explorers would remember for the rest of their voyage.

In the custom of the Hyac, they ate outdoors, before the hour of Darken. *Skyreaver* was anchored on the steppe just beyond the town, which itself sprawled through a series of terraces near the upper rim of the great canyon, Riven Deep.

From these plazas the travelers and their elven hosts looked into the vast gulf and shared a sense of wonder at the immense space, the mist-shrouded view.

Unlike most elves, the Hyac were herders, and their large beasts—also called hyacs—stood placidly around the canyon rim, just beyond the low wall demarking the town.

"We came here by horse, that time a century ago," Natac explained to his shipmates as he sat beside the khan and sipped a gourd of warm hyac milk. The stuff was rich and creamy, seemed to infuse him with strength and energy as he drank. "That was part of my attempt to map the area around Circle at Center. Roland and I rode into the Nullreach for a few days and found this canyon, too deep to traverse, too wide to see more than a haze on the other side . . . and then I met some elves, who invited me to their town."

"We captured you, if you remember," said one elf, Lord Hellenkay, who sat beside Janitha. "I still remember how surprised you were."

"Indeed," Natac agreed with a laugh. "But it was a hospitable imprisonment, and I would like to think that we became friends."

"And so we shall stay," the lord replied cheerfully. "So long as you don't try to take the other khandaughter when you depart!" He laid his hand upon Janitha's, and the elfwoman smiled.

"Someone has to stay and mind the affairs of Shahkamon," she said. "And that will be me—except of course for next week, when I ride with the herders to the grazing lands."

"But only for half a year," the khan said. "And then you, at least, will come home again."

"Yes, father, I shall."

"And you stayed for a year that first visit," Lazzutha remembered, addressing Natac again. "Always looking at the canyon . . . wondering."

The warrior nodded. "It's a thrill to think that we'll finally see what lies beyond."

"Little did I think the day would come when man and elf

would fly through the skies of Nayve in such a ship. It is a wonderous and miraculous craft." He turned to Sirien, who sat at his side. "It makes me proud, daughter, to know that you are a part of such great endeavors. Your eyes will see far corners of the world. But know that you will always have a home here, with me, and with your sister when my time has passed."

"Always," agreed Janitha, who looked very much like a more savage version of Sirien. Her skin was bronzed by the sun to a leathery brown, and her hands were wiry and clearly strong. When she walked, she moved with the rolling gait of the natural rider. It seemed to Natac that her life on the edge of the known world had hardened her yet had done nothing to dull her pure elven beauty.

After dark, the milk was put away, and flasks of wine came forth. Elven maidens danced, their movements sinuous and sensual in a way that was also unlike any other elven folk Natac had encountered. Janitha produced a lyre and plucked the strings with rare skill, drawing notes in chords that seemed more complex than anything he had heard in the city.

"Do you remember the tale of the Horn?" asked the khan, as he passed the flask of wine to Natac and signaled for another. In a Hyaccan custom, they would open a single bottle and pass it among the guests, then open another, rather than pouring into flasks or goblets at each place.

"I recall that it was a great epic. The details, I'm afraid, are lost to my memory," Natac admitted.

"I was hoping you'd say that!" The khan was beaming. He clapped his hands and drew Janitha's attention. "Our guests . . . they go beyond the chasm on the morrow. Tonight let them hear the story of the Horn, when that which is beyond the chasm tried to come to us!"

"Of course, my father," said the khandaughter. She plucked a minor chord, drew out the notes into a long harmonic, and then began to play an elaborate strum. From somewhere nearby, a flute began to play, and the soft resonance of drums whisked a rhythmic accompaniment.

But when Janitha began to sing, all of the instruments seemed to fade away. So dynamic was her voice, so powerful and evocative and heartfelt, that the listeners were in a matter of moments transported to a distant time, a long-ago realm.

"It was the Time Before . . . the Birthing Age of Nayve," she told them, and it was a time when the elves were young upon the face of the world. There was no temple in the center, indeed, no city at all on the island upon the lake. Instead, there were clans of elves dwelling around Nayve, in places of sublime beauty and transcendent natural power.

One of those places was here, upon Riven Deep, at the edge of the world. The Hyaccan elves herded their great beasts, and sang, and watched over the valley that lay below their realm. For in those days, it was not a spectacular canyon but rather a deep vale, coursed by a wide river. All the land beyond was mountain, and unknown.

The drums spoke again, a sterner cadence, a sound of marching, and war. Janitha sang of the legions of enemies, as the Worldsea drained away, and creatures of lethal intent came from beyond the borders of the world. Most lethal of all was the horde of the Deathlord, shades from Loamar, the land that was neither metal nor wood. And the host came in such a tide that all the world would have been overrun, and Nayve would have succumbed to darkness, except for the valor of Lath-Anial.

Lath-Anial was the first khan, the one who had led the Hyac to their home, and he had been their patriarch for more than a thousand years. At last he perceived the danger that was coming, and so that he could warn the peoples of the world, he asked the Goddess Worldweaver for a gift. She bestowed upon him the great, spiraling horn of a mighty ram. She blessed the instrument with all the power of her magic and named it the Horn of Lath-Anial.

When at last the hosts of the dead came, they blackened the valley with their ghastly numbers, and they swarmed up the slope, a tide ready to spill upon Hyac and the world. Lath-

Anial stood atop the ridge, and he blew his horn, and in the great blast of sound, the enemy's host was routed, and the elven patriarch himself fell dead.

None of the rest of Nayve came to the aid of the Hyac when the horn was blown, and so it was that these elves determined themselves to be a breed apart. They built their city, Shahkamon, and turned their backs on the rest of the Fourth Circle, and contented themselves with their lone and prideful existence.

As for Lath-Anial, he was buried in a great ceremonial barrow, a cave at the headwaters of the Sirenflow River. His horn was laid to rest beside him, and they were blessed by the protection of the goddess. So stern was her guardianship that she laid a lethal curse, a condemnation to death, for any who dared to disturb the horn "so long as Shahkamon shall stand."

The last mournful notes faded away into the darkness that had come with full night. Applause was neither necessary nor appropriate. Instead, the explorers reflected upon the story they had heard and shared a final drink.

Finally, pleading the need for an early departure, Natac and his companions made their way back to the gondola. Khan Lazzutha and Janitha came with them, seeing that their water barrels were topped off and sending enough gifts of food and drink that Natac finally had to politely decline additional provisions, under the argument that they would never be able to get off the ground.

At least five hundred Hyac, accompanied by their princess and king, came forth the next morning to witness the airship's departure. The lines were cast away, and *Skyreaver* rose into the sky with stately grandeur. Quickly the vessel slipped into the stream of wind still rising from the druids in Circle at Center. As quickly as that, the steppe fell behind, and the ground below plummeted into this chasm of almost unimaginable depth.

"It looks like the end of the world!" Juliay declared, pointing into the gray light that began to brighten the world as the sun commenced its descent toward day.

Indeed, such was the gulf of space coming into view that Natac momentarily had the same impression. He glanced back; the steppe faded into the distance, a flat plain extending like a blanket until it reached a precipice as abrupt as the edge of a tabletop. The rim was an irregular line, jagged and twisting from the effects of erosion, and as *Skyreaver* drifted farther, cliffs of red, gray, and black came into view below, marking the edge where the land fell away.

The plazas of the Hyac were like long, slender shelves, just below the rim. These were lined with elves, and for a few minutes, the travelers could hear the sounds of their flutes and lyres, the cheers and songs rising on the morning breeze.

The immensity of the canyon almost defied belief. Within, shelves of barren rock descended in a series of terraces, each thousands of feet or more below the previous level. The base of the gap was lost in the mists that, Sirien said, were an eternal feature of the shadowy gorge.

"I don't blame you for not trying to cross that on a horse," Owen said with a chuckle. At the same time, he clutched the edge of the hull so tightly that his knuckles whitened. Sirien, Juliay, and Roland were similarly awestruck.

Natac leaned over the blank sheet of paper he had fastened to his exterior drawing table and began to sketch the outline of the canyon. He used a telescope and a compass to measure bearings to several known summits in the distant hills, triangulating to give him an approximation of the canyon's size, and he let out a low whistle.

"It's easily twenty miles across," he said. He looked at Sirien. "Is it this wide along the whole length?"

"There are places where it narrows," she said, "but you still can't see to the bottom."

"Should we take the ship down for a closer look?" Roland wondered.

Natac considered, tempted, but they would have to release

a lot of helium for the descent and then lots of ballast to come back up. In addition, they would drop below the level of the windstream that still bore them along. He shook his head. "Let's not take the time. Now that we're this far, I want to see what's on the other side."

The others were in full agreement, and the warrior concluded his preliminary sketch. He would draft a more careful version in his cabin later. They passed over the middle of the canyon near midday, saw that the deepest section of the gorge was concealed by a churning mist, that permanent fog.

That vanished from sight quickly, and throughout the afternoon, the far rim of the canyon drew closer. He leaned out over the side, staring into the impossible depths below as the opposite cliffs took shape before them. "Riven Deep. It's like a hole in the world."

And he would be among the first to see what lay on the other side.

It was a peculiar thrill to him, this knowledge that he was discovering, exploring parts of the world that had never been seen by the people of the Center. Would there be elves here, a new civilization of that graceful sylvan race? Or giants, perhaps even bigger than the hulking humanoids of Granitehome and the Lodespikes?

In his heart, he had a hope he had shared with no one . . . that this would be a part of the world that was pure wilderness, untouched by elf, goblin, giant, human, or any other race. In his explorations toward wood and metal, he had never found such a place, but neither had he encountered an obstacle such as this. It was a selfish hope, he recognized, but one that tickled his anticipation every time he imagined it.

Finally, near Darken, *Skyreaver* approached the rampart of cliff marking the far side of Riven Deep. It seemed as though the skyship was going to plunge right into that precipice, and Natac was prepared to drop ballast, but the effect was an illusion. As they actually crossed the line, they were safely aloft, several hundred feet above the rolling terrain. They drifted through the night, over a shadowy landscape of rolling terrain, and by the following Lighten, the rim of the canyon was out of sight behind them.

"Looks like a kind of scraggly forest," Owen said. "Stunted trees . . . no water that I can see."

The hills were steep, with many outcrops of crumbling, grainy rock, apparently sandstone, jutting between the branches of cedars or pines. The ground, where it showed between the sparse trees, was covered with yellow grass and dark, thorny bushes.

The wind that had borne them from Circle at Center still coursed along, though distance and time were beginning to leaven the effect of the druids' casting. Still, they were moving along nicely, and Natac was content to travel more slowly for a while now that he was sketching. Roland and Juliay might as well save their strength until their windcasting efforts were really necessary.

By late in the day, as the sun began to recede upward, the barren hills gave way to a string of shallow, marshy lakes. Just beyond, the hills reached higher, and dark mountains loomed beyond. Natac opened the valve to drop some water ballast, easing the airship so that they drifted five hundred feet above the valley floors, although some of the crests drifted past only a hundred feet below. He quickly saw that the scrubby pines of the chasm edge had given way to an open forest of immense oaks, the biggest trees growing on the crests of the hills, while many more oaks of more normal size clustered on the hillsides and floors of the winding valleys.

"Those are the biggest trees I've ever seen," Juliay said wonderingly, as she brought Natac a cup of tea on the foredeck. "Do you think they're really oaks?"

"Same leaves, same shape," Natac replied. "But you're right; I've never seen any so big before." He looked into the distance, saw the beginning shadows as the sun moved toward Darken. "Let's find one of these hilltops where there's enough room to set down. We can anchor *Skyreaver* to a couple of trees, and tomorrow, have a good look around."

They started seeking a likely place, and Sirien's keen eyes

quickly picked out a summit crowned by a large meadow fringed by several of the monstrous oak trees. Roland spun a stuttering little gust of wind that pushed the skyship sideways, until they were directly above the clearing. Then the wind spiraled downward, and Natac released just enough helium to bring them gently to ground. He and Owen leaped over the sides of the hull, each carrying a coil of sturdy rope. The Tlaxcalan went to port, the Viking to starboard, and in a few minutes, the balloon was secured against the force of nearly any natural breeze that was likely to arise.

By dark they had eaten and agreed upon a watch cycle that would have at least one of them awake at all times. Roland, who would stand first watch, took position on the high deck.

"I'm going to sleep on the ground," Natac announced, carrying his bedroll, dropping over the side to land on the soft ground. "Wake me when it's my shift for the watch."

"Be careful," Juliay called, and he waved his assurance as he strolled away from the hull.

The grass was soft and lush underfoot, and he found a flat space not far from one of the grand oaks. He wondered what the next day would bring. What would they see or find here? The limbs swayed softly, leaves rustling, as he lay down and quickly fell asleep.

"Awfulbark! Hey, king! King Awfulbark! Wake up!"

The pounding on the oaken door somehow perfectly matched the cadence of the throbbing in his skull as the great king, lordly monarch of the forest trolls, finally groaned and opened one eye.

"Go away!" he roared—or tried to roar. Actually, it came out as an inarticulate croak.

"Hey, get up! It's Wartbelly! Wake up!"

"Go talk to him!" It was Roodcleaver, kneeing him sharply in the small of his back. "Let me sleep."

Awfulbark rolled off his sleeping pallet and pushed himself groggily to his feet. He clumped to the stairway and started down, making it all the way through the second-floor storeroom before he tripped and tumbled down to the kitchen.

"I'm up!" he snapped as the pounding—still in perfect beat with the throbbing of his head—resumed. He threw open the door and reached out to grab Wartbelly around the throat. "Give me a good reason why I shouldn't strangle you right now," he growled.

"Urk—grtl!" Wartbelly choked. A chubby, weak troll who frequently tried to ingratiate himself with Awfulbark, Wartbelly now struggled in the king's powerful grip. Finally, Awfulbark relaxed his hold enough that his underling could draw a breath. "Something came!" he croaked. "Gotta see!"

"What came?" The king was in no mood for riddles. It was dark outside; he had no idea how late or early it was.

"Gotta see . . . somethin' big! Came!"

"I'll see it in the morning," Awfulbark retorted, pushing Wartbelly, knocking the troll onto his back outside the king's oak tree house. He was about to slam the door when he saw a sly look cross Wartbelly's knotted, woody face. "What?" demanded the monarch.

"Could be food," Wartbelly suggested. "Free food. And treasure."

Now Awfulbark was intrigued. Despite his best efforts, he just hadn't been making any progress in his attempt to collect food and treasure. The other night he had been forced to settle for a lone deer haunch, after he gambled away the milk. Last night, he and Roodcleaver had finished the last of the venison, and he couldn't muster enthusiasm for a routine shopping trip.

"All right. Show me."

They collected Breakwind on their way out of Udderthud, the three trolls plodding along the valley floor in sullen silence. Awfulbark wasted no time trying to imagine what it was they were going to see. Instead, he kept a close eye upon Wartbelly, suspicious that the fat troll would change his mind about sharing knowledge of this mysterious find with the king. For an hour, then another hour, they plodded through the dark woods, their trollish eyes having no difficulty spotting the numerous irregularities in the twisting path.

"Up here," Wartbelly finally whispered, when they came to the base of one of the area's many steep hills. "Be real quiet now."

With a minimum of tripping and cursing, the trio climbed the grassy slope. Quickly they reached the summit and, skulking and darting, moved behind the cover of a sturdy oak trunk.

Awfulbark let out a grunt of astonishment and grabbed Wartbelly's arm. "What *is* that?" he demanded, louder than he intended.

Wartbelly only shrugged. "Dunno," he croaked indignantly.

The king of the trolls studied the immense shape, clearly visible in the light of Nayve's bright, shifting stars. It looked kind of like a monstrous wineskin, filled and then inverted. The great length of its shape was high in the air, looming even above the lofty oaks. A webbing of ropes connected that long, massive object with a much smaller form, like a long box, on the ground.

"Did it *grow* here?" asked Awfulbark.

Wartbelly shook his head. Then he gestured, pointing and moving his hands, and repeating the motions again. Awfulbark clopped him on the head, drawing an "Ow!" of pain. "You try to tell me this big thing came down from the sky?" he demanded in disbelief.

"Do you hear them?" Natac asked in a conversational tone. He was standing on the ground, next to the hull, while his four shipmates were gathered at the railing above and behind him.

"Yes," Owen said. "I can't make out where."

"Behind that big tree," Sirien said, pointing with assurance. "There are three of them. They act like they're trying to hide, but they keep standing up to look at us."

The warrior considered climbing into the hull, but he

wasn't really very worried. In all his explorations, he had been violently attacked three or four times by large predators, but not once by any one of Nayve's peoples. And these strangers, judging by the fact that they were talking, even bickering, were clearly some kind of people.

"Here's your sword," said Owen, and the warrior reached up to take the sheath and the blade. "We've got the longbows out," the Viking assured him.

"You worry too much," Natac said quietly, nevertheless glad to know he had protection behind. He considered strapping on the sword but didn't want to make a warlike impression, so instead he leaned it against the hull where *Skyreaver* rested on the ground. "I'm going to talk to them," he said.

"Be careful," Juliay whispered.

He advanced toward the looming silhouette of the tree, barely making out the shadowy figures as they pulled back to disappear behind the stout trunk. The warrior crossed half the distance between the ship and the tree and then stopped.

"Hello," he called. "I bring greetings from Circle at Center."

He heard a startled gasp and then a smattering of dull, agitated whispers.

"I am called Natac," he said, keeping his tone calm. He hoped that these strangers could understand him, and he believed they would, since all the peoples of Nayve he'd thus far encountered spoke similar dialects of the same language. "What kind of people are you?"

He saw movement then as something surprisingly large moved around the bole of the tree. The thing had a creeping, surreptitious air about it that put the warrior on edge, though he didn't yet start to retreat toward the airship.

"Who are you?" he called.

Abruptly, that moving figure rushed forward, sprinting with surprising speed out of the shadows, reaching toward the man with arms that seemed as long and gangly as stout tree branches. He had a quick image of a large round head atop a lanky body, with a grotesque mouth opened into a broad leer of unmistakable hunger.

"Run!" cried Sirien, though Natac was already doing just that. He sprinted back to the side of the airship, hearing footsteps pounding the ground behind him. Lurching up to the hull, he pulled the sword from the scabbard, and whirled to face his pursuer, blade extended.

There were three of them, he saw, and they had not come after him as fast as it had sounded. Now they approached warily. They stood perhaps eight feet tall, and within their gnarled faces were spotted a pair of deep-set eyes, utterly black and lightless. Even so, the warrior felt that triple gaze upon him, knew that they were appraising him, wondering what to do.

"Show yourselves—and your weapons," Natac said, hearing the rustling as his four shipmates adjusted their position to stand on the deck. The monstrous pursuers turned their gazes upward, and the warrior was startled to see a flash of something that looked like a grin cross the mouth of one of them.

"We got four arrows aimed and ready to fly," Owen said. "We'll get the two on the flanks, and you have the one in the middle."

The Tlaxcalan nodded. "Who are you?" he demanded, sword extended before him. "We come in peace—but will defend ourselves if you attack."

The beast in the middle snuffled, a loud, wet noise. "You trolls?" he growled, his voice deep but understandable.

"No . . . we're humans, and an elf," Natac replied, relieved that some sort of communication had begun. He lowered the sword fractionally, still keeping his eyes on this grotesque woodsman. "Are *you* trolls?" he asked.

The one who had spoken made no reply. Instead, he nodded slightly, a gesture that was watched by his two cronies. "Get 'im!" he snorted, and rushed forward with those gangly arms outstretched.

The other two charged at his flanks, and Natac heard the sharp *twang* of bowstrings as his companions let fly. Instantly, the outer pair of trolls tumbled to the ground and thrashed in convulsions, each with two arrows jutting from its barklike chest. They shrieked and groaned piteously, while the troll in the middle halted and looked, dumbfounded, at his two cohorts.

"*I* get him!" he snorted contemptuously, advancing to reach those long arms toward the warrior.

Natac ducked and swung his sword hard, slicing through the forearm of the troll, lopping off the grotesque, flailing hand. The beast stopped and gaped at the wound.

"Back away from here," the warrior declared, "and I won't hurt you again."

Instead, the troll growled, a menacing, rumbling sound, deep as any bear's voice. That mouth spread wide again, revealing an irregular array of bent but sharp teeth. The creature leaped with a quick spring, the remaining hand clutching toward Natac's sword. The man chopped savagely, mangling that hand, then slashed a vicious backstroke across the face, carving deep into woody flesh, sending the grievously wounded creature staggering backward. Once more the sword slashed, this time cleanly chopping off that monstrous head.

The two trolls who had been dropped by the arrows were still moaning piteously on the ground, drawing gurgling breaths, flailing desperately with their long, sticklike hands. Grimacing in disgust, Natac stepped close and ended the suffering of first one, then the other, with sharp down blows of the sword.

"Trolls," said Owen in amazement, as Natac kicked the bodies, making sure that each was dead. "Not a very nice welcome, eh?"

"It's a good thing there's Riven Deep between them and Circle at Center," Natac agreed. He noticed that daylight was growing, as the sun had begun its descent toward Lighten. "Make ready to launch. I'm going to see if there are any more of the bastards," he said.

Owen and Roland scrambled over the sides and went toward the trees where the ship's lines were lashed. Natac made his way to the edge of the bluff and looked downward, seeing no sign of any movement in the growing daylight. He heard Sirien's gasp of alarm just as he was ready to turn back to the ship, and he whirled to see what had startled her.

The three trolls had risen, unnoticed, near the ship. Trotting quickly, they spread out and advanced toward him. The two on the flanks had plucked the arrows from their flesh and now cast these disdainfully to the ground.

The third, the one Natac had decapitated, was holding his head atop his shoulders. The warrior stared in disbelief as the stringy flesh of the neck knitted together, attaching the head to the body with knotty cords of muscle that connected and grew before the human's stunned view. Finally, the creature let go of its head, and that toothy mouth broadened into a wide, hungry smile.

5

Delvers of the Dark

Darkness gathers,
Shadows clothe,
Lethal deeds,
And nothing loathe.

From *Song of the Delvers*

"Don't you want to at least clean up, put on a fresh uniform?" Darann asked. "This is the *king* you're going to see!"

"You've got to understand," Karkald declared, shaking his head so hard the dried mud broke from his beard and crumbled to the floor of the palace entry hall. "I have urgent news. The king will want to hear from me right away. He isn't going to care what I'm wearing!"

The dwarfmaid looked imploringly to Borand, but her brother only nodded in maddening confirmation. And Konnor had already rushed ahead to make sure the lift was ready when they reached the base of the vertical tube. Sighing, she adjusted her blue frock and tagged along.

They followed a long, smooth avenue toward the lofty column that was the Royal Tower. Twin battle pillars, each a hundred feet high, studded with batteries, lookout posts, and coolfyre beacons, flanked the roadway. Royal guards gathered along the road, bearded faces watching in grim interest as the hero of the Nayve War all but trotted toward an interview with the king.

The great marble gates on the ground level of the palace rumbled apart before them. Despite the bright beacons throughout the city, a great wash of brilliant illumination spilled from the widening gap. A full company of guards, sixty axemen in blue tunics and silver helmets, stood at attention as Karkald, Darann, and Borand hastened toward the royal lift cage, across the great reception hall.

They hurried into the cage, where Konnor was waiting. The operator held open the door, then slid the grate smoothly closed when the trio had boarded. For the first time, Karkald seemed to take note of his appearance, running his fingers through this matted beard, swiping the caked mud, now dried to dust, from his shoulders, chest, and legs. Darann helped, turning her face away as she swept his back and hips. Clucking, she pulled out her silver comb and ran it through the tangled locks running across her husband's shoulders.

"Thanks," he said, turning to face her, taking her arms in his strong hands.

Suddenly she was so glad that he was home, and so proud of him. She pulled him close and kissed him, falling into the embrace of his long arms as he pulled her tightly against him. The hardness of his body seemed to mold her, and for a moment she knew nothing except joy.

With a hiss of steam, the lift lurched upward and they leaned against each other, the promise of intimacy in their comfortable closeness. Borand, Konnor, even the lift operator awkwardly shifted and looked away. Too soon, however, Karkald broke their embrace, standing straight, drawing several deep, slow breaths as he prepared for the meeting.

"King Lightbringer will see you immediately," declared a herald, a stout, gray-bearded dwarf in golden livery who met the lift as it glided to a stop.

Darann had been here many times, but she felt the familiar thrill of awe as the huge doors of solid gold parted with a hiss of steam power. Each portal ran in an oiled track, and they quickly separated to reveal the vast throne room of Daric Lightbringer, king of Axial. He was seated now as he had been every time she had come here, with a throng of attendants, lords, musicians, and citizens gathered before him. This group magically parted in two, creating a wide aisle leading Karkald, Darann, Konnor, and Borand right toward the throne.

The king was a stout dwarf with long hair and a beard of frosty white. His face was lined, and the big hands resting on the arms of his throne were weathered and gnarled with age. But his eyes were clear and sharp, and his mouth formed a welcoming smile as the famed hero approached. A heavy crown of platinum studded with jewels sat regally upon his head, and robes of rich purple draped from his shoulders to flow outward around the throne. His boots were of polished black leather, fastened with straps that were also made of gleaming platinum, the precious and silvery material that was known as "the royal metal" in Axial.

Her husband took a few paces into the lead, Darann, her brother, and Konnor following behind. At the foot of the great throne they knelt and bowed low.

"Rise, Karkald Watchcaptain . . . and make known your news," declared the king, his voice a sonorous rumble in the vast, marbled chamber.

Karkald stood and clasped his hands behind his back. Any trepidation he might have felt—and, if he was anything like Darann, he felt plenty—was masked behind a façade of professional concern. He cleared his throat and spoke in strong, resonant tones.

"Sire, I fear that I bring dire tidings. Five cycles since, my field company came upon a Delver excavation party in the Baserock, some three dozen miles from Axial. We attacked the enemy party, which was not accompanied by an arcane. Our attack was successful, and none of the Delvers escaped."

"Splendid work," declared the king approvingly. "Did you suffer any losses of your own?"

"Alas, yes, sire. Barton, from Jordon's company. And four goblins."

The king winced as if in physical pain before gesturing with his hand for Karkald to continue.

"My lieutenants, Hiyram Goblin and Jordon of the Coal-catchers, maintained their position in the cavern, and we investigated a new kind of digging tool the Blind Ones had been employing. It proved to be a giant auger, with the capability of being raised for vertical drilling, or horizontal drilling, into a position some fifty or sixty feet above the ground."

"And was this tool in use when you discovered the Delvers?"

"Actually, sire, it had already been used. The Blind Ones had bored a hole through the ceiling of the main cavern, and this new route had revealed a hitherto undiscovered passageway extending for a great distance through the Midrock over our heads."

Daric Lightbringer's eyes narrowed in alarm. "Did you follow this passage?"

"Indeed, Your Highness, several of the Rockriders and I made our way for a long distance along the cavern. It is the cause of my emergency arrival here . . . of my urgent request for an audience, when dignity and respect—not to mention the sage advice of my dear wife—would otherwise compel me to bathe and dress myself for a royal meeting."

The king's face softened momentarily into an easy smile, and several of the attendant dwarves chuckled until Karkald continued. "The grim news, sire, is that the new cavern leads to a terminus directly above the city of Axial. Thus, if the Delvers successfully make their way down that cave, they will be in position to attack our city from above."

The levity melted away in the space of his explanation. The king closed his eyes and drew a long, deep breath through his nostrils, while murmurs of concern rippled through the gathered dwarves.

"Are your companies still posted at the terminus of this route?" asked the monarch.

"Indeed, sire. And they are brave men, to the lowest private. But fifty Seers and fifty goblins are precious little protection against a Delver army," the captain reported frankly. "I have a platoon of Rockriders there as well, and others of the 'riders are patrolling even deeper into the Baserock. I feel confident saying that we will at least have a few cycles' warning of a major Delver movement. But that is all I can promise at this time."

Again the king pondered for a time, and the dwarves in attendance waited quietly. Daric Lightbringer's eyes swept across the throng of his people gathered below his throne, until they fell upon the one he sought.

"General Paternak . . . what is the readiness state of our army?"

The gray-bearded dwarf, high commander of Axial's army, cleared his throat as those around him imperceptibly moved back, leaving the general alone in his small space. Alone except for one, anyway—Darann recognized Marshal Nayfal, standing close beside the general. The marshal's eyes met hers, and he smiled thinly, tilting his head in a slight but formal bow.

She flushed with a strange sensation of guilt and immediately looked away, saw Paternak's eyes flick to Karkald with an expression Darann couldn't read. She knew little about the man, save that he had been fighting Delvers for more than five centuries. He had been an adamant opponent of Karkald's plan to train the Rockriders for fighting in small-unit tactics, and several times she had heard her husband griping about the elder warrior's stubbornness. But he was revered by the people of Axial, and though he had not marched to Nayve during the war three centuries earlier, the Seer army that had come there had been dispatched upon his orders. In that way, he had saved Karkald's and Darann's lives, so she was inclined to be sympathetic.

"Sire, as you know, the troops have been preparing for the Festival of Fyre. Many of them are posted on the watch stations around the city, in preparation for the illumination that will culminate that event. Those are troops from the Second and Third Legions, for the most part. The First Legion, as well as the brigade of the Royal Guard, is still here in the city."

"Very well." The king stroked his long white beard, nodding almost imperceptibly.

"Forgive my impertinence, sire," added the general, "but I believe that it is worth pointing out that the display planned for this celebration is unprecedented in all the centuries since the discovery of coolfyre. The royal treasury has been expended in the preparation of the fyreworks, and many of those installations are time sensitive."

Warming to his topic, the general huffed again with immense dignity, thoughtfully stroking his long gray beard. "Sire, I would further suggest that the, er, captain's report, although useful, should not be taken as a sign of immediate threat. Rather, we have the advantage now of knowing the enemy's secret. Prudence demands that we take precautions. May I suggest that the full regiment of the Rockriders be dispatched at once? With those bold and speedy Seers posted about the periphery of our realm, we would have ample warning of any Delver activity."

"No!" Darann yelped, before clapping her hand over her mouth and staring, aghast, at the king. She heard gasps and clucks all around as the noble dwarves reacted to her temerity.

As to Daric Lightbringer, he chuckled, and it was as welcome a sound as Darann had ever heard. "I beg Your Majesty's pardon," she said, bowing humbly.

"Do not apologize," said the monarch. He raised his hand in a gesture that the dwarfmaid found physically soothing. "Your husband has been gone for a long time in the service of this crown, and you deserve a chance to be together."

"Th-thank you, sire," she said. Only then did she notice Karkald, who was blushing furiously and glaring at her in a way that made her very glad that they were in the midst of such an illustrious assemblage. Resolutely, she looked back at the king, who was addressing her husband again.

"Where does this tunnel originate?"

"In the midpoint between the direction of metal and the direction of neither," Karkald replied.

"They come from the Slatemont, then?" The king spoke of a tangled region of gulleys, ravines, and broken hillocks. Though open to the "sky" of the Underworld, the area, hundreds of miles square, was virtually trackless, full of countless box canyons, precipices, and other obstacles.

"It's only logical, sire. Where else can the Delvers move an army through the First Circle with a reasonable chance of remaining undetected?"

King Lightbringer frowned, and the lines of worry creasing his forehead and cheeks suddenly made him seem much older. His eyes moved from Paternak, the general of his army, to Karkald, the captain of his scouts, and back again. "Old warrior," he began. "Know that I value your judgment and your experience. I give weight to your words. But in this matter, it seems that the cautious course is only sensible. I want you to recall the Second and Third Legions, bring them back to the city. All of the First Legion should immediately be placed upon alert. I want every battery manned, each frontline of defense held by at least a regiment."

"Yes, sire. It shall be done at once," said General Paternak, his voice and face expressionless.

"When the Second and Third are here, in position for defense, I want the First to march into the Slatemont. It may be that we can interrupt the Delvers in the process of mounting their onslaught."

"A spoiling attack? Indeed, sire, a splendid idea," the general noted. "May I request the honor of commanding that expedition?"

Daric Lightbringer nodded. "The task is yours, old warrior." Shifting his gaze, the dwarven ruler turned to Karkald and Darann. "Good Captain, rest for two or three cycles. . . . I am sorry it cannot be longer. Then mount your brigade and deploy them as escort to the First Legion on the march. If the enemy is discovered, you will help in the attack."

"Of course, sire."

Again the king cleared his throat, and as he took a deep breath, he sounded tired. His voice was strong, and though he looked toward the lofty, arched ceiling, his words were clearly directed to everyone in the vast room.

"Shortly we would have commemorated the anniversary of a great discovery. Five hundred years ago, the secret of coolfyre was made known to our people. In that moment of revelation, our lives were given hope, our civilization a chance of wonderful growth. This splendid palace where we all convene . . . the wonderful city beyond, where tens of thousands of my subjects go about their lives under a canopy of brightness made possible by that long-ago discovery . . . all of these things we owe to the light that protects us, that reveals the Blind Ones for the corrupt Delvers that they are."

Daric Lightbringer's voice hardened, and he swept his clear eyes across the assemblage. Darann felt his look as a personal command, and her willingness to obey brought a lump into her throat.

"But that freedom, those blessings, come to us with a price . . . a price in vigilance and, when necessary, blood. I knew Barton, of Jordon's company, and it grieves me that I will not see him again. Yet he died for a cause, and we must take the lesson learned and apply it.

"Is it better to joyfully celebrate the thing that makes us free . . . if that very celebration jeopardizes our freedom? I think, no. Therefore, the Festival of Fyre shall be postponed, and my orders regarding the army take immediate effect."

VICIERISTN, called Nightrock, was more like a hive of termites than any kind of city known to the civilized denizens of Earth, Nayve, or Axial. For the latter were all places of light, where the people were warmed and cheered and illuminated in a fashion that drew them outside of their homes into plazas and gardens and streets where they could gather and share in the benign brilliance of the sun or, in Axial, coolfyre.

In Nightrock, there was no need for such congregating, for Vicieristn was a city of utter, unchanging darkness. Located in a porous mountainside that rose to merge with the sidewall of the First Circle, lying in the direction that was neither metal nor wood, the dens and caves and tunnels of Nightrock honeycombed the soft rock in an area a dozen miles wide, two miles deep, and a full mile in height.

It was impossible to know how many Delvers lived here. Zystyl had tried to count, once, but had given up after a full interval of laborious census-taking. Even though he had conducted much of the count from his own chambers, probing through the paths of the city with his mind alone, the forty cycles of constant probing had been utterly draining. He had tallied more than fifty thousand, and at the same time realized that he was seeing just a small fraction of the entire, hivelike metropolis.

So he had allowed this project to lapse, as he had allowed every other task that had threatened to interfere with his real life's work. Since that time, at least two centuries earlier, he had devoted himself with single purpose to the destruction of the Seer Dwarves and the concurrent raising of the Delvers to mastery of the First Circle.

But he would not be hasty, would not be rash. Thrice since the founding of the hated city of light, the Delvers had attacked Axial, waged furious onslaughts aiming for nothing less than the utter destruction of the hated citadel of their enemies. Two of those attacks had resulted in massive disasters, as the Blind Ones tried to come ashore on the island of Axial only to be slaughtered en masse, many before their boats had even touched ground.

The third attack had been made three hundred years ago and had been commanded by Zystyl himself. He still believed that they could have been successful, might have finally destroyed the enemy stronghold, if they could but have waged the campaign he had planned. Instead, the First Circle had been wracked by a great earthquake, and well over half of

Zystyl's army had been lost at sea. The survivors had found the path to the Seer city blocked by massive cave-ins. Instead, the arcane general had led them upward, through the caverns of the Midrock, and into Nayve.

There, in a world of food and plenty unlike anyplace they had ever imagined, the Delvers had campaigned for twenty-five years until, finally, treachery and defeat had sent them reeling back into the caverns of their sunless domain. The elves of Nayve had shown no willingness to pursue, and so the dwarves of the First Circle had withdrawn to their eternal campaign. The Seers still held the lighted central reach of Axial, while the Delvers roamed freely through the periphery of the world.

But for all that time, Zystyl and his Delvers, and especially his fellow arcanes, had been plotting, planning . . . and waiting. Waiting for the present moment, the opportunity that now lay before them with such stunning, perfect clarity. Now he clutched his Hurtrock, felt the power swell through his fingers, and knew it was time to act.

Zystyl swaggered through his council hall, accepted the clapped salutes of hundreds of his loyal retainers. Ignoring the throne of gold, he passed through an iron door, which was opened by an attendant who felt his master's approach. The metal portal clanged loudly shut behind him, and Zystyl drew a deep breath, confirming through scent and telepathy that the others were already gathered. They were tense, alert, suspicious, and guarded but also very intrigued.

"Hallion, my Bold Warrior, how good of you to come." He addressed the nearest, a strapping, metal-clad warrior of immense stature.

The burly arcane snuffled loudly, and Zystyl sensed the suspicion and resentment in his voice. "You commanded my presence. I am no fool, that I would ignore your summons."

"Nevertheless, you are a welcome ally." *And you shall sit at my right hand, Bold Warrior.*

He felt the other arcanes stirring at the unspoken exchange. The keenest among them would know that a silent message had been sent, but they would not know what that message was.

"And Jarristal, Lady Arcane, you also do me honor . . . Lastacar and Bienifist as well. And young Fieristic, welcome to your first Council of the Mighty. May there be many more to come."

"It is my sincere hope, Lord Zystyl. And may our next meeting be held on the dead bodies of our Seer foes." Fieristic's voice burned with palpable hatred, and Zystyl was pleased to let the emotion simmer and tingle in this room of keen senses.

"Know, my arcanes, that such a consummation may be closer than we have been able to hope for a very long time."

"How can it be close?" demanded Hallion, his tone scornful. "I have it on good authority that you lost a whole work party just a short time ago. Is this how we defeat the Seers— force them to fatigue themselves as they slash our people to pieces?" *I have heard rumor that this loss is part of your plan, Lord Zystyl. I am skeptical. But if you can show me how it is so, then you shall have my loyalty and my army at your side.*

"I welcome your challenge," Zystyl said, to emanations of disbelief from the rest of the arcanes. He chuckled, a moist and gurgling expression of pleasure. "No doubt some of you have sampled the mood of our foes this cycle . . . probably just before you came to this conference. What have you discovered?"

Jarristal, the lone female in the group, spoke first. "There is great fear in the Royal Hall. . . . I tasted the emotions of several goblin slaves there, weak-willed fools who don't even know they are being studied. All of the Seer army has been called back to their fortress city, and they are making every preparation to defend against attack."

"Aye, it is the same as I have learned," chimed in Bienifist. He was a Delver arcane who had lost his left arm in battle and since then had worked his right into a limb of muscular, even unnatural, power. Zystyl could sense the tautness in his voice, knew that he was tensing the bulging sinews of that arm even as he spoke. "I entered the city through the mind of a drunkard, one who was cast out of the Royal Guard and now spends his days begging for silver, that he may drown his senses in ale. Rest assured that, even drunk, those senses are keen enough for me to watch the Seer city."

"So pray tell, wise Zystyl," asked Lastacar, in a tone as oily as the sweaty stench characterizing that arcane's small, wiry body. He tried to conceal his sour odor behind an array of unguents, but despite the perfumes, his natural rank presence seemed always to win out. "How exactly does placing our foes in a state of high alertness enhance the prospects for a successful attack?"

"That is the crux of the matter," Zystyl replied with a wet snicker. "And I am disappointed that none of you have been able to divine the reason I find this news pleasing. It is—"

"—because you do not intend to attack Axial at all." Fieristic's interjection provoked thoughts of astonishment and outrage from the others, in part because of his poor manners, and part because of the arrogantly confident tone in which he made his announcement.

But Zystyl allowed a hint of respect to creep into his voice as he replied. "You are correct, young warrior. This is absolutely the wrong time to attack the stronghold of the Seer Dwarves, and so we shall not do so."

"You tease us, lord of dark battles, and I have little patience for teasing," Bienifist growled, his impatience stabbing through the air as a sharp, cutting blade.

Zystyl carefully masked his furious response, even as he took note of the impudence, the potential for insurrection that lay beneath the one-armed arcane's voice. He would watch that one carefully.

"Very well," replied the lord arcane. "You have indulged me with your presence, and the least I owe you is an explanation of my plan. Young Fieri has started us in that direction, as he has correctly noted that this is not the time to attack Axial.

Yet our army is as numerous, as strong, and as well trained as it has ever been. We have rock cutter drills that will carry an assault through any palisade. And we have a generation of warriors with no memory of real war—and they are only too willing to learn!"

"Still you speak in circles, Lord." Jarristal's tone was intrigued, and the emotional undercurrent, tendrils of thought directed to Zystyl alone, was rife with excitement and, there at the end, just a hint of desire.

"Then let me be straight, able arcanes. For the enemy will go to war, but they will not fight us. Rather, they will smash themselves against our agents, and they will die." He drew a deep, satisfied breath and turned to Jarristal. "Are you ready?" he asked.

"Indeed, lord," she replied. She rang a small bell, and one of the doors to the chamber rumbled open. Something else rumbled then, something that all the arcanes could feel.

A creature of iron took a step forward, one stride covering six or eight paces. The floor shook slightly when the heavy foot came down, and then the metal monster stood still. The arcane Delvers all but quivered with excitement as they expanded their senses to examine this construct. They felt the steam pulsing through the innards, the fire burning hotter than coal in the small furnace in the monster's belly.

"This is my new warrior, good arcanes, the golem of metal. He shall be at the forefront of our armies, and his power shall smite our enemies."

"And you have more of these?" asked Fieristic, his tone full of awe.

"Soon I shall have many more. And they will make the destruction of the Seers a certainty. So, you see, our army will gather, not for an attack on Axial, but to await the enemy's reaction. I have laid a trap for the Seers, and in their arrogance they cannot perceive the danger.

"First, I shall cripple their army. Then, I shall tighten the noose, and then, when all the preparations have been laid . . . only then, will the real attack commence."

"I'VE got to get my companies mustered," Karkald said, his mind filled with worries and obstacles. "There's no time to lose."

"Yes, there is," Darann said, taking his hand and pulling him close in the crowded aisles of the great plaza. "On the king's orders, you have to wait three cycles before you begin preparing for war."

He chuckled. "I'm sorry." His own strong finger entwined in hers, and he looked into her green eyes, those eyes that always seemed to see every fiber of his being. "Have I told you yet how beautiful you are?"

"No," she said, affecting a pout. "You were in too much of a hurry to tell the king why he should cancel the Festival of Fyre!"

He sighed and shook his head. "It *is* awful timing, isn't it? Believe it or not, I have some idea how much this was going to mean to you, when my 'riders led the parade before the king. But you know, the whole thing will be rescheduled, after—" He suddenly found himself groping for something to say, realizing that he didn't know enough about what was happening even to begin to predict what would occur afterward.

"Did you see how mad General Paternak was when the king ordered him to bring the legions home?" Darann asked.

"No," Karkald said. "I didn't notice. Why would he be mad?"

Darann sighed and gave him a hug. "You're smart, but such a child sometimes. Are you aware that you embarrassed him in front of most of the nobles of Axial? That those who weren't there will be hearing about it by the end of the cycle?"

"Because the king took my advice over his? But it was the right thing to do!"

"And you think that matters to people, don't you?" Darann kissed him. "Just stick with me, and you won't get into too much trouble."

"I plan to stick with you . . . all the way," he said, reaching an arm around her waist. He was acutely conscious of her breasts pressing against his chest, her blue dress that swirled so enticingly, and felt so feathery light under his touch.

"That's more like it, soldier," she said with an intimate smile. She kissed him long and deep. "Welcome home."

6

The Bastion of Karlath-Fayd

King of darkness,
Lord of death;
Liege of sickness,
Thief of breath.

Hunter's master,
Warrior's lord;
Everlasting,
Lethal sword.

From *Faces of the Deathlord*
Ancient Elven Chant

The outer battlements formed a semicircle more than a hundred miles in diameter. This parapet was a barrier along the entire coast of Loamar, the Fifth Circle, sometimes called the Deathrealm. For eons, the Worldsea had battered that wall, but wherever the rampart cracked or splintered, the minions of Karlath-Fayd came forth to rebuild the barrier even stouter, higher, stronger than it had been before.

And this was only the initial protection to the realm of shadow and magic, of foul spirits and restless, menacing ghosts. The wall was pierced by a single gate, this opening into the Gulf of Ah-Truin, where the death ships were moored in all their infinite ranks of darkness. Within the gulf were vast wharves, each overlooked by massive dark towers and huge ramparts, with steep ramps ascending to narrow, well-fortified towers, all linking to the one wide, lofty gate.

The first plateau of Loamar was a belt some twenty-five miles wide, scored with towers and plunging ravines, negotiable only by a twisted maze of roadways, all of which ran along the heights, every length and curve visible from a dozen strong points. Mighty castles stood astride each of the three roads that finally extended far enough inland to meet the second wall.

Here the battlements rose hundreds of feet into the air, and even so, they were mere garnishes at the base of a sheer barrier reaching fully a thousand feet above. A lofty balustrade of cliff blocked access here, sheer and seamless except at the trio of huge, unassailable gatehouses. Massive gargoyles, greater than the tallest giant, peered from the ramparts of the second wall, and their wrath could be mighty and would fall against any who dared challenge that parapet. Within the gatehouse castles, steep ramps spiraled upward, all continually exposed to defensive fire from above.

Beyond the second wall, moving still closer toward this realm of eternal shadow, the land rose steeply, every pathway overlooked by balustrades, ramparts, and parapets. Towers jutted from the shoulders of grim rock, and great siege engines lurked in lofty caverns, resting upon wheels that allowed them to rumble forth in time of war . . . should war ever come to this bastion of stone and darkness.

Past the rising land, which sloped upward for ten thousand feet across a breadth of only a dozen miles, the Third Wall rose as an utterly impassable barrier. Fully fifteen hundred feet high, carved from the living bedrock of Loamar itself, it was pierced by but a single gate. That gate, aligned toward the Center of Everything, far away across the Worldsea, was the focal point of a massive fortification, a series of sprawling castles overlooking a winding roadway down in a chasm so deep that it remained shrouded in eternal darkness.

Before the gateway, the road coursed back and forth, a dozen switchbacks across the face of a slope, exposed to view—and attack—from twice as many vantages. Any intruder reaching this point would come under fire from a hundred mighty engines of war, catapults and trebuchets that could rain fire and stone and steel across the tortured landscape.

Beyond the Third Wall lay the strongest fortification of all. The Keep of the Deathlord rose like a mountain against the black sky of the cosmos. Twenty thousand feet high it was, and ten miles across at its base. Walls upon towers upon gates upon ramparts crept ever upward across the vast face, each overlooking those below, successively commanding higher and higher ground. Routes and corridors turned back among themselves or reached dead ends. Many passages were fitted with elaborate traps, so that a whole regiment of attackers might be dropped into caustic acid or a searing lake of fire.

Indeed, fire was a common element here, spilling in liquid spumes from sluice gates high on the fortress walls, bubbling and chortling in lethal moats, or spilling downward to fuel the infernal heartland of the Deathlord's realm. Geysers of flame erupted in many places, and frequent clouds of noxious gas wafted across the landscape, often settling into low sumps and dells.

The walls of the Keep were a mile thick or more, often with layers of iron or steel clad across the eternal granite. Within, passages twisted and curved and rose and fell with chaotic imprecision, until at the very last they converged into the heart of the realm, the great hall of the Deathlord.

Here the brooding master of Loamar sat, a presence felt but not seen upon a massive throne. Only visible there were his eyes, orbs of fire and fury, seeking through the darkness, ever burning, penetrating water, cloud, and stone. These eyes could see anything, anywhere upon the Seven Circles, save a place or thing under the glare of sunlight. And so throughout the worlds, among all peoples, death became known as a thing that stalked the night.

The Deathlord was an eternal presence, master of the realm in the way that no goddess, dragon, or arcane could claim to master any other circle. He brooded here and studied the worlds of the cosmos, absorbing the dead when they came to him, fostering violence in any way he could. For ten thousand years, even during all of the Time Before, Karlath-Fayd had ruled this world. And for all those centuries, he had resented the other realms, worlds of light and growth, and ever did he plot to extend his reign. Once, four thousand years ago, he had tried and failed.

So he waited, knowing his chance would come again.

Across all the plains and crags and walls and valleys of Loamar, there was nothing alive. No trees grew, no grass softened a slope, nothing grazed, for there was no fodder, and nothing ate, for there was no hunger.

But do not mistake: The realm of Karlath-Fayd, though it was a realm of oppressive, inescapable death, was not a place of stillness. For here had gathered the shades of the dead for ten thousand years, those souls who had perished in violence and were doomed to existence as the Deathlord's slaves. They shimmered and marched across the realm in great companies, and ever did they fight and wound and maim, but never could they kill.

Great battles were enacted in fire and smoke, legions standing firm in line against the onslaught of massed barbarians, phalanxes with disciplined spears arrayed against the charge of bronze-plated horses. Artillery thundered in long batteries on one crest, and catapults hurled crude missiles of rock and fire on the next. And when the tide of battle passed, the wounded, even those grievously torn, arose from the field. Suffering the pain of infinite wounds, they nevertheless closed ranks and marched toward the next campaign.

When they tired of these pointless combats, the shades of Karlath-Fayd gathered upon their lord's walls and ramparts and watched the steady procession, the new souls who emerged from the sea, passed through the opened gates, and made the long ascent through the Fifth Circle, until at last they came before their new lord and learned their grim and timeless fate.

From all the Circles came these shades, drawn only by the common bond: a death rendered by violence. There were the ghosts of Delver and Seer Dwarves, locked in eternal hatred, waging battles now for the Deathlord's amusement. Elves and other faierie folk of Nayve were here, most of them remnants of the great casualty lists of the Crusader War, though some had been here for thousands of years, and bore dire memories of strife even dating to the dawn of that reputedly peaceful realm, the war in the Time Before. There were harpies and griffons and even dragons who had perished in the skirmishes of the Overworld, and ironmen and treefolk who had been felled in the occasional strife marring the Second and Third Circles.

But far and away outnumbering all the rest in the vastness of their ever-swelling numbers were the shades of the dead who came from Seventh Circle. The wars of Earth were waged with monstrous regularity, a relentless fury that diminished to almost nothing any other conflict in the Seven Circles. Even in times of relative peace, violence on the world of Earth commended dozens, even hundreds of souls every day into the maw of Loamar's darkness. During the great wars, such as had happened twice in the current century alone, the numbers swelled into gruesome thousands, whole ranks of men slain under the flags of France or Prussia, England or Spain, the United States, and the Confederate States of America. Napoleon had led many into the halls of Karlath-Fayd, as had U. S. Grant and Robert E. Lee.

The shades came in their numberless ranks to Loamar, and here they closed formation again. Waterloo and Ligny, Gettysburg and Shiloh again shuddered under the onslaught of brutal violence, while stony mockeries of the fields at Hastings and Pharsalus were fertilized with blood and meat but never yielded a crop other than the next wave of slaughter.

Yet great as was his host, the legions of ghost troops eternally patrolling his realm or awaiting his commands, Karlath-Fayd was not without external allies, as well. In two cases he had pushed his will through the ether, connecting with the beings of other circles, quietly and patiently turning these beings, each a leader on his own world, to the will of Karlath-Fayd. He had created the *dakali,* mighty gems of power, containing all the elements of his will in a multitude of facets and hues. By careful and patient means, he had caused these stones to be delivered into the hands of the two unwitting souls he sought to ensnare.

These were souls already wicked and debased, nurtured in death and lustful of cruelty and blood, and so they were ready recipients of the will of Karlath-Fayd. One of these was the blind dwarf arcane, Zystyl of the First Circle, and loyal servant of mass slaughter.

Zystyl first encountered the dakali while he had been attempting to map out and decipher the entire maze of vast Vicieristn. Alone in a winding corridor, deep in the bowels of the tunnel-city, he had felt the compulsion to explore a natural, wet cave. Normally, he would have dispatched lackeys for such a job, but some unrecognized compulsion caused Zystyl to perform the search himself. He had crawled through a trough of slick mud, scaled a perilous cliff, and at last closed his hand around the hard, multifaceted surface of the gem. The arcane had exulted at the find, even as he kept it a secret. Smugly, he disdained the interest of lesser creatures, knowing that none of them would have had the senses and the wherewithal to locate such a treasure. Never did he realize that it was the stone that had found him, not the other way around.

The other servant of the Deathlord lurked high above the other circles, in the realm of the Overworld. He was a withered and ghastly creature, great in size and ancient in years. He dwelled in a darkened cavern in the clouds, and he was Vultari, lord of the harpies. The dakali had summoned him to devour the carcass of a skywhale, and there the harpy lord had discovered the glowing gem. Delighted by the find, he had clutched the trinket to his chest and spread his broad wings. None of his minions dared to challenge mighty Vultari, and he had flown aloft with his treasure, never suspecting that, in reality, the dakali was the finder and Vultari himself the prize.

For a long time now, more than four thousand years measured in those realms where such counts had meaning, Karlath-Fayd had fortified his bastion. His own land would be proof against conquest of any kind, and never mind that there was none who had inclination to attack. The shades that guarded his gates and patrolled his walls maintained constant vigilance, and vast regiments of undead warriors waited in barracks throughout the realm, ready to sortie against any threat.

For those four millennia, the Deathlord had nursed a dire hurt, the wound that had been rent in his power during the War of the Time Before. Then he had hurled his legions against Nayve, after using much of his power to raise the bed of the Worldsea. His troops had crossed en masse, but they had been slaughtered on the plains of the Fourth Circle, and Karlath-Fayd had retreated to his bastion.

There, he had nursed his wounds, strengthened his defenses, and made his plans. Now, at last, those plans had taken form. Again the Deathlord had sent forth a great swell of his strength to tear at the fabric of the Seven Circles. This time, he had not tried to raise the bed of the sea.

Instead, he had created the Worldfall.

VULTARI stirred in the depths of his aerie. He yawned, stretched wide his fanged jaws. Feathers lined the cloudy floor, and the stink of carrion was rank in the air, proof that food was at hand in the lair.

But, for once, the lord of the harpies was not interested in food. Instead, he rose, waddling awkwardly on his taloned feet, as he kicked through the sleeping figures of his wives, bringing them—hissing and screeching, of course—to wakefulness. He ignored the cacophony, ignored everything but the sudden urge that sent him toward the mouth of his lofty nest.

Around his neck, suspended on a thong made from the woven hair of a pegasus tail, his precious Starstone glittered, warm and pleasant against the harpy's feathered chest. He touched the stone with a four-fingered hand, the clawed digits curling protectively around his treasure. He spat a fiery gob, watched it sizzle through the floor, and then he waddled on.

Soon he emerged, perched on the balcony of cloud near the foot of a vast, roiling mountain of dark vapor. He shrieked, a keening cry that echoed from the nearby summits, sank into the valleys, and reverberated over ridge and through swale. Again he cried out, and then Vultari took to the air.

Gaining altitude, he circled above his lair, watching as his mates, still cawing, emerged from the nest and flew in response to his command. Higher he flew, as he saw the harpies coming over the ridge and up the valley, in flocks of dozens, then hundreds, ultimately in the thousands. All of them keening and shrieking, they circled through the air in a dark cloud, numbers swelling as the vicious carrion eaters came from all across the Overworld.

Still Vultari climbed, until he was level with, and then above, the nearby ridges. The Starstone glimmered on his breast, a caress of his master's will, and he set course for the direction that was neither metal nor wood. His minions in their thousands came behind, wings flapping steadily, hasty flyers crowded together in the sky.

They were a cloud of darkness as they flew, and they saw an even darker cloud billow before them. Many were afraid, and shrieked and cried their protests. They tried to turn, to dive away, but their master's will was too strong.

And all of them followed Vultari into the Hillswallower Storm.

ZYSTYL admired his creations as they stood before him, a row of iron monoliths, capable of such deeds as the arcane could scarcely imagine. He clutched his Hurtstone with a rush of pleasure and then slowly turned so that he could stalk along the line of metallic giants.

"You will serve me well, my golems," he said breathlessly.

He stopped and drew a deep breath, relishing the slow inhalation, letting each bit of air tickle the sensitive membranes of his nostrils. He could smell iron and coal, steel and tin, and fire and soot. Pausing, he reached out a hand, caressed a monstrous foot, a solid, trunklike leg. Though Zystyl could not reach as high as the knee, he could clearly remember the rest: the iron breastplate, the fists with metal fingers ending in spikes, curving blades, and crushing bludgeons.

The faces were blank, save for a single hole where the nostrils of a person might be. Through that hole the golem could sense its world, in its own peculiar mix of scent, sight, and sound.

For these were machines of war, but they were machines unlike anything the Seven Circles had ever known. They could sense, and they could think, at least after a fashion. Zystyl had created them, and the magical essence of his Hurtstone had shown him how to bless them with cognizance.

"Now is the time to march," declared the arcane. "I want you to go to the place I have shown you, in the direction that is neither metal nor wood."

With immense dignity, the golems wheeled and, in a file, began to march across the plain of the First Circle.

"There, my pets, you will go . . . and await my command. And there we will commence the destruction of our enemies and the triumph of darkness at last!"

KARLATH-FAYD lifted his invisible hand and moved his fingers through a broad circle in the air. The Worldfall raged, tearing away the fundament of the Sixth Circle, tumbling downward, a great spilling of air and cloud and water and storm, plunging through the cosmos, past the sun, and crashing the ground in the desolate mountains of Nayve, in the direction that was neither metal nor wood. He was pleased at the chaos, the pure, fundamental destruction, that his magic had wrought.

The Deathlord had expended great power to create this

storm, but the symmetry of the plan now became apparent. He no longer strived to disturb the equilibrium of worlds. Instead, the cycle of destruction he had set in motion had become self-sustaining, the weight of plunging world stuff creating a crush of energy upon the Fourth Circle, and that resurgent counterforce was enough to power the storm.

An effect Karlath-Fayd had not anticipated also began to occur. As the Midrock was relentlessly pounded, battered by the pressure of the Worldfall, the stony bedrock of the cosmos began to crack. Fissures shot through the multitudes of strata, and earthquakes rumbled through once-stable ground.

And the roof of the Underworld began to crumble.

7

Hillswallower

In these confines with a monarch's voice,
Cry "Havoc," and let slip the dogs of war.

From *Julius Caesar*, by William Shakespeare
Bard of the Seventh Circle

The angel Gabriel dwelled at the summit of the highest peak in the Thunder Range. Regillix Avatar needed all of his strength and endurance to make the long climb. He spent hours gaining altitude through the foothills and lesser peaks, powerful strokes of his massive wings marking a very gradual path of ascent. He fully circled the vaporous massif of his destination three times before he neared the lofty summit.

Finally, he banked sharply and stroked for all he was worth, climbing steeply as he forged closer and closer to the spire of stormy cloud that marked the very crest of the immense mountain. Craggy shoulders jutted to the sides, small ledges leading sharply upward, a series of steps ascending steeply into the great vault of the skies. The mighty wyrm directed his course toward the highest of these ledges, knowing there would not be room for him to land on the summit itself.

He had spent much time in the air during the last two days, and his flight was much more deft than it had been when he first awakened. He banked to the side, lifted his head and neck to burn off some of his speed, and settled to the shoulder of

cloud with a sharp downbeat of his wings. Mist swirled off
the semisolid surface, and the dragon's talons gripped easily
to the cloudy flatness of his narrow ledge. His long tail dangled down the face of the peak, but he furled his wings and
found that he could stand quite comfortably.

Rearing back, Regillix braced his forefeet against the face
of the cloud before him and lifted his long neck. His broad
wedge of a head reached to the very summit, and he huffed
slightly, a gust of breath steaming from his blue nostrils, as he
looked for Gabriel.

"All right, have a little patience, and I'll be out."

The voice came from a small hut, a little dome of cloud
with an arched doorway. The interior of the domicile emitted
a wash of golden light, but Regillix was slightly off to the side
and couldn't see within.

In moments a small, white-haired man came into view,
stooping to exit the low door, then standing to stretch, arching
his back, thrusting his fisted hands out to either side. As the
dragon watched, two large, white wings emerged into view,
spreading outward and up from the man's shoulders. At the
same time, the man seemed to grow stronger and younger, his
white hair brightening to shiny gold, his stature increasing
into a physique of rippling muscle and dextrous, easy motions.

"Ah, Regillix old friend, I have been expecting you,"
Gabriel said, using his wings to glide across the summit in a
single step. He settled to a rest before the dragon's head, seating himself on the lip of his cloud peak.

"You have?" rumbled the dragon in a deliberate expression of surprise. "Then the danger is worse than I thought."

"The danger is worse than any of us could have thought,"
Gabriel confirmed. "But I am too hasty. . . . Please, tell your
story. What is it that brings you to my lofty nest?"

Regillix drew a deep breath and collected his thoughts,
while the angel waited a minute for him to begin speaking. "I
have slept for thirty years and would have slept half again as
long. But something called me from slumber early, awaken-

ing me with a sense of danger. There is no threat to my cave, so the danger must be toward the Sixth Circle itself."

"Indeed . . . to the Sixth Circle, at least," Gabriel murmured.

Regillix was startled by that comment but continued with his explanation. "I spoke to a pegasus stallion, and he told me of a terrible storm, a thing he called the Hillswallower. It rages in the direction that is neither metal nor wood, and I intend to fly to see for myself. But first I thought to come here, to see what the wisest of all the angels has seen from his lonely mountaintop."

"Wise?" Gabriel chuckled wryly, reached up to stroke the long whiskers beside the dragon's mouth—a mouth that could have engulfed the angel in a single gulp. "Would that I could advise you. But as it stands, for all my meditations, I know little more than a sleek stallion."

"This Hillswallower storm, then, is what awakened me?" Regillix pondered.

"Of that, I am certain. I have looked at this storm myself and watched its progress from my hut." The dragon didn't bother to ask about that; Gabriel's knowledge of all matters on the Sixth Circle was a commonly accepted fact. No one knew how he could see what happened in harpy dens and dragon aeries, in sunlit gorges or atop shadowy thunder peaks, but if Gabriel said it, you knew it to be true.

"And how does it eat the hills?"

Gabriel looked into Regillix's near eye, and the angel's gaze was direct and deeply troubled. "I fear that it eats the hills as it eats everything else . . . for this is not just a Hillswallower. It is the Chaos Storm."

The great dragon shivered, an instinctive reaction to a word he had never heard before. "Chaos . . . a cold word, for the direction that is neither metal nor wood."

"A cold, strong word," Gabriel noted. "But it is far more than a direction. If it is not contained, null is the end of all things. It swallows the hills and carries them away into nothing. It has been growing from a small whirlpool fifty years ago to a swath of the Sixth Circle that is the size of a small mountain range. Ever it sweeps outward, slowly but consistently, and each new tendril seizes clouds and creatures, engulfing them, carrying them into chaos."

"Are such creatures killed?" Regillix wondered. "Pegasus told me that many harpies have been swallowed into the vortex."

"That is a strange thing," Gabriel said. "As you know, I have an understanding of death. When anything, from the lowest cloudfish to the mightiest dragon, perishes, I sense the fading spark of life. If it was a worthy life, I can offer comfort, bear that soul to deserved rest. But when one is trapped by the Chaos Storm, I sense nothing. Those harpies swept away are gone from my awareness."

"Perhaps they are not killed, then?" speculated the wyrm.

"Perhaps not. I cannot see into the storm. Nor do I have the strength to fly into the maelstrom and bring myself out again. I am too small, too weak."

Regillix huffed in dry amusement. "Never would I presume to think of Gabriel as weak."

The angel smiled sadly. "I do lack your strength, old friend. You have the wings to carry you where I dare not go."

"And this is why I was awakened," understood the dragon. "So that I may fly into the Chaos Storm and see what is happening to our world."

"That may be," replied Gabriel. "Though I do not know if I should go *into* the storm, if I were you. It is best that you observe it from the periphery and learn what you can thusly."

"Perhaps . . . but in any event, I must see it. I shall go there at once," declared Regillix Avatar with a decisive nod. "Thank you for sharing your wisdom."

Now the angel chuckled ruefully. "Do not be so hasty. It may be that my 'wisdom' does nothing less than lead you into terrible danger."

Snorting skeptically, the serpent shook the broad chisel of his head. "There has not been a storm in all the Seven Circles that is a menace to me."

"Be careful, old friend," counseled Gabriel, "for never in the Seven Circles has there been a storm like this."

Those words echoed through his mind with uneasy portent as Regillix winged his way down from the great summit, plummeting with headlong speed, soaring like an arrow in the direction that was neither metal nor wood. Banking gracefully around vast summits, diving through the shadowy heights of a plunging cloud canyon, he at first allowed gravity to carry him. The dragon swelled his speed through a whistling dive, wind tearing at his wings, scouring his scales, filling his nostrils and rasping past his huge, leather-lidded eyes. The roiled slopes of Gabriel's mountain tore past until the great dragon lifted his head, angled his wings, and slowly began to pull out of his meteoric descent.

He felt the solid pressure of his weight as he knifed the great pinions through the air, curving slightly to steer. He relished the speed that bore him away from the peak faster than any other being in the Sixth Circle would dare to fly. He came upon a flock of griffons and swept past, leaving them tumbling and squawking in his wake before they had even detected his approach. Harpies appeared in the blink of an eye and vanished as quickly.

The Thunder Mountains extended for a great distance, but the dragon's speed carried him into the foothills by the time the sun began to sink toward Darken. He passed over the shore of the Cloudsea in the twilight, with the rainbow bands of beach shimmering iridescently far, far below. The momentum of his great dive had finally burned away, and he winged under his own power, long strokes pulling him through the air with relentless speed. For hours he flew, the surface of the sea fading into darkness that occasionally flared into fluorescence when some mighty denizen of the vaporous waters breached the surface in with tendril or fin.

Before dawn, he detected a fluff of whiteness off to the side, one of the numerous cloud islands that floated above the surface of the sea. He was not fatigued, but if he didn't rest, he knew that he would be quite tired by the time he reached the far side of the sea, so he curled through a gradual turn, lifted himself slightly with vigorous strokes, and finally settled to the surface of the island.

Immediately he heard a hiss of alarm and blinked at the sight of a young dragon, rearing back with jaws agape and wings buzzing in agitation. "Begone from here, or I will burn you with fire!" snarled the little serpent.

"I don't think you can do that. And know, if you belch so much as a puff of smoke at me, I will pick my teeth with your bones," growled Regillix, in no mood for such a challenge.

With a yelp, the youngster vanished beneath a fold of cloud. A few moments later, a hesitant head poked outward, eyes clear and bright and wide in the pale light.

"Begging your pardon, great sire," whispered the little wyrm. "Please forgive my impertinence. I heard you approach, and spoke before I saw to whom I was speaking."

"Have a care, little wyrm. Such impertinence might cost you more than an apology, next time."

"Oh, great sire, I shall!" said the little dragon, wiggling forth from his hiding place. Regillix saw another dragon head, with the larger eyes and soft jowls of a young female, also emerge into view.

The big serpent coughed and cleared his throat in acknowledgement of his own embarrassment. "It is my sincere hope that I did not interrupt a moment of, er . . ." He wasn't sure what to say, but the young dragon stammered and shook his head.

"Oh no, most wonderous wyrm! That is, I thought you were Daristal's sire, and I was prepared to . . . that is, he doesn't know that we . . . that she . . ."

Regillix snorted impatiently.

"Please, no!" squawked the female, coming forth to fan her wings beside the young male. "Do not eat poor Cantrix, nor crush him, nor tear off his wings! For he is bold even though foolish, too, and I love him very much!"

Regillix snorted in exasperation. "I was not going to do any of those things to poor Cantrix. I only came here for a rest, perhaps even a nap. I would be sleeping now if it weren't for all the clamoring from the two of you."

"We extend our deepest apologies, great sire," said Cantrix, bowing his head.

"And we wish you the finest of rests," offered Daristal. "A nap of unparalleled comfort and repose, undisturbed by bad dreams."

"Thank you," said the great dragon. He stretched across the island, which was small but offered plenty of room for him to curl up. The great wyrm coiled himself on a flat shelf near the edge of the floating islet and closed the heavy outer membranes over his eyes.

"Only . . . there is one thing," Daristal said hesitantly.

With a huff, Regillix cracked open one eyelid, just enough that he could see the female dragon sitting up, regarding him with an expression of mingled fear and hopefulness. "Yes?" he sighed.

"Do you know what happened to Plarinal?"

The name sounded vaguely familiar, but Regillix wasn't in the mood for puzzles. "Who in the Sixth Circle is Plarinal?"

"He is my brother, the elder of our nest, and a fine and brave and beautiful dragon," explained the female in a rush, as if she feared the great wyrm would go to sleep before she could finish.

"But he flew off to the White Hills, and he promised to return, but he didn't," Cantrix added.

Now Regillix had both eyes open. "I remember Plarinal . . . a fine young male, not yet ten centuries old, as I recall. He went to the White Hills, you say. And when did he make this flight?"

"It was three days ago," Daristal contributed. "He went to see about the Hillswallower Storm."

"The Chaos Storm," Regillix noted, with that same shiver of apprehension that the word had caused him before. "How did you come to know about it?"

The two young dragons, neither of which was a day over five hundred years old in the elder serpent's estimation, looked at each other sheepishly. Finally Daristal spoke, "It was my sire, Red Fixwhisker . . . he forbade Plarinal and me to fly across the Cloudsea. He said anything that could swallow hills in a single bite would make short work of two foolish little wyrms."

Regillix remembered Fixwhisker as a short-tempered bully of a dragon. "And so, because you were forbidden to go there, you absolutely had to disobey, to find out what all the fuss was about?"

"No! Well, yes, I suppose," Daristal admitted.

"That is, only to the islands, to here," Cantrix added, puffing out his chest and raising his head on its graceful neck. "At least, for Dari . . . I came to give her company, while Plarinal flew in the direction that is neither metal nor wood, to see the storm for himself."

"But he was to return yesterday, and there has been no sign of him," wailed Daristal.

"And when I arrived, you thought that I might be Red Fixwhisker, coming in pursuit," Regillix concluded, lifting his head with a groan and fixing the two young wyrms with a baleful glare. "Not that you don't deserve to be captured and punished!"

He puffed scornfully at Cantrix, forming a waft of smoke that clouded around the serpent's nostrils and eventually provoked a strained, single cough. "Do not think that you fooled me with your talk of 'company.' I was young once, and I have sired offspring who have since sired offspring who are older than you. I know why a young male comes to a lonely cloud with a pretty female, and I do not approve."

"I am sorry, Grandfather," said Cantrix, lowering his head to the misty ground. "Please understand that I have behaved with honor and made no encirclement about the lovely Daristal."

"He has been perfectly genteel," agreed the female with a bob of her head.

From the glow in her yellow eyes as she looked down at

Cantrix, Regillix suspected that it wouldn't be long before there was some encircling going on, and the thought brought back some pleasant memories of his own youth. But he quickly banished those in consideration of this new evidence.

"I want you to wait here," he said to them both, with a brow-furrowing glare to indicate the seriousness of his charge. "I shall forgo my rest and fly on, seeking sign of your nestmate. You two should realize that there is real danger abroad in the world, and this Hillswallower is harbinger of that peril."

The two were still gratefully promising obedience as Regillix Avatar launched himself from the island. Once more he dove, using the altitude of his launching point as an impetus of speed. With deliberate wing strokes he accelerated, bearing toward the White Hills while remaining a thousand feet above the surface of the sea. Unnoticed, Lighten began to illuminate the surface, and it was full daylight when he saw the rim of smoky horizon, a brackish murk in the air obscuring the place where the pastoral range of hills should rise.

Ahead, the strand of beach marked the end of the stormy, surging Cloudsea. Breakers of white foam smashed against that shore, spuming over many dark lumps scattered across the ground. The rainbow hues were faded here, only visible as pale images, chalky colors viewed through a dirty window.

A stink of rot permeated the air, and as he drew closer, the serpent saw why: The dark specks on the beach proved to be carcasses, skywhales and cloudfish that had somehow been cast upon the shore. Beyond the beach, where the ground rose into the first of the hills, there was only a wall of roiling vapor, a dark face with lightning flashing in the depths and great faces, like whole mountains, simply rolling past and vanishing into the chaotic cyclone.

The storm made a dull noise, a roaring din that initially seemed a vague background but, as Regillix neared the beach, swelled to a cacophony like steady thunder, a rolling crash that never ceased, stuttered only enough to allow here and there for a monstrous crescendo. The Chaos Storm seemed to pull the ancient wyrm closer, almost as though he was making a steep dive, even though he still advanced in level flight.

Harpies scattered all across the beach as Regillix banked to fly parallel to the storm, their dirty feathers bristling as they hopped awkwardly into the air. The vulgar creatures had been feasting on the carrion, and now they took wing in panic. No doubt they were shrieking in alarm and outrage, but their usually shrill noise was utterly swallowed in the raging storm. Gray wings fluttered and flapped, and taloned feet flailed in the wind. The ancient dragon looked down onto an array of those bony hag faces, saw the grotesque leers, the spitting tongues, the hateful eyes of the vile scavengers.

One after another, the harpies were swallowed by the Chaos Storm, the sucking wind proving much too powerful for winged bodies no bigger than large eagles. As Regillix coursed along the beach, more and more harpies were startled up from their feasting, and nearly all of them vanished into the horrific maw of storm. The dragon saw three of them blackened by a jagged bolt of lightning, and another was smashed onto the beach in a powerful downdraft. Only a few escaped, flying low, skimming the top of the Cloudsea in desperate flight.

Regillix was beginning to enjoy the sport—in one span of flight, he had gotten rid of more harpies than he might typically kill in a dozen years—when some vague noise reached his ear, a disturbing tremor penetrating the deep tenor of the storm. He glanced at that turbulent face and saw something solid there, a writhing tendril of tail that abruptly vanished into the moving surface.

There it was again, tumbling along the cloud, moving rapidly sideways in the opposite direction of the dragon's flight. He saw taloned forefeet, then a neck and a dragon's head. The serpentine jaws parted, and the frantic bray for help just barely tickled Regillix's hearing. Then the trapped dragon was gone, once more vanished in the roiling murk.

The ancient wyrm tipped his wings, veering away from the

cloud, spiraling through a backward loop, and diving to gain speed. He emerged from the maneuver going the opposite direction, chasing the storm's current, looking for any sign of the struggling serpent.

Was it Plarinal? He couldn't know, though it seemed as likely as anything. And it didn't really make any difference, for now he knew that this Hillswallower, the Chaos Storm, was capable of devouring dragonkind as well.

NATAC'S sword was in his hand, but his mind still hadn't accepted the truth. These trolls were dead! He had prodded each lifeless body himself. By the goddess, he had cut off the head of one and slashed the others through the throat! Yet the leering beasts were swaggering toward him right now, certainly a little more cautiously than their first impetuous rush, but with grim purpose, nonetheless.

Bowstrings twanged from *Skyreaver* as Sirien and Juliay, belatedly noticing the danger, each let an arrow fly. But the trolls immediately sidestepped at the sound, turning to snort derisively as the two arrows whispered harmlessly past to thunk into the ground. Already at the extreme range of the archers, the trolls simply hastened their advance toward Natac, trotting along with gangly steps that nevertheless carried them swiftly across the ground.

The warrior saw Owen and Roland hurrying back to the ship, each trailing the heavy guylines that had been used to secure *Skyreaver* to the big oak trees. The Viking reached over the side of the hull and pulled back, holding the long steel of his sword.

"Take off!" cried Natac, waving to make sure he was heard. Owen hesitated. "Get aboard and get up in the air. Trail me a rope!"

Shaking his head in disbelief, the bearded warrior did as he was told. Roland, too, scrambled aboard, and he and Juliay quickly took their casting bowls, while Sirien opened the valve to release a tank of water ballast. Ever so slowly, *Sky-*

reaver started to drift upward, the gondola gradually rising from the grass, swaying like a gentle swing.

Natac turned his attention to the trolls, who had shrewdly spread out to block off any attempt he might make to get back to the ship. He took only a moment to consider his options. He stood near the edge of the crest of the steep-sided hill, his back toward the descending slope. Any advance toward the skyship would quickly have sent him against all three of the trolls at once, and—having already seen their ferocity and proof that they had learned from their mistakes in the first battle—he wanted no part of those odds.

Instead, he spun on his heel and sprinted off the hilltop, starting himself down the slope with three long steps. As soon as he had dropped out of sight of the trolls, he darted to the left and raced along, breathing hard, carefully watching his balance as he traversed the steep side slope, fighting the urge to drift down the hill. He ducked as low as he could while maintaining his speed, hoping to delay discovery for another few seconds.

"Hawrph!" roared one the brutes indignantly, and the man knew he'd been spotted. A quick glance showed that, as he hoped, all three trolls had converged on the spot where he had disappeared. Natac picked up his pace, even veering slightly downhill to put distance between himself and his pursuers as he continued around the side of the hill. He dodged between a pair of stout oak trunks and then started scrambling to gain elevation again.

Thudding footfalls sounded from behind, spurring the warrior on to greater speed. He curled around the trunk of another tree, surprised by how quickly the trolls were gaining. Another glance showed him one of the brutes, mouth spread in a fang-baring grin, was loping along just uphill, using its long arm almost as a third leg as it paced along a horizontal contour. The second troll was directly behind Natac, while the third was out of sight—hopefully it had fallen back following his surprise deflection.

With a sudden burst of speed, the man turned his path

straight uphill, cutting across in front of the upper troll while leaving the second one skidding to a halt, scrambling more slowly to climb. Natac's sword was in his hand, and he slashed it quickly, slowing the nearest of his pursuers enough so that he could scramble the last few feet up toward the crest. Still he couldn't see the third of the trio.

Until he lunged over the rim of the hilltop and halted, seeing that he had been outsmarted and outmaneuvered. The third of the trolls was standing right in front of him, big arms outstretched to block any evasion he could make. He heard a grunt and a scuffing behind, knew that the first of his pursuers was scrambling up the last bit of the hillside.

Instinct took over, and Natac attacked, driving toward the standing troll with his blade held out before him. At the last minute, he pulled back, anticipating a defense even as the troll skipped sideways with surprising agility. The steel blade slashed through a sideways attack, chipping into that woody skin, and the warrior rushed past. He saw *Skyreaver* hovering eight or ten feet off the ground, with a rope ladder dangling, and he dashed toward the escape.

But somehow the pursuing troll lunged forward, reaching far enough to sink wicked talons into the man's heel. Natac cried out in pain as his foot was torn, and he tumbled to the ground, catastrophically tripped by that flinging grab. Rolling onto his back, sword raised above him, he kicked and slashed, determined to fight to the last. It seemed utterly inconceivable that his life's journey across two worlds and four centuries would end here, in such tangled chaos.

A troll loomed to either side of him, while the third of the brutes, puffing and staggering, came lurching up the hillside to stop just beyond his feet. With a flex of his arms and shoulders, Natac bounced into a crouch, grimacing as a lance of pain shot up the leg from his injured foot. The trolls instantly closed in. The keen blade flicked right, cutting a sinewy arm, while cruel claws tore at his left shoulder. Before he could twist away, the third troll lunged, grasping his sword arm and pulling Natac relentlessly toward those widespread jaws.

Fetid breath wafted over his face, but he had no leverage, no way to hold that deadly bite at bay.

Abruptly, one of the trolls shrieked and spun away, flinging its hands backward while a pair of dirty white wings, like those of a large eagle, fluttered and thrashed behind the brute. Natac broke the grasp of the other troll, but as he slashed his sword, a burning, oily ooze splashed onto his arm. The agony was so fierce it was all he could do just to hold onto his blade.

But the trolls seemed to have forgotten him. Each was fighting savagely in the taloned claws of what at first looked like large, malformed vultures. One troll turned, bashing at its own shoulder. Wings beat through the air, one of them slapping Natac's head, dropping him to his knees.

Then he heard the noise, keening shrieks that jabbed into his ears like steel spikes: a changing sound, like "harp-*ee*, harp-*ee*." The birdlike attackers screeched, and for the first time he saw their faces. One, with taloned feet sunk deep into a troll's shoulders, looked at him in an expression of tortured hatred—and it was an expression from a *human* face! Natac was reminded of an old crone he had known in Tlaxcala, wrinkled face, a wild tangle of gray hair. But the eyes were utterly inhuman, black and huge, with tiny specks of fiery light glowing hellishly in each. When the monster opened its mouth to cry, the human comparison vanished entirely; the flying beast had long, sharp fangs and a serpentine tongue that thrust rigidly forward, wriggling obscenely as the beast let loose a horrid shriek.

The winged monster spat a brown blob into the air, and as that spittle flew, it burst into flames, trailing stinking black smoke. The gooey fireball smacked onto the back of a troll, and the brute immediately howled in pain, to that mocking chorus of "harp-*ee*, harp-*ee*." At the same time, the creature tore at the troll with clawed hands on the ends of skinny arms, limbs that extended grotesquely from the shoulders below its wings.

Still on his knees, Natac scrambled backward. He held his sword in numb fingers as his arm, where the hag bird had scorched him, burned with excruciating pain. All three trolls were thrashing about, each of them under the attack of two or three of the bizarre flyers. One was burning over much of its body, as the flying brutes spat more and more of the incendiary bile onto the wretched creature.

Another harpy swooped in, wings pulsing, gaunt body swiveling downward to bring both taloned feet lashing toward Natac's face. Frantically he slashed, almost dropping his sword as the keen blade cut into the thing's feathered belly. With a wrenching scream, it fell to the ground, toppling sideways, thrashing its wings in a pool of its own gory entrails. An eerie plume of smoke belched from the deep wound.

Staying low, Natac continued to move away. The burning troll, bellowing in rage and pain, shoulders ravaged by smoking fires, pulled one of the hag birds apart with its hands. With that violence the others closed in, bearing the gangly beast to the ground beneath an enclosing shroud of beating wings and rending claws.

The two trolls thus spared of their tormentors quickly turned and dashed away, fleeing off the hilltop, long strides carrying them between the oak trunks and out of sight. Natac withdrew more cautiously, flipping his sword to his strong left hand as the fiery pain transformed into a frightening numbness as his right arm swelled and stiffened.

The vicious flyers, at least a half dozen of them, bore the remaining troll to the ground. Their talons tore at the beast, and their fanged jaws lashed in to tear bites right out of the creature's living, burning flesh. The struggles of the troll faded to a limp kick, a halfhearted thrash, all marked by dull moans.

By the time Natac had reached the ladder dangling from the skyship, the troll's struggles had ceased altogether. The warrior sheathed his sword, grasped the highest rung he could reach with his left hand, and pulled himself weakly upward. As they drifted from between the oaks, away from the hillside, he saw more of the horrid scavengers, scores of them, circling like vultures or winging from the distance to swirl around the dead troll and his shrieking killers.

MIRADEL took the strands of yarn and allowed the fibers to play through her fingers. Before her, looking deceptively small, was the Tapestry of the Worldweaver. She remembered the amazement that had always moved her in the past: the knowledge that this spool, no larger than a typical brewer's keg, could contain the histories not just of each of the Seven Circles but of each being who had ever lived on any of those worlds.

She looked up, into the interior of the great spire, the Worldweaver's Loom. That silvery space was bright now, shimmering with filtered sunlight. Fine threads drifted downward through the dazzling space, swirling into an inverted cone like a tiny cyclone, though no breeze brushed against the druid's skin. As these threads finally settled toward the top of the spool, they were bound together with instantaneous magic into a multicolored strand that coiled, eternally, onto the roll.

The threads were pulled directly into the great fabric, magically woven by the goddess far faster than any human could have done—indeed, even faster than Miradel could see. Now, as she tried to watch, to imagine, that spontaneous weaving only served to heighten her sense of superfluous activity. She needed something to do.

Originally she had come here to view the tapestry, but once the crystal doors had whisked open and she had found herself within the great, circular temple, she had been strangely reluctant to take up one of the viewing glasses, to peer too closely at the fabric of lives and deaths that spiraled so many loops around this eternal axis.

Of course, the pictures on the tapestry were too fine, too infinitely detailed, to show as visible images even when she looked closely at the threads. From here she saw only a splendid blend of brilliant colors, with emphasis on blue and green, but also containing little dashes and sparks of every other color imaginable. A druid needed one of the lensed glasses in order to view the tale of a specific thread.

For a time, Miradel had wandered around the temple and its gardens, through the great room, the chamber surrounding the garden where the goddess had so recently returned her to Nayve. Some time later, she found herself again at the forward edge of the great history, watching the threads fly upward from the spindles, mingling themselves into the material, imperceptibly moving forward with the progress of time. Miradel could have studied that edge for a long time without seeing any movement, for—just as each spiral of the tapestry represented a thousand years—it took a full millennium for the new weaving to advance through a full circumference of the room.

Finally, she stepped close, picking up one of the many viewing glasses that were placed on a velvet-covered table near the loom. These were used by druids who sought specific insights from the tapesty, and Miradel had finally made up her mind.

She started at the near edge of the tapestry, at the place where present met future. She knew from her previous studies that a druid could view present and past throughout the Seven Circles here, but on Nayve, the Fourth Circle, at the center of existence, it was also possible to catch a glimpse of a very short stretch of future.

She held the glass before her eye, and in a quivering moment he was there, before her as a living, breathing image. Natac was sailing in his skyship. She saw that he was hurt; his arm was being tended by druids, while his shipmates gaped at something on the ground, something below and behind the graceful skyship.

"When will you come back to me?" she wondered, barely whispering the words. She moved the glass, seeking a glimpse of the future.

And then she could only freeze in horror, for that solitary look showed her the very short span of time remaining to Natac. His thread twisted close to the spool, then shredded and came to an end.

8

Down the Worldfall

In days of worlds' breath,
In blush of spring;

In birth of growing,
And rattle of death;

In truth of knowledge,
In bliss of light;

Came the Worldfall to knock it down.

From *Days of the Worldfall*
by Sirien Saramayd

From the Log of the *Skyreaver:*

> We drifted away from the troll hill on a wind raised
> by Roland and Juliay together. We saw more of the vile
> harpies, but our altitude and size seemed to be enough
> to dissuade most of them from aerial pursuit. One did
> dare to fly near, and Juliay—who is certainly our best
> archer—felled it with a single arrow.
> Juliay also tended my wounded foot, which had been
> gashed deeply by the troll's blunt but powerful claws;
> talons, it seemed, that were more like a bear's than a
> lion's. With the aid of some druidic enchantment, I was
> free of pain and standing on the deck again after an

hour. My arm, too, she tended and healed, though it was badly burned by the vile spittle of the harpy.

The repairs to flesh, however, could not assuage a lingering darkness that has fallen over our mood. Attacked by monsters of two previously unknown types, we were chastened and dismayed by what we had seen of the natures of both the trolls and the harpies. Most particularly, the utterly astounding recuperation of the former and the fiery spittle of the latter seemed to make these adversaries well worth avoiding.

Nevertheless, we persevered on our course in the direction neither metal nor wood. After our initial escape, our two druids took turns vigorously maintaining the wind. The oak-covered knolls extended for dozens of miles, but we soon drew nearer to the array of jagged peaks that had earlier occupied our attention.

Somewhat surprisingly, the hills did not rise into the mountain range. Instead, after a series of ragged and worn ridges, where the trees became thin and withered in appearance, the ground fell into a broad, flat morass. We saw patches of ponds and great swaths of reeds. The open water, where it appeared, was weed-covered and stagnant; there was no sign of any flowage. Typically, I would have expected such a wetland to teem with wildfowl, but there was an utter lack of bird life, an absence that struck us all as strange and foreboding.

Only after a dozen miles of this bog, through a sump of still air that seemed fetid and oppressive, did the land rise into mountains. Then it ascended abruptly, creating a belt of cliff along the far side of the wetland. We dropped ballast and climbed, and now Roland steers us into the winding highway of a lofty vale. . . .

The mountains drifted past, below and, in some cases, beside the airship *Skyreaver.* The bedrock was black, a granite as dark as obsidian that seemed to absorb the rays of the sun and reflect back only a much-diminished illumination, like a pattern of long, tenebrous shadows. No trees grew here, not even in the most sheltered valleys or beside the numerous streams and lakes. For their part, those lakes were lightless mirrors, windows of still, black water that seemed to promise great depths but then concealed those depths in a mask of impenetrable murk.

"Does anything live down there?" wondered Roland, leaning on the rail beside Natac. The druid held a windcasting bowl at his waist and stirred with the paddle in his hand, easily raising the slight breeze needed to guide them along.

"Who's to say? We've drifted beyond the realm of the trolls," replied the warrior. "And, thank the goddess, it's been a long time since we've seen any more of those harpies."

"I'd almost be willing to go back, just for the sight of a few trees," noted the druid. "This . . . this is just strange. It brings my spirits down just to look at it."

"A direction neither metal nor wood . . . perhaps not much of anything at all," Natac mused.

"And look at that," Roland noted, pointing toward the sky beyond several successive ridges to the crest of the rugged mountains. "A storm building?"

"I've been watching it," replied Natac. "It's like a wall of cloud there, rising higher than any storm I've ever seen. If it's a storm, we'll want to get onto the ground, but it hasn't moved all day. I don't like it, but at the same time, I want to get a little closer."

Scrutinizing the dark distance of the sky, Natac felt a compelling curiosity tinged with an undercurrent of dread. That murk did not look like a storm, at least not like any storm he could remember from Nayve or even Earth. It occurred to him that they could be looking at the end of the world, some kind of physical barrier, and he had to know more.

Or perhaps it was just a continuing extension of this lifeless landscape, rising impossibly high. Already the Mountains of Moonscape, as he had called this range, seemed the most barren landscape on Nayve. He wondered if these summits were young in the scope of the world's life. The slopes of black rock were slick, and little rubble was collected at the feet of even the steepest cliffs. Not only were trees lacking, but even where it was flat, the ground looked like fields of boulders; no grass, wildflowers, or bushes marred the rocky terrain.

Besides the dark lakes, even the streams flowing through the valley bottoms seemed somehow subdued. They tumbled over falls and churned along steeply tumbling cascades, but the white froth of lively spray quickly settled back into an almost oily smoothness. The rocks below the falls were slick and shiny, but wherever the water gathered into eddies and pools, it remained smooth, black, and featureless.

"I've been thinking about those harpies," Natac said. "They seem to defy the logic of Nayve. After all, I can understand the fact that we've never encountered trolls before—Riven Deep makes a perfect boundary between these reaches and Circle at Center. But the harpies can fly. Why is it we've never heard of such a thing before?"

"Good question. And a plague on both," declared Owen, climbing the short ladder to join the two men on the forward deck. *Skyreaver* bobbed only slightly as the big man moved forward, and a moment later, the airship steadied and drifted along, still propelled by Roland's wind. The Viking leaned against the rail, scowling fiercely at the nearest summit, a needle of indigo rock rising from a base of smooth stone to pierce the clouds a thousand feet over their own altitude. Water glistened on the sheer face, here and there spreading downward in shiny swaths, but there were no cracks, nothing that would suggest a long pattern of erosion.

"A plague on this treeless landscape, as well," growled Owen, spitting over the side.

"A plague on everything?" Natac asked pointedly. "You seem to be spreading a lot of disease around today."

The big man looked shamefaced behind the immense spread of his beard. He cast a surreptitious glance down into the middeck, toward his cabin door that remained shut, and sighed. "Truth is, I am unfair to you. And to her, who means

life itself to me. I seem to not be able to do aught without pro-
voking her into a temper." Owen glowered again, and Natac
was reminded of the fierce warrior lurking within this tame
façade. "Though there was a time I wouldn't have had 'no'
for an answer!"

"And you wouldn't have Juliay, either," Roland reminded
him, not missing a beat in his windcasting.

"True enough. Aye, it was a gentleman she wanted, and
she gentled me," said the big man, unusually somber. "Now I
wonder if she dislikes what she has wrought."

"All of us are on edge," the Tlaxcalan suggested. "No
doubt Juliay is frightened and unsettled by what we have
seen."

"Would that were it!" Owen said. "But I fear not."

"She has changed you over these last centuries, and for the
better," Natac observed.

"I know! But how is it now that I wonder if she has
changed me into someone she no longer desires?"

PALE rays of light slipped beneath the cabin door, feeble
enough so that she knew it was still early in Lighten. Owen
had left, impatient and frustrated, and she had been glad to
hear him go.

More than her irritation, indeed most likely a cause of that
ill temper, was the other reason that she had been grateful for
his departure. Wistfully, her thoughts drifted across worlds, to
one who suffered far worse than the trivial frustrations vexing
Owen or any of them.

She didn't know if Jubal Caughlin sensed her comforting
hand, her caring thoughts, but she wanted to believe that he
did. And even if he did not, she could not stop dreaming. The
maelstrom of war was tearing his soul, even as his flesh survived. She had lived his nightmares: Sharpsburg, Gettysburg,
Fredricksburg . . . so much killing! Yet still she had to know,
to follow the story to its end.

She took the pinch of wool from her purse, the tiny tuft of

threads she had drawn from the Worldweaver's Tapestry.
Turning onto her side, she laid her cheek on her hand, with
the wool of time resting on her palm. Almost immediately,
consciousness gave way to the familiar trance, the sensory
journey of her mind. Her thoughts, her sensations, her love
reached out, through the mists of space and the boundaries of
worlds, until she found the spark, the thread, of the one she
sought. . . .

*Cold Harbor. It seemed a good name for a place where
men came to die.*

*And Jubal was certain that there would be some killing
here, and very soon. As they had died not far from here, at
Spotsylvania Court House, and beyond that, in the tangle of
woods and hills known as the Wilderness. Throughout this
grim season, the spring and summer of 1864, the Confeder-
ates had fought the Northerners to a standstill at so many
crossroads and streams and fields . . . but for what?*

*In past campaigns, in '62 and '63, the bluebellies had also
been fought to a standstill. In those years, they had retreated
north, across their beloved Potomac, and spent many months
licking their wounds, repairing their battered army.*

*But this new commander, General U. S. Grant, seemed
determined to ignore this time-honored practice. Each time
Lee's rebels halted his advance, Grant simply moved his army
sideways and went around the Southerners, always moving
closer to Richmond, to the great prize of Virginia.*

*And so each time Lee had been forced out of his fortified
positions, Southerners hurrying along in front of the invaders,
stopping again to throw up hasty breastworks, dig shallow
rifle pits, and prepare once again to meet the enemy's onslaught. Now they had come to the place called Cold Harbor,
and the Army of the Potomac had gone into camp on the far
side of the little crossroads.*

*Jubal had set his men to digging with a vengeance, and
they had thrown themselves into the work with the fervor of
troops who knew their lives depended on good work, done*

fast. The general took a shovel in his own hands, strained his own back hauling logs, helping to raise the breastwork, in a space of twelve hours, into a formidable wall. It was a wall that zigzagged back and forth, a jagged array of strong points and flanking positions.

Over the night, as rain washed enemy and friend alike, the rebel guns were rolled into place, battered but reliable cannon trundled into redoubts, blunt barrels turned toward the ground the Yankees would have to cross. At the same time, they heard the sounds of imminent battle, the marching, cursing, clanking of a great army taking up a position.

The attack came at dawn, long lines of blue-uniformed men emerging from the woods, plodding resolutely into the ground before the Confederate entrenchments. They did not come in a rush nor with a great shout; instead, they advanced as men who were reluctant to go to their deaths and finally understood that to advance was to die.

The rebel artillery opened the firing, but the rifles and then the muskets soon followed. Sheets of flame rippled forth from the entrenchments, and the first line of blue-coated soldiers was ripped to pieces. Those who weren't killed turned and tried to flee, but their retreat was blocked by the second and third lines. More and more fire fell onto those hapless corps, even the general taking up a rifle, resting the barrel on the parapet, shooting as quickly as he could reload.

He was awed by the bravery of those sad, doomed men, even as he fired. He saw blasts of artillery, double-shot charges of canister cutting swaths thirty, forty, fifty feet wide through packed ranks. His men fought with the bravery, the tenacity he had come to expect, and in less than an hour there were thousands upon thousands of Union dead and dying, scattered across the gory field.

The attack was broken. The men of the two sides would glare in weary hatred through the rest of the steaming summer. Then Grant would move again, and Lee would be forced to hurry, again, to block his way, this time south of Richmond at a place called Petersburg.

Juliay awoke suddenly, to a sense of stark fear. She cried out softly, mourning the broken contact. And then she heard shouts, real shouts in her real life. Sitting up in alarm, she listened, then spun out of bed.

"BRING my sword, Juli!" roared Owen, staring in disbelief at the misty sky. The mountains were taller here than ever, at least a dozen nearby peaks rising higher than the airship, which had been coursing an easy path through this stony forest. "Make haste, woman!" he added.

Natac busily curled the draft of his map into a tube and thrust it into the long pouch he wore at his belt. He strained to look along the slope of the nearby mountain, blinked as he tried to recall every detail of the sight that had caused such alarm: the thing he had glimpsed momentarily, before it vanished behind the shoulder of the nearby mountain.

"Like a lizard it was, with wings," he said aloud. "And big as an elephant, at least."

"I caught a glimpse of the size but not the shape, before it disappeared," Owen declared.

Juliay rushed out of her cabin, handing the longsword up to Owen, who knelt on the upper platform to grab the weapon. He snorted in frustration. "Of course, I'd like to have my big sword, but no time to get it out of the hold now."

Roland and Sirien, who had had the watch for the latter half of the night, also emerged onto the middle deck in response to the alarm.

"String the bows," Natac called down. "Arrows ready. There's something going to come into view around the side of that mountain at any moment."

"Do you think it's hostile?" asked the druid.

"After the harpies and trolls, I'm not taking any chances," Natac declared.

"There!" cried the elfwoman, pointing. "By the goddess—what?"

The flying lizard came into view suddenly, banking around the slope of a steep mountain. It appeared in a shallow dive, angling directly toward *Skyreaver*. Natac saw jaws reminiscent of a great crocodile's, though the movements of this soaring monster were more suggestive of a bird than a reptile. The wings were broad and smooth, like great, leathery sails.

Roland had readied the bows and passed two of the weapons and a full quiver up to Natac and Owen. The two druids and Sirien also took up bows and stood side by side on the middle deck.

Natac drew back the shaft, wondering how effective the little dart of his arrow could be against such a monster. He hoped that it would veer aside, dive or bank or somehow change course, offer at least some hope of peaceful intentions. Perhaps it was simply curious. But somehow, this foreign serpent aroused an instinctive antipathy. Too, every other creature they had encountered past Riven Deep had proven to be vicious and aggressive. He would assume the same of this one.

The toothy jaws spread wide, and the monster uttered a barking roar that shook the air and echoed through the high valleys of the Mountains of Moonscape. It came on. Instead of bearing for the great bags of helium, the creature was shrewd enough to dive toward the hull, where the five explorers stood on the deck. The mouth stretched wide open, big enough to bite a person in half.

"Shoot!" cried Natac, as the wyrm swept into range. Five arrows hissed outward, and battle was joined in the sky.

"I came as soon as I could," Quilene said breathlessly, joining Belynda in the garden below the Worldweaver's Loom. "You said lives depended on haste. But what—" The normally serene elfwoman froze, then gasped and clapped a hand to her mouth.

"Miradel?" she said, seeing the third person in the little grotto. "But . . ."

"It is I," said the druid, "And I thank you for coming so quickly. I only hope we can prevent disaster."

"Disaster . . . yes. To business, then," said the sage-enchantress, with a sideways look at the druid. "Though later I should very much like to hear your tale."

"You shall. But now it's Natac," Miradel said. "And the airship. They're in terrible danger. I've seen it in the Tapestry. The ship will not survive the day."

"We might be able to save them, to bring them out of there. Let us prepare. I see you brought paddles, Belynda. Good. You two, each take one and begin swirling the water in the pool, counterclockwise. And tell me, what exactly did you see?" asked Quilene.

Miradel explained. "Perhaps you know that the Tapestry reveals many truths, lives and places and occurrences on all the Seven Circles, to a druid who knows how to read the Wool of Time. Here on Nayve, however, the power goes even beyond that. On all the other worlds, the Worldweaver spins her threads to record the tales of lives as they are lived. But here, on the Fourth Circle, parts of the story are actually spun before they occur."

"So that one can see something that is about to happen?" guessed the enchantress.

"Yes . . . though such witnessing is forbidden by the goddess. But I violated her commandment, so hungry was I for the sight of Natac's life, his thread. And I saw that his story ends sometime during the morning of today."

Miradel had no need to look up; she knew the sun had been fully descended, blazing at bright daylight, for several hours already. She kept the paddle stroking the water on the opposite edge of the small pool from Belynda. Between them, they had coaxed the still liquid into a gradual, stately whirl.

"I will try to perform the teleport spell. It is the only chance I can see to save him."

"Yes—save *them*," Miradel added. "There are five in *Sky-reaver*."

Quilene sucked the breath through her teeth, a startling display of agitation for an elf, but she nodded grimly. "Bringing one through the ether who is not a participant in the casting of the spell is a challenge. It does not become significantly more difficult with two or three souls. I have never attempted five before."

The enchantress turned to a glass ball that was resting on a patch of moss near the pool. "I have my Globe," Belynda said. "I hoped it would help."

"It will," Quilene agreed, curling her legs beneath her and sitting on the ground before the crystalline sphere. She placed her hands upon either side of the ball, then blew a soft breath of mist over the surface. As the vapor evaporated, Miradel needed all of her discipline to keep swirling the water. She desperately wanted to rush over to the enchantress and see what Quilene observed.

"They live," said the sage-enchantress after a heart-stopping minute. "But they are hard pressed." Abruptly she looked up, and the urgency was apparent in her voice and her face. "Spin! Move the water, quickly now! We have no time!"

REGILLIX Avatar sailed the sea of air surrounding the storm called Hillswallower. For three days he had remained aloft, flying constantly, seeking to understand the size of the murky turbulence. Though he flew in the same direction as the wind, that roiling face of cloud spilled past faster than he could fly. Lightning crackled within dark and gloomy canyons, and those gaps then pressed shut in an eyeblink of time. Wind howled even outside the storm, but the dragon could see that these gales were as nothing next to the power that twisted and spun that vortex of storm.

He recalled the glimpses he had had upon his first arrival here, the wing and tail and talons that had flailed from the darkness, as if frantic to escape the grip of the storm. Regillix wondered if that had been Plarinal, the elder brother of the female Daristal. He regretted his initial hesitation, the fright that had suggested he, himself, could be overwhelmed by this storm, that had prevented him from trying to rescue a smaller, weaker wyrm.

Since that time, there had been no sign of Plarinal or any other dragon. He had encountered many harpies, and when possible had startled these into the maw of the storm. The periphery of the storm still ran through the White Hills, and where the sinister vortex loomed, the land was littered with the corpses of the dead: griffons, pegasi, stormcows, all the creatures of the Sixth Circle represented in ghastly abundance. The carcasses, in turn, had drawn harpies in unprecedented numbers. At the very least, the dragon reflected, the storm allowed him to cleanse the Overworld of many representatives of its most repulsive pests.

Something solid caught his eye, a shape like a dragon's neck extending from the whirling cloud. Immediately, Regillix banked, braved the buffeting winds to fly up to the face of the storm, peering into the turbulent depths. There, again! He was sure he saw a glimpse of black, scaly skin.

With a pulse of his wings he darted, pulling up short as thick murk roiled past his face. He stretched his head forward, the serpentine neck lashing him into the cloud. With widespread jaws he sought the touch of that trapped, elusive dragon. His wings beat again, pushing him backward, fighting to hold him back from the powerful suction.

In the darkness he saw something darker, and he snapped his jaws, seeking to take a grip that was firm but not crushing. Instantly, he realized that he was biting carrion, the rotten flesh of a skywhale; the dragon's neck had been the dead tail of this rank carcass! Sour meat stung his tongue, and he spat the thing away, striving to pull back his neck, pulsing powerful wings to break from the cyclonic might of the storm.

But a wild arm of wind reached out, curled behind, pulled him with startling power. Tendrils of wind wrapped themselves around his limbs, and he felt a physical pull. He squirmed in the grip of a mindless foe, contested the strength of his ancient being to the strength of wind and air . . . and he lost.

Blackness surrounded him, and the assault of the gale was a series of punches along his flanks, his limbs, his wings.

Shaking his head, the dragon turned so that he tumbled with the storm, and some of the pain diminished. Lightning flashed past his face, leaving his eyes blinded by afterglow, the scent of ozone lingering in his singed nostrils. Regillix felt the wind tear at his wings, knew that he was locked in the grip of a storm of immortal force, with power greater than his own, supernatural might converging against venerable, but ultimately mortal, flesh. He strained with all the power in that huge body, driving his wings through the churning air, pulling himself back to the rim of the great storm.

He drew near that edge, caught a glimpse of the ground very close below him. With every fiber of strength, he tried to pull himself free, but again the Hillswallower pulled him back. He was tumbling downward, to the level of the Sixth Circle's cloudy terrain, then below, into the hills that had been destroyed. Regillix braced himself for the impact against the ground, but there was none, no resistance, no barrier to his descent.

And he was still falling.

THE arrows slashed into the approaching serpent, Natac's shot striking the broad nostrils, Roland's taking it in the neck, and the other three piercing the vast, leathery wings. The monster roared and immediately veered downward, vanishing below the airship before the explorers could ready another volley. They all stepped across the narrow deck, bracing against the lurch of the hull as their weight shifted to the port rail.

"There it goes—it's so fast!" Juliay declared, as the serpent swept back its wings and plunged along the shoulder of the mountain, following the curve of the slope into the vast gorge yawning below. Any hopes that they had seriously injured the creature were dispelled quickly, as it flew along the valley with powerful wing strokes, then spun through a tight turn and began to climb along a course parallel to *Skyreaver*'s.

"What is it?" Natac asked, his eyes never leaving the sinister shape as he placed another arrow against the string of his bow.

Only after a long pause did Sirien speak. "I think it is a dragon. There are old legends of such. But they are not of Nayve. It was said that dragons were lords of the Sixth Circle."

"Well, this one has designs on *our* world," growled Owen. He held his mighty bow at the ready, his longsword on a strap over his broad shoulder. "Trolls, harpies . . . now this? I aim to bring at least one of these outrages to an end!"

They watched in trepidation as the dragon climbed higher, making a wide circle around the airship, all the while remaining beyond the range of the longest bow shot. The serpent reached the level of the explorers and continued to climb, still circling, until it was far above them. Only then did it fly toward *Skyreaver,* and it remained very high. Before long, it vanished from view, their line of sight blocked by the large tube of the flotation bags.

"Wind!" cried Natac. "We need to move!"

The two druids snatched up their bowls and began to cast, spoons whirling into a blur from the urgency of their movements. A gust of air stirred, pushing *Skyreaver*'s nose to the side.

"Be ready with an arrow," Natac said to Sirien, who nodded. Owen, his bow slung with his axe and a quiver, was already starting up the rope ladder leading to the starboard side of the great sack. Wearing his own bow and sword, the Tlaxcalan started up to port. Hand over hand he climbed, fearing with every heartbeat that the monster was even now diving to rip into the sack with fang and talon.

He scrambled on top of the great balloon in record time, feeling the silken surface give under his feet. Ropes were draped to form simple railings, but he was well aware that a fall, coupled with a missed grab at a lifeline, would send him tumbling to inevitable death. Owen was there, too, coming up the far side of the flotation tube, like Natac, intent on the sky.

The dragon was diving, but with a measured patience that

allowed it to spiral downward in tight loops. When the men came into view atop the balloon, it roared and dipped into a steeper descent, angling toward the Tlaxcalan. Natac told himself that it wasn't as big as he had first thought; the body was more like the size of a big horse than an elephant. Even so, it was a terrifying monster.

The warrior's bow was in his hands, and he let fly instantly, seeing the dragon expand in his view with horrifying speed. The hasty shot caromed off a bony knob atop the monster's skull, and the creature tucked its wings for the last, meteoric descent. Natac dropped his bow, watching in frustration as the weapon skidded down the curved side of the balloon and was lost. Seizing one of the rope handrails with his left hand, he drew his sword with his right. He stood tall, the blade extended forward and upward, directly at the open jaws of the wyrm.

"Take that, spawn of Loki!" cried Owen, shooting an arrow that took the serpent in the jowls, puncturing the serpentine throat.

At the last instant, Natac dropped to his back, still holding the rope. As he hoped, the dragon pulled up to avoid crashing into the bulk of the balloon. Jaws snapped in the air where Natac had been standing, and talons lashed downward, scoring rips in the silken surface.

The man stabbed upward as the smooth belly glided past. Keen steel cut the dragon's skin at its breastbone, and the pressure of his thrust carved a long wound all the way to the groin. The monster shrieked and twisted, but momentum carried it on. As soon as the wyrm was past, Natac bounced to his feet, saw Owen shoot another of his long arrows right into the creature's flank. Meanwhile, blood trailed into the air, trickling from the long gash.

Then it was gone, diving out of sight beyond the curve of the great balloon. Natac took a quick glance at the torn fabric. The sack, one of seven supporting the great airship, was rapidly deflating, and he knew they would have to land

for repairs. But only one of the bags had been ruptured, and
he also knew that *Skyreaver* was still airworthy.

He and Owen scrambled down the ladder, all the while
watching as the dragon flew along the course of the valley
floor, this time gliding away until it disappeared around the
foot of a mountain ten or a dozen miles away.

When he reached the deck of the ship, he was about to re-
count the story of the battle, when he noticed Sirien staring,
awestruck, in the direction that was neither metal nor wood.
His own eyes followed hers, and he grunted softly, an unconscious expression of astonishment.

"It *is* a storm," he whispered. The sky had grown black, a
solid-looking wall of cloud rising to the loftiest elevation but
surging past with stately movement, enough so that he could
be sure this wasn't solid ground. As if in confirmation, great
bolts of lightning crackled through the murk, and a noise like
constant thunder rumbled in his ears. The monstrous gale
loomed much closer, and as he watched, he saw tendrils of
cloud reach out, surrounding several peaks.

And then there was something else there, a wicked form
now strangely familiar, a flying shape that tumbled out of the
storm and fought with powerful wing strokes to stay aloft.
The serpentine body righted itself, then dove right toward
them.

"The first one was a baby," the elfmaid whispered.

Another of the winged serpents was flying at them, soaring
between the peaks with a span of wings that seemed capable
of embracing a large mountain. It so much dwarfed the other
serpent as to seem like a different scale of being, something
cosmically removed from men and elves. Great jaws spread
wide, revealing a mouth that looked ready to swallow *Skyreaver*'s hull in a single gulp.

But the monster disdained the use of those jaws or even its
curved, sword-sized talons. Instead, it stretched out a wing
tip, the end of a membrane that was as large as a playing field.
The tip sliced into the first of the flotation sacks, cutting it al-

most in half. In rapid succession, it ripped through the second, and then through following balloons. Natac stared in horrified disbelief, feeling the deck canting under his feet.

The gondola lurched to the side. Owen and Juliay skidded across the deck as silken shreds filled the air, and the skyship and its passengers abruptly started to fall.

The druidess hit the edge of the railing, and Owen made a desperate grab for her hand, but the momentum of the fall carried them apart, and Juliay's scream was all that lingered in the air when she vanished over the side.

The deck plunged away below him, and Natac knew he was falling. His last glimpse was of that monstrous dragon, slowly, contemptuously flying away. It didn't even turn to look back.

"Now!" shouted Quilene, suddenly rising to her feet. Her eyes closed, she turned her slender face toward the sun, and spread her arms wide. Magic crackled in the air, the power of the spell pulsing audibly.

Miradel didn't dare look up. She paddled the water like some frantic canoeist, except that she still knelt at the bank of the pool, and the goal was to move the water itself, not an aquatic conveyance.

Then, suddenly, Sirien the elfmaid was standing there, her face pale, her fists clenched in panic. She gasped and stumbled away to sprawl in the grass, crying. Owen was there next, thrashing so wildly that he tumbled from the rim of the pool to splash wildly into the middle.

Desperately, Miradel paddled, fighting the frantic fear that Owen's splash would disturb the rhythm of Quilene's spell, would somehow break the bond of magic that was reaching through space, even now trying to bring Natac and his companions here.

And then he was standing there . . . her Tlaxcalan warrior, bronze-skinned and chiseled and no older than he had been that day she had first brought him to Nayve. She gasped and almost hesitated, continuing her stirring movement only by instinct, as the warrior looked wildly around, staggering as he tried to keep his balance.

Another man arrived, the druid she remembered as Roland Boatwright. But Miradel was still looking at Natac. His eyes were open and he was trembling, standing in a crouch as if he was ready to spring in any direction. At first he didn't see her; his eyes seemed fixed on something much farther away. The magic faded around them, as the spell dissipated.

Only after a moment did the warrior blink and shift his focus and stare. "Miradel?" His voice was a croak. "Miradel! But . . . where am I?" He looked up at the spire of the World-weaver's Loom, still not comprehending.

"Yes, I am Miradel, my warrior," she said, dropping the paddle, standing, stepping close to him. "And we have both come home."

9

Centered Again

Through the ages,
Two survive;
Birthing stages,
Lovers thrive.

Flesh departed,
Sorrow bloomed;
Broken heart,
Eternal gloom.

Came the goddess,
Touched her hand;
Silken bodice,
Faithful man.

From *Love's Epic: The Ballad of Miradel and Natac*
by Sirien Saramayd

"Juliay!" Owen cried in despair, sitting on the edge of the pool and holding his head in his hands. "She's lost . . . surely she is," he groaned.

"I am sorry," Quilene said, shaking her head with grave sorrow. "The spell was cast in utmost haste. . . . We tried . . ."

"Lady, I know . . . I wish only that she could have been saved in my stead, and I could fall with the airship!" He looked around, blinking, his face and beard wet with tears.

"We four owe you a life debt," Roland said somberly. He knelt beside Owen, put a hand on the big man's shoulder. "That in itself seems only a miracle."

"A miracle . . . twice," Natac said. Since arriving here, in the garden of the Worldweaver, his gaze had not left Miradel's face. He was lost in those violet eyes, in that transcendent beauty that was so much more intense, so undeniably perfect in every way, that his long years of memories seemed like pale and illusory imitations. "Am I mad? Or do we both live? Or is this delirious death?"

"You and I both live, my warrior," she replied, and even with the proof of her voice, he found himself disbelieving. "We are here, in the Center."

He stared, still reluctant to move, fearing that any alteration in his surroundings might break this wondrous spell. Finally, he exhaled, tore his gaze away from Miradel to look at Quilene. "But how . . . what has happened, for you to bring us here at the instant of doom?"

"Miradel spied disaster in the Tapestry," Belynda explained. At last he noticed her, seated on a stone bench, holding a crystal sphere in her lap. Quilene, of course, must have worked an enchantment of teleportation. . . . Suddenly he understood how he and his three companions had come to be here and how Juliay must have tumbled away in the chaos of the crash.

But still, he couldn't bring himself to believe it, to accept the sudden, shocking shift in his circumstances.

"The danger is not over," the sage-ambassador said. Belynda set her Globe down on a pillow of soft green velvet and stood to join the others beside the pool. "I could see *Skyreaver*, and then it was as though a shadow fell across the sun. What happened?"

"A dragon," Sirien said, her face pale, her elf eyes even larger than normal. "A beast of legend, and a thousand times more horrible than any nightmare."

"She speaks the truth," Owen said grimly. "The creature could claim, could waste any part of Nayve. It struck down the airship and killed Juliay, would have killed us all, with scarcely a notice. There's no bow, no sword could kill a thing like that. But by Odin and all the gods false and real, I will find me a weapon, and I will try!"

"Good words, old warrior," Miradel said with a sad smile. "This is not the Owen Viking I remember."

"Aye, lady druid," he said, lowering his head in shame. "It was Juliay, blessed by the goddess herself, who changed me. Sorry I am for the carousing, the wenching that I did in your presence. You would have been well to shun me then."

"You have nothing to be sorry about," Miradel replied. "And know that we share your grief. Juliay was a precious friend, a wise druid, and she will be mourned and missed."

"And avenged," growled the Viking. "I will go back and kill that cursed beast, and the cost of my own life would be but a small price!"

"But how can you slay such a thing?" the sage-ambassador said quietly.

"More important, perhaps: How did it come to Nayve?" asked Quilene. "Dragons are the masters of the Overworld, the Sixth Circle, but never has one been seen in the Fourth."

"There was a monstrous storm beyond the Mountains of Moonscape," Roland said. "It rose into the sky, higher than we could see . . . and when we first encountered the dragon, it was coming from that vast cloud wall. Could that be the conduit that allowed the monster to descend to Nayve?"

"It is not impossible," the sage-enchantress said. "Though if true, then this mysterious storm may prove to be a danger greater than that represented by the rogue wyrm. We must research and meditate upon this."

"Do you think the dragon will come here, to the Center?" Miradel asked.

"We can't know. But Riven Deep will not stop it, if it decides to fly in this direction."

"I will see that warning is given in the Senate," Belynda said. "And then seek the monster in the Globe of Seeing . . . perhaps we can track its movements and learn if it draws near to the Center."

"The Tapestry holds secrets of all the Circles," Roland said. "The Fifth and Sixth are little known, because in most ways they are the most remote of all from Nayve. But the Sixth, the Overworld, is the birthplace of dragons, and I will see what the Worldweaver's fabric will tell me about them."

"And I will send word to the enchantresses across Nayve," Quilene said with a pointed look at Owen. "For if this beast must be battled and slain, then I suspect we shall need to wield magic as well as steel."

"Is it possible that the attack was an accident?" wondered Miradel. "Could the dragon have simply struck the airship in passing?"

"No!" declared Owen. "You only have to see that wyrm to know that it is the very essence of evil."

"All the same, we shouldn't assume that it is hostile or aggressive," Natac pointed out. "For all we know, the blow to *Skyreaver* might have been an unavoidable collision. It happened very quickly after the monster spilled out of the storm."

"Then we will also take care to try to speak to this dragon," Quilene said. "Better it is, by far, that we communicate and understand instead of attack and face ruin."

"There are other preparations," Natac said. "We should alert the city . . . gather the troops from the old regiments. Especially archers and artillerists. We'll have to send for Galluper in the Greens. . . . His rolling batteries are stored in the Center Arsenal. . . ."

"Yes . . . we can't be certain, but we should be prepared," Belynda said. "I'll send a faerie for Galluper Centaur. We have at least a week, more likely two or three, before the serpent can fly through the space you just passed in an eyeblink."

Natac felt the touch of Miradel's hand on his own. He looked at Owen and saw that the Viking's eyes were warm at the sight of Miradel and Natac together. "You two . . . go for a while, across the lake or wherever you want. I will see to the ordering of the troops. It is as the lady sage-ambassador has said: We have some time. You can be summoned when you're needed."

Natac felt a rush of relief, as if his old friend had lifted a burden of complications from his shoulders. He looked at Miradel, swam in the purpled vision of her eyes.

"Come, my warrior," she said softly. "Let us go home."

THE gondola hung, bow downward, twisting and spinning as it fell, trailing shredded silk in the sky overhead. Juliay clung to the side rigging of the airship in terror. She knew Owen was gone. He had tumbled past, his expression terrified, his hands coming up short when he had grabbed for her arm. Sirien had screamed, the sound snuffed out by the gale of the storm, and the druidess knew that Natac and Roland must also have plunged to their deaths. The giant dragon was flying away, a serpentine vulture gliding effortlessly through the skies.

And Juliay alone was still alive, clinging to the netting along the port rail, her legs dangling above a thousand feet of space. The mountainside rushed past, frighteningly close, as the wreckage of *Skyreaver* fell. Desperation and instinct propelled her into action.

With a pull of her arms, she lifted herself up the rail, tumbled onto what had once been the vertical bulkhead of the forward cabin. Now it was a horizontal platform, with the middeck of the gondola rising like a wall beside her. She looked up, expecting to see the black sky, and was heartened to realize that a couple of the flotation bags had somehow remained intact. They were slowing the descent just enough to give her a chance.

The gondola crunched into the slope of the mountain and bounced violently. Juliay tumbled up and away from her small perch. Frantically, she grabbed a flailing rope, and immediately hauled herself back to the bulkhead. The black rock, as smooth and shiny as polished coal, grated past as the airship skidded downward.

With both hands entwined through ropes, the druid lay flat on the bulkhead, staring upward, bracing herself for the brutal crash that would mark the bottom of this plunging descent. Again the gondola lurched, this time twisting sideways as it bounced from an outcrop on the mountain. Only her desperate grip on the ropes kept her from flying into space until the remaining flotation bags, with lines connected to the stern of the gondola, once more pulled the hull into a nose-down fall.

Still the wrecked ship tumbled downward, but she allowed herself to believe that the momentum of the fall had slowed somewhat. Those two inflated sacks, the purple and violet spheres at the stern of the great tube, remained overhead, adding some braking pressure to the friction of the slide down the mountainside. But additional peaks came into view across the valley now, a wall of dark stone rising upward, and she knew the bottom must be very close.

The ultimate impact came with a solid crash, a splintering of timber, and a great explosion of destruction. Her body smashed the bulkhead with brutal force, then bounced upward. The gondola tipped sideways, and Juliay fell a short distance to the ground, landing on her face, trying to break the impact of the fall with her hands braced before her.

The *snap* of breaking bone was a surreal sound coming from her wrist. An instant later, a wave of pain ripped through her body with nauseating power. She sobbed and lay on her face, holding the agonizing arm utterly still. Slowly, she drew a deep breath, but when she tried to move, even to turn onto her side, the excruciating pain froze her helplessly in place.

Only very gradually did she realize that the violence of the crash, the noise and chaos of the long fall, had settled into utter silence. Somehow she, alone of her companions, had survived. She couldn't even know where Owen's body or those of her other shipmates had plunged to their sudden end. A sense of solitude overwhelmed her, an utterly hopeless feeling that, for a little while, made her wish she had simply hurled herself from the airship and perished with her companions. She cried, for her friends, her lover, for herself.

But after a while, the pain began to fade, as shock numbed her senses. Her mind became more focused, and, still lying motionless, she tried to analyze her wounds. Her forearm or wrist was broken, and her chest and face were bruised and scraped, but for the most part, her body was intact.

"I will *not* die here!"

She hissed the words through gritted teeth. Wincing, she again tried to roll onto her side, gingerly supporting her broken arm against her hip. Finally, she used her good hand to push herself into a sitting position, slumping against a smooth face of rock. Again, pain stabbed up from her wrist, so intense that her head grew light and blackness closed her vision into narrow spots of light. Drawing short, urgent breaths, she refused to yield to unconsciousness, and slowly, illumination broadened out to her full view.

She lay at the very bottom of the steeply sloping mountain, on a small strip of flat, stony ground. Before her, a stone's throw away, was a creek, as black and lightless as every other waterway in these forsaken mountains. Just beyond, the slope of the next summit rose abruptly, steep and obsidian black like the peak at her back. The stream flowed from her right to her left, curving around the shoulder of the mountain until it was lost from her sight. The skyline all around was a vista of steep, barren, and smooth-sided heights.

When the next spasm of agony tore through her arm, she fought back, clenching her teeth, leaning her head back against the rock. She reminded herself that she was a druid of Nayve, blessed by the Goddess Worldweaver. There was power in that knowledge, and she resolved to call upon it to draw the strength of the immortal power that had brought her to the Fourth Circle, that had carried her through nine hundred years.

"Goddess Worldweaver, hear my prayer," she said, placing her right hand over the twisted flesh of her left wrist. "Grant me healing, in your name, from the blessed Center of All."

Immediately, the pain faded, not disappearing, but dying back like a bonfire doused with a bucket of water. The wound steamed and hissed and seethed beneath her consciousness, but now the discomfort was magic at work. The power of the goddess flowed from her strong fingers, knitting and binding, stanching and sealing flesh and vessel and bone. For a full minute, Juliay clutched the wound, until at last she slumped back, exhausted.

Hesitantly, she lifted the hand, flexed fingers, and rotated the wrist. A dull ache extended all the way up her arm, but that was no matter. At least her flesh was whole, and she could move.

She looked at the shattered gondola. The hull had smashed, bow first, into the ground at the base of the mountain, splitting wooden timbers, tearing a great crack along the middeck, reducing the forward platform to so much kindling. Beyond and to the side were swaths of bright silk, red and orange here, green and blue stretching across the mountainside like some kind of enchanted snowfields.

But those two flotation sacks in the stern, the indigo and violet, remained aloft, like spherical banners marking the wrecked airship. Unquestionably, their buoyancy had saved her from a fatal plunge. Furthermore, they had prevented the gondola's utter destruction; she had no doubt but that she might find many useful things within the broken hull, now that she was strong enough to look.

Looking around, she saw that she was deep within a steep-walled valley, those black and barren peaks rising in every direction. The place was almost like a canyon, the valley floor curving away to either side, quickly vanishing behind the steep balustrades at the base of the mountains. The stream seemed to tumble along rapidly, marking a fairly steep descent, but it was eerily devoid of rapids, ripples, eddies, or other marks of the current.

Juliay realized that the darkness was not entirely caused by the obsidian landscape. Pale sunlight reached far down in the valleys, indicating that the sun was rising toward Darken. With no feature offering an especially likely place to camp, she decided that she would remain beside the wrecked airship at least for tonight. A sense of utter loneliness surrounded her, and she whispered a memorial prayer for her four fallen companions.

Looking at that oily stream, she shivered, then climbed onto the bulkhead atop the supply cabin. She lifted the two pieces of the broken door, exposing a tangle of ropes, casks, broken wood, tumbled arrows, and other supplies. The first thing she looked for was water, and she was relieved to see that one of their casks had survived the crash intact.

After a long, refreshing drink, she pulled a crate of hedras out of the mess so that she would have something to eat. Finally, she found a bow and several quivers of arrows. Then she lifted herself back onto the bulkhead and turned to the door of her and Owen's cabin. That portal, too, had been broken free by the crash. Lifting herself through the opening, then standing on the wall within, she gathered a few quilts and blankets, as well as a thick bearskin, enough to keep her warm through the night. Next she found her lockbox, still closed, and after checking the contents, she left it near the door, feeling that it was as safe here as anywhere else.

She would have preferred to find a place to sleep in the gondola, up and off the bare ground. But here fate conspired against her, and there was no unbroken flat surface large enough for comfortable rest.

Instead, she dropped her quilts and the bow and arrows onto the ground. She thought about bringing the crate of food and cask of water but decided they would be safer in the wreck. Then Juliay scrambled down the steep hull. With a little effort, she spread her bedroll on a flat stretch of ground a short stone's throw from the broken airship.

Finally sitting back against the mountainside, she turned her eyes to the sky, where stars were beginning to sparkle into view. She chewed on a wafer of hedras, feeling the restoration of strength and energy that came from that elven morsel. Cool water washed the crumbs down her throat. What could she do? Where should she go?

And then she froze, seeing the great shadow gliding through

the night. Wings spread wide, seemingly across the whole valley, the serpent glided along. The wickedly reptilian head tilted down toward the ground. With a moan of terror, Juliay shrank against the slope. Dagger and bow were forgotten as she watched the dragon fly closer and closer, still looking, searching along the valley floor. All she could do was crawl under the imaginary shelter of her bedroll, pulling the quilt over herself and lying utterly still, thinking about all the ways a person could die.

"WHAT *was* those things?" groaned Awfulbark, as he and Wartbelly cowered under the shelter of an overhanging bank in the valley bottom. They looked through a curtain of roots and vines into the grassy floor of a narrow vale.

"I dunno. They make that bad sound—'harp-*ee,* harp-*ee*'! And they kilt Breakwind!" his companion muttered, touching some of the ugly red blisters marking his arms and torso, places where the oily spittle had burned his flesh. "An' I hurt!"

"Too many flying stuff," the King of Udderthud complained, remembering the strange creature with the metal hand that had so cruelly lopped off his hand and his head. While neither wound had been fatal, both had been excruciatingly painful. The decapitation, in particular, had been a nasty attack, having left Awfulbark with a sore throat that was sure to linger into the next day.

But for all that, the smooth-skinned person would certainly have been edible, and the trolls had it surrounded, would certainly have killed it, except for the intervention of the flying hags. As to those horrid invaders, the burning spittle, tearing claws, the maddening and relentless shrieks, and needle fangs had formed a nightmarish veil of violence. The hurts caused by fire were wounds that would not heal, and the burns had been awful enough to kill Breakwind.

The two surviving trolls stayed under their bank throughout a full day and another night, and even when the Lighten

hour came again, they were reluctant to move. Fear would
have kept Awfulbark there for much longer, except that the
pangs of hunger finally growled loudly from his skinny gut. It
was time to go home.

"Look and see if they are gone," ordered Awfulbark, giving his companion a sharp push.

Squawking, Wartbelly tumbled into the floor of the narrow
ravine. He threw his arms over his face and looked upward
with an expression of terror. Finally, he blinked and sat up.
"They gone," he grunted.

"Let's go," Awfulbark declared, striding out of the dank
shelter, blinking in the daylight. Here and there, stately oak
trees scattered the floor of the winding valley and dotted the
slopes rising steeply to each side. The troll king ducked his
head and raced to the shade beneath one of the trees, where
his companion joined him.

They started in the direction of Udderthud, Awfulbark
darting quickly from tree to tree, eyes constantly scanning the
skies. With Wartbelly hastening behind, he jogged through
the maze of twisting valleys. They made their way with haste,
fear mingling with hunger to propel them at a steady run.

They came around the last bend before the city and saw
that the sky was black with soaring, sinister shapes. Hundreds
of harpies dove and spat fire and swept exultantly back into
the sky, keening and shrieking in delight. Even from a mile
away, his ears were stabbed by the hideous noise of their
cries, and he could only stop, aghast, as he watched this nightmare flock attack his city and his world.

REGILLIX Avatar winged through these bizarre, ferrous
mountains, utterly confused and dangerously irritated. No
matter where he flew, he could not get his bearings after that
long plunge. The Hillswallower storm had spewed him out
here. He had burst from the clouds so violently that he had
fought desperately just to stay aloft, careening wildly until he
righted himself and flew on.

Immediately, he had noticed the sun, shining in the sky *above* him, and this fact had been enough to shatter his sense of reality. Such a thing was impossible, he knew, for the sun lay *below* the Sixth Circle! At zenith, it brought daylight to the Overworld and left Nayve in darkness, while the nadir created the opposite conditions.

And with that connection of logic, he had confronted the truth: The storm had swept him from his home, from the realm of his birth, the place that was his by ancestral right, and it had hurled him into this bleak and forbidding environment of a completely different world. He considered the location of the great Chaos Storm and reasoned that he had either fallen to the Fourth Circle, Nayve, or the Fifth, Loamar. Nayve, he knew, lay directly below the Overworld, at the center of all existence, while Loamar was across the Worldsea from the Fourth Circle in the direction that was neither metal nor wood. Loamar was also known as the death world, and that seemed consistent with the lifeless nature of these black mountains.

However, the sun had provided evidence that suggested this was Nayve, not Loamar. He knew that the Fifth Circle, as well as the Second and Third, lay far from Nayve, separated by the gulf of the Worldsea. Those realms would be subject only to feeble daylight, whereas the brightness of the current day suggested that the dragon had entered the world that was directly under the sun. Therefore, he concluded that his long descent had brought him to Nayve.

Knowing where he had come did not make Regillix Avatar any happier to be here. For a full day he had soared through this place, flying above black mountains that rose like jagged teeth into the sky. Even the air seemed heavier, like a blanket that tugged at his wings, closed like thick vapors around him, forcing him to work hard even to maintain level flight. Nayve was reputedly a world of strange magic, and the dragon wondered if the beings of this world had somehow harnessed that magic to create the Chaos Storm, tearing at the very fabric of the Seven Circles.

After he had emerged from the maelstrom of the storm, he

had skirted the edge of the great wall of cloud here, seeing the same roiling face of cloud that had marred the Overworld. Here the storm formed a wall, a great barrier in these mountains. Winds whipped rocks from the summits, and in two hours, the great dragon had been witness to at least a dozen crushing landslides. It almost seemed as if the scouring winds bored right into the stone of Nayve, just as they had penetrated the cloud land of Arcati.

When it became apparent that the storm here was at least as big as it had been on the Sixth Circle, Regillix had reversed his flight, deciding to fly back to the place where he had emerged from the storm. Now he was growing tired, and light was fading fast.

A spot of color attracted his attention to a deep valley, and he saw something that looked familiar. Two spherical objects floated there, globes of the rainbow spectrum that he had encountered earlier. Other swatches of color, now limp and deflated, were spread across the nearby mountainside. He remembered the strange cloud he had flown past upon entering this world, the surprisingly solid shape that had caused a painful sprain in his right wing tip. Here was some remnant of that thing, which was clearly not a cloud at all. He wondered if it had been some kind of creature but decided against that as well; there had been nothing vital about the thing then, nor did this pathetic scrap look to be anything more than windblown refuse. In any event, he wasn't about to land to investigate, for it lay deep in a narrow valley, and he would have had to climb high onto a mountainside, a tedious ascent on foot, before he would have gained room to return to the air.

But the draining fatigue could not be denied, and as distasteful as the thought was, he had no alternative except to land on this foreign and unnaturally solid world. He flew across a broad plateau and decided that was as good a place as any to set down. Wheeling around above a wide river valley, he soared back toward the precipice rising to the plateau. Skimming over the top of that cliff, he stretched his legs below and dropped his tail.

His forefeet hit ground that offered shocking resistance, stopping him cold until his legs bucked and he skidded onto his breast. Roaring in rage, he scrambled to his feet, stepping as gingerly as his vast size would allow. Immediately, he realized that there was no comforting cushion to the land here; it was as solid as the ice that, occasionally, formed around the fringes of the Cloudsea.

Snorting in disgust, he tried walking across the plateau. After a few steps, he found that it was not difficult, though he could imagine that any more of this than was absolutely necessary would result in some very sore feet. Still, it was a relief to furl his wings, and despite the unyielding surface, he tucked the wide membranes at his sides and settled onto his belly, allowing his fatigued muscles to rest and rejuvenate.

He found himself looking at the great, surging face of the monstrous storm. It seemed impossible to imagine, but this was a disturbance that clearly bridged across worlds. Hill-swallower . . . Chaos . . . these were inadequate names, for this was greater than any threat to mere landscape or climate. Like a massive cataract it had borne him downward, and then he understood.

"It's a worldfall. . . . My world is spilling over the brink and pouring into Nayve."

How had such a thing been created? The question had no ready answer, but the very pondering filled the ancient dragon with a deep, seething rage. He vowed to learn who was responsible for this desecration and to exact punishment for this act of cosmic vandalism.

Regillix was still thinking of that villainous power, trying to imagine the effrontery required, when he was distracted by a faint, bleating cry. Lifting his head, he listened, trying to hear through the wail of the wind. A minute later, the sound was repeated, a deep, thrumming moan of pain that touched familiar nerves deep within his soul. There was a summons in that call, and it seemed to be rising from below, reaching this plateau from some unseen place at the foot of the mountain.

Rising, he crept toward the rim. He sniffed, but smelled

only the dry, featureless air of these barren peaks. The wind swirled around him, not the tearing chaos of the worldfall, but enough of a mountain breeze to mask sound and scent. At the edge of the plateau he looked down, into the broad valley of the river, the vale now masked in a cloak of evening darkness.

He saw something moving, ever so slightly, at the bottom of the lofty precipice. Again he heard that bleating cry, and with the sound coming directly to his ears, the source was clear.

That was a dragon down there, and it was injured, perhaps badly. With that realization, Regillix spread his wings, already rested and strong, and leaped off the edge of the cliff. He soared outward, cutting a long, banking turn along the face of the mountainside. Quickly he dropped through the thick air, over the river that seemed very still and dark, though the smooth waters reflected little of the starlight or the lingering glow of fading Darken.

He saw the other dragon then. The creature was curled at the base of the precipice, watching the ancient one's flight with head just slightly upraised. Regillix came to rest on the ground, this time anticipating the hard surface by leaning backward just before he touched down. He squatted before the other wyrm and looked down from the great height of his neck.

"Who are you?" he asked.

"I . . . I am Plarinal," croaked the smaller serpent. "I was trapped by the Hillswallower Storm and came here."

"And I, too," Regillix replied. "In part because I was looking for you. I spoke to your young sibling and her companion, on their isle above the Cloudsea."

"Cantrix and Daristal . . . you saw them? I am glad," said Plarinal weakly.

Only then did the great wyrm smell blood, lots of it, and he knew that his fellow dragon was sorely hurt. "What happened?" he asked.

"I escaped from the storm, but I was here, where the sun is wrong and the surface cruelly hard. All was black, save a small cloud I spied, a cloud of splendid color, like the seven strands of the rainbow. I flew toward this mystical thing, and I was attacked."

"How?" probed the giant serpent, leaning closer, sniffing along Plarinal's body. He smelled the stench of entrails and knew the wounds were dire, probably fatal.

"Darts of fiery pain they hurled at me through the air. Then, I flew past, and saw a being—a creature like a harpy, only lacking wings." Plarinal paused, drew in a great, rasping breath. "I flew past, and this wingless harpy reached out with a sharp claw, a shiny claw. He tore me open, and I came to the ground here."

"A harpy without wings? What foul land is this, to give breeding to such?" asked Regillix. He well remembered the colorful cloud himself. "Know that you are avenged, at least in part," he said to the young dragon. "For I destroyed this rainbow cloud. . . ."

He paused, waiting for Plarinal to draw another rasping breath. But there was no sound, no movement from his smaller counterpart. He leaned down, sniffing, nuzzling with his scaly snout, and then he knew.

Plarinal was dead.

THEY climbed the hill together, as the sun rose into the sky and the myriad patterns of stars emerged, shifting and whirling and spinning about in the cosmic display that, so far as Natac had been able to tell, was different every night. Yet never had the Darken sky looked so beautiful, and for a few minutes they stood together in the darkened garden, looking upward, awestruck and silent.

But then she took his hand, a gentle but insistent tug that brought him quickly along at her side. They entered the door and paused to light a small lamp. In the flaring light, Miradel's face had the luster of pure gold, her black hair the sheen of finest silk.

"Wait," he said, and she turned to him expectantly. He

lifted a flower, a blossom he had taken from the garden, and wove the stem through the strands of her hair, leaving the poppy a scarlet decoration behind her ear. "You were wearing such a flower when I first laid eyes on you," he said.

"And you have waited for me since then," she said quietly. "I know. . . ." She put her arms around his neck and pulled his lips to hers. Her tongue was a dancing flame, teasing and licking at his mouth, and his hunger swelled. Fiercely he pulled her close, and she clung to him with desperation.

The lantern flickered as Natac moved, still holding his woman to his side. They were at the door to that room, then, the place where he had come to Nayve. Inside, the pallet awaited, layered with plush furs. He took only enough time to set the lamp in a niche, and Miradel was already slipping out of her long druid's robe.

Natac's throat tightened as he beheld her beauty, the perfect breasts, round and high, each centered with a dark nipple. Her skin flowed smoothly, even more precious than gold, and he touched her at first with gentle reverence and then with powerful longing. She melded to him, her own hands pulling at his shirt, tearing it away. For an instant, she groped at the unfamiliar laces of his breeches, until he tore away the string with an impatient pull.

They fell onto the pallet, faces together, lips and tongues gently stroking. His fingers traced the smoothness of her breasts, squeezing, caressing, while she held his face in her two hands. Then she lowered her touch, tickling across his belly, finally taking his manhood in a grip so firm and compelling that he groaned aloud.

His own hands touched her more urgently, feeling warm flesh, the heat of her desire. They had all the time they needed, but Natac could no longer be patient. His lips pressed, his hands clutched her tightly, and she responded with an urgency that matched his own.

He was on top of her then, and she rose to meet him, frantically took him into her as their passions exploded into a monumental whirlwind of love. All of life, existences on two worlds, centuries apart and moments together, finally focused into their ultimate sharing, the conjoined being of their flesh linking in spirit and mind as well.

For a time, they lay together in shared silence, gentle touches conveying more than any volume of words. A thousand thoughts stirred his mind . . . how many nights and days had they been apart. That time meant nothing, now; he was whole again. The beauty of this night left him speechless and drained, and finally they slept in each other's arms.

It was a rest of such contentment as Natac hadn't known for more than three hundred years.

10

Into the Underworld

Came a Seer to look for the light.
When he saw that light gave him a fright.
Said the Delver who lurked,
In steely black shirt,
Tasty Seer, I liked every bite.

Seer Dwarf Nursery Rhyme

Styril had no idea why he had been commanded to make this mission. Like a good Delver, he obeyed orders, and so he had followed Lord Zystyl's commands to the precise letter. He, a lowly sergman, had been placed in charge of two dozen sightless dwarves, the detachment ordered to transport a caravan of goods and supplies to the fringes of the realm, all the way beyond the Slatemont to the Oilsea.

Surely the mission was strange. The warriors were too few to put up other than a token defense against attack, and their cargo was valuable enough to warrant much more effective protection. Styril had not inspected the carts, but he could smell gold as clearly as could any Delver, and he knew that three of the small wagons were loaded full of the precious metal. And the others, too, were strange: from the clinks of sound, the scents of old sweat and fresh burnishings, he understood that in those other carts he carried enough armor breastplates to outfit an entire legion of Delvers.

Yet he was marching into an uninhabited wilderness, so far as he could tell.

Styril had never touched a map in his life, yet he knew that they were going in the direction that was neither metal nor wood, and that was enough to frighten him further. Certainly there were many dangerous places in the Underworld—some claimed by Seers, others by cruel and bullying Delvers—but this! This was a place that welcomed no one.

At least the route was clearly marked. Centuries ago, the Delvers had cut roads through most of the uninhabited sections of the Underworld. Now Styril's party followed a route across a series of rough hills, but the smooth, curved pavement underfoot ensured that the sightless dwarves remained on track. They were in the vast cavern of the First Circle, with the stone ceiling vaulting more than a thousand feet overhead. Somewhere to the right, Styril knew from the echo, rose the mountainous wall that marked the border of the realm. Of course, many caverns honeycombed that stone bedrock, some passages leading hundreds of miles or more into the foundation of worlds. Furthermore, the great bulk of the Slatemont, an underground massif rising all the way to the ceiling of the world, loomed to block direct access.

But Styril much preferred the open spaces, the vast hill and swale and plain of the Underworld. The air seemed fresher, and the lakes and streams spilling across the rocky terrain gave rise to bountiful fields of mushrooms, deep pools thriving with tasty blindfish. So he set his shoulder to the bar of the leading gold cart and trudged resolutely up this latest steep hill. He heard the puffing breaths of his mates behind him, two per cart on this long climb.

Finally, he crested the rise and caught the scent of water coming from the other side of the ridge. There was a foreign scent there, as well, and the Delver froze in alarm. The odor suggested wyslet, but was not so foul. . . . There was no hint of carrion.

Only then did he hear the clink of metal. Immediately, he sensed the danger and shouted the alarm. All around him,

Delvers scrambled to set brakes on the heavy carts and to draw their triple-bladed knives.

"Form line!" cried Styril, turning his back to the cart. He was still standing there, ready for battle, when a Seer arrow tore through his throat and dropped him, choking, into a growing pool of his own blood.

"Do you *have* to go?" Darann asked, already knowing the answer.

Karkald didn't answer. Instead, he kissed her again, and she tried unsuccessfully not to cry. Her tears glistened amid the bristling hairs of his beard as, at last, he broke their embrace and turned toward his sleek ferr'ell.

"Be careful!" she said, putting a hand on his arm.

"I will." He smiled, his hand covering hers, and then he took hold of the saddle and hoisted himself onto the back of his mount. The ferr'ell—she wondered why in all the circles had he named it *Bloodeater*—pranced eagerly, baring sharp fangs in a wicked grin. Karkald pulled back the reins with one hand, while he kissed the fingertips of the other, then waved the kiss at her.

She waved back, feeling forlorn, as the mount wheeled briskly and trotted toward the Nullgate of Axial. Guards at both sides saluted, and Karkald returned the gesture as he rode through the portal onto the light-washed plain beyond the city. Bloodeater pounced forward, and with a series of sleek hops quickly raced toward the formations of the First Legion, forming up on the field.

Darann watched until Karkald and his ferr'ell joined a company of the Rockriders, a mile or more away. Then she turned and started the long walk back to their tower. Even from this distance, the quarters she shared with Karkald seemed like a bare and lonely destination. How long would he be gone? What terrible dangers might he face?

She pondered these questions all the way through the Axle Ring, the great plaza that lay in the heart of Axial. Legend had it that it lay directly below Circle at Center, the focal point of all the worlds on Nayve, far above the First Circle. Now the bustle of the market fair had been cleared away. She saw goblin workers gathering up debris, all that remained of the throng that had gathered here in such anticipation.

The king's announcement canceling the Festival of Fyre had been greeted with many mutters and a few loud shouts of discontent. Merchants who had laid in great stocks of food and drink complained about wasted goods. Entertainers and peddlers who had counted on the gathering to make a year's worth of profit griped about missed opportunities. And many a dwarfmaid moped about the absence of a spouse or lover, gone to full-time service in the king's legions.

Indeed, Darann had heard mutters in the streets and plazas of the city blaming Karkald for these inconveniences. "He craves the attention," one acid-tongued wench had proclaimed, knowing full well that Darann could hear. She had merely straightened her back and walked away, but it had taken all of her dignity to avoid a confrontation.

She felt strangely, disturbingly uneasy as she rode the lift toward her home, the home she should be sharing with Karkald but that would once again be an overlarge abode for her solitary life.

Opening the door to her apartment, she found a letter on the floor, and her mood brightened a little at the sight of Aurand's penmanship. Her younger brother was stationed in a distant watch post, and his notes were few and infrequent.

> *Dearest Big Sister,*
>   *You should know that things are still quiet, here in the end of the world, the place "that is neither metal nor wood," as they say. I miss you, and Bor, and Mum and even our beloved patriarch. . . .*

She chuckled at memories. Aurand had always been a rebel, defying her father in ways that Darann admired but would never dare attempt herself. Yet she had often found her-

self standing up for the hotheaded youngster, and more than
once her humorous mockery had even coaxed a chuckle from
an angry Rufus Houseguard. She would go to see her parents,
she decided, and soon. A visit to the sprawling house above the
still and beautiful waters of the lake would be just the tonic.

*One thing of import: there was a pretty big cave-in just
the other cycle. It seemed like about a square mile of
the roof fell in, smashed up a big part of the cavern, and
blocked the main roads to wood and Axial, both. We
sent a detachment over to check it out. Nobody was
hurt, but another mile in our direction, and there would
have been some real damage done.*

    *Now I hear the king is sending more troops our way.
I don't know what they'll do here; we spend more time
fishing and hunting than on duty, as it is. (My captain
took cave lion with one shot! The brute's mouth is
big enough to hold a dwarf's head; makes quite a tro-
phy.) But we'll welcome some new blood. I wonder if
Karkald will be among them?*

Aurand closed with a request that she pass his love on to
their parents and to Borand. "I will," she said sincerely, fold-
ing the paper and tucking it neatly back into the envelope.
Then she got ready for bed, already missing Karkald more
than she could stand.

KARKALD and the other officers met at General Paternak's order. The legion commander convened his council on a low
bluff of rock overlooking the martial plain beyond the city.
The regiments were formed in blocks below and around
them, each illuminated by a tall staff capped by a globe of
coolfyre. The wheeled batteries of the artillery companies
were ranked neatly at the base of the steep-sided block. The
Rockriders and their chomping ferr'ells were gathered on the
opposite side of the bluff.

An aide ushered Karkald into the ring of officers, some hundred Seers in march dress, forming around General Paternak and Marshal Nayfal, his second-in-command. The lesser officers waited expectantly as the commander cleared his throat and looked them over with a scowl.

"We will be marching on the king's orders, into the direction that is neither metal nor wood," he began. "We have received evidence of a Delver massing, here in the nether reaches of the Underworld. Our mission will be to discover this gathering and then to deliver a mighty blow. When we find them, understand this: I do not want a single one of the Unmirrored to crawl, walk, or swim away from this field."

His determined remarks were greeted with mutters of assent. Karkald nodded along with his comrades, knowing that the Rockriders, with their speedy ferr'ells, would be invaluable in such a fight.

"We don't know exactly where the enemy is massing, but we have spied them on the march. Just two cycles ago, we ambushed a supply train. . . . Not only were they hauling gold, but they had enough breastplates for two regiments of men. And we've had confirmation of several large formations gathering in the direction that is neither metal nor wood."

"When do we march, General?" asked a grizzled captain of artillery.

"We're waiting on two wagons of flamestone, should be out to us within the next six hours. As soon as they arrive, we march."

The officers stirred; all were ready for action, but the prospect of a near departure automatically brought to mind numerous tasks needing attention.

"Are we marching straight into the Nullplains, then?" asked Karkald. He knew the terrain on that side of the city, mostly wide flats of rock, scored here and there by deep, wide ravines.

"Good question," grunted Paternak, nodding gruffly. "And no, we're not."

Karkald was surprised but waited quietly with the other officers for the explanation. "This is going to be a march conducted in stealth," explained the general. "And so I intend to take the Rimroad. By skirting the edge of the plain, I expect to avoid the pickets that the Delvers will certainly have posted all across the flats. When we get to the Slatemont, we'll circle around to the shore of the Oilsea. With luck, we'll catch the Delvers with their backs to the wall. Failing in that, we can maneuver through Arkan Pass."

A palpable tremor went through the officers, though none raised his voice in question. Few of them had seen the place, but all knew the pass by reputation: a narrow cut through the vast peninsula of stone called the Slatemont. It was a shortcut that led deep into the wilds of the Underworld, but at the same time, the constricted nature of the ground and the narrow options for egress and exit offered clear problems for maneuver.

"Sir?" The question was asked hesitantly by Captain Barstan of the supply corp. "Er . . . that is, the Rimroad may be fine for marching infantry, but my wagons will have a tough time with some sections. You know how steep it is, and cursedly narrow at some of the highest points. As to the Arkan Pass—is it even passable to wagons?"

"To answer your second question first, Captain, over the last fifty years, the pass has been thoroughly surveyed upon my orders. I have anticipated a need such as this. It is a rough road, but we will pass.

"As to the steepness of the Rimroad, I've considered this, as well," said the general. "And made arrangements for help. Captain Karkald?"

"Yes, General?"

"Your Rockriders will be attached to the supply corps. Those ferr'ells are nothing if not strong. It will be your task to help get the wagons over the tougher parts of the road."

For a moment, Karkald was too flabbergasted to speak. And then the words came pouring over themselves in a jumbled torrent. "But sir! My men haven't trained for work like that! And our mounts are restive enough with a rider. Who knows how they'll fare if they have to pull alongside the darkbulls?"

Paternak's bristly brows lowered, fully shading his eyes from the coolfyre globe above. "Your words border on insubordination, Captain. Do you refuse to carry out my orders?"

"No, sir, of course not," Karkald said, waving his hand. "But you don't understand—"

"Get this straight, *Captain* Karkald. It is you who don't understand, if you think I care to waste my time with your complaints and excuses. Perhaps you should know that Marshal Nayfal has mastered the art of ferr'ell riding. If you find it impossible to follow orders, I'm sure he would be quite capable taking over your regiment."

"I—I'm sorry, General," Karkald said, dropping his hand. "I meant no disrespect." He kept his voice as humble as possible, though his mind whirled with thoughts of pure dismay. How could the proud, fast steeds of his riders serve as plodding beasts of burden? And why wouldn't the general listen and learn that he was wasting the most mobile force at his command?

"Just so we're clear, there has been a lot of attention given to some of these new ideas—dwarves riding weasels being just the most outrageous. Well, I've been making war on Delvers long enough to know what works, and this enemy is too dangerous to be playing around with untried theories. So you Rockriders will be staying in the march column, just like your more disciplined comrades."

Karkald kept silent through the rest of the planning session, learning that the marching order would follow the same tactics the Seers had employed for the last five hundred years. Half the light infantry would go in front, followed by half the heavy infantry and the artillery. The supply convoy would come next, followed in turn by the rest of the heavy and the light foot soldiers.

"Speed and stealth will be of the essence," Paternak concluded by saying. Again his eyes found Karkald. "Another reason that we'll keep those beasts of yours in the middle of the column. I don't want your men riding all over the plains— they're sure to be noticed."

Karkald thought, *At least, if we sent out scouts, we'd find where the Delvers might be hiding!* But he said, "I will follow orders, General; you know that."

"I know what my eyes and my ears tell me, and that's all," growled Paternak. His glowering gaze swept across the whole band of his officers, but Karkald still felt as though he commanded an inordinate amount of the general's attention. "Be ready to march in three hours," the general concluded. "You are all dismissed."

ZYSTYL marched with only one of the five Delver armies that had sallied forth from Vicieristn. The other four were under the command of his fellow arcanes, but he knew their movements would be coordinated with his, just as he had outlined in his plans. They were taking circuitous routes, but all of them would be formed around Axial within a half an interval's time.

The arcane touched the Hurtstone, momentarily craving some comforting response, some indication that the gem's power sensed and approved his plan. But now, as it had been for some time, the precious bauble remained cold and lifeless. Could it be that the power had faded, that the stone had been reduced to mortal properties?

Zystyl would not accept that. Instead, he believed that, for some reason, it had gone dormant for a while. But he was utterly convinced that, when he needed it again, it would once more pulse warmth and comfort against his skin.

And for now, he was perfectly capable of handling matters himself. His beautiful golems, steaming and smoking and resolutely obedient, had marched into the darkness as he had commanded. Even now they were taking positions, ready to perform the task for which they had been designed. His fellow arcanes, too, had accepted their roles with surprising enthusiasm, perhaps because Zystyl had been shrewd enough to give them authority and to place them in positions for which each was well suited.

Proud Hallion had willingly consented to command of the first army, the linchpin of the great maneuver that Zystyl had planned. Lastacar and one-armed Bienifist led the second and third, respectively, marching together in a great flanking movement that, for a half an interval, would take them far out of reach of the rest of the Delver troops. Fieristic, the impatient one, had control of the fourth army, with instructions to advance in reserve of the other three and to throw his force into the battle when the enemy had already been sorely pressed.

Jarristal had at first protested when informed that she, alone of the council of arcanes, would not be granted independent command. But when Zystyl had privately explained his plans and also privately demonstrated that his interest in the female arcane went beyond her military capabilities, she had become a willing accomplice.

Willing in very many ways, he reflected, as a tendril of thought reached his mind from Jarristal, who marched near the rear of the column. He paused, sent a lascivious caress wafting toward her brain. Then he chuckled aloud at the perfection of his plan.

The Delvers marching behind him made no reaction to his expression of humor; indeed, he would have harshly punished anyone who dared to make a vocalization. But the blind dwarves plodded on, tromping footsteps merging into a dull rasp as the whole army, twenty thousand strong, followed the lead of their arcane.

"My lord," reported a voice, a scout from the darkness. He was miles away, but his words reached the arcane's ears in a well-directed whisper. "The Seers have taken the bait. An entire legion, the First, has departed Axial on a route toward the Slatemont."

"Excellent," murmured the arcane, the word intended for himself and Jarristal. She allowed a bubble of pleasure to

simmer up from her mind, and he welcomed the response
with his own warm stroke of thought.

For indeed, things were going even better than he had
hoped.

"LASH that line—pull, dammit!" shouted Karkald, frustration
causing his temper to slip yet again. Bloodeater snorted and
lurched, straining against the traces that connected the proud
cavalry mount to the brace of darkbulls pulling the supply
wagon. Slowly, the great vehicle crept upward, wheels
crunching on the smooth road, Seers cursing and groaning as
they pushed from the rear.

The two darkbulls snorted and bucked. They were broad-
faced, generally stolid creatures, hoofed and wide and strong,
but the proximity to the ferr'ells made them nervous. Only
with liberal use of his whip did the driver keep the beasts
hauling forward. Higher and higher they moved, rolling along
a road that had been carved into the face of a lofty cliff.

Coolfyre lanterns flared from each of the supply wagons,
illuminating the column like a procession of fireflies. To the
left, space vaulted into darkness, a downward plummet that,
by now, marked a drop of at least five hundred feet. To the
right, an equally steep face led upward, rising all the way to
the roof of the First Circle.

Finally, the road turned to the right and crested in a narrow
saddle, a notch that had been carved over a rib of mountain
sweeping outward from the great wall. Here Karkald pulled
Bloodeater to the side, pausing to dismount and unhitch the
line that had connected his steed to the heavy wagon. He nodded to the driver, who set the brake and guided his team onto
the gentle descent beyond the notch.

From here, Karkald could see the vanguard of the legion,
six thousand dwarves marching in a slender line, confined to
this steep, winding road. Each company had its bauble of
coolfyre, and these strung out to mark the force for two miles
or more beyond this notch. To the rear, an equal number of

dwarves climbed after. The artillery had already rolled through, and now the wagons, one by one, lumbered past. Weary foot soldiers welcomed the prospect of a downhill march, while several more of the Rockriders gathered beside Karkald, resting and watching in this narrow saddle of pass.

"Enough of this cow work," snorted Vayshun, a young Rockrider, pulling his restive mount off to the side of the narrow road. "When are they going to let us run?"

"Keep your mind on the task at hand," Karkald said sternly, masking his own frustration behind the face of a loyal subcommander. "We need to get the wagons past the worst part of the road."

"Aye, Captain," said Vayshun, chagrined.

"Ah, dammit anyway," groused Karkald. He felt sorry for the young rider who, after all, had only expressed the opinions that the captain himself had been feeling. Knowing that this pass was only the first in a long series of obstacles, he felt worn down by fatigue and by frustration, realizing that his elite unit was being badly misused.

Another wagon rolled by, starting the slow descent, and Karkald, together with Vayshun and two more Rockriders, rejoined the column. The high-strung ferr'ells were listless as they plodded down the road, which descended for a mile before leveling out along a broad shelf that skirted the base of the high wall.

It was Bloodeater who reacted first, the mount raising his head and staring intently into the darkness beyond the Seer column. The ground sloped down here in a hillside, no longer the steep precipice that had loomed along the high stretch of the route. Immediately, Karkald tugged the reins to the side, his three comrades following him off the road. The ferr'ells were taut and attentive now, heads upraised, round ears pricked upward.

"What was it?" whispered Vayshun.

"I didn't hear or see anything. I think Bloodeater caught a scent." Karkald's eyes strained, penetrating the darkness, looking for any flash of movement.

Abruptly, the animal took a quick step forward and froze, one forefoot raised, curved backward in a natural point. Wagons rumbled along the road behind them, and a darkbull snorted, but the dwarf's attention was on the darkness. There was danger, some kind of threat out there, he was absolutely certain.

And he knew what he had to do.

"Go!" he hissed, and Bloodeater sprang like a bolt from a crossbow. Two leaps took him beyond the rim of light, and then the ferr'ell was skidding and bounding down a gentle slope, a rock-strewn hillside. Stone clattered behind, and Karkald knew that his comrades were coming after.

Even here, down the hill and beyond the sight of the Seer army and its column of lights, Karkald found that he could discern details in the extended glow of the legion's coolfyre lamps. A flat rock loomed, and the ferr'ell came to rest on top, then leaped across a narrow gully and up the opposite hillside. His three companions were right behind, their ferr'ells streaking purposefully.

A dark shape moved on the ground, spitting curses. Karkald's pick was in his hand, and he struck, driving the spike right through the blank mask of a Delver's helm. Another Blind One died as Bloodeater pounced on his chest and then bit the screaming warrior in the neck.

There were more of the Unmirrored, tumbling out, knives whirling as they slashed toward the ferr'ells. Steel clanged, blades bouncing off armor. One of the animals yelped and recoiled, and Bloodeater dashed close. Again Karkald's pick penetrated black armor. The others were also hunting, pouncing, and killing across the stretch of hillside. One Rockrider chased into the darkness, and the ferr'ell's jaws snapped. The mount then shook its head, a limp Delver hanging from its jaws.

It turned out that fifteen of the Unmirrored had been hiding here. All of them were killed in the swift attack. Karkald dismounted, touching off a light as he looked over the corpses. The nearest was a limber Delver, armored only in helmet and breastplate instead of the steel greaves and girdles common on most of the enemy warriors. Karkald noticed that the fellow clutched some kind of purse in his hands, and when he bent down to investigate, he found a pouch divided into eight small pockets. The pockets had various numbers of stones, pebbles differentiated by weight and texture.

Looking up the hill, he realized that the road followed by the army was not very far above. The rock was solid, and when he leaned down and placed an ear against it, he could hear a steady rumble, loud as a wagon rolled overhead, then fading, then rising again as the next rumbling freight cart was hauled past.

"They were counting," he said, looking at the stones and the pockets, as one of his riders, also dismounted, came up to him. "These must mark batteries, and wagons . . . maybe foot companies, too." Only then did he realize that his man hadn't heard, was staring at the captain with anguish on his face.

"What is it?" demanded Karkald.

"Vayshun, sir . . . he's over here."

The young Rockrider lay on the steep hillside where he had fallen. Blood slicked the ground, an oily kind of black in the darkness, but Vayshun's eyes opened as Karkald knelt at his side. "We got 'em, Captain. . . . That was a proper job for us. . . . Killed the bastards . . ."

"Don't talk, son! We'll get you up the hill—" Karkald realized that it was too late. Gently, he closed his comrade's eyes.

It was a somber trio that brought Vayshun's body up the hillside and back onto the roadway. Karkald saw that General Paternak and his marshal, Nayfal, were waiting for them beside the army column. The last of the wagons had trundled past, and now came a long column of heavy infantry. These Seer veterans, armored from scalp to toe, marched by with a ground-shaking tread.

"I see that you chose to disobey my orders," snapped the general, as Karkald dismounted and saluted. "And, it seems, at the cost of a good man's life."

"Sir—" Karkald was appalled at Paternak's words and forcibly restrained the wave of fury that swept through him. With a powerful effort of will, he spoke coldly. "We detected a Delver spy post within sight of the road. I did not abandon my post; instead, I simply acted to protect the army. None of the Delvers escaped. I regret to report that a good man, a young rider named Vayshun, was lost."

"And the enemy knows, beyond all doubt, that we have the 'riders with us," the general declared. "Because you could not follow orders and remain within the column."

"General, they were *spying* on the column. They were counting our troops as we passed."

"Your insubordination has cost you more than a comrade," growled Paternak, as if he hadn't heard. "I told you that I would trust my eyes and ears . . . and they tell me that you have let me down. I am giving Nayfal command of your regiment. You will march in the ranks with the heavy infantry . . . where I can keep an eye on you."

11

Chaos Wyrm

Creatures of transnatural beauty,
Beasts and birds in sight of grace;

Mountain peak of lofty grandeur,
Mead and swale in life's embrace.

Song and tale and sculptor's wonder,
Faith and love and virtue true;

Lest it all be torn asunder,
O'er all worlds the Master flew.

From *The Song of Draco Minstrel*
Epic of the Sixth Circle

Juliay couldn't move, could barely breathe, for a full hour after the dragon flew past. She huddled in her bedroll, the blanket pulled up to her eyes, watching the sky. Finally, full darkness settled over the mountain valley, shadows thickened to oily shrouds by the blackness of stone and water in this rocky abode. In one direction—the direction that was neither metal nor wood, she understood intuitively—the vast, churning wall of storm filled the sky, darkening her view as high as she could see.

Directly overhead, however, and across the whole stretch of sky toward the Center, stars in greater numbers than she had ever seen blinked into view. They swerved and arced through the night in a display so vivid that it seemed frighteningly unfamiliar.

At last she stirred, sitting up, then cautiously rising to her feet. Immediately, she felt the coolness of the air, an unusual chill for a calm night. She lifted the blanket of quilted down and draped it over her shoulders, remembering the jackets in broken *Skyreaver*'s hold. The gondola still lay at the base of the mountain, bow forlornly smashed, stern jutting upward, leaning against the steep slope, though she could barely make it out in the darkness. The balloons were easier to see, the two spheres clearly outlined against the stars.

She had no stomach for going there in the night, so she pulled the quilt around her and turned away from the wrecked airship. The stream whispered off to her left, and the mountainside rose to the right, but there was a fairly level strip on the valley bottom that, for now at least, was well above the water level. Walking carefully, feeling with her toe before placing each step, Juliay made her way along the hard, rocky ground.

Despite the fact that she had seen no evidence of plant or animal life in this valley, the surrounding night seemed to be full of secret whispers, stealthy footsteps. She froze and listened. On the surface there was only that soft hiss of the stream. Dissecting the sound, she felt its abnormalcy even more keenly. There was no trill or splash, none of the bubbling, churning noise that should characterize a mountain creek. Instead, the sound was sibilant but low, constant in pitch and tone though, as she concentrated, it seemed to grow louder and louder.

"Don't be silly!" she whispered to herself. "You're too old to be afraid of the dark."

But she *was* afraid, and with the memory of the dragon and the crashing airship, she knew she had good reason to fear. Reversing course, walking a little more hastily over the ground she had crossed, she made her way back to the pad of her bedroll. Dropping the quilt, suddenly feeling that encumbrance was more dangerous than cold, she wished that she had a weapon more useful than her bow and arrows.

Something scuffed against the mountainside, the steep slope rising above her sleeping place. A tiny pebble rolled down the rocky face, ticking against the ground. Juliay strained to hear, to see, but the black night offered no clues. She remembered Owen's bastard sword, the huge weapon in *Skyreaver*'s hold, and started toward the wrecked airship, trotting as fast as she dared over the remembered but unseen ground.

Air swirled to the side, a slight puff of wind, as if a great bird had flown past. Again she heard a scuffing sound, this time something stepping on the valley floor, toward the stream. She picked up her speed, running toward the dark shape of the gondola, which was barely visible on the black ground.

A spark of brightness startled her into a gasp, and she flinched and ducked as flames burst from the darkness, a small ball of smoky fire that flew over her head and smacked into the ground like a ball of mud. The flames sputtered and died, but in that brief light, Juliay caught a glimpse of a ghastly shape with two legs and two arms like a person, but a pale, skeletal face. Beyond the shoulders, so dark she could have imagined them, rose a pair of wide, feathered wings. But she knew those wings, and the rest of the horrid beast, were all too real; she recognized this as one of the harpies such as had attacked Natac and the trolls.

The druidess screamed aloud and broke for the ship at a full sprint. Another flare of fire broke the night behind her, as she tripped over an unseen rock and sprawled painfully on the ground. This time, the fireball flew right over her; it would have smacked her in the small of her back if she hadn't had the fortuitious fall. She heard the *whoosh* of powerful wing strokes and knew the harpy had taken to the air.

Frantically, Juliay rolled to the side, unmindful of the sharp rocks poking her ribs. Her hand fell upon a stone, and she picked it up, pushing herself up to a squat. Movement flashed past, and a hard wing smashed her shoulder, but she was well braced, and the monster caught her with only the tip of the long wing. With a hiss of rage, the harpy pivoted, landing awkwardly, tumbling to the side.

Heaving her rock with a scream of instinctive hatred, Juliay turned and sprinted the last few yards to the gondola. She heard a smack as the stone struck flesh, and an inarticulate shriek of pain sent shivers down her spine. Then she was crawling up the rigging, over the broken planks of the hull, to tumble into the wreckage of the deck.

Another fiery missile flew over, smacking into the bulkhead. She was actually grateful, for the bit of light showed her the yawning door to the forward hold. Dropping through that, she reached to the left, frantically groping for the hilt of the great weapon she had seen before. She touched rope, casks, broken boards, tangled blankets, seemingly everything but a sword. Only as her eyes adjusted to the Stygian surroundings did she see a faint glimmer, six inches to the left of her left hand.

The diamond on the hilt! Immediately, her hands closed around the rough leather handhold, and she pulled with all her strength. The blade was startlingly heavy, but it came free from the scabbard with a smooth hiss. Falling backward onto a coil of rope, she used all of her strength to lift the steel weapon, angling the tip on a direct line toward the hatchway. The fire outside had faded to almost nothing, but she saw tiny traces of ember-red reflection shimmering up and down the long, metallic blade.

Maintaining her grip, she shifted around, gathering her feet under her as she watched, unblinking, for some sign of the pursuing monster. A blinding flash of flame caused her to flinch and close her eyes, but she held the sword firm. One of the sticky fireballs tumbled into the hold; she heard it *thunk* wetly into the side of a barrel.

She looked again in time to see that horrid face—it *was* a skull—leer from the darkness. Long arms reached, hands with clawed fingers gripped the edges of the hatchway, and then the horrid body pivoted through. Juliay saw short legs, feet like the talons of a vulture, and a small, smooth belly.

That gut was her target as she thrust the heavy sword with all of her strength. Her attacker's momentum added force to the thrust, and the harpy fell onto the blade with a gurgling shriek. Juliay gagged and backed away as claws raked, limbs flailed, and those huge wings, still trailing out the hatchway, thrashed and flexed in dying frenzy.

The beast met her gaze with eyes of deep, impenetrable blackness, tinged with a glow of fire. The bony jaws, more bestial than manlike, with sharp teeth and a rounded, protruding muzzle, clacked. Abruptly, the monster belched a choking death cough, and the bile that spilled from its mouth burst into flame as it trickled across the bony chest to drip onto a coil of rope. The harpy flailed again, clawing with hands and feet at the sword piercing its vitals. Twisting violently, it convulsed, pulling both wings through the hatch to spread behind it.

Moaning and whimpering in terror, Juliay kicked it away, then rose and jumped toward the hatch. She pulled herself through, onto the deck, and looked back to see the monster lying in the flaming gore of its own death. The harpy rolled back so that the hilt of the sword jutted upward, toward the open hatchway. The ember light in those eye sockets faded, and all the limbs—arms, legs, and wings—twitched a few times, then lay utterly still.

The druid fought nausea, clutched the edge of the hatch with hands that wouldn't stop trembling. Flames flicked across the barrel, feeding into the wreckage of shattered supply crates. The ropes were burning, filling the cabin with a thickening cloud of gray smoke. As her shock gradually faded, Juliay suddenly perceived that the entire gondola would inevitably be consumed by this fire.

Immediately she thought of the treasure in her cabin, then realized that the fire would burn the hold first. She focused on action. Reaching into the cargo compartment, the druid tried to seize the handle of one box of hedras. Smoke swirled around her face, and she fell back, coughing and choking. The box of nourishing elf cakes was out of her reach. She took a breath and stretched her hand in again, seeing little except the smoke backlit by spreading fire.

The hilt of the sword was the only thing she could touch and, with a shiver of disgust, she leaned in to grasp it with both hands. Leaning backward, then rising to her knees, she pulled the blade out of the grotesque body and up and out of the hold.

Only then did she run to her cabin. She gathered up the lockbox containing her candles, mirror, and her precious wool, then took a heavy cloak and her druid's pouch of herbs and unguents. She crossed the deck for the last time, ducking under the thick cloud of smoke. Lifting the sword and her other possessions over the rail, she set them onto the ground. She slid down herself, then dragged her burdens away from the hull, over to the tangle of her bedroll.

Finally, she pulled all of her belongings into a tumble of large boulders at the foot of the mountainside. She pushed them out of sight and found an overhanging rock that would conceal her from view.

Then she sat down in this crude shelter, watched the airship burn away, and cried.

REGILLIX regarded Plarinal's body sadly. He was vexed by an uncommon feeling of helplessness. In Arcati, he would have known what to do: He would bear the remains to a deep sungorge, or perhaps to the Cloudsea, and commend Plarinal's life to the sun and the goddess and the great, eternal cosmos of the Seven Circles. Other dragons would be there, and they would all fly a long, ritual circle over the place, singing songs and reciting deeds from the deceased serpent's life and the lives of his ancestors.

But here, in the Fourth Circle, such a ceremony was impossible; there was no way to drop a body *up* to the sun. Though it seemed a monstrous crime, the only thing the great wyrm could do was gather many rocks from the surrounding

terrain and pile them in a cairn over Plarinal's cold flesh. He
instinctively disliked the stones. They were far harder than
anything he had experienced, save only ice and the tooth and
talon of dragonkind, and handling them caused unpleasant
sensations. Yet it seemed even worse to leave the poor dragon,
dead at such a young age, exposed to air, where any of the vile
beasts of this world might come and abuse his flesh.

Most vile of all those beings, Regillix had no doubt, were
the "wingless harpies" of which Plarinal had spoken.
Whether they were the elves, of which he had heard but never
seen, or some other repellent creature, he couldn't know.
Whatever the nature of these foul beings, they had committed
an unspeakably grievous offense by the slaying of a dragon.
The great wyrm was determined to exact revenge.

Well did Regillix remember the oddly solid cloud that had
been among his first sights in this new world. His wingtip had
scored it, sent it tumbling to the ground, and he felt certain
that had been the end of any flightless creatures within. Yet he
remembered the wreckage and decided that he would begin
his search there, even if it meant landing in that narrow valley
and climbing out on foot.

There was plenty of room to fly here, in this wide river
valley. Regillix began to trot into the face of the steady wind.
He hurried into a lope, then a full run, and finally leaped upward at the same time as he spread his vast wings. Those sails
caught the air and lifted, and with powerful strokes, the dragon
bore himself upward, following the gradual curve of the valley until he was high enough to glide over the neighboring
ridge.

At least his keen sense of direction seemed to function
here; he knew that the Center lay to his left, and the direction
of metal to his right. He had no difficulty remembering the location where he had seen the wreckage of the colorful cloud,
in the direction that was neither metal nor wood. Skirting the
great plateau where he had first landed, he followed a narrow
valley, curved around an obsidian peak, and looked for the
twin spheres he remembered floating above the place.

Surprisingly, one of the spheres, a dark purple in color, was rising into the air before him. He dove past and saw a series of threadlike lines, many of them smoldering from some kind of combustion, dangling below the thing. But there was no sign of any creature, harpylike or otherwise, around the odd cloud.

Regillix circled around several times and finally dove close, slicing a wing tip through the skinlike membrane of the sphere. Immediately it sagged and began to tumble downward.

When he dove lower, a smudge of smoke caught his eye. Beside the dying fire, he saw several sweeps of colorful skin, undoubtedly the membrane of the other cloud-spheres, scattered across the ground. But again there was no sign of any creature.

This now seemed a very unpromising place to search, so he banked away, letting his momentum carry him past the looming peak. There was nothing here in these bleak mountains to interest him. Instead, he set his sights, and his bearings, toward the Center.

"THERE it is," Belynda said, whispering unconsciously though she knew that the massive creature pictured in her Globe of Seeing couldn't hear her. Even so, there was something so supernatural and timeless about the great dragon that she pulled back and shivered, worried that the thing might sense her inspection.

"Good. Can you see where?" Quilene asked. The sage-enchantress had been dozing on Belynda's couch, but now she rose and crossed to the table, looking into the crystal sphere over her friend's shoulder. "By the goddess—it's huge!"

"I can see how it destroyed *Skyreaver*. It's a miracle you were able to bring any of them home." Belynda shivered again, then turned away from the Globe, rising and crossing the airy room until she stood before the open doors leading to the garden. Quilene stayed in the viewing alcove, frowning as she studied the frightening image.

The sun was bright, and birds harmonized cheerfully, but the sage-ambassador couldn't escape the sense that there was some kind of ominous shadow across her vision, a darkness more spiritual than real.

"The dragon is flying toward the Center," Quilene said, coming to join Belynda at the door. "We had better send word to Natac."

The sage-ambassador nodded sadly. The warrior and his druid had returned to the villa only two days ago, and she had wanted them to have so much longer, so much more time to begin making up for the centuries they had been apart. But it was not to be.

A part of her envied the closeness, the obvious passion that had linked the two humans as soon as they had seen each other. She thought, a trifle wistfully, of Tamarwind Trak, the elf with whom she had sired two children, so long ago. They came and went from each other's lives with casual connection, as if they would have limitless time together whenever they wanted it . . . only now, most of the time, they didn't seem to want it. That was their elfness, she knew, and the knowledge brought her a sense of melancholy. Her people were blessed with countless years; why was it impossible, in all that time, for them to truly share their love?

Of course, Belynda remembered another, darker aspect of human passion. Sometimes, in the dark of the night, she would wake in a sweat, remembering the stinking arrogance of the Crusader, Sir Christopher . . . the brutal violence and spiritual violation she had suffered when he had forced himself onto, into, her. Christopher was long dead now, but sometimes the hatred she felt was like a deadly snake coiled inside her, and she wished that he lived for the sole purpose of suffering her vengeance.

"Should we send a message?" Quilene asked gently, laying a hand on Belynda's shoulder, stroking her tense neck muscles with strong fingers.

The sage-ambassador nodded. She took a small golden bell from the shelf beside the door, held it outside, and shook it several times. The music tinkled at a high pitch, almost inaudible to elven ears. "We'll have a courier in a few minutes," she said.

Quilene nodded, though she didn't remove her hand. Belynda relished the soothing touch, wondered if her friend was using a little magic to enhance her massage. Either way, she felt much more relaxed when, a short time later, a small figure buzzed into view.

The faerie flyer was a young man, barely a foot tall, with a pair of wings on his shoulders that buzzed like a hummingbird's as he swept up to the doorway and halted, hovering at eye level with the two elven women.

"Dahrt, of the Courier Dahrts, at your service," he said with a midair bow. "Is there a chance I heard the music of the faerie summons?"

"A good chance, and thank you for your quick response," said Belynda. "Do you know the villa of the warrior Natac and the druid Miradel?"

"My lady sage-ambassador, of that fabled house I well know. And there is not a courier on Nayve who would not be honored to carry a message thereto."

"Good." Belynda drew a breath, composing the message that the fairy courier would carry, verbatim, to Natac and Miradel.

"The scourge comes toward the Center," she said. "Quilene and Belynda will mark its course, but feel that haste is imperative. Please come at once."

"It shall be my privilege to deliver your message. I shall return with a response before the hour is out!" pledged Dahrt before spinning around and taking off like an arrow shot from a bow. He flew up and over the hedge surrounding the garden, and in three seconds, he was gone from sight.

AWFULBARK and Wartbelly parted ways as they ran into Udderthud. All around, the harpies shrieked and cawed and screeched. They hurled their flaming balls of bile, and several

ancient troll homes were already engulfed by fire. Wartbelly
ran, howling, up the nearby knoll to his wife and clanhome.
Awfulbark raced down the ravine-bottom trail at a gangly,
loping gallop, making for his own oaken domicile. He gagged
at the sight of a dozen troll bodies, some of them youngsters,
charred and blackened and permanently killed by the harpy
fire. Elsewhere, trolls were trying to battle, but the harpies
dove and swooped and then climbed away, for the most
part avoiding the frantic blows of Udderthud's would-be defenders.

The king scrambled up the last slope and found harpies
soaring among the trees. Several trolls swung wild punches in
the open, while others battled in the large windows venting
the upper rooms of several houses. Awfulbark saw that his
own door was intact, but then he groaned at the sight of
harpies, three or four of them, crowding into the upper room.
Abruptly, the door burst open.

"Aeeiii!" cried Roodcleaver, tumbling out of the house.
She wielded her great kitchen knife in wild slashes, hacking
at the winged horror that chased her outside, that struck her
with raking talons.

"Run!" cried Awfulbark, racing up to the burly oak of his
home. He heard a heavy limb crack overhead, and hurled
himself upon Roodcleaver, bashing the attacking harpy to the
ground and covering his wife with his own body.

The timber crashed to the ground, a painful smack against
his shoulders, but he shrugged off the pain and the branch as
he scrambled to his feet. The harpy hobbled away, hissing
hatefully at the troll, baring sharp fangs. Awfulbark saw that
the creature trailed a broken wing. More wings and ghastly,
red-eyed faces thronged in the nearby doorway of the king's
house, and Roodcleaver groaned at his feet.

The king of Udderthud reached down and hoisted the tree
limb, which was stout and long but devoid of leaves. "Stay
down!" he grunted at his wife, swinging the timber through a
circle as the harpies tumbled out of the house. He caught one

of the monsters with a stunning blow to the side of the head and sent it sprawling. Momentum carried the beam into the next two, both of which went down in a tangle of flailing wings and furious shrieks.

Finally, he threw the log, splintered end first, at the broken-winged harpy. The creature raised an arm to try to ward off the blow, but the branch was too heavy. The impact knocked the monster down, and there it lay, moaning feebly, kicking one taloned claw.

But the troll king could take no pleasure from his small victory. One of those hateful fireballs came spurting down from above, landing with an oily splat on the ground. More of the harpies winged past, lighting in the branches of the trees on this lofty elevation, the Crowned Knoll of Udderthud.

Roodcleaver stumbled to her feet, her knotty face screwed into a strange mixture of anger and fear. "What *is?*" she cried.

"Come," replied Awfulbark, taking her wrist in his hand. "We run!" She bounded along beside him as they joined other trolls from nearby houses, all of them fleeing in panic, tumbling down the steep slope into the ravine.

There they could only join the file of miserable trolls, pushing and jostling and hurrying along. Some harpies swept past, and others spat their fireballs at the retreating trolls, but most of the shrieking attackers seemed content to gather on the tops of the knolls, looting the houses and thronging around the feast fires.

One harpy swept low enough to cut painful scratches in the scalp of a young troll. Awfulbark found another log on the ground, this one solid and thick along most of its length, tapering to a narrow but sturdy end. He picked it up by the narrow end and swung it at the next harpy, knocking the creature to the ground. Furious trolls quickly tore it to pieces.

After that, the harassing fliers kept a safer distance, shrieking insults, spitting from high up in the trees. Finally, as the trolls plodded into the dark forest, they saw no sign of further pursuit. The shrill cacophony of triumphant screeches, however, lingered long after Darken.

JANITHA trotted along the balcony, ready for the departure of the herd. But she had to see her father once more before she left Shahkamon for a half a year of nomadic wandering, following the great hyac around on their leisurely grazing and migration. She hurried down the steps, barely taking note of Riven Deep yawning through space beyond the royal balcony.

Her father was already up, of course, and had completed his meditations in the steam room. She met him on the wide plaza and gave him a kiss on the cheek.

"My daughter, can you share my breakfast table?" asked Khan Lazzutha, leader of the Hyac. "Fast riders from the Metalreach have brought an array of sweet grapes from the Kankish Hills."

"I can't take the time," she said breezily. "The herders have been up for hours, and I know they want to get moving."

"They'll wait for you; you're the daughter of the khan!" Lazzutha declared.

"I know they *would* wait, but I don't want to *make* them wait," she said. "Give me a bunch of grapes I can eat in the saddle, won't you?"

With a mock sigh, the khan agreed. He couldn't complain too much, he knew; after all, he was the one who had taught her to be considerate of the needs, feelings, and pride of her countrymen. Lazzutha had been the nominal ruler of the Hyaccan elves for the last five hundred years, and Janitha could only hope that she would be as worthy a leader if she had the chance to assume the khanate.

"All my daughters gone from me—Sirien to the ends of Nayve, and you for a half year of herding!" her father wailed in mock anguish. "What will I do? Who will I talk to? More to the point, what will I listen to . . . indeed," Khan Lazzutha concluded thoughtfully. "Perhaps I shall avail myself of the silence!"

"Papa, it's *your* fault! You taught us to learn about the world and to spend our lives *doing* things. 'Don't make the mistake of so many elves,' you said—I don't know how many times! 'Don't expect to sit around and watch as life passes! Go out and experience that life!' Didn't you say just that?"

"Ah, it's a cruel child who takes the words of a doting father and turns them back on him like a sharp knife. But yes, I did say just that. And those were wise words, even then."

Janitha took pity on the old elf and embraced him. "Besides," she consoled. "I'm coming back in six months, after the herds have grazed on the Barkmont. Who knows how long your *other* daughter will be gone."

"And I am proud, so proud, of you both," said Lazzutha, heartily returning her hug. "I will miss you, and welcome you home with a grand feast. Now go. What kind of princess are you, to keep your companions waiting thus?"

She laughed and pulled away. "And I am so proud to have a father like you," she said, looking seriously into his eyes. For the first time, she noticed tiny lines webbing outward across his temples. She had to mask her surprise and sadness at these signs of the khan's advancing age.

"Then remember what I have taught you, and take care, with yourself, and your people, and your animals," her father declared. "And do not forget us here, on the Rim of the World."

"I won't," she said, then laughed. "But can we call it the Rim of the World now, since Sirien and Natac and the explorers have sailed on to the other side?"

"I can call it whatever I want," huffed Lazzutha in mock seriousness. "I am the khan of the Hyac! But please, daughter . . . just keep us in your thoughts."

"Always, father," Janitha said, giving him another kiss, as one of his servants brought a bunch of the grapes for her. She started up the steps when another voice hailed her from the nearby smithy.

"Janitha!"

It was Lord Hellenkay, wearing the leather apron of the metalsmith, the sign of his true occupation. "I wanted to say . . . farewell. I will count the days until you return!"

"Why, Alric," she said coyly. "That's very flattering!"

"You know I will," he said seriously, coming closer. "And when you are back, let us speak to your father, about . . . us."

She gave him a kiss on the cheek. "When I return, let us speak to each other about us," she teased. "We have lots and lots of time before we talk to the khan!"

"I will think about you every day!" he pledged, as she skipped up the steps and raced past the barns to join the herders who had gathered with their fast, wiry ponies. The herd of hyacs, more than a thousand of the hulking brown shapes, shaggy with long fur, many with the long, curved horns marking the males, waited placidly beyond.

"The khandaughter is here!" cried one elf, a lanky hunter named Falri. He flashed her a dazzling smile and whirled his nimble pony through a quick circle. "Let us ride!"

Janitha sighed at his antics, while her friend Beval, astride her own black pony, hooted with laughter. "At least the khandaughter will lead us in a straight line!" she cried, to Falri's amused protest.

In moments, Janitha had vaulted into the saddle of Skyrunner, the sturdy gold-colored stallion that was her favorite mount. She looked at Beval, saw the keen enthusiasm in the elfmaid's smile. "Let's run!" she called.

Skyrunner reared, and his forehooves pawed the air, then he sprang across the prairie. The other herders galloped behind, following the rim of the canyon toward wood, as they gave the eager ponies free rein. More than a hundred elves of the Hyac rode with her, all of them young, all looking forward to the months of freedom, the idyllic wandering that would lead them all the way to the rich grasses of the Barkmont, in the shadow of the Ringhills, and then back to the Rim before the passing of a half year.

With shouts, whoops, and whistles, the mounted elves circled the great bulk of the hyac herd, and the hulking herbivores started shuffling across the grass. Like a sea of brown fur, they pitched and surged and rolled back upon themselves, then started woodward in a slow but inexorable tide. Janitha inhaled the earthy scent of the great beasts and allowed Sky-runner to sprint at his own pace. The wind blew back her golden hair as she whooped and waved her hand, until the stallion finally slowed to a trot at the head of the vast, irregular mass of hyac, ponies, and elves. They moved along the rim, with the canyon to their left and the towers and barns of Shahkamon still visible, but shrinking behind.

More ponies rushed past, a loose herd of riderless mounts driven by several younger elves. For general purposes, the ponies would be kept separate from the hyac, encouraged to graze on the harsh grasses of the hilltops while the great cattle took sustenance from the broad valley floors. They would spend many weeks traveling in the direction of wood, meandering along with Riven Deep on their left and the great extent of plains to the right.

One of the herders, a youth named Rosto, a young herder just embarking on his first migration ride, turned and rode toward Janitha with sudden urgency, his eyes focused on the town that was already fading into the distance.

"What's that, my princess?" he asked, an undercurrent of fear in his voice.

Janitha followed the young elf's pointing finger, staring into the hazy distance of the great canyon. Something moved there, a shape in the air. "A cloud . . . ? No. . . ."

What *was* it? The thing soon became defined as large and winged.

"What can it be?" she asked. "I've never seen anything like that."

The young riders gathered their ponies near the rim of the canyon, all of them resting uneasily in their saddles as they watched the flyer come closer. The hyac went back to grazing, while the steeds snorted in agitation. Soon Janitha realized that the winged creature was even bigger than she had first imagined. Those massive wings looked to cover a span as wide as Shahkamon's cliff-side marketplace.

"It's a monster!" whispered a young herder, her voice hushed with terror and disbelief.

The creature's approach had been observed from the town, she saw, as elves were racing from the buildings, gathering on the rim of the lofty plaza. A great roar emerged from that horrible shape, as huge jaws spread wide and the creature dove toward the elves gathered on the king's plaza. Several hyac bellowed in the barnyards near the town. One great bull broke its tether, then tossed a rail fence into splinters with a sweep of its long horns. In panic it rumbled onto the plains, fleeing the canyon's rim and the approaching horror. Ponies raced back and forth in their corrals, neighing and shrieking in terror.

The monster flew above Shahkamon, the massive wings casting a broad shadow, a shade that rippled across the houses, plazas, and streets, swept onto the grass, then narrowed as the monster banked and turned back to the elven community. With a dip of its tail, the wyrm flew upward, slowed to a stall, then dropped down into the midst of the town. Janitha gasped aloud, and all around she heard her companions sobbing.

From this distance, across the bay of the canyon side, the attack was strangely soundless. They could see stones and timbers flying through the air, whole buildings crushed by that lashing tail. With a mighty spring, the dragon took to the air again, diving into the canyon, then curling around to climb back toward the rim. A shelf of the town, bearing several inns and a market, broke away, trailing dust and screams as it plummeted into Riven Deep.

A volley of arrows sparkled in the sun, tiny missiles launched in a concentrated volley. Many of those barbs struck home, but they did nothing to slow the monster's approach. Instead, it roared again and landed heavily on the plaza in the midst of the elves. Dozens were crushed under that great body, while the tail swept many more from the edge, small bodies tumbling soundlessly into the gulf of the canyon.

Janitha was rooted in place by horror. She saw great jaws lash forward, crushing the façade of her father's palace. Stone columns fell, and wooden doors and walls were splintered like kindling. Back and forth on the terraced shelves did the great beast bound, clawing at the stones, tearing and clawing and biting any elf too slow to get out of the way.

From the corrals suddenly came a sweeping charge, golden-haired elves on horseback racing close to the monster, casting spears, chopping with swords. Janitha saw the silver helmet, knew that Lord Hellenkay led this charge. And she cried aloud when that dashing elf and his horse were smashed flat by a crushing blow of the wyrm's taloned forefoot, the bodies swept into the Deep by a casual flick of the great tail.

More elves came rushing forth, from every barn and inn and house and hall. They brandished pitchforks and axes, spears and clubs with heroic courage. Their cause was hopeless, and they perished instantly under the great serpent's lethal attack. Still more attacked, and still more died, all the people, the wreckage, the whole place swept into the canyon.

Finally, the monster launched into the sky with a great, rending twist of its rear legs. Janitha screamed and covered her face with her hands, unable to watch as the remainder of Shahkamon, her people's abode for a millennium, broke from the canyon's rim, toppled forward, and plunged in wreckage and chaos down the sheer precipice of Riven Deep.

12

The Druid's Soldier

Oh I wish I was in the land of cotton,
Old times there are not forgotten,
Look away, look away, look away,
Dixie land.

Folk Anthem of the Seventh Circle
Confederate States of America

Juliay knew that the Lighten hour had passed, but she could find no strength, no purpose, for stirring within her small, rock-walled shelter. It was like a small cave, with a fairly spacious chamber around a narrow, bending passageway connecting to the outside. Daylight filtered through the looming tumble of boulders, and even though the druid remained deep inside the stony cairn, in several places beams of sunlight found cracks and penetrated to strike the floor with spots of glaring and incongruous brightness.

She pulled her quilt over her body and curled up on the bearskin, chilled more deeply than any cold could penetrate. The great sword lay forgotten near the mouth of her niche, next to the unstrung bow and the quiver of arrows. Her lockbox was in her hand, clutched tightly, pressed against her belly.

Hours passed, and finally the dull craving of thirst grew to a parched reality. Juliay sat up and let her quilt fall away, shaking off the lethargy that had paralyzed her for so long. She moved to the side, let one of the light shafts fall over her, used the warmth to steel her determination. Perhaps there was a water cask in the ruin of *Skyreaver,* one that had somehow survived the fire. If not . . . she shuddered, remembering the oily smooth water in the stream.

On her hands and knees, she made her way around the curve to the mouth of her shelter. From here she could see the smoldering wreckage of the gondola, blackened and broken, collapsed into an unrecognizable smear on the ground except for the riblike skeleton of the main hull timbers. The shrouds linking the two remaining balloons had burned away, and those flotation spheres were nowhere to be seen. Only on the mountainside, where silken sheets and great tangles of rope were scattered, had any of the ship escaped total destruction.

Next she turned her attention to the sky, which was a pale blue, screened by a morbid film of gray. Mostly she feared the glimpse of wings, feathered or leathery, each betokening its own lethal threat. Thankfully, that vista was clear.

She emerged in a crouch and quickly spun to scan the rest of the sky. No deadly fliers soared there, but she gasped at the sight of the monstrous storm cloud, looming upward to the limits of her vision. Black and boiling it was, a churning murk of lightning-tinged violence that covered the full expanse of the horizon in the direction that was neither metal nor wood.

The stream slid past, forgotten, as she leaned against the rock and let out a sob. She pushed herself away and wandered listlessly toward the remnants of the hull. Even a cursory glance indicated nothing intact within the scattering of ashes and coals. The contents of the storeroom, fueled by the cask of oil, had burned away to a smooth, featureless mound.

Something slammed Juliay's feet out from under her, and she tumbled to the ground in a spine-jarring fall. She rolled, knocked helplessly to the side, felt unforgiving rock smash her face. On her belly she sprawled out her limbs, trying to grab or kick something. The ground convulsed, and she landed on her hands and knees and balanced herself desperately.

A quake! It was the ground itself that attacked her, tossed and smashed and punched her with uncaring cruelty. It seemed like forever that she braced herself against the temblor, and when the ground stopped moving, she was crying again, head slumped in defeat, shoulders trembling from her sobs.

Finally she became aware of other sounds, rumbles and crashes and violent thunder. She saw a shelf of rock break from the opposite mountainside, plunging down the steep slope in an explosion of debris. More slides tumbled up and down the valley as the mountains themselves reacted to the rude pummeling of the quake.

Only once before had Nayve suffered such a quake, Juliay knew, and that time it had been the precursor of violence and war. Now she looked again at the storm and wondered if she bore witness to the end of all existence.

And then a more immediate concern penetrated her shock as a trio of winged shapes glided through her field of view. One screeched, the horrid song of the harpy, and they all dove toward the lone druidess on the valley floor. Frantically, Juliay sprinted toward her makeshift shelter. The harpies swept lower, and she looked into the black eye sockets of the nearest, saw hungry sparks glow there.

She reached the cave mouth, diving headlong into the narrow niche under the boulder. Ignoring the further assaults on her bruised flesh, she kicked and clawed and vanished underground before the first of the vicious scavengers landed heavily just outside. Within, Juliay picked up the hilt of the sword, using all of her strength to lever the blade toward the entrance. Clenching her teeth, she waited, fully prepared to drive the weapon into another of the monstrous creatures.

But the harpies seemed content to leave her alone, for now. At least, they made no attempt to enter the cave. Throughout the rest of the day, Juliay lay there. When she looked out the entrance, she was unable to see any sign of her tormentors, but she had no difficulty imagining them perched just above, waiting for her to emerge.

In the night she listened, and once or twice thought she heard the scuff of a taloned foot on the stones. She was hungry, thirsty, and terrified. Terror won out, and she stayed right where she was. Finally, fatigue overcame thirst, and she slept.

Once more, she held her lockbox. This time she had it pressed to her heart.

The order to retreat was delivered by a dust-stained courier, as gaunt and unshaven as every other man around here. Jubal Caughlin read the orders dispassionately, knowing the import: The siege of nine months would end in rebel defeat. With the retreat, Grant's army would be marching into Richmond, and Lee's would be hard-pressed to escape and survive.

Surely there could be no crueler order that had ever been delivered to the loyal soldier. The signature at the bottom— Robert E. Lee—only served to heighten the hopelessness, the all-encompassing despair of the moment. The remnants of Jubal's division would have to pull back, joining the straggling survivors of the once proud Army of Northern Virginia.

And yet, now that it was time to act, he faced his decision with a kind of lethargy that frightened him as much as had the greatest bombardments over four years of war. He wanted to rail against injustice, to cry out to God for righteous retribution. He was a faithful man. All his life he had attended church and prayed, perhaps not as often as he should, but with sincerity. Now he came to the end of all endeavor, a bleak terminus of defeat and despair.

But he still had a duty. He sent messages summoning his brigade commanders, and began to plan for an orderly withdrawal. And if he despaired at the situation, he did not find it surprising, because it had seemed inevitable for so long. After the carnage of Cold Harbor, the Union armies had started to squeeze the great city, capital of Virginia and the Confederacy, as cold blooded as any python crushing its prey.

In the shadows of his command tent, he watched the light of the last pale candle flicker and wave. It was hypnotic, really . . . a summons to sleep, it had come to seem. More and more, lately, he found the urge to sleep irresistible. He attributed it to fatigue, malnutrition, and the toll of a long, bloody war. Now he laid his head on the table, cushioned by his arms, and as awareness slipped away, he felt the comforting embrace of peace.

He was awakened by a gentle cough and looked up wearily until he recognized the white-bearded figure, stooped and worn but still somehow embodied with all the pride of the Confederacy. "General Lee!" he declared, rising to his feet, saluting. "I . . . I'm sorry, sir."

"No need to apologize, Jubal," said the man who would always be The General. "We need to take our rest as we can get it. It is I who offer regrets for thus disturbing you."

"My division and I stand ready to do as you command, General," he said.

"I know. I need to ask you for one more favor, old soldier."

"Anything, sir."

General Lee went to the map table while General Caughlin turned up the wick on the lamp. The grim siege of Petersburg was depicted there, jagged lines marking the fortifications that had held up the Army of the Potomac for nine months, the latter half of 1864 and now the first three months of '65. Like an indomitable dam, those fieldworks had sheltered Lee's men and stood firm against the relentless attacks of the Yankees. But now the enemy had captured the last rail junction, west of the city, and closed in with cavalry and infantry, an envelopment that would mean the end of the rebel army.

"I need you to take this fort, here, on Larchmont Hill. If you knock the Yankees out, even for half a day, I will be able to pull the army out of Petersburg and up the valley of Appomattox Creek. With a little luck, we might be able to link up with Johnston down in Caroline, continue the war from there.

"And Richmond . . . ?" Jubal already knew the answer.

"The capital, the government, is moving to Danville right now," Lee replied. He sighed wearily. "As for Richmond, she shall have to fend for herself."

"I . . . I understand, General." Truly, *Jubal couldn't understand how it had come to this, but he knew the armies and the terrain as well as anyone else. Indeed, Richmond would have to fend for herself.*

By nightfall, thirst was an angry talon clawing at Juliay's tongue. She judged it likely that the harpies were still out there, but she also recognized that she would waste away and inevitably perish if she didn't get some water.

And she knew that the strange liquid in the mountain stream was her only option.

She considered charging forth with the sword but immediately discarded the notion; the weapon was too heavy to do anything but hold her back. Instead, she decided she would simply race to the stream . . . and then she realized that she had nothing with which to gather water.

Her eyes went to the precious lockbox, and she knew what she had to do. Gingerly she turned the key and lifted out her three candles, the small mirror, and the vial containing her precious threads. These items she set on a small shelflike ledge on the rock wall. With a touch of her finger and a whispered prayer to the goddess, she lit the longest of the candles and then critically inspected the box.

It would be waterproof, she believed. At least, it would have to do. The container had as much volume as a good-sized drinking gourd, and she reasoned that she could race to the stream, scoop water, clap the cover shut, and scramble back to the shelter. With luck, the harpies wouldn't be able to react before she made it to safety.

Her tongue was like a piece of dry bark, and every move provoked aching from her abused flesh. Crawling back to the entry, she tried to move with utmost silence, though each scuff of hand or knee sounded like a falling rock to her straining ears.

Darkness again shrouded the mountain valley, and the growling storm clouds blocked out half of the starlight. Juliay could make out the surface of the stream, vaguely luminous, ten or a dozen paces away. Fearing that hesitation would only give rise to greater fears, she pushed herself from beneath the rocky shelf, leaping to her feet and running toward the stream. She was crouched, and not just from fear; spears of pain, from muscles stiffened by long confinement, stabbed down her back and legs as she tried to straighten.

The water was before her, black and smooth and swiftly flowing, and she dropped to her knees, taking the time for one look around. Wings suddenly fluttered atop the rock pile, and she heard a screech of alarm. She dashed the box through the water, shut the lid on a solid weight of precious liquid, and sprinted for all she was worth back into the little cave. Sliding onto the ground, she scrambled under the rock, clutching the box upright as the diving harpy whooshed past the entrance. A gob of flame struck the ground, spattering loudly, hissing and sputtering and spewing vile smoke.

Only when she was all the way into the deep niche did she draw a deep breath and sit, with her back against a smooth rock face. Carefully she pushed back the lid and relished a long drink.

The water touching her mouth created a sensation of pure ecstacy. Wondering, she took a second drink, and a third. The freshness of the liquid seeped into her limbs with a wave of soothing. In that instant, her pain diminished and then vanished entirely. She drank again, half finishing the box before she set it down in a sheltered corner.

Amazingly, the barren shelter looked safe now, even snug. Along with her physical ailments, some of her emotional pains had been eased away. Terrible danger lurked without, but she was safe within . . . safe, and even comfortable now.

She laid out the bearskin, which covered most of the ground in the central chamber of the little cave. Checking the candle, she was pleased to see that it burned very slowly.

Then the tuft of wool caught her eye. She had the fire here, and the mirror . . . and she could escape her own miseries, for a time, by following her warrior . . . her Jubal.

The tiny thread was in her fingers. Placing the mirror upright, near the candle, she touched the piece of yarn to the flame, and drew the picture, and the story, from the Seventh Circle . . . from her warrior of Earth.

The division formed with its left flank resting just above Appomattox Creek. General Caughlin gathered his brigade and regimental commanders in the center of the line. The ranks of his proud division, which numbered barely a thousand men left of the original nine thousand four hundred and twelve, wearily awaited the command. Dawn had only begun to blue the sky on this day in early April.

"At least they won't be expecting us to attack," he said. It was the only hopeful aspect of the whole, mad situation. "We knock them out of there, and the general will get us out of this bluebelly trap. But for this morning, it's up to us."

"Reckon we've got one more charge in us, Gen'rl," said Hoskins, the colonel of Caughlin's First Brigade.

"That's what I told Mister Robert E. Lee," Jubal replied.

He took up a position in the middle of the line, standing just before the front rank. The division standard bearer would follow behind that regiment; Jubal's orderly and headquarters sergeant stood at either side of the general.

They started out at a walk through the misty field that was barely touched by dawn. Their guns were unloaded, in that tactic copied from the Yankees: When attacking entrenched positions, men with ready muskets would invariably go to ground and shoot rather than press the assault. But with no ammunition in the guns, the bayonet became the only weapon, and the men would drive the charge home.

The fort was a massive block against the skyline, grim and dark and silent. It was that silence that gave them hope of success, even of survival. For that silence meant that the enemy could still be surprised. A thrush warbled in the woods, and a multitude of frogs peeped in a nearby marsh. Jubal took a moment to relish the sounds of peace, knowing that they would be the last such for many of his men.

The division entered a band of saplings, and inevitably

some noise was made, trees and branches snapping, men stumbling over unseen roots, cursing quietly. Still there was no reaction from the Yankees. When the regiments emerged from the trees, they took a moment to dress the lines, reserve companies coming up behind, all three brigades orienting themselves for the final approach.

They started forward again, and Jubal broke into a trot, knowing the men behind him would match his pace. From the darkness before them, a voice shouted a challenge, an enemy picket out in front of his own lines. A single shot sounded, a rifled bullet whistling past overhead, and in that instant, the priority changed from stealth to haste.

Now he was running, and the men came behind. From somewhere the cry began, the yelping "ki-yi, ki-yi" of the rebel yell. It had been a long time since he had heard that sound, and he found himself shouting, too, adding his voice to the din echoing across the misty field.

The first cannons fired, but like the sentry's rifle, their aim was high. Shells whined above, fused charges that exploded well past the thin rebel line. Still yodeling their battle cry, the attackers scrambled over the first of the abatis, barriers of logs and ditches. They ran through trenches that were mostly unoccupied, bayoneting a pair of sentries who had only just awakened to the reality of their doom.

The First Brigade charged up the sloping wall of the fort, with Jubal racing in the lead. They came over the parapet between a pair of belching cannon and saw with a flash of hope that the ramparts were barren of infantry; the surprise was complete. Union artillerymen tried to flee, but they were clubbed and stabbed to death beside their guns. The men of the Third Brigade swept over the eastern wall, taking another battery by storm, scouring the defenses with their bayonets. A few Yankees were in the yard, but they wasted no time in fleeing out the back entrance. Some of the rebels chased them, while others began to swivel the captured cannon, turning them to face the lines of their original owners.

The rest of the men loaded their guns, looked to their com-

rades, and settled down to wait. Everyone knew that the Yankees wouldn't delay long before trying to get their fort back.

"No!" Juliay gasped. She stared at the thread in horror, seeing the frayed end, just a scant inch from her fingertips. She knew what it meant, though at first she tried to deny the truth. But there was no other explanation; the life thread had turned to ash.

And Jubal Caughlin was going to die.

In the next instant, she made her decision . . . the decision no druid had made since Miradel, more than three centuries earlier. She drew a deep breath, and the power of the goddess was in her. Taking only the time for another sip of that vibrant, revitalizing water, she went about her preparations.

One candle she placed at her head, finding a niche in the cavern wall that allowed it to be placed three feet off of the floor. The second she placed to the left, half that height above the smooth surface where lay her bearskin and quilt. The third and final candle completed the equilateral triangle, set on the floor itself.

Within that triangle she would work the spell. She felt the magic, the power of Nayve and all the Seven Circles, rising through her flesh as she breathed deeply, meditated on the Worldweaver, on the history of worlds. The cost to herself was immaterial, a sacrifice she would make willingly, to give life to another.

Finally, she was ready. She took the thread, aligned the mirror, and touched the strands to the flame. . . .

"Here they come!" shouted Colonel Hoskins unnecessarily. The advance of the Yankee divisions, at least three of them, would have been obvious to a blind man; thousands of Northerners yelled their own battle cry. It was a deep-throated roar, and it came from three sides of the fort.

Jubal looked east, into trampled ground underneath the harsh glare of the midmorning sun, and he saw that bright-

ness reflected off of ten thousand bayonets. To the south, however, he saw the brown line making its way along the road in the valley of the Appomattox. Lee was bringing his army out of the trap, through the gap opened by Jubal's charge.

Guns boomed to either side of him, captured pieces called Napoleons, now turned on their original owners. Shells blasted the ground and the bodies but had no visible effect on the blue tide as a whole.

Yankee artillery opened up, and Jubal dropped behind the bulwark of the fort's rampart, standing just high enough to peer over the upper timber. A shell screamed overhead and burst in the air; one of the rebel gunners cried out and fell, writhed on the ground, his chest ripped open by hot metal. Another gaunt scarecrow of a man took his place with the muzzle rag.

The volume of guns rose to a deafening thunder, an insane violence of shattering breastworks and smoky, churning air. Through the chaos, the men took their places at the rampart, muskets laid across the interwoven logs. Jubal watched the Yankee tide rush closer, knowing that the first volley needed to register a shocking impact if they were going to halt the charge.

The bayonets wavered and dropped, the blue-shirted attackers running now, shouting wildly. A glance to the side showed them coming from each direction, sweeping into the rear of the fort that was, after all, built to face attack from the opposite direction.

"Fire!" he shouted, and the nearby men released a crashing volley into the enemy charge. More shots rippled around the perimeter as all of the rebel troops fired, then smoothly reloaded. The enemy rushed closer, but the second volley rattled across the front and flayed hundreds of men from the first rank of the attack. The rest continued on, some swarming around to the back of the breastworks, others scrambling up the timber-tangled forward slope.

Now the shooting was every man's task, as fast as he could

load. Gray and white smoke boiled through the air, here and there streaked with black where creosote sputtered and oily timbers burned. But that forest of bayonets was unstoppable. Men poured over the ramparts, while others scrambled up the platform from the other side.

Jubal's sword was in his hand, and he chopped at the nearest Yankee, cutting off the man's hand, then hacking his arm to the bone. Three more took the screaming soldier's place, and the rebel general struck hard enough to knock two bayonets to the side. The third lunged, and Jubal hissed with pain as the cold metal punctured his thigh. Leaning on his good leg, he stabbed his enemy through the heart.

The Yankee fell, but the weight of his heavy Springfield cruelly twisted in the wound. Jubal's leg collapsed as he tried to pull his sword back. He grunted as another bayonet pierced his ribs; suddenly it was impossible to breathe. His hand, strangely insubordinate, released the sword and dangled loosely. Blood bubbled into his mouth, rising from his guts, and then he knew he was dying.

The ground was surprisingly soft, and the noise of the battle faded to a pleasant hum. He watched another bayonet come down, piercing his chest, sticking him to the ground, and was vaguely surprised that he felt no pain. His vision went black, though he had the feeling his eyes were still open.

And then he had the strangest memory. . . . He recalled a ball in a grand plantation manor, the sight of a dazzling belle in a low-cut gown. They had danced, and she had clung to him, and the sensation of her creamy breasts, pressed tightly to his chest, was a memory he had vowed never to forget.

He was as confused and helpless as a newborn babe. His eyes registered astonishment as Juliay, naked, pulled back the quilt and rose to her knees. She knew what to do. . . . She reached out and took his genitals in her cupped hands. He stared in wonder, tried to touch her . . . gaped as his hands passed right through her hair, her flesh. Leaning closer, she bestowed a soft kiss, felt him harden in her gentle fingers. He writhed, disbelief mingling with delight on his face, and in moments she had the proof that joy had prevailed.

The magic continued to work, solidifying his presence here. Now he touched her head, caressed her soft hair, touched her breast. Then he could speak, but she touched a finger to his lips, denied his questions as she pulled him down beside her on the softness of the bearskin, beneath the warm embrace of the feathery quilt.

For a time she held him close, felt the comfort of his returning embrace as he lay wonderingly. His eyes remained open, looking with wonder upon her face, upon the three candles flaring brightly in the cave. When she reached over and touched him again, he seized her with a kind of desperation, a hunger that sent shivers of wonder through her body, for it had been long since a man had taken her like that.

She lay on her back and he rolled atop her, desperate. Their lips met, tongues dancing, alternately frantic and gentle. She rose to meet him, and her world grew bright and hot and magnificent; she held him close for long moments after their combined release.

A thought intruded. She remembered what this night would cost her. And she smiled wistfully, knowing that she didn't care.

"Where are we?" he asked drowsily.

"You are here, with me. . . . That is all you can know tonight. Tomorrow there will be time for questions and answers."

He shook his head and sat up, the quilt sliding down to his waist. His body was lean and sculpted, with broad shoulders and sturdy, muscular arms. He held out his hands, looked at his physique in astonishment. "By God, I was starved, thin as a rail. You could see each of my ribs. . . . What sorcery is this?"

"Tomorrow," she said.

"Very well . . ." he replied, lying down again. "If this is a dream, may my awakening be a long time hence." He leaned his head back, closed his eyes, and sighed deeply.

"And your sleeping need be delayed, as well," Juliay said, reaching for him with intimate fingers. "For the dream to become real, warrior, you must have me once more before the dawn. . . ."

13

Angels of War

Pebble'd pool,
Or blossom's pollen;
Salmon's spawn,
And love's caress;
Scandal rumored,
Violence rendered;
Linger long
Beyond the nest.

From the Tapestry of the Worldweaver
History of Time

"The dragon flies toward the Center," Belynda explained, as soon as Natac and Miradel reached the College. The warrior nodded, reaching for the satchel of maps he had brought, until something in the sage-ambassador's eye caused him to pause. "What happened?"

"The Hyaccan elves," she replied, tears welling. "Shahkamon is . . . *gone*. The monster pulled the town right off the precipice . . . all of it . . . everything fell into the canyon."

"The khan . . . ?" He couldn't ask the rest of the question, but Belynda's grim head shake confirmed his worst fears. "Janitha?"

"I don't know," replied the golden-haired elfwoman. "The town is no longer there, and if she was at home when the mon-

ster attacked, she is certainly dead. Whether or not she left
with the herders for the migration, I can't say."

"Does Sirien know?" Natac asked.

"Yes . . . she's with Owen, at the Willowfield. Roland was
going to meet her there. He was studying the Tapestry, but he
left the temple as soon as he heard."

"I'll go there at once," the warrior said, sickened at the
thought of Shahkamon's destruction. "Has Owen started to
muster the troops of the old regiments?"

"Yes . . . he's put out a call, though of course people have
been slow to respond. But I know Rawknuckle Barefist is
there, and Nistel has been gathering the gnomes. I don't know
how many goblins we'll have. Most of them have taken to living in the Midrock, since the war."

"Have you heard from Gallupper?"

"The messenger found him the same day and flew back to
report. Gallupper and his clan are coming here as fast as they
can travel."

"Good." Natac was thinking about the rolling batteries, the
wheeled, spring-powered bows of heavy steel that had been
designed by the dwarf Karkald during the war. These were the
only weapons he knew of that might have a chance of inflict-
ing a serious wound upon the monstrous serpent.

"Quilene has gone to the Lodespikes to convene with the
other enchantresses. She will bring as many of them as will
come back here, as soon as she can."

Natac nodded. He could only hope that the notoriously
suspicious and solitary enchantresses, masters of Nayvian
magic, would perceive the danger and rally to the defense of
Circle at Center. He turned to Miradel. "Can you go to the
Grove and take word to the druids? Ask Cillia and the others
to gather at the Willowfield. We'll make our plans there. And
send a message to Socrates, too. . . . I want to know if he can
make another balloon, just a single sphere, but something that
can get me up into the air."

"He was already here," the sage-ambassador said. "He anticipated your request and has the gnomes working on stitch-

ing up the silk. He also said he had something he needed to experiment with ... some kind of explosive, or bomb, that might be able to help."

"Good," Natac said. "We've got to do everything we can to get ready for this thing."

"And if it comes ... ?" Belynda couldn't finish the question as she and Miradel followed Natac out into the garden. He stopped at the gate and turned back.

"We'll kill it," he declared, hoping that he sounded determined and purposeful. But as he looked at the sky, the real, unanswerable question rose to the surface of his attention.

How?

THE wingless harpies had stung him many times with their flying darts, but Regillix Avatar was content that he savaged their nest with catastrophic impact. He had torn the very hives themselves from the walls of the great cliff and cast every such structure into the depths. The smooth plazas he had rent, so much so that his talons were still sore from the effort of ripping at this strange fundament.

Countless of the strange denizens had plunged downward as well, screaming and kicking and pathetically flailing about until they skipped off the precipitous slopes far below. He had seen enough of them to realize that they were, in fact, considerably different from harpies. One such had dared to stand and challenge the dragon. That one had worn a crown of gold and bore a golden staff in his hand. He strode to the very edge of a plaza, after Regillix had destroyed half the town, and raised his hands, speaking some squeaking sounds.

He had died with a swipe of one taloned foot, and seconds later, the plaza itself had been torn apart, sent as rubble into the depths. But even in the midst of the chaos, Regillix had known that no harpy would have dared to challenge him thus. Drawing on ancient legends of Nayve, he suspected that this place had been the lair of elves.

Finally, the dragon had plodded away from the ravaged

town, too tired and hungry to immediately fly. He came upon several creatures, larger than any beasts he had seen in this place, and brought down two of them with swift pounces. They were covered with shaggy brown fur, with four hoofed feet, and broad skulls from which sprouted a pair of long, pointed horns.

Once he tore away the pelt, he found the meat to be sweet, rich, and plentiful. Consuming both, he curled up in a niche between a pair of low hills, and finally he slept. Fatigue allowed him to slumber through several days, but eventually, after four or six or eight cycles of the sun—he was not exactly sure—he found the warmth of Lighten to be a discomfort. Groggily he opened his eyes and lifted his long neck from the coil of his serpentine body.

The day was indeed uncommonly hot, and he sniffed in irritation. Normally, when overwarmed by the sun, he would merely retreat to a lofty cloud summit, seeking shade from the brightness and warmth in the valleys. Here, however, even if a cloud would have supported him, that high vantage would merely bring him even closer to the sun.

A scent of moisture reached his nostrils, borne by the warm wind, and abruptly he felt his thirst. Slowly, regally, he rose and stretched, extending his legs, wings, neck, and tail, relishing the sense of vitality returning to his limbs. From this height he could see over the hills that had sheltered his grassy bower, and he caught a glimpse of a silvery reflection some good distance away.

Strange though it was compared to the misty lakes of his own world, he knew this was water. Loping up the hillside, he sprang from the crest and spread his wings, gliding just above the surface of the rolling ground. Almost immediately he passed over an encampment of people, two-legged beings running about in panic, pointing and shrieking at the sky. They were accompanied by many of the shaggy, horned beasts such as the dragon had recently eaten, as well as many small hoofed animals. The latter were sleek-furred and fast, and he saw several people riding on the backs of these mounts.

They could offer him no harm, for he flew by too fast for them to launch any stinging darts, and the dragon's thirst was more pressing to him than any desire to wreak further havoc. But it occurred to him that people might be a fairly populous denizen of this world, and they would bear watching. Only when he had flown far beyond this band did it occur to him that, perhaps, they had seen him land and had been approaching to attack while he slept.

The pull of the center was off to the side now, but the dragon didn't mind the detour. The more he discovered about this place, the more sinister and dangerous it seemed. He decided that he would drink, and hunt again if he had to, and show a little more caution as he continued toward the Center of Everything.

He came to rest in the shallows of a wide lake and found the waters to be very much to his liking. A mere sip of the rich liquid was enough to quench his thirst, whereas in the Overworld he would have spent hours soaring through the mists of a skylake. And the cooling effect on his belly, indeed over his whole body, was refreshing and remarkable. The plenitude of water was a miraculous delight, the first and only thing about this world that the serpent found actually preferable to Arcati.

For hours he lay immersed, his head and upper neck on the grassy shore, wings floating like massive lily pads, the rough scales from his spine and tail jutting like a string of islands above the glassy surface. Only when the sun began to recede toward Darken did he move, emerging onto the shore, buzzing his wings with an energetic hum to dry them off.

Again he took to the air, circling over the lake, climbing higher and higher above the rolling landscape. Again the sense of direction was strong, compelling him to fly toward a line of jagged hills in the darkening distance. He straightened, sniffed the night air, and made a mark for the Center of Everything.

IT started to rain after Darken, and the column of trolls plodded miserably through the mud, slipping and cursing, some clawing each other while others moaned piteously. Udderthud was a mile behind them, their ancient home now infested with shrieking, fire-spitting harpies. Roodcleaver slipped and fell facedown onto the gooey track, and Awfulbark seized her shoulder and hauled her roughly to her feet.

She sniffled loudly, wiping the mud from her face and looking around in despair. "Where to go?" she asked plaintively.

Many of the trolls, those who had been walking within earshot, shuffled to a halt and looked at Awfulbark through the murk. The rain fell in a heavy shower just now, spattering from the king's face, obscuring visibility into the distance.

"Yeah. Where?" asked a troll named Rumblegut, his tone belligerent.

"Where?" cried a third, shaking her head mournfully. "Where is there?"

The question was taken up by others, dozens, then scores, grumbling and muttering and crying. All of them seemed to be looking at Awfulbark, and he had the clear, dismaying understanding that he didn't know the answer. At the same time, a dim voice suggested to him that he shouldn't reveal his ignorance to the others.

"Follow me!" he said, hoping that he sounded more confident than he felt. "That where to go!"

He paused, scrutinizing the dull, woody faces around him. Water streamed from every nose, and the gorge bottom at their feet was starting to flow with the runoff of the storm.

"Follow King Awfulbark!" said Roodcleaver, looking at him with something shining in her black eyes, something that wasn't just the rain.

"Make way for king!" Rumblegut added, whacking several trolls out of the way. "Follow King Awfulbark!"

Roodcleaver gave him a push, and Awfulbark stumbled into the gap cleared by Rumblegut's blows. He started walking, trying to think, and found that the trolls in front of him were now shuffling to the sides, staring at him with unreadable expressions as he trudged past. The cries from behind followed him—"Make way for King!"—and he plodded along until there were no more trolls in front of him.

He had reached the head of the line, and when he continued, the other trolls scrambled to follow along, to stay as close behind him as possible. They moved with more spirit than before, and he vaguely understood that this was because they, for some reason, had placed their faith in him.

That thought made him very frightened, but he could do nothing besides continue on through the rain. He came to a low place in the trail, where the water had pooled atop a bed of sticky mud, and found himself wallowing. Kicking his way to the side of the pool, he skirted the water on the slope above the gorge bottom.

Almost immediately he realized that it was easier to walk here. There was no reason, after all, to muddle along in the riverbed, just because that's where the road had always been.

The realization was strangely liberating, so much so that Awfulbark turned his course up the hill, and the rest of the trolls followed. They reached the crest, and the file of miserable refugees followed along a broad, grassy ridge. The ground was much drier here, and almost immediately the rain eased back to a steady drizzle.

Yet when the king paused and listened, back in the distance he could still hear the screeching noise of the harpies, and he knew that he didn't have any idea what the trolls of Udderthud should do next.

THE Hyaccan ponies were capable of traveling great distances without rest, but never in her memory had Janitha known the sturdy steeds to make such a run as they had in the last three days. She and her fellow herders had dozed now and then in their saddles, and taken drink and food while they rode, but the valiant horses had not even had that respite. Instead, they had loped along at a steady, miles-devouring pace, through the hours of light and dark, bearing steadily along the path taken by the monstrous serpent.

The elfwoman herself, daughter of the khan, had barely closed her eyes during that same stretch. Her eyes had marked the horizon where the serpent had disappeared, and she understood that it flew, unerringly, toward the Center. In her breast burned a hatred such as she had never felt before, a fierce compulsion that drew her after the beast, filled her with such thirst for revenge that, for a few days, concerns such as food and drink faded into unimportant details.

But at last her endurance and that of her faithful horses compelled a halt. Skyrunner stumbled as he tried to step down the gentle bank before crossing yet another of the plains' meandering streams, and Janitha lurched forward, clutching the shaggy neck and pushing her feet in the stirrups to prevent a fall.

All around she saw the weariness in the faces of her companions, and the wobbling, unsteady gaits of the ponies. "We'll stop here for the night," she declared, even as the decision tore at her, for it thwarted the vengeance that, really, was the only thing that mattered.

"Lady Khandaughter?" It was Falri, speaking hesitantly, with unusual respect.

"Yes?"

"I know of a hunters' cache nearby, less than a mile up the stream. There we have stored crates of hedras and many spears, bows, and arrows. Shall I take a few of the elves, go there, and return with arms?"

"Good idea. Yes, please do so," Janitha said, surprised by the news. She had been determined to strike at the wicked serpent but had not as yet determined how that blow would be struck; now it seemed that arming themselves was a very good place to start.

The Hyaccan party numbered one hundred elves and some two hundred and thirty ponies. A few of the herders, the youngest dozen or so, had remained behind with the herd. Each of those elves had voiced loud objections to Janitha's plan—they wanted vengeance, too—and in the end she had been forced to state her decision as an order.

"This herd represents all that is left of our possessions, our

prosperity," she pointed out. "You will remain here to watch
over the hyac, to keep them together so that when we return,
we have a chance of starting over."

"But how will you avenge your father?" one had asked, a
youth nearing maturity, who clutched his hunting bow and objected loudly. "And we deserve the chance to ride with you!"

"No! You will do as I say," Janitha retorted, and the younger
elves had grudgingly acceded. In return, she had agreed that
they could direct the migrating herd toward the Center, inso-
far as possible. In that way they could at least stay on the trail
of the riders, the elves who rode for vengeance against the
monstrous dragon.

Finally, here, they rested. Falri, Rosto, and a dozen young
men returned within two hours, laden with crates of weapons
and food. Janitha was content, for now, to let her war party
sleep. Tomorrow, when they resumed the ride, there would be
time enough to make a plan.

THE massive steel doors to the arsenal were too heavy for any
small group of people to move, and they stood within a narrow, arched tunnel that was too narrow to allow access to a
larger group. They were secured by no lock, no barrier other
than their great weight, but for centuries this had proven ade-
quate to keep any unwanted intruders away.

Every ten or twenty years, Natac, Owen, and a group of
their veterans had entered the armory to inspect the weapons
stored there. They had oiled the great springs of the batteries,
greased the wheels, rasped away any developing patches of
rust. On those occasions, as now, they had employed the help
of powerful druidic magic to part the doors.

It was Cillia and Roland who stood before the twin portals.
Each of the druids held a short, metal rod that was highly
magnetic. Placing one of these magnets against the edge of
each door, the druids stood side by side, close enough so that
the reverse polarity of the metal rods caused a strong repul-
sion. Natac watched, amazed as ever, as with the catalyst of

druid magic this polarity infused the large, steel doors. Slowly, propelled by the antithetical magnetism, the two great slabs rumbled apart.

An hour later, the first of the rolling batteries was trundled into the daylight, hauled by Rawknuckle Barefist, who had the traces over his broad shoulders. The giant turned back to the gaping doorway, while Natac and Owen started looking over the weapon with critical eyes.

"Quite a layer of dust she's gathered," observed the Viking, sweeping away a cloud of grit that had settled atop the great spring.

"But I think the oil has sealed the metal," Natac noted. "Sure, it's a mess, but I don't think it's gotten rusty."

"Do you think . . . can it be trained to shoot up into the air?" questioned a voice from behind the two warriors. Natac turned to see Sirien Saramayd, regarding him with a narrow, determined expression. Her eyes remained red-rimmed, as they had been since she had learned of her homeland's destruction, but her voice and her hands were steady.

"We might need to prepare some ramps," Natac said, eyeing the weapon critically. Designed as a battlefield missile weapon, for casting explosive spheres or powerful, steel-headed bolts against an enemy formation or strong point, the battery could be raised to no more than a forty-five-degree elevation. "It looks like we can alter the sighting screws enough to shoot a little higher, but that won't help if the target is right overhead."

"How many of them do we have?" asked the elfmaid.

"There are a dozen of them," replied the warrior. "Galluper's company used them in three sections of four apiece."

"And here comes our centaur gunnery master," said Owen, clapping Natac on the shoulder and pointing across the Willowfield, near the terminus of the Highway of Wood. Tiny figures came galloping into view, feathered hooves drumming across the smooth, grassy turf. At first indistinguishable from riders mounted on horseback, very soon the centaurs raced into clearer view.

Each was marked by the head, arms, and torso of a strapping man, with bearded faces, long, flowing hair, and chests like sinewy barrels. At the waist, these human forms merged into the forequarters of large horses, and these hoofed bodies hurried along with long, cantering strides.

"Ho, friend Natac!" cried the leader of the centaurs, hauling back to rear before the warrior. "I, Gallupper, have heard the summons of my general! My company has ridden like the wind to meet you here!"

"Many thanks, from all the peoples of the Center," replied Natac. "As you can see, we're preparing for the worst." He regarded the faithful centaur with affection. Gallupper had been a mere stripling when first he had gone to war, and the interceding centuries had aged him into a powerful stallion. His beard was rich and brown, and a mane of curling hair cascaded over his shoulders to blow about in the wind. He nodded his head as his forehoof pawed the turf, and already the warrior felt encouraged.

"Aye, these old shooters have held up pretty well," Gallupper noted, frowning as he looked over the two batteries that had been trundled into the open. "Here, good Rawknuckle," he said to the giant. "Let my lads do the work of bringing the rest of them out."

"Good enough," said the giant, whose head rose to about the same height as the centaurs'. He regarded the equine bodies with appreciation. "Never did I understand how much weight you were pulling around when you ran into position during the fray."

The centaur chuckled, and he directed a dozen of his companions into the arsenal. Almost immediately his expression darkened again, and he looked at Natac with frank apprehension. "The summons from the faerie was brief. Can you tell me the nature of this attacker?"

The warrior described everything they had learned of the dragon, from its appearance over the Mountains of Moonscape, to the attack on Shahkamon, and the fact that it had last been observed flying a course almost directly toward the Center.

"Belynda saw it fly a great distance and then set down in a forest near the fringes of the Ringhills. Perhaps it needs to eat and rest, but we have to assume that it will soon resume its flight."

"And that could bring it here as soon as tomorrow?"

"It's possible," Natac agreed. "A few more days than that, seems likely."

"But dragons are not creatures of Nayve," pressed the centaur. "Do you know how it came to be here?"

"Our best guess is this tumult, a great storm in the direction neither metal nor wood. We saw the thing, like a wall of cloud reaching into the highest vault of the skies, dark and forbidding. The dragon seemed to come right out of it."

"Indeed," Roland said, the druid coming to join them. "I consulted the Tapestry of the Worldweaver to see what I could learn about these serpents. At the same time, I saw a great tangle of threads, mingling the Fourth and Sixth Circles in the direction of null. It seems likely to be the avenue the dragon used in coming to Nayve."

"Could you learn anything about the likely weaknesses of such creatures? Is there anything we could exploit in battle?" wondered Natac.

The druid's grim expression presaged his discouraging answer. "The Tapestry was imprecise, at best. It seems that the Sixth Circle is a more ethereal place than Nayve, a trait that carries into the details I could glean about the denizens of the Overworld. There was little in the way of specifics."

"Tell us what you can," encouraged Natac. Owen, Gallupper, Sirien, and Rawknuckle all listened attentively as the druid recounted his observations.

"Dragons, for the most part, like to remain aloof from the affairs of the Seven Circles. They can live, apparently, just about forever, and they keep growing for every year of their lives. The older they get, the more they like to sleep. It seems that they're likely to hibernate for years, even decades, at a time. The only references I could find place them on the Sixth Circle, which they call Arcati.

"You know about their strength, and size . . . and flight. I found reference to dragons with breath of fire, though in a context that sounded almost legendary . . . as if that happened thousands of years ago. And these are more than mere powerful brutes. A dragon may be five thousand years old, yet he will still remember in crystalline clarity details of his youthful existence. They are reputed to be patient and wise.

"But another thing," Roland continued, "and these tidings are no more encouraging than the other: Those harpies that attacked when Natac was battling the trolls . . . they, too, are native to the Overworld and have never been known to dwell in Nayve."

"Lending credence to the idea that this Chaos Storm is somehow providing a conduit between the two worlds," Natac said. "Do dragons have a warlike history?"

"Not so far as I could tell," the druid replied. "Indeed, they are rather portrayed as the peacekeepers of the Sixth Circle. They are held in lordly esteem by the griffons, the pegasi, and the angels. Everyone in Arcati, from the furry little creatures called batfrey to the lofty cloud giants themselves, treat the dragons as the sages and adjudicators of their world. Everyone but the harpies, I should say. . . . Those are universally reviled, by all accounts the scourge of that world."

"And now, perhaps, ours," Natac muttered. "But they must be considered a secondary danger to this dragon."

"Do we have other allies mustering to the Center?" asked Gallupper.

Belynda spoke up, emerging from the crowd of onlookers. "I have word from Tamarwind Trak. He has marched from Argentian with five thousands elves, coming here. It will take them weeks, of course, but he wanted me to tell you that he is on the way."

"That *is* good news," Natac acknowledged. "And we have the regiments from the city re-forming in their old ranks, lots of elves, and some of the gnomes, too."

"Quilene has communicated with the enchantresses," Belynda continued. "They are watching the situation, discussing courses of action."

Natac looked across the field to the dazzling waters of the lake. His view was clear, far in the direction that was neither metal nor wood, and he could see the horizon of the Ringhills, rolling and tumbling beyond the lake.

Somewhere, from there, an implacable enemy was approaching. And he didn't know what to do.

JULIAY awakened and was immediately aware of his naked body next to hers. Jubal's breathing was gentle and deep; clearly he still slept. She remembered everything, each detail a thing to be cherished, now, until the end of her days.

And with that, her thoughts turned to the price of the spell, the knowledge that she had given up her youth, even her immortality, in order to work the magic of the summoning. She remembered the horror she had felt when she had first seen Miradel, after her casting: The white hair, the wrinkled face and posture stooped by age and weariness had seemed like a monstrously unfair cost. Indeed, she had hated Natac at first, for she could not help but blame him for her friend's sudden aging.

All of those effects, she had learned, had occurred even before the druidess awakened from the night of the summoning. Of course, the matter of that sacrifice was a little different in her case. Alone in the mountains, without food, she had already accepted that she had little chance of surviving. Perhaps she had merely brought Jubal here to suffer the same fate . . . but the alternative was his ending, on the enemy's bayonet, in the trenches of Petersburg. Here, he would have a chance. Perhaps he would even be able to help her reach safety, if her newly withered flesh had the strength to follow him out of the mountains.

Strangely, she didn't feel any weaker than she had been the day before. She held her hands to her belly, unwilling to look at the skin that, overnight, must certainly have become blotched and wrinkled with age. She thought, with a sense of dread, about Jubal's reaction. Would he be horrified? Repulsed? Almost certainly both, of course, but what would he do? From watching him in the Seventh Circle, she knew he was a good man, fair and brave, but nothing could predict a matter such as this.

She decided to move away from the bedroll. It would be awkward, and difficult in any event, but at least she would not be lying beside him, their naked flesh pressed together. Slowly, she sat up, rather surprised that the aches that she had anticipated did not seem to plague her limbs.

Drawing a breath, she lifted her hands, looked in wonder at fingers that were as smooth and supple—and young!—as they had been the night before. She touched her chest, feeling the firmness, the full breasts of a young woman. Finally, she sat up in agitation, and as the quilt fell away from her naked body, she saw that she looked like the same person who had fallen asleep. With trembling fingers she lifted her mirror, looked back at herself with a face that was smooth, unlined, youthful. It was true: She hadn't aged!

"But . . . how?" She felt a pang of fear. Could the effect be delayed? Would she age when she rose, when she ate or drank? Perhaps . . . but again, that was not how it had happened with Miradel.

Last night, when she had briefly contemplated the spell, the decision had been easy: She would willingly make the sacrifice for this warrior. She accepted that fate as the cost of her choice, the decision that was hers alone to make. Now, however, when her requisite sacrifice seemed unaccountably delayed, she was suddenly terrified that the magic would take effect without warning, withering her while she writhed in misery.

She looked down, saw that his eyes were open. His whiskers had begun to show, darkening the previously smooth skin of his cheeks and chin. His expression was full of wonder, but at once he smiled, sat up, and took her in his long arms. She felt strangely paralyzed, as though she should pull away but was unable to make herself move.

"Questions," he said. "Last night, you said they must wait

for the morrow. And indeed, fair lady, you drove all such thoughts from my mind. But I must know: Where am I, and how did I come here? Can this be the Purgatory before my journey to Hell? And if it is, how cruel a God to show me such a glimpse of heavenly charms!"

Gently, she broke from his embrace, held him at arm's length, and met his curious, bemused gaze. "You have learned many falsehoods, common to humans, but untrue. There is no Hell, nor Heaven, nor Purgatory," she began. She told him of the Goddess Worldweaver, of the Center of Everything, and of druids who were brought here by the goddess, rewarded for lives and labors lived on the Seventh Circle. "I once dwelled on Earth . . . in a place called Provence, in the country of France, nearly a thousand years before your time," she said. "Until the goddess brought me to Nayve."

"And you have lived here, as a young woman, since then?" asked Jubal. "D'you mean to say you're immortal?"

She smiled wryly. "Immortal? Hardly. I fully expect to die, eventually. Indeed, that is one reason I dared to bring you here." She commenced an explanation of their circumstances, the forlorn mountain range, the deadly harpies and dragon, the loss of her brave companions. She did not, for now, mention the price she had expected to pay for casting the spell. "So it may be that I have only postponed your fate, for I cannot promise you survival here."

"I like my chances," said the warrior. His hand cupped her breast, and she felt a thrill of remembered pleasure. "And I reckon I'll have me a look around, before too long. But first, there's something else. . . ."

She saw that proof of that other thing as the quilt lying over his lap suddenly stirred. The spell was over, and her fears were forgotten as she reached for him, fell into him. His urgency matched her own, and in moments they were entwined and alive upon the bearskin, smooth and soft on the rocky ground.

14

Arkan Pass

Hold drum,
March done,
Eat, sleep, fyre.

Bang gun,
Blind run,
Blood, slay, dire.

Marching Chant of Seer Army

In King Lightbringer's Army, the heavy infantry was the anvil upon which all other formations struck. As such, the sturdy dwarves of the "heavies" were armored in steel, from caps to cuirasses, hauberks to greaves. Each dwarf wore gauntlets of heavy leather, with steel reinforcements for the back of the hand and each finger, and boots with metal cleats and armored uppers. They were trained to fight in close order, forming a wall of shields against any attack.

Most of the dwarves were armed with a pair of short spears, usually worn on the back, and a short, double-edged sword good for slashing or stabbing. A few of the heavies, about five per company of one hundred, were called Axers. They carried no shields and were armed with long-hafted battle axes, weapons of ancient enchantment and keen edge, wielded with skill and mastery. The Axers formed the corners and linchpins in the battle line and would frequently stride in the lead when the time came to advance.

Karkald was given command of a company that had lost its captain to a broken leg when he had fallen from the high road. These dwarves, the Fifth Company of the III Heavy Infantry Regiment, regarded him with sullen and angry eyes as he caught up to them in the line of march, huffing and sweat-covered from his haste. He bore the orders signed by General Paternak, giving him command, and he presented these to the sergeant, Gaynroc.

"Welcome to the Third, Captain," grunted that doughty veteran, offering a grudging salute while he inspected Karkald from beneath the low-fitted brim of his steel cap. Gaynroc was large and broad for a dwarf, with a body like a barrel and bristling brows that seemed locked in a glower of displeasure.

"Thanks. I'm sorry about Captain Swordmender."

Gaynroc offered a shrug, suggesting that the previous captain's fall was not a matter of great concern to him, one way or another. He stomped his foot and barked at the company, which was shuffling along, two abreast, in the midst of the army column.

"Line up, you toads! This is Captain Karkald, and he's coming along to look you over!"

The armored dwarves made a halfhearted attempt to dress their ranks, as Karkald strode past on the side of the road. He knew they were inspecting him as much as the other way around, and he felt strangely exposed to their sight. His leather shirt and breeches, the soft boots rising almost to his knees, were no burden at all compared to the steel carried by the lowliest footman of the heavies.

"Sergeant Gaynroc!"

"Cap'n?" The dwarf was right behind him, still glowering. Karkald wondered, perhaps, if that was just his natural expression.

"Can you see that I get an issue of equipment at tonight's bivouac? I'm going to be living in this neighborhood. Might as well dress up like a tin can."

"Aye, sir. Our extras is strapped onto the back of the battery wagons, just ahead. I'll see you outfitted proper."

Karkald held his place at the head of the company for the rest of the cycle's march. He hoped that one of the Rockriders would come by. He felt concern for his old company, guilt for abandoning men he had commanded for decades. He longed for news of his company, but apparently the new captain, Marshal Nayfal, was keeping the men on very short leashes. For the rest of that cycle, there was no sign of any of the ferr'ells coming as far forward as the heavies.

When next they broke camp, the general ordered several coolfyre beacons illuminated, and the Seers saw that the cliff wall to the right, the boundary of the Underworld, was split by a great gap in the massive precipice.

"This is Arkan Pass," declared General Paternak, as he stood, brightly lit on a pinnacle of stone, speaking to his assembled army. "I intend to march right through the Slatemont. When we come down on the shore of the Oilsea, we will deploy for attack and take the enemy in a single, sweeping assault. Now, brave dwarves, we fight!"

Karkald, good soldier that he was, joined in the cheer raised by his company and the rest of the army. To his ear, the hurrahs sounded a little hollow, and he was not surprised. No doubt many others, like himself, were startled and a little concerned by the general's plan.

These misgivings lingered as the III Heavy Infantry Regiment started to move, filing into place behind the I Heavy, preceded in turn by many companies of light infantry, as well as skirmishers armed with deadly crossbows. The army found entrance to Arkan Pass by marching up a long, ramplike slope of debris, rubble that had spilled from the lofty pass over the course of millennia. The stones skittered and slid underfoot, drawing curses from the armored troops. Karkald was astonished by how much he was sweating inside the confines of his metal plate.

A flare brightened the air, arcing high and casting coolfyre through the gap of the Arkan Pass, just ahead and above.

Strangely, the illumination spilling so brightly from the narrow notch only seemed to highlight the constricted nature of the passage. Niches, cracks, and ledges scored the walls on both sides, with plenty of shadowy alcoves where the light didn't reach—and where numerous enemies could lurk, completely safe from observation.

Watching in alarm, Karkald saw the first light company disperse and move into the pass at a trot. He almost groaned aloud. How could Paternak be so goddess cursed blind to the uses of the Rockriders? In a few minutes, the mounted dwarves could have explored the passage for miles, poking into crevasses on the wall, even investigating cracks in the ceiling. The foot troops, nimble and well-trained as they were, could only hope to scout a fraction of the terrain.

Yet this was the tactic the Seers had employed for centuries, so this was the tactic Paternak would employ today. Karkald knew the folly of even trying to speak to the army commander, but he found himself stomping his feet in his anger. He noticed Gaynroc marching beside him and casting an interested eye in his captain's direction.

"D'you smell a trap, sir?" asked the grizzled sergeant.

Only then did Karkald sense the real nature of his agitation. He looked at the looming gate of the pass, twin cliffs of black rock rising, swelling outward to merge into the mouth of a lightless hole. "Yes . . . in fact, I do."

Gaynroc sniffed, a sound of agreement. "If you don't mind me sayin', I'm not too fond of this close-in kinda place. Too many hiding places, too nearby."

"We'd best keep our eyes open and our swords sharp," Karkald noted.

He was distracted by sounds of movement coming along the path behind, claws skittering over loose rock. The familiar musk of the ferr'ells reached his nose before he turned around to see Nayfal, on a sullen, snarling mount, leading the column of Rockriders in single file.

The marshal cast a sneer in Karkald's direction as he rode

by, then whirled in his saddle as the rest of the file came up. "Eyes front!" he snapped.

Many of the dwarves ignored the marshal, turning a sympathetic eye toward Karkald. It was with a heavy heart that the captain turned his own face away, denying the men this chance to get into trouble with their new commander. For a moment, at least, he hoped that Paternak was sending the Rockriders ahead to scout the narrow passage, but even that was denied when the regiment of ferr'ell-mounted dwarves merely went into closed ranks near the front of the column.

Soon the cavalry and the leading light infantry had vanished into the pass, and a few minutes later, Karkald saw the enclosing walls looming before him. "We'll have to narrow the ranks," he observed, eyeing the twisting pathway. "Let's make it six abreast."

"Dress that column!" Gaynroc ordered, and the dwarves of the heavy infantry smoothly obeyed. "Sixes wide, lads!"

Now it was more of a snake than a series of block, but the First Legion of the Army of Axial continued forward at a fast march. The tromp of thousands of boots formed a soft, dull background, a *crunch, crunch, crunch* of measured footsteps. More flares drove back the darkness, and Karkald saw that the gorge of the Arkan Pass twisted and wound through the Slatemont, a serpentine series of bends that prevented observation for more than a quarter mile or so before them.

He wondered where General Paternak was, and if the army commander was feeling the same disquiet that had settled like a cloying blanket over Karkald's shoulders. A look at Gaynroc's frowning face indicated that the sergeant, like his captain, wanted nothing to do with this shortcut. But then, Paternak hadn't bothered to ask their opinion.

The braying sound of a battle horn suddenly rang through the deep, and it was almost with a sense of relief that Karkald knew the enemy had been seen. Moments later, he heard a clatter of falling rock, and then the ringing clash of steel—the sound clear proof that many blades were bashing against the armor of a foe. The column continued forward, dwarves instinctively picking up the pace, moving closer to the sounds of strife.

"Eyes up, men! Have a care now," Karkald barked.

But almost immediately the company before them slowed and halted, and Karkald's men had no choice but to do the same. The steep walls, bases lined with rubble, prevented any kind of deployment, so the captain could only hope that the troops at the head of the column would be able to deal with the resistance. A glance to the rear showed that the gates of the pass were already out of sight behind them—a fact that surprised Karkald, for he hadn't realized they had advanced so far into the narrow cut.

Then, as if to underline his surprise with dismay, the clash of battle sounded from the rear of the column as well. He needed no further evidence to convince him that they had marched into a trap.

"Backs to the center!" he called. "Face flanks, and keep your eyes open!"

Immediately, the dwarves of the Fifth Company, III Regiment, pivoted in response to the order, three ranks turning to the right and the other three turning to the left, so that all were facing outward from the center of the trail. Shields were up and swords were drawn, while the axemen moved to the fore of each line. The stone walls rose before them, not as cliffs, but as steep slopes strewn with many broken rocks. More flares sparked into light, but even the multitude of lights couldn't penetrate the numerous shadows. Karkald strained his eyes, seeking any sign of Delver activity.

Something moved, but at first his gaze passed it by; it was far too large to be one of the Unmirrored. Then stones clattered downward, and his attention was drawn like steel to a magnet. Massive, stout limbs pushed the rocks out of the way, revealing a dark, armored figure looming twenty or thirty feet high. It was manlike, with two mighty legs that kicked forward to carry the great body free from the niche where it had been concealed. The great metal helm had a single hole where the face should be, and within that gap, red light reflected, like the flare of a churning furnace.

Though manlike, this thing was not a man . . . it was not even a creature of flesh. Karkald could see the rivets connecting the iron plates that seemed to form the being's "skin." The head was the size of a large barrel, set atop broad, metallic shoulders, and it had two arms terminating in fists of articulated steel. A possible explanation darted through the Seer's mind: Could this be a giant of unprecedented girth, somehow encased in a suit of black iron?

One of those fists crunched into an obstructing shelf of rock, shattering the hard granite into a thousand shards, and Karkald knew this was a thing far exceeding mortal strength. A platoon of the Fourth Company, just in front of his own men, charged the giant, and one massive foot kicked through the armored dwarves, scattering them like toys, crushing armor plate and shattering flesh.

"Form shield wall!" cried Karkald, more out of instinct and training than from any real hope in the tactic. His company responded with precision, each man's shield protecting himself and the gap to his left. A volley of crossbow bolts flashed through the air, clattered against the giant's armored breast, and bounced harmlessly away. Swords flashed as it took a step closer, and then with another step, it planted a great foot right in the middle of the line.

Karkald heard the screams of doomed dwarves, was horrified by the sight of three men vanishing under the cleated boot, crushed like bugs under unspeakable power. Swords chipped and hacked against the iron, but even when they scored the surface, they couldn't penetrate the heavy plate.

More lights flashed, before and behind, and from his position, Karkald saw at least a dozen of the metallic giants. Each strode forward with lethal force, kicking the tightly packed Seer army into disarray. An Axer rushed in, gouged at the iron ankle, and his weapon scored a deep gash in the metal plate.

The monster simply kicked hard and sent the brave dwarf smashing into the wall of the pass. Others advanced to the right and left, crushing, killing.

And there was nothing the dwarves could do to stop them.

FAR away, shadows lingered across the bastion of Karlath-Fayd. The sun was low across the Worldsea; Nayve lay under the fullness of midday Lighten. Precious little of that life-giving warmth reached across the water into the murky realm of Loamar.

But Loamar had no need of life-giving warmth, for Loamar, of course, was the realm of death. Within his great citadel, the Deathlord was insulated even from the little energy that found its way into his land. His thoughts and his powers were turned elsewhere now, reaching low, through the sunless depths of the Midrock, toward one of his faithful allies—an ally who, as yet, remained unaware of the distant master he served.

The Deathlord sat upon his grisly throne, and his will was a force, unseen but potent, that stretched from the Fifth Circle, sank through the depths of the Worldsea, and came at last to the talisman of the one who was summoned.

"THE Seers entered the trap, and the golems have attacked as planned," reported the breathless scout. The Delver lay face-down on the cavern floor, in the position he had flung himself as soon as he had reached Zystyl's position in the center of the camp of the army.

Zystyl snorted, a sound of pure delight. He and his troops were in commanding positions upon the heights surrounding Axial, but the news from the distant Slatemont had been carried to the scout through the pulsing of shade-magic; he knew that the message had been sent but a few minutes before.

He reached for Jarristal, knowing that she was a foot away to his right, and his hand found the pleasing narrowness of her waist. Her own excitement was a palapable emotion, hot across the skin of his body, and for a moment he toyed with the notion of a halt, an interlude for the two of them away from the press of twenty thousand blind dwarves.

But duty prevailed. He traced her flesh with a firm grasp and mentally projected his intentions for their later—but not too much later—tryst. Now it was time to make plans, to put the army into motion, commencing the attack upon the hated capital of the hated Seers, the offensive that he had spent three centuries preparing. . . .

Yet now, strangely, he hesitated.

Unusual doubts began to assail him. Was it possible that he had been tricked, that the Seers had maintained a great force in reserve, were even now waiting for the assault so they could smash the Delver army for once and for all? Or was it that the prize, the city of light and gold and fire, was not the cherished objective he had long believed it to be? Indeed, what use had he and his people for the kinds of treasures that were there for the taking?

And then his Hurtstone flared, hot pleasure penetrating, shivering through his flesh. He wrapped both hands around the precious gem, elated that, again, it had warmed in his presence. With an inaudible sigh, he held perfectly still, savoring the delight.

"Do you have orders, my General?" asked Jarristal, verbalizing the question because, for the moment, Zystyl's mental communication had been fogged by the ecstasy that had suddenly beset him. His fingers remained wrapped around the stone, holding tightly, and nothing else mattered very much.

"We will pull three of our four armies back from the city and form them on the Plain of Magma. There we will make ready for a march . . . no, an invasion." Yes, now he began to understand! He needed them there, together, concentrated into a close circle . . . sixty thousand dwarves, gathered around Zystyl. . . .

Around his Hurtstone.

"But . . ." Jarristal bit back her words as Zystyl's anger,

never far from the surface, rose as a tangible wave. "Yes, lord, it shall be as you command."

"Good," Zystyl said, touching her with a wave of affection, a reward for her swift compliance. He felt her pleasure at the mental touch, knew that she still belonged to him.

Then he turned his thoughts forward and upward. Such a great movement of his army would not be accomplished with ease; there were logistics to resolve, routes to plan, diversions to maintain. Yet, as the fervor for the onslaught rose inside of him like steam brought from a quick boil, he knew that he wanted nothing so much as that great gathering of Delver numbers.

A thunderous crash echoed through the Arkan Pass, and the air filled with such a cloud of dust that the coolfyre flares vanished in the murk. Karkald felt the ground shake and heard screams of pain, the sickening crunch of breaking bones, and he knew one of the monstrous attackers had crushed more of his men.

"Fall back!" he cried, though there was precious little room to move.

"Back, you apes!" roared Sergeant Gaynroc, his voice rumbling above the level of the din. "Up the hill with you!"

Karkald tripped over a rock and felt a strong hand pull him back to his feet. "This way, sir," said the doughty Gaynroc, lifting him onto a flat-topped boulder. Some of the dust settled, and the Fifth Company was coming into view, armored veterans following the command, moving onto the rough slope that rose from the floor of the pass, retreating from the iron monster.

He heard the twang of a powerful spring, and immediately the narrow gorge brightened by an explosion of bright light. One of the batteries had swung into action behind them, casting a spray of metallic shot against one of the steel-plated giants. Magnesium flared into white heat, and the monstrous attacker staggered backward, pounding at the fire with mighty blows of its iron fist. A clanging noise, a cacophony of monstrous gongs, resonated through the air, squeezing Karkald's eardrums with physical pressure. The giant toppled, flailing, into the midst of a Seer company, crushing a dozen or more dwarves as it flailed, finally weakened, and lay still.

But another of the giants had moved in reaction to the danger. The huge brute reached down and seized the wheeled gun in both of its hands. Karkald saw the fists close like massive pinchers, and the frame of the battery crumpled like tin. The wheels, bent and mangled, tumbled to the ground, and then the hulking beast hurled the wreckage into the crew, the artillerymen who had taken shelter in the loose rubble of the floor. They vanished in an inferno of killing heat as ammunition exploded.

The fireball was hot enough to kill dwarves a hundred feet away, and Karkald felt his brows and beard singe from the pure heat. He threw himself onto the rough ground as the blast tore through the confined space. Rocks tore free from the cliffs, and the lumbering giant nearby was knocked down by the force. A sluice of debris tumbled past, crushing a half dozen fighters of the Fifth Company and half burying the monster.

"Take it!" cried Karkald, lifting his head, seeing the opportunity. The monster flailed with a free hand, trying to shift a slab of rock that pinned its other side. "Use fire, steel—anything!"

He was skidding down from the rocky slope, his hammer in his hand. He saw the hinged flange on the shoulder, where that arm moved to gain purchase on the slab, and he put all of his strength into a precise blow. Steel rang on iron, and the flange twisted, angled hard enough to prevent the creature from drawing back the metal limb to its full extent. Delivering a series of rapid blows, he bent the metal farther, pinning the arm tightly against the ground.

Other dwarves of III Regiment rushed to join. One stuck a flare into the single opening on the giant's metal face, and immediately fire spurted from the hole. The monster kicked like a physical being, smoke and green, vile-smelling vapor pouring from the opening. Other Seers stuck swords into the gaps of the creature's plated surface, or, like Karkald, set upon hinges and joints with crushing blows of hammer and axe.

Whether it was the fire or the blows that finished it off, the metal giant suddenly became rigid and utterly still. Smoke still poured from the hole, brightened by flames that outlined the dark circle of a metal maw—some material even stronger than steel, for the ring neither darkened nor melted under the furious assault of white heat.

Karkald looked around. Still more of the giants stalked through the dying army, kicking and crushing. Here one leaned forward, swiping with a blade-studded hand to cut down a dwarf climbing the wall. Another dropped to its knees and then lay flat, crushing a dozen dwarves before quickly pushing itself upward and striding on.

To the rear, the artillery section was a shambles, ammunition boiling and exploding, noxious smoke rising to fill the upper sections of the pass, heat so intense that soft rock turned to liquid on the walls, and the air quickly reached the temperature of a hot oven.

"This way," cried Karkald, knowing that any chance of survival meant first escaping from that lethal fire. He and Gaynroc gathered the pathetic remnant of his company, as well as survivors from the units before and behind, both of which had lost their captains. Climbing as high as they could on the sloping rubble at the base of the cliff, they moved farther into the pass.

Karkald was appalled at the carnage on the floor of the narrow gorge. The corpses of the heavy infantry were all but unrecognizeable, a gory tangle of flattened armor, grisly bone, and slick, bloody flesh. Here and there the wounded moaned in the midst of the chaos. One strapping warrior crawled along, trailing legs that had been flattened to pulp. Another was not visibly wounded, but he lay on the ground choking and gurgling, spitting up a torrent of black blood.

The giants, having completed their butchery, were moving

forward along the Arkan Pass, traveling in the same direction that the army had been marching. Karkald and his men were at the tail end of this column, which included at least a dozen monstrous figures, and possibly—probably!—many more, unseen beyond the bends of the passageway.

Indeed, as they moved along, they saw that the light infantry had been similarly mangled. They found one more fallen giant, lying still and spewing smoke out of every crease in the plate armor, amid more than a hundred broken, bleeding dwarves.

Next they came upon a ferr'ell. The beast was hissing and clawing with its foreclaws, struggling to lift itself, though its back was clearly broken. The rider, still in the saddle, had been crushed, and with dull horror Karkald looked at the brutally twisted face and recognized Darmant, a young recruit he had personally welcomed to the regiment.

The ferr'ell, brown flanks slicked with blood, snorted and snapped. Karkald saw the creature's pain in its bright eyes, and his own misery was reflected there. With a grimace, tears staining his eyes, he drew his sword and slashed the steed through the throat, ending its pain.

The next few minutes were a nightmare for Karkald as he led the survivors through the carnage of his Rockriders. They had fought well—here, two of the giants had been pulled down, burned and smashed into ruin—but they had paid a terrible price. The cliffs on both sides showed gouges, where the ferr'ells had climbed and the giants had pulled them down. Dozens of the loyal mounts were dead, and most of these still had the corpses of their riders strapped into the saddle.

One of the giants looked as though it had lost its arm to some unimaginable force, but moments later, they located the limb across the pass, where it had smashed into two Rockriders and killed both mounts and both dwarves. "Like it shot it off, some kind of monster crossbow bolt," growled Gaynroc.

A few more of the beasts were cruelly wounded, and these the dwarves put out of their misery as mercifully as possible. A few injured dwarves they found as well, and those who could walk joined the shambling ranks of the survivors, while the rest were made as comfortable as possible and then, at least for now, left behind.

Karkald kept his group just in sight of the last of the tromping giants. The creatures seemed to take no interest in anything that might be happening behind, but still the dwarves moved as cautiously as they could. They found that they had to trot, however, and sometimes break into a full-out run, just to keep the monsters in view.

Finally they reached the end of the pass, and here the giants filed down from the narrow gap and gathered on the shore of the Oilsea, the swath of thick black liquid that marked the far border of the Underworld in the direction that was neither metal nor wood. Spots of brightness flared and faded across the sea, flames rising from bubbling whirlpools or shooting upward from churning currents.

Carefully, Karkald and the surviving dwarves, several hundred in number, came after. Ordering his men to take shelter across the broken ground, the captain and Gaynroc together made their way to a low promontory, where they could overlook the shore. The gouts of fire spouted brightly across the sea, providing sporadic, reddish illumination. The air was thick with smoke, acrid to breathe, leaving a film of soot on tongue and lips.

"I count thirty of them," Gaynroc whispered after a few moments' observation.

Karkald was about to reply in agreement when a dull tremor shook the ground upon which he knelt. He grunted in shock and felt the convulsion grow much stronger, a quake rumbling through the fundament of the cosmos. Shouts of alarm, even panic, rose from dwarves shaken by this rare, unnatural phenomenon. In the next instant, it seemed as though the cliffs of the Arkan Pass, the ceiling of the First Circle—indeed, the whole of all existence—were collapsing into a pile of rubble.

And his dwarves were going to be on the bottom.

15

Elven Riders

Shahkamon,
Living ledge,
Bountiful home
On world's end.

Yawning chasm,
Fatal deep;
Ere the darken,
Lives will keep.

Speedy hooves
And lethal hearts;
Spears a-glimmer,
Elves depart

O'er the prairie,
Through the sky,
Ride to vengeance,
Wyrm must die.

From *The Ballad of Janitha Khandaughter*
by Sirien Saramayd

Juliay felt his gaze upon her, and she opened her eyes and smiled languidly. He was sitting up in the little cave, and the light of day was still streaming through the cracks in the stony ceiling. The bearskin was a soft blanket underneath her nakedness, and she didn't care that the quilt had been pulled away. Instead, she spread her arms in a gesture of clear invitation.

Only then did she see the frown upon his face, sense the uncertainty that made him hesitate.

"What is it?" she asked, sitting up, pulling the blanket across her breasts in a token of modesty.

"I'm remembrin' that you told me of many things: this goddess you called the Worldweaver . . . this place, Nayve. And I believed you, of course. The proof was here, in my living flesh. Only now something makes me wonder." He turned and looked at her frankly.

"Was this a test?" he asked, his voice thick. "Are you temptation? For if you are, lady, I know that I have failed." He hung his head, clearly despairing. "Is my weakness to cost me an eternity of salvation?"

She laughed, gently, so he would know she didn't mock him. "No, you have succeeded in the only test I have to offer. As to salvation, there is none to be had, not from me nor from the god your people worship on the Seventh Circle . . . upon Earth."

"Tell me, then. What is the meaning of a lifetime of faith?"

"Perhaps that faith helped you to survive. I have watched you. I know that your time and place in the world is torn by violence, terrible war."

"Yes. Battles like none the world has ever known. War has become a faceless machine of steel and trenches. It has brought the ruin of Virginia, of all the South." Another thought occurred to him, and he looked at her again. "Is mine the fate of all who die . . . or all soldiers, then?"

She told him that he was unique among warriors of his century, that no human had been thus summoned in over three hundred years. Still she made no mention of the historical cost of the spell, though as she spoke she took note, again, of her own youth and vitality. This was late in the day following the night of passion that had brought her warrior to Nayve, and as yet she suffered no sign of aging. The mystery was deeply puzzling, but the result was nothing that she wished to question.

"You tell me there's no Heaven . . . no Hell . . . no God Almighty?" asked Jubal. "And I can sense the truth, in my being . . . in your beauty. But it is a hard change, all the same."

"And it may become harder," Juliay said. "Remember, we're stranded in a barren mountain valley. Dragons and harpies fly through the air. Trolls stalk the forests at the foot of the range. My four companions perished here . . . and there is a great storm out there, unnatural in power and portent. You have come to a part of Nayve that is dangerous, and you have been brought here at an unsettled time."

Jubal laughed caustically. "Reckon I come from a place and time more unsettled than any. No, I think I'm ready to face your world. But dragons? These are beasts of legend and myth in my own world, fearsome creatures of ancient days. And you say they live here, they fly through these same skies?"

"Never before now, but yes . . . I saw a great one and a lesser one, though even that was bigger than a large horse."

He nodded toward the sword, the bow and arrows. "I see you bear arms."

The druid shrugged. "I can shoot the bow. The sword proved too heavy for me."

Crouching, the man crossed the small space and lifted the sword with both hands on the long hilt. "A fine weapon. I'd like to see it in the light of day. How did you come to have it?"

She was startled by the question, as though it related to a previous life. "It . . . it was Owen's . . . he was a shipmate, on *Skyreaver*. He—all of them—died when we crashed."

"I'm sorry. I would have liked the chance to thank him," Jubal said. Abashed for a moment, he looked down at himself. "I'd feel a little better going out of here if I had some clothes."

"I know where there's a lot of silk," Juliay said. "We can fashion something for you. But we'll have to go out there to get it."

He flashed her that easy grin, and she was suddenly, for the first time since the crash, utterly hopeful. She pulled her own shirt and leggings on and sat down to string the bow. "I have an idea," she said. "If those harpies are still there, they'll expect me to be by myself. I'll go out first, and move away from the entrance. If they come after me, that might give you a chance to attack with surprise."

Jubal frowned. "I reckon that seems rather less than gallant—to use a lady as bait, as it were."

She shook her head impatiently. "It's practical. And we'll want every advantage. You've got to trust me."

Reluctantly he agreed, and, picking up the sword, followed her to the mouth of the little cave. She readied an arrow on the bowstring, then sprinted into the open. A dozen paces away she stopped, lifted the weapon, and spun about while scanning the sky. A moment later she saw it, a single harpy, perched on the mountainside fifty feet above.

The creature squawked, a shrill cry of cruel delight, and sprang into the air. Dirty gray wings spread wide as it soared downward.

Juliay released the arrow and the monster, noticing the weapon at last—too late—shrieked in dismay. The harpy was too clumsy to veer out of the way, and the missile caught it in the breast, at the base of the leathery throat. With a choking gurgle it plummeted to the ground, smashing onto the rocks a few feet in front of the druid.

Only then did she notice Jubal, who had emerged from the cave with the sword held in both hands. He came over to gape in shock at the dead harpy. The ghastly face was turned toward him, and the monster gagged reflexively, spewing a trickle of oily bile onto the ground. The discharge smoldered, and then burst into flame.

"That's the ugliest son of a bitch I've ever seen," the man declared with a grimace. He looked around, half raising the big sword, and she noticed that he bore the heavy weapon with easy strength. "The only one around, for now?"

"I think so. But let's not waste time wondering."

The Chaos Storm still loomed into the sky, black and whirling but apparently fixed in the same location it had been several days ago. Jubal studied that murky face of cloud and shook his head. A few minutes later, she had formed a toga-like tunic for him from a swatch of green silk. A little more effort produced a belt from the rigging cords, as well as a harness that allowed him to carry the great sword strapped to his back. Finally, they took many layers of the silk, wrapped in bundles of cord, to create makeshift sandals. After cutting and coiling a long length of the light rope to carry along, they were ready to go.

They decided to follow the stream downhill, reasoning that, eventually, it would bring them out of the mountains. As they knelt to drink before they started out, Juliay froze and stared at the smooth surface of the creek.

"The *water* . . . that must be the reason! Somehow it protected me from the effects that should have followed the Spell of Summoning!"

"Effects . . . you mean, besides me?" the man asked with a smile.

In a rush she told him about the dramatic aging that had been the lot of every druid who had ever cast that spell. He listened quietly, then stared at her with an expression mingling disbelief and awe.

"You have a life here, forever . . . and you were willing to give that up, to bring *me* here?" he asked.

She looked at him without speaking, for the answer was known to both of them. He closed his eyes, then looked at her with an expression of reverence. "I will do everything I can to prove myself worthy."

"I know," she replied, and touched his rough cheek. "I know," she repeated.

Side by side they started down the valley, taking turns looking skyward, alert for harpies or dragons.

"My lady, surely we have to rest. There can be no catching a beast that flies with such speed!" Falri's pony cantered along next to Janitha on Skyrunner. The loyal animals were staggering with weariness, shaggy flanks streaked with foam, tongues dangling from their mouths. The elven riders were in no better shape, each of them staying in the saddle only through sheer force of will.

The party was slowing down as they approached another shallow dip in the plain, a gentle descent into the vale of a wide, flat stream. Janitha begrudged every moment of delay, but she had to admit that the Hyac had reached the limits of their endurance.

"We'll camp here through Darken," she said. "What river is this?"

"I believe we have come to the valley of the Sirenflow," Beval said. "We're nearly to the Ringhills."

The khandaughter nodded, dismounting and then grasping her saddle as her legs immediately cramped violently. Grimly she ignored the pain, pulling the reins and tack off of Skyrunner as the others did the same with their fatigued, lathered mounts. Only when the ponies were tended did the elves allow themselves to drop to the ground.

The sun was climbing away from them, shrouding the plains in twilight. Every fiber of her body cried out for sleep, urged her to collapse on the soft grass, but Janitha wouldn't allow herself to yield. Instead she limped from one group of her people to the next, until she had spoken with every one of the hundred or so elves who had ridden with her. All were uncomfortable but in good spirits. She told them all to get something to eat, and she set the example by pulling a box of hedras out of her provisions. She passed the nourishing cakes around, while the ponies grazed on the lush valley grass. Afterward, elves and mounts alike drank the sweet waters of the Sirenflow. Finally, the elves unrolled their blankets underneath the cloudless sky.

Despite her weariness, however, Janitha couldn't sleep. Instead she lay there on the ground, watching the stars wheeling overhead, and thinking about the monster that had come to destroy her world. Had Nayve ever faced a threat like this?

Perhaps it had, she remembered. Once before, the legends

said, during the Time Before, invaders had come from beyond Nayve, ultimately repelled by the artifact of the an-
cients. She recalled the ballad, the song she had sung about
the Horn of Lath-Anial. That ancient artifact was at rest in the
funeral barrow at the headwaters of the Sirenflow, this very
river, she remembered. It would remain there forever, of
course, protected by the curse—

Abruptly she sat up, remembering that curse in its specific
details. A sheen of sweat slicked her brow, despite the cool
night. Surely there was hope there! The hand of the goddess
must have brought her here, now, and let her understand!

Quickly she rose to her feet, moving silently among the
sleeping forms of her fellows. She found Skyrunner, and the
pony, despite the fatigue of the long, steady run, stomped his
feet in eagerness to be off. In moments, she strapped the simple saddle into place, mounted, and eased her loyal stallion
along the river, moving upstream.

Her heart was pounding as she went over the words to the
song, the words of the prophecy. What if she was mistaken,
and the curse struck her down? She was prepared to take that
risk. . . . Even more, she felt certain that she was right.

After a few hours, the river had dwindled to a small creek,
and it was not yet early Lighten when at last she halted before
the graven stone doors, twice as tall as her head, marking the
ancestral barrow of the ancient khans. A few times before, she
had been here, camping with her father's household on one of
the periodic expeditions to honor the dead. Never before had
she sensed the powerful aura of this place, the sense of history, destiny, lineage.

She dismounted, suddenly dismayed, knowing that she
would never be able to move the great slabs. But as she
walked closer she gasped as she saw the great portal slowly
rumble open. The doors swung inward, revealing a shadowy
alcove vanishing into the depths of the tunnel.

Janitha Khandaughter walked forward, and torches came
to light in each wall. They burned with clean white flame and

issued no smoke. The farther she walked, the more torches burst into flame, illuminating her path all the way into the musty, hallowed hall.

The floor was smooth marble, and a series of arches led into small chambers along each side of the hall. But she kept going forward, for her objective was the last bier, the honored cairn at the very end of the hall. Finally, she approached and, with a sense of awe looked up at the resting place of Lath-Anial himself. Marble pillars stood to either side, and a large stone sarcophagus occupied all of a raised dais.

From within that coffin, Janitha heard the braying of a horn.

PROPELLED by a storm of wind, wind that was the fetid breath of Karlath-Fayd, the death ships gathered at the wharves in the deep harbor of Ah-Truin, enclosed by the protective shores of Loamar. A thousand black hulls sliced the cool waters of the Worldsea, and on each hull a thousand shadows would ride.

The silent fleet came into the harbor like a tide of blackness, cruel prows thrusting forward, lifeless eyes fastened over the bow toward the land. And on that land, the shadow legions of the Deathlord gathered, marching in numberless waves toward the wharves and the embarkation.

The fleet was assembled, and the shades stood in file. The winds of violence swirled around, driving the ships up to the rocky docks, and the restless troops pushed forward, seething with eagerness, impatient to board their vessels. They had an objective now, a goal that would hurl them across the sea, a talisman that would draw them.

Soon they would sail upon the Worldsea, and thereafter they would land upon the far shore and bring the wave of death across the Fourth Circle. They would march upon the Center of Everything, for there was the key, the object that their master craved, the only thing that held his power back from absolute mastery of the Seven Circles.

And the Deathlord, in his bastion, dreamed of the Tapestry and knew that with the fabric of the goddess in his power, all the worlds would be his.

"WHAT's the latest word?" asked Natac, as he reached the entrance to the tent where Belynda had been studying the Globe of Seeing. He remained outside as he saw her rise from her table and come out to join him. Quilene came from another compartment within the tent to join their conference.

"The dragon paused to hunt again when it reached the fringe of the Ringhills," she said. "Then, like before, it went to sleep in a small valley. That was last Darken, so we can hope it'll stay there another day."

Around them, the Willowfield was bustling with activity, elves and gnomes gathering, re-forming into their ancient companies. Weapons that hadn't been unsheathed for three hundred years were again reflecting the light of the sun. Whetstones rolled, and sparks trailed down from the flinty wheels as armorers restored edges to swords, spears, and axes.

"If only we could strike it while it sleeps," Natac declared, his mind whirling, seeking a plan. He looked at Quilene. "Could you teleport a group of us right there . . . perhaps with some of Gallupper's batteries?"

The sage enchantress shook her head regretfully. "We need a pool of water to set the spell into effect, and another such pool at the far end. If conditions are perfect, I might be able to send five or six of you. But nothing so large as a battery. Nor do I think there's a suitable pool in the valley of the dragon."

"Nearby?" he asked hopefully.

"I can look through the Globe," Belynda said. "But that's a pretty arid section of the hills. I'm not optimistic."

The warrior turned away, walking a few paces from the tent. His eyes went to the horizon, in the direction that was neither metal nor wood. How soon would it be before the monster came into view, flying this way with implacable hatred in its heart and utter destruction its intent?

And when it came, what in all Nayve could they do to fight it?

"Ahem . . . Natac?"

He turned to see the wizened elf hesitantly standing behind him. "Socrates! Please, tell me you have some good news!"

"Well, of a sort, yes. You see, the balloon is being stitched by gnomish tailors even now. They should have it completed by Darken."

"And the helium?"

"There seems to be enough in the reserves left from inflating *Skyreaver.* I daresay we will have a floating ship within twenty-four hours. Not terribly big, mind you, but with a simple gondola, it should be capable of lifting two or three passengers."

"At least we might get some advance sightings of the beast," the warrior stated. "And what about the . . . the other thing, the explosives?"

"That was rather surprising, to me and all of those who have—er, had—classes in my wing of the College. You see, it was rather dramatically successful, quite beyond my anticipations, in fact."

This, at last, seemed to Natac like a promising development. "What did you learn? And can it be used as a weapon?"

"Well, indeed, I learned that the metal will explode, quite violently, if two pieces of it are clapped together with some force. For my test, I dropped one small shard, no bigger than a coin, down a long tube, where it fell atop another piece of the same substance. The resulting explosion quite destroyed my laboratory, I am afraid."

"Then a larger blast could do the same to the dragon!"

"Indeed, I believe it could. Though there is the awkward matter of setting it off. You see, the collision must be quite precise. You could achieve it by holding the two pieces in your hands and smacking them together. But that has obvious drawbacks for the one who must wield the bomb. There would be no way to survive the resulting blast."

"I see," Natac said. "And there is no way to do this mechanically?"

"Well, certainly there is . . . and in a year, maybe as little as a few intervals, I could design a way for that to occur. But I was under the impression you needed something soon."

"Yes." The warrior bleakly considered the prospect. "Indeed, old scholar, you have done good work. It may be that we will have to use this bomb. For the loss of one person, compared to all of Circle at Center, is a price we would have to pay."

"Of course," said Socrates. "Though the cost to that person, it might be noted, is the same, either way."

Natac nodded silently. He was asking himself the question: If he bore these two pieces of metal, and he could destroy the dragon at the cost of his own life, would he do so? He knew he would, but he was startled by how much he wanted to avoid that drastic choice.

"There are the gnomes, on Dernwood Downs," came a soft voice behind him, and he turned to see Quilene regarding him intently. "King Fedlater's realm lies in the path of the wyrm's flight, if it continues toward the Center."

"We sent warning of the serpent's approach by faerie. There is nothing more to be done about them," Natac replied, dismally considering the prospect of another halcyon realm succumbing to the monster's predations. "I hope the king has the sense to order his people into shelter. Let the creature destroy marble and wood, rather than flesh."

He was distracted by Miradel's arrival. She looked stricken, and he took her hands and held her for a moment, feeling the uncanny trembling in her strong body. "What is it?" he asked.

"The Tapestry," she said. "I have looked in the direction that is neither metal nor wood . . . and I have seen an army of the dead . . . an army that follows in the wake of the Delvers and comes to conquer Nayve."

"From the Chaos Storm?" Natac asked grimly.

"No, it musters across the sea. The enemy is not the dragon, not from the Sixth Circle at all. It is the Deathlord, master of Loamar. He rules the land where the dead go . . . but only those dead who are killed by violence. That's why he wants to come here, to get the Tapestry."

"Why?"

"Because if he takes the Tapestry of the Worldweaver, the protections of the goddess are lost. Karlath-Fayd will become the master of all souls, everywhere . . . in each of the Seven Circles."

16

Darkbringer

Shadowed highway,
Darkened path
Evil's byway,
Villain's slash.

Lofty hero
Virtue's blade,
Best the fear, ere
Vict'ry's made!

From the Tapestry of the Worldweaver
Legions Under Coolfyre

"Go!" shouted Karkald, his voice shooting through the cacophony of tumbling rocks and breaking stones. "Get out of the pass!"

His dwarves needed no encouragement. Despite the group of lethal metal giants, which stood still, as if the quake and cave-in was a matter of utter irrelevance to them, the Seers knew that to remain in the crack at the end of the pass was to die. They scrambled outward and down, more concerned with the threat of crushing rock than with the danger presented by the giants on the shore of the Oilsea.

The exit from the pass was a steep-walled trough in the bedrock, cliffs rising a hundred feet high to the right and the left. The gap itself was above and behind them, and the short valley descended steeply toward the shore of the slick, fiery Oilsea. There the way opened out to either side, a flat shore bordering the sludgy liquid to the right and left. But there, too, stood the giants, thirty of the implacable monsters, patiently immobile, positioned astride the only exit from the narrow valley.

A flash of quick, liquid movement, brown pelt shining in the fading glow of oily flares, attracted Karkald's attention to the other side of the narrow valley. A ferr'ell bounded toward him, saddle empty, reins flopping loosely. His heart surged with the first sensation of hope he had felt in hours. "Blood-eater!" he called.

The ferr'ell sprang across a thirty-foot slope and pounced to a stop before the dwarf, fanged jaws gaping in a caricature of a grin. "You're alive!" Karkald declared in disbelief. He was further encouraged as he saw more of the mounts, gliding like shadows along the base of the cliff wall. Dozens of the Rockriders had made it out of the pass, it seemed, and they were as delighted as Karkald at the mutual discovery of their survival. The mounted dwarves joined those on foot in the valley before the exit from the pass. Rocks still crashed downward in the defile, but they seemed, for the moment at least, relatively safe out here.

He looked at the faces, spotted Jordon, his old lieutenant. "How many of you made it out?" asked Karkald.

"Maybe fifty," replied the dwarf. Jordon's helmet was gone, and his head was wrapped in a bloody bandage. Now he cast a glance at the ferr'ells that milled about in the shadows, then he spat contemptuously. "And that was no thanks to that boot-flapper the general put in your place," the wounded warrior growled. "Soon as them giants come out, he ordered us to dismount! As if we'd do better on foot, than fightin' on our steady 'ells!"

Karkald was dismayed at the mental picture: his company, lightly armored and trained for speed and maneuver, compelled to abandon their greatest advantages while facing an implacable foe. "What happened?" he asked, his own eyes scanning the other Rockriders.

"Well, them few as obeyed were smashed in the first stomp," Jordon declared. "The rest of us mounted, then—the marshal's orders be damned, I said, and I would say again!—and took off up the walls. Brought a couple of those big steel bastards down, we did . . . though not without dire cost. And then the affair was lost, plain to see. The marshal was riding again, and we followed him, makin' our way high on the walls till we came out here. Those giants come after, and we parked in the shadows over there, real quiet like. Though it don't seem as if they're much on the hunt right now."

Karkald looked at the metal giants, which were still standing in an apparently perfect circle, all facing inward, on the shore of the still, black Oilsea. Gushes of liquid fire boiled up here and there from the smooth surface, and though a haze of smoke lingered in the air, these flashes were bright enough to provide some semblance of illumination.

"How many did you bring out?" asked Jordon, looking at the dwarves gathering on the slopes below the pass. Tremors shook the ground, and large rocks still bounced out of the gap, some of them skittering dangerously close to the surviving Seers.

"Maybe three or four hundred . . . didn't have time to get a count," Karkald said. "And I think we'd better move the whole lot of us down the hill here. Some of those rocks are coming too damned close. You get the 'riders," he told Jordon. "Stay on the left flank, and I'll bring the infantry down the center of the valley."

The loyal veteran nodded, and his mount sprang across the rocky slopes, returning to the mounted company. Karkald felt a nudge against his shoulder, and as he staggered to the side, he saw that Bloodeater remained at his side. Again, that pointed snout pushed against the dwarf, and he took the reins.

"Thanks for the ride," he said, swinging into the saddle as the ferr'ell bobbed eagerly. Feeling strangely hopeful again, he directed Bloodeater back to the dwarves spread along the mountainside. Already, rocks were bounding and crashing down here, as the level platform directly outside the pass began to overflow with debris.

"Sergeant Gaynroc! We'll be moving down the valley, farther away from the pass. It'll be safer down there."

"Follow me," ordered the doughty veteran, and men hastily moved lower, forming a series of ragged columns. "Begging the captain's pardon," Gaynroc said conversationally as Karkald rode beside him. "But it's only safer as long as those tin crushers don't take note."

"I know," Karkald replied. He had been studying the strange creatures for several minutes but remained at a loss to perceive their intentions. He could see the rivets and overlapping plate and remembered the pipes and internal furnaces in the wreckage of the felled giants. "Do you suppose the Delvers made them?" he asked.

Gaynroc shrugged. "As like as anything, though *how* they could do it is a mystery. And I'll tell you this, sir . . ." He looked at Karkald levelly, but his voice was low enough only for the captain's ears. "If they've got more of the bastards, then we—I mean, the army, Axial, everything—is in for a powerful bitch of a time."

"I'd been thinking the same thing," Karkald agreed. "I think we need to learn as much about them as we can."

Another convulsion rocked the ground underneath them. Several dwarves cursed quietly as they slipped and tumbled or scrambled for purchase on the descending slope. Oily waves surged onto the shore of the sea, and fires erupted into sustained blasts in a dozen places, revealing a surface of clumpy swells and roiling murk.

"Keep together now," the captain hissed, conscious of the fact that they drew closer and closer to the giants. Still, those mechanical foes seemed to take note of neither the dwarven survivors nor the pitching landscape.

Only then did Karkald see that some of the Rockriders were holding back, dwarves engaged in a quiet but heated exchange. Impatiently, he urged Bloodeater over there. The powerful ferr'ell cleared the dry streambed with one leap, and another easy jump brought him into the fringes of the group.

Karkald saw that it was Marshal Nayfal, on his restive mount, who was ordering the riders to hold back. "I gave an order, and I expect it to be obeyed!" he snapped in the face of the bandaged Jordon.

"I gave a different order," Karkald said, as Bloodeater shouldered his way through the ring of mounts. He confronted Nayfal, saw the shock and anger register on the other dwarf's face. "The rockfall, right now, is a greater danger than the giants. Besides, we have to get closer, get a better look at them, see if we can find any weaknesses, flaws."

"Weaknesses?" Nayfal's tone was scathing. He gestured back to the pass. "Weren't you in there? Didn't you *see*—"

"I saw plenty. I saw dead Seers in the hundreds. And there were dead 'riders by the score, brave men you ordered out of the saddle. We have only a fraction of the army left to us, and we have to keep it together and use it as best we can to defend our nation!"

"I am in command here," declared the marshal, beard bristling as he straightened in his saddle. "And you will bring those others back up here. Then you will dismount and take your place with your command."

"No, Marshal. This situation is too critical to let an ass like you take charge. You'd doom us all in five minutes! Rockriders, my orders are to proceed down the valley, on the flank of the infantry. Form up at the very end of the cut."

Immediately the dwarven riders moved their ferr'ells down the sloping valley floor, leaving Nayfal to splutter indignantly. "You can remain here," Karkald snapped. "I won't presume to order you—but your best bet lies with the rest of us."

With that, he turned and let Bloodeater bound past the rest of the mounted dwarves. A clatter of stones told him that Nayfal came behind.

Before them, the giants still loomed, a ring of statues. The dwarves would have to pass within a dozen feet of one or another of the brutes to get out of the valley. But for now, Karkald would be content to sit, wait, and observe.

THE Worldsea crashed against the rocky shore of Loamar with a flood surge of epic proportions. Sections of wall that had stood for three thousand years toppled and fell, washed away by the unprecedented pounding. The warrior-shades stationed along the coast, a million steadfast and deathless troops, quailed at the fury of the storm and wondered what was their master's plan.

For they knew—all in Loamar knew—that it was Karlath-Fayd who had summoned this storm. The Deathlord worked great magic in his citadel, drawing upon powers of elemental fury. This storm of lunging surf was but a part of it. There was also the wind, a dry blast of air that scoured the world of the Fifth Circle, drawn ever inward, toward the great bastion. There were plumes of fire, burning lava, and infernal gouts of gas erupting from the ground within the great citadel, the heat funneled directly into the master's throne room.

And there were the lives sacrificed, a hundred thousand of them or more, shadow warriors who had marched under the iron gate of the bastion's inner circle and then continued, driven by their master's immutable will, directly into the furnaces that roared and growled and spumed. Their spirits, thus condemned, were the final key to the spell, the catalyst that allowed the Deathlord to extend his power outward and down, through the Worldsea, into the depths of the firmament sustaining the cosmos itself. He used the Worldfall as his conduit, bearing the power, building the sorcerous might, preparing to cast his greatest spell.

The magic was a power of deep and abiding force, an immutable call to those who were sanctified to the Deathlord's cause and his name. It swelled as an aura of whiteness, but it was not the whiteness of purity and light. Instead, it was the pall of death, the smoke of ashes, the miasma of dire purpose and foul intent.

It sank through the Midrock like an arrow pierces the air, swirling, seeking, finding. At last the power of Karlath-Fayd swept into the Underworld, where its magic was directed, its purpose finally understood.

THE multifaceted gem pulsed against his chest, a sensation of exquisite pleasure, and Zystyl seized it, felt the thrill of power and destiny in his hand.

"Form the armies around me!" cried the arcane, his command piercing the air, and—much more potently—penetrating into the consciousness of his blind warriors, an instruction that each Delver could feel and was determined to obey.

The three formations had withdrawn from their deployments smoothly, forming march columns, proceeding across the Underword to assemble here on the Plain of Magma. Sixty thousand strong, the great army of Vicieristn now assembled in three great wings, one in each of the main directions, all the dwarves standing at attention and facing inward, toward the arcane who stood atop a monolith, a squat tower of rock rising some forty feet from the plain.

Zystyl took in the scent, the aura, the *power* of this great force—three times the size of the army he had commanded centuries before—and his heart pulsed with excitement. With great anticipation he descended the steep pillar around the steps that spiraled once about the face. He found the female arcane, Jarristal, waiting for him at the foot.

"My Lord Zystyl," she asked, her tone hesitant and beseeching, but the question palpable even before she spoke. "Please forgive my impertinence. But tell me, why are you bringing the armies to this place? We were poised to close in upon Axial at your command . . . but now I sense that we have withdrawn far from that objective."

He was impressed by the courage she showed in daring to ask the question. After all, he had slain underlings for less, and even Jarri had felt the mental whiplash of his impatience. Twice already he had left her cringing and whimpering on the floor, blood running from her flaring nostrils. Both times he had turned his rage toward her in a telepathic blast because she had not been quick enough to respond to his wishes.

Yet now, uncharacteristically, he did not respond with anger. In fact, he recognized that she asked a very pertinent question, and furthermore, it was not a question that he could answer. Though he didn't know *why* he had brought his army here, as his hand closed around the Hurtstone, he understood again, with perfect clarity, that the maneuver had been absolutely necessary.

"I have ordered this deployment because it is right," he replied. "I cannot say how I know that, but we must march together, here on the plain. And we must do it now."

"Very well, lord," Jerristal replied, bowing so that the crown of her helm brushed his knees. "I shall attend to the stragglers."

"Good, my pet . . . that is good. We must march inward, closing the ranks as tightly as possible."

Within an hour, the well-disciplined Delvers had massed around the monolith, leaving barely enough space for the officers to walk between the individual companies and regiments. The arcanes Hallion, Fieristic, and Lastacar each stood at the front of their respective wings. Zystyl could sense their curiosity, tasted their misgivings in the ether. Lastacar's acrid stink was a pungent wave, though the sweating Delver stood fifty feet away. But the commander ignored them all. For another hour the blind warriors stood at attention, not one warrior wavering among those vast ranks. The army commander alone took a seat, Zystyl reclining on a flat stone at the base of the stone tower.

Finally, he rose to his feet. "It is almost time," he said, placing his foot on the bottom step of the flight spiraling up the squat monolith. He felt the ripple of anticipation move through the ranks as the troops stirred slightly, though there was no wavering in the discipline of the formations.

"Master, may I accompany you?" It was Jarristal, her hand

just touching his foot as he prepared to ascend. The contact, though it was through her gauntlet and his heavy boot, nevertheless sent a thrill of pleasure running through the arcane's leg.

"Yes," he said. "It will be pleasing to have you there."

Atop the monolith, he suddenly turned his face upward. There was a brightness there, a fullness of light that now, somehow, penetrated his blindness. His companion, his armies, were forgotten as he stared in wonder at a descending spiral of light, knowing a sensation—*seeing*—that he have never experienced before. He beheld an aura of consummate and consuming beauty.

"My lord!" gasped Jarristal, and he knew that she saw the same thing. The magical effect swirled across the troops in their tight ranks, and many of them cried or prayed or gasped in wonder. It surrounded them, blazing but cold, unforgiving and merciless, yet gentle and inviting at the same time.

There was nothing at all fearful in that light. Instead, it was an embrace, a shelter and protection for all who came within its blinding rapture. Zystyl felt himself lifted from his feet, borne upward through the air. Jarristal was at his side, her hands clutching his arm with delightful pressure. His amulet, the Hurtstone, was pulsing in cadence with his pounding heart.

When Zystyl extended his own senses again, he knew that his army was rising with him. This white light was bearing them upward, away from the First Circle, through the barriers between worlds, on a journey of discovery and power. . . .

And to a destiny of glory and blood.

"By the goddess and glory of coolfyre—what in all the circles is that?"

The question was gasped by Jordon, and it echoed in the minds of every dwarf among the Seer survivors. The object of their awe was a cloud, swirling gray white, descending in a great spiral from the vault atop the First Circle. Karkald had seen whirlwinds during his time in Nayve, and this reminded him of nothing so much as a vast, pale tornado.

The point of the cone seemed to drop toward the middle of the ring of metal giants, the animated creatures that, for hours now, had not stirred from their positions beside the Oilsea. The appearance of the bright cloud coincided with a new round of tremors, convulsions rocking the ground and bringing further rubble tumbling from the cliff walls and the exit from the Arkan Pass.

"What should we do, Captain?" asked Gaynroc, his tone laconic.

"Flee—back to the pass!" cried Marshal Nayfal, who sat astride his ferr'ell, as far from the giants as possible. "There's dark magic in that foulness!"

"No!" Karkald declared. "Look at the cave-ins up there! We'll have dozens of men crushed by rockslides." He looked at the giants again, knowing they needed to learn, to understand the lethal creatures, and he knew that this light was somehow key to that knowledge.

"I'm taking that chance!" cried Nayfal, putting spurs to his mount. "Come with me if you would live!" The animal bounded up the slope, nearly dropping the officer from his saddle. Nayfal clung to the reins grimly, as the steed nimbly pounced out of the way of first one cascade of stones, then another.

"Stand firm!" growled Gaynroc, though Karkald was heartened to see that none of the dwarves, whether afoot or mounted, showed any inclination to flee with the marshal.

Again, Karkald's eyes were drawn back to the spiraling cloud. It was clearly descending and was wider than he had at first thought. Abruptly, the tip of the cone expanded into a great halo, a whirling cloud of light that swelled to a much larger diameter than the ring of metal giants. And then the swirling brilliance plunged to the ground, encompassing, overwhelming.

Karkald felt a sense of wonder and disorientation, realizing that he and his dwarves had been trapped within that swirling ring. Yet he felt no fear, no compulsion to flee. Even Bloodeater and the other ferr'ells, though they pranced restively, remained in place.

The light swept closer, a blinding storm that masked view in every direction. And then Karkald had the strangest sensation: as though he was staying in one place, but the ground, the firm and eternal surface of the Underworld, was falling away until it was far, far below.

DARANN took one look at her father's face, and her worst fears erupted in a wave of shock that weakened her knees and sent her stomach surging with a wave of nausea. Staggering, she leaned on the table, then sank into one of her sturdy, low chairs.

"No . . ." she moaned, looking into Rufus Houseguard's eyes, hoping against her fear to see some hint of mistake, some acknowledgement of error, to deny the news that she could not bear to receive.

"I wish I could say anything but what I come to tell you," her father said with a bleak sigh. He looked as though he had aged half a lifetime since the night before, when he had supped with his daughter. Now his hair and beard seemed somehow more white than gray, and the creases around his eyes seemed like dark cracks of weariness.

For long moments, Darann stared vacantly, while her father shuffled into the apartment and took a seat on another of the stout chairs—Karkald's chair. "What happened?" she asked finally.

"Disaster," Rufus Houseguard replied. "A military disaster of the worst magnitude. General Paternak marched his army into the Arkan Pass, and there our men were annihilated in ambush."

"Were there . . . are there any survivors?" she asked, suddenly, wildly hopeful. "Kark was riding his ferr'ell. Surely they could have gotten away."

Rufus winced as if he had been struck, but she leaned forward and took his gnarled hand in both of hers. "Well? *Couldn't* he?"

"Even supposing he would leave his comrades in danger—and I think you know your husband would be the last one to do that—the entire pass was buried by a landslide. There was a rear guard, men Paternak had posted outside the place when the rest marched in. They are the only Seers who got away. They ran all the way back to Axial and reported to the king, not two hours ago. But they say the devastation was complete. There were no other survivors."

For a long time, Darann did nothing except cry, and as he held her close, her tears mingled with her father's in the bristling hairs of his tangled beard. But then, finally, she drew away, dried her eyes, and shook her head. It was unthinkable; surely there was some mistake! Her mind groped for possible explanations, but each thread of promise she recognized as irrational, born out of her own desperation, not from any real prospects for her husband's survival.

Questions came, then, and anger. "Why were they over there, in the depths of the Underworld?" she demanded. "Karkald thought the danger was here, at the city!"

"No doubt General Paternak would have to answer for many decisions," Rufus growled, "had he the ill fortune to stay alive. But he is lost with the rest of his men."

She was seized with a sense of wild energy. "I must do something, prepare a memorial . . . no . . ." Nothing seemed right; nothing made any sense.

"You should come home, to your mother and me, at least for a few cycles," said Rufus gently. "This is no time for you to be alone."

"No . . . no, it isn't," she agreed numbly. Then she started to cry again. "This is no time for me to be anything at all!"

KARKALD felt Bloodeater beneath him, the ferr'ell taut and utterly still as the white magic blossomed around them. He could see nothing through that brightness, but he sensed that his companions were nearby, too, hidden within that cloaking illumination. He had little sensation of movement, no sense at all of whatever lay beyond the blanket of magic, no feeling for the passage of minutes or hours.

Except that vaguely, and very slowly, he began to realize that the dwarves had been ensnared within the magic for a very long time. He tried to shout, calling out to his mates, but it seemed that the sound of his voice was swallowed even before it left his mouth.

He was rather surprised to realize that he wasn't frightened. Perhaps the magic numbed his emotions as it masked his senses. That thought came to him rationally, and he gave it some credence. He looked at Bloodeater, the animal's brown fur milky and vague in the wash of light. The ferr'ell's forefeet splayed to either side, as if expecting a landing at any moment. The round ears pricked upward, and the whiskers bristled along the sharp, toothy muzzle.

Finally, the light began to fade, and the ferr'ell started to twitch and kick, straining for contact with a solid surface. Karkald looked around and saw Gaynroc with the mighty axe held before him. The sergeant met his eyes and blinked, as if he slowly awakened from a trace. All around were others, heavy and light infantry, and ranks of steady crossbowmen on the right, Rockriders on their bucking mounts to the left.

At last the light was swept away, spinning around them one last time and then whisking upward to vanish into the darkness, like a silken cloak tossed and trailed by a skilled dancer.

Bloodeater snorted and crouched, taut as a coiled spring, and Karkald could see that the ferr'ell was standing on hard, rocky ground. The terrain was broadly flat, nothing like the narrow vale at the mouth of Arkan Pass.

And then he noticed the wind, smelled the scent of rain, and realized with a sudden sense of comprehension that he had been borne out of the First Circle completely. He leaned back, saw the gently dancing constellations that he remembered from three hundred years earlier, and gaped in shock.

"We've come to Nayve!" he said softly, as his dwarven troops, like sleepwalkers awakening, looked around at each other and their surroundings. Some groaned or cried out, others dropped to their knees and prayed or stared numbly around. A few, like Gaynroc and Jordon, checked their own weapons and equipment, then issued quiet, calm orders, telling the rest of the dwarves to do the same.

It was dark night, but the stars provided enough illumination to reveal a mountainous horizon, lofty peaks enclosing in a semicircle across half the sky. Beyond, high above, loomed the greatest storm cloud Karkald had ever seen, pitch black against the night, with wind howling audibly around it, the sound a dull roar even at this distance. Lightning played back and forth across the mass, electrical bolts brightening the rocky valley, outlining features in harsh relief.

"The giants!" grunted Gaynroc, pointing.

Karkald saw them outlined in the flashes, standing still in a ring on the valley floor, in the same position relative to the dwarves as they had occupied when the curtain of gauzy magic had descended. For the time being, at least, they showed no more sign of movement than in the Underworld.

"Orders, Captain?" asked Jordon, astride his ferr'ell a short distance away.

"What? Yes . . ." The dwarf looked toward the mountains, saw several wide valleys opening beyond this place, rising steeply into the massif. He immediately distrusted those, knowing that any one of them could end in an unclimbable cliff. To either direction along the floor, however, he saw a belt of land that looked flat and passable. He took out his compass, saw the needle swivel toward the direction of metal, and triangulated on his head.

"If this is Nayve," he said, speculating aloud. "Then we've come to land very far from the Center, in the direction that is neither metal nor wood." He pointed down the valley, where it presumably led to a terminus on the shore of the Worldsea. "That is the direction of Loamar, of chaos and decay."

"The giants—they're moving!" hissed a low voice, as one of the dwarves caught sight of activity. Karkald instantly saw that the metal beings had pivoted in the circle, and were starting to march outward, a path that sent several of them directly toward the dwarves.

"Come on!" urged the captain, waving to his men. Immediately, the veteran troops started to move, trotting at a steady jog, moving quietly but with impressive speed.

"Rockriders, deploy to screen," said Karkald, and his mounted warriors bounded away, interposing themselves between the striding giants and the retreating dwarven foot soldiers. Fortunately, the survivors of the Seer army were able to move quickly. Furthermore, it soon became obvious that the giants were not intent upon pursuit. Instead, they simply moved so as to greatly expand the size of their circle. When they had formed a ring nearly a mile across, they paused again.

By then, the Seers were partway up the slope, on the Center side of the big valley. Karkald sent several riders to explore the ground higher on the ridge, and they came back to report that, after an easy climb through one or another ravine along the bluff, they could rise to a flat plateau that seemed to offer passable travel in several directions.

It took only a short time for the irregular formation to make the climb, which was steep but not especially challenging. At last the dwarves gathered on a promontory overlooking the vale. Eyes attuned to the darkness by now, they could easily make out the giants, who remained rigid, in their great circle.

Karkald was about to order a renewal of the march—he decided they would look for shelter first, then some sign of civilization—when he was distracted by a disturbance on the ground in the middle of the iron giants' ring. The rolling, rocky terrain began to glow, emitting a soft white light very reminiscent of the magical veil that had brought the Seers here. The illumination brightened, as if a large bubble of light was rising through impenetrable rock. Even as he watched this, Karkald realized that the ground was solid, but he couldn't shake the impression that the brightness was coming toward them from a great depth.

Then the surface of the light bubble broke through the ground, spilling brightness into the air. The same white fabric of sorcery, the cocoon that had brought them here from the Underworld, erupted from the rocks and coiled like a brilliant cyclone in the valley. It whirled in the middle of the circle formed by the metal giants.

Like that earlier silken veil had whirled away by a deft motion, the shimmering magic spiraled into the air and vanished, plunging the shoreline and the looming mountains into a darkness that seemed deeper, more sinister than before. Karkald strained to see, gradually made out dark patches on the terrain, huge expanses of blackness that lay like a blanket—like three distinct blankets—on the ground.

Only when those areas of darkness began to move, to wheel and to march and to advance and form columns, did he at last perceive the truth. "Delvers," he growled, instinctive hatred thrumming in his voice. "They have been brought here with their giants, by some power of magic like we have never seen!"

"But why?" asked Jordon, struggling to quiet his suddenly restless ferr'ell.

"I can only think of one reason," Karkald said, trying to imagine the tally of individuals in those huge, blocklike formations. It was a number beyond comprehension, but surely numbered many tens of thousands.

"What's that?" asked his fellow rider.

Karkald shook his head, strangely unwilling to verbalize his grim thought, but finally he spoke.

"It looks like they've embarked on another invasion of Nayve."

17

Cultures and Chaos

Wilding river,
Untamed sea;
Lashing thunder,
Crashing surf.
Graven power,
Erosion's kiss;

All flowers are bright
On the altar
Of destruction.

From the Tapestry of the Worldweaver
Bloom of Entropy

For two days, Juliay and Jubal followed the winding course of the mountain stream, through a valley that remained as barren of plant and animal life as it had been where they started. However, they moved steadily away from the looming bulk of the Chaos Storm, and for a while at least, that was enough to brighten their spirits.

At least, until hunger started to gnaw with a persistence that could no longer be denied.

"I reckon this water is about as refreshing as anything—save, maybe, some North Carolina lightning," Jubal said with a chuckle, as he leaned over the stream and cupped a drink in his palms. "But my belly's getting right impatient with all this drinking. What do you suppose we'll do about food?"

Juliay had been wondering the same thing. She looked at the barren, black peaks and wondered what lay beyond the next bend in the valley. "We've got to get to the lowlands. They were lush and fertile, at least they looked that way from the skyship." She remembered that they were inhabited by rather vicious trolls, too, but she was reluctant to remind Jubal of that just now.

Indeed, more and more she had been torn by feelings of guilt. Had her whole impulse in casting the Spell of Summoning been mere selfishness? She had convinced herself that she was sparing Jubal from a gruesome death upon the Seventh Circle, sacrificing her youth and future so that she could bring him to a better place. But if they wandered in these mountains until they ran out of food, how much good had she done him?

In balance, it seemed like: none whatsoever.

Of course, when she had made that decision, she had fully expected to suffer the dire cost of the spell, the cost that had been exacted from those few brave druids who had worked the magic in the past. When Jubal's predicament was contrasted against her grim fate, none could have questioned her motives.

But now she felt as though she had brought him here, into grave peril, merely so that she could have a protector, a companion . . . a lover. Surely, as the perils of dragons and harpies and trolls became manifest, he would see her as a selfish coquette, and he would come to resent her. These fears grew with each step they took, and now she found herself trudging along, bleakly wondering what fate the future held for her . . . for them both.

"Trees! I see trees!" Jubal's voice, and his clear delight, snapped her out of her melancholy. The stream valley, continuing to curve around the base of a craggy mountain, had begun to open outward. The narrow waterway spilled over a steep rill to form a deep pool. Following a meandering course of less than a mile, it merged with a larger river and a broad, grassy valley. And on the far side of that river sprouted several lush groves.

She cast a glance at the sky, noting that the sun had not yet begun its ascent. Still, her sense of time told her that it was late in the day. "If we hurry, we can get down there before Darken," she suggested.

"Then let's hurry, and hurrah for all that!" cried Jubal, all but skipping as he jogged along the rock-strewn path. He had the long sword strapped to his back, and his green kilt swirled wildly as he turned back to wait for her.

She couldn't help laughing as she trotted to keep up. "There's never been someone who looks like you in the whole history of the Seven Circles," she announced.

"I declare, miss, that I shall take that as a compliment," Jubal replied with a bow. "Besides, you look to be pretty handy with that bow and arrow. I wouldn't want to be irritatin' you, now."

They found the slope next to the spilling cascade to be a neat series of stony steps, irregular, but none of them too high for an easy hop down. The water, Juliay noted, here splashed and swirled, but where it gathered in eddies it lacked the bubbles and froth that she would have expected. This was still that stream that they had followed from the site of the crash and her spell.

Abruptly, a new fear tugged at her, and she hesitated.

"What is it?" Jubal immediately sensed her change in mood.

She looked at the water, then at him. "I was just wondering . . . if it's the water that altered the Spell of Summoning, then perhaps the aging effect is just delayed . . . postponed until I'm away from here."

Jubal frowned, met her eyes. "Do you want to stay here, then? I shall not abandon you, of course."

She smiled sadly, again felt that gnawing guilt, and tried to cover it up with a joke. "No, certainly not. This mountain range is no place for an old lady to live!"

He laughed, which was all that she had hoped for, and then

continued down the stairlike slope, pausing to offer her his hand at some of the longer drops. Soon the ground leveled out, and they strode over grass—the first vegetation either of them had seen since the mountain camp—toward the small river.

"I think we can wade it," Jubal suggested, standing on the graveled bank and looking at the clearly shallow flowage. His gaze lifted. "And I declare, those look like apple trees! And I see birds—fresh meat!" He turned and squinted at Juliay. "That is, if you're as good in the use of that bow as you are in carrying it."

"I could fancy a quail," she said. "And if one comes within a hundred feet of me, we'll have a taste of something good."

The water barely came to their knees. The current was moderately strong, and as the water swirled around her legs, Juliay noticed that it seemed normal in every respect, frothing and splashing and sparkling like the water she had found everywhere else in the world, except . . .

She looked back at the mountain valley, at the bright rill spilling down the last steep cascade, and again perceived the oily smoothness, the dark and somber patina that distinguished that flow. Something was unique about that place, and she was more convinced than ever that it had given her protection from the dire cost of her magic. But if it had, would that protection last?

There was no way to know, and in fact she forgot all about the question as she and her warrior emerged from the stream to find another meadow of lush grass. The trees rose, tall and green, just a dozen paces away.

And sure enough, they were laden with bright, ripe apples.

"YOU see them?" Roodcleaver asked, nudging Awfulbark with a sharp elbow.

"Yup, yeah," he snorted, waking up. "See who?"

"There! Skinny folk, two." The female pointed a bony finger through the tangle of underbrush in which they had sought concealment. Around them, other trolls were currently sleeping off the effects of a veritable feast of apples, the first food the refugees of Udderthud had come upon in several days.

"I see," said Awfulbark, his skin tingling in alarm as he observed the man and woman drawing near to the trees. These were not harpies, but instead seemed akin to the strange being with the long silver claw, the one who had hacked his head off with a single blow. Others of those people had stung his companions with the flying darts, a wooden shaft similar to the one carried by the female.

When the male turned, Awfulbark all but groaned, for he saw that this man, too, bore a silver claw. Indeed, the weapon, which was strapped to his back, looked to be even greater than the one that had so painfully decapitated him.

"What you do?" hissed Roodcleaver, lying beside him as he wormed forward to the edge of the brush. "They take our apples!"

Awfulbark snorted, seeing with his own eyes. The male took the female's hands and spun her around, while she emitted some kind of shrill cry. Perhaps it was a mating ritual, he speculated. But instead, the two simply plucked several apples from a low-hanging limb and sat on the grass, backs to the tree trunk, contentedly munching.

The strangers had picked a tree on the outskirts of the grove, away from the trolls, so the king didn't worry about them coming upon his people by accident, at least not so long as they stayed where they were.

"That's meat," Roodcleaver suggested pointedly. "Better than apples, all the way."

Awfulbark's belly growled, and he nodded. Hunger battled with fear in his slow, thick mind. He thought about the large grove, concealing hundreds of trolls right now, and speculated that, if they all attacked at once, the chances of the silver claw cutting *him* again were probably quite slight. It seemed realistic to expect that they could overpower these two bizarre creatures. And his wife was right. A meal of meat would be a fine improvement over apples.

Worming back into the shelter of the underbrush, he sat up, then looked through the branches into the sky with a critical eye. "Darken's coming," he said. "Let skinny folk sit there, fill up on apples."

His broad mouth curved into a wicked smile, then, as Roodcleaver licked her lips in anticipation of his next words. "In the night," he continued. "We hunt, and we kill, and we eat."

SOCRATES had seen to the rapid inflation of the hastily constructed airship, though he had to use all the extra helium he had stored. The whole project had been completed with remarkable haste, and the alchemist wasn't particularly happy about it.

"Not proper, not proper at all," he muttered to Natac, as the warrior inspected the light, wicker gondola. "To work with such reckless speed, why, it's an affront to the dignity of science!"

"Perhaps," the Tlaxcalan replied genially. "But it's essential to prevention of disaster. Wise Socrates, I thank you from the bottom of my heart for your endeavor."

"Well, of course . . . you know you're welcome. Indeed, these trips of yours . . . well, they've given me some great opportunities for experimentation. I do wish you had been a little more careful with *Skyreaver,* however. She was a special one."

"Yes, I agree. And I wish to all the Circles that I could have saved the ship . . . and Juliay, as well," Natac said, gently chiding. "In truth, our druid is the one who cannot be replaced."

"Er, yes, well, quite right," said the wizened elf. His white hair bristled in all directions, and he shook his head mournfully. "Indeed, I didn't mean to forget . . . now, with you and the druid, and that lovely Sirien going aloft into such danger. Truthfully, can you forgive an old fool?"

"You're anything but an old fool, and of course you are forgiven," Natac said. "Without your efforts, we wouldn't even have the chance that we've found."

"Indeed . . . the matter of the . . . well, I guess it's a bomb, isn't it? Though I shouldn't like to be remembered as the one who made it. Discovered it, really . . . Of course, there's not much making to it at all, is there? Really just two rocks, smashed together, and then heat and light and . . . a nasty blast, all told."

Natac nodded. He had seen the two "rocks," and he, too, was amazed at the potential power Socrates had described. And he hoped to the goddess, and every other power of the Seven Circles, that the bomb would not have to be used.

The warrior looked up at the airship. Unlike *Skyreaver,* this was but a single balloon, a sphere perhaps twice as large as any one of the earlier airship's seven flotation bags. But the gondola below the flotation bag was much simpler, little more than a hull of strong, light wicker. There was no need to plan for storage or for the transport of provisions. In the back of his mind, Natac wondered if there would even be a chance for this balloon to return to the Center.

Owen, Roland, and Sirien came down the winding path through the garden, joining him in the clearing at the Center of Everything. The Worldweaver's Loom rose, a silver spire to the heavens, nearby.

"Is the ship ready?" asked the druid. "Sirien and I have everything we need."

"Yes. We can launch in a few minutes." Natac turned to Socrates. "Do you have the, er, rocks?"

The elven sage looked at him seriously. "Yes . . . yes, I do. They are small enough that one can wield them in his own two hands, if necessary. And the destructive force, from our tests, looks as though it will be sufficient. But I warn you again, it is an awesome power, and I should hate for it to be used at all."

"I would hate that, too," Natac said sincerely. "We're going to try to talk to the dragon first."

Roland spoke earnestly to the warrior. "I must ask you again. Please, stay behind here. Sirien and I can do this ourselves! And you, now that Miradel is here . . . you should stay behind and be with her."

"I have told him that, many hundreds of times," said the druid, as she, Belynda, and Quilene came up to join them. Natac thought how the small gathering, those who had come here to the flowered garden for this departure, was so very different from the festive throng that had gathered for *Sky-reaver's* embarkation from the Willowfield. Again he felt that tug of destiny, the sense of duty that would brook no deviation from its implacable course.

"I'm the only one of us with the experience to keep the airship leveled. We all hope that we will be able to speak to the wyrm, reason with it. But if the worst comes, Roland can spin wind, I can level the airship . . . and Sirien has offered to wield the rocks. We need all three of us to insure that the beast does not reach the Center . . . or the Tapestry."

"No," Owen said sternly. He looked from Sirien to Natac. "I should go instead of either of you. I can clap two rocks together as well as anyone, and I've seen you work the ballast, the gas, a thousand times. I can do that myself, as well! And as to the bomb . . . well, we all know that I have lost the one who was the world to me. If one of us is to perish, let it be me!"

"I'm sorry, my friend," Natac said, realizing very much that he wanted to stay here, to go to the villa and seclude himself with Miradel. A frantic voice deep inside of him coaxed treason: Even if the dragon came to the Center, devastated the city, what were the chances it would bother with a lone house on a hilltop across the lake? Surely they could be safe there, could have those years together that they so richly deserved!

But the voice of duty was too strong. He turned to Miradel, speaking quietly, but knowing the others were listening as well. "I remember when you brought me here . . . remember it like it was yesterday. When I asked you why, you said that

Nayve needed a warrior—needed *me*. The Fourth Circle was facing a great danger, a disorientation of worlds, and my duty was to protect this world."

"But you did that, and so much more," she said, those rich violet eyes swimming with tears. "Why must you fight again—in such a manner that, if you fight, you die?"

"It's the only way to battle such a beast. And besides, we won't fight if we don't have to. We'll try to talk to the monster, reason with it. Dragons are old and wise. I have no doubt but that he will respond to reason."

"*I* have doubts!" she cried, and pulled him close.

Gently he disentangled himself. He and his two companions hugged their friends, and he again had to dissuade an insistent Owen. "Look at the basket," Natac said quietly. "You would leave barely room for the others—and not to mention you weigh twice what I do. No, I am the right man for this task."

He drew a breath and looked at the grieving faces. "Besides, we know this dragon rests frequently, and for long periods. Even if we have to face him, it might not be in the air . . . and on the ground, only one of us would have to close in for the attack."

"And that one should be me!" Owen insisted. "I have lost my beloved. I have no place in this world without her. While you—" The Viking put an arm around Miradel. "—You have to return!"

"I have every intention of doing so! And you'll be coming after me as fast as you can, remember? Bring the army, Gallupper and his guns, Tamarwind Trak and the elven regiments, everyone, across the Causeway of Wood before Darken. With any luck, we'll meet in the Ringhills in three days' time."

"Yes . . . any luck, at all," Owen said glumly.

"We've sent a faerie messenger to King Fedlater," Belynda said. "He is to order his gnomes to take shelter, underground if at all possible, and if he spots the dragon, he will send word to us immediately."

"Good. I hope he has the sense to keep out of sight," Natac said.

He would take his sword, and Sirien was armed with a bow and several quivers of arrows. Roland had his windcasting bowls and paddles. Their only other cargo was the small box Socrates had brought with him from the College. He opened it to display the contents, two round objects that looked like lumps of lead, each about the size of a clenched fist. They were separated by a sturdy divider, and the inside of the box was lined with plush velvet.

"We tested on a very small amount, as I told you," he said. "When the two lumps are brought together, the fire and the heat are remarkably powerful. If the dragon is close, the resulting explosion will surely be enough to slay it."

None of them voiced the corollary, as the balloon lifted off and Roland steered them toward a windstream that all the druids in the city were casting from the Grove. But each of them, on the ground and in the air, knew full well the truth. As well as killing the dragon, the explosion of the two rocks would annihilate the weapon's wielder and any nearby companions, as well.

REGILLIX Avatar took his time flying across the rugged hills that bordered the lush plain. His internal compass told him that the Center lay beyond this rough ground, but he was intrigued by the sight of such an exotic landscape, unique in all of his experience.

He delighted in the view of the streams that meandered through so many of the valleys, waters often gathering into serpentine lakes or spilling down dazzling waterfalls across faces of sparkling cliff. Too, he relished the sight of the sunlight upon the land, a light that was noticeably brighter and more direct than the illumination that graced his own world. It seemed as though he could see things more clearly, and even the air tasted and smelled of exotic odors and rich, intriguing scents.

The game animals of Nayve he had found particularly palatable and very easy prey. Most rewarding had been the grazing beasts of the steppes, probably because one or at the most two of those hulking herbivores were enough to quench his monstrous appetite. Now, in the forested hills, he pounced upon deer, boar, and sheep, but he found that he needed to eat a dozen or more of these lesser beasts in order to stave off the pangs of hunger.

Still, the land was rich with game, and the creatures of Nayve seemed to have no instinctive fear of a flying predator, not even one so large as himself. Many times he had spotted a creature grazing in a sheltered meadow and had simply dropped on top of the hapless beast.

But finally he realized that such a pastime, while rewarding and delectable, only served to delay the purpose that had brought him winging toward the Center ever since his escape from the Chaos Storm. When next he took to the skies, after a restful sleep of several days spent in a wet, soft-bottomed marsh, he circled for a long time, slowly gaining altitude, sensing his surroundings.

The call to the Center was clear, and he turned his course in that direction. His wings sliced the air with powerful strokes, and his neck craned forward, as if the sooner to catch sight of his destination. Yet at the same time, doubts and questions assailed him with more fervor than ever before.

Indeed, he was becoming increasingly curious about this place, the Center of Everything. His initial rage had been leavened somewhat by the passage of time. He was determined to punish those who had slain Plarinal, but he was no longer quite so certain that the elves must be to blame for the existence of the Worldfall itself. Even if they could create such a thing, what would their purpose be?

He flew on as Darken began to descend. Momentarily, he considered landing—so much had he enjoyed this place that he didn't want to glide past any undiscovered wonders in the night—but quickly he decided that his mission should finally take precedence over his curiosity.

Several hours later, however, he was surprised to see sparkling lights brighten the sky, many miles away to his right side. He banked around and watched, seeing tiny sparks rise from a hilltop, then burst into blossoms of fire when they were high in the sky. The display was quite attractive, and the dragon flew closer. Colorful explosions continued to brighten the air, all of them apparently launched from a lone hilltop that rose a little higher than the surrounding summits. Gliding past that crest as he watched, Regillix then circled around for another look.

More and more of the bangles burst in the air, trailing multicolored sparks, sometimes popping with a large boom and other times going off with a whistle or a long hiss. He saw that the initial sparks seemed to be emerging from tiny holes in the hilltop, and for a moment he wondered if this could be a natural phenomenon. On his next pass, however, he saw several small figures scurrying about, briefly illuminated by the flares, then vanishing into the shadows.

Intrigued, now, Regillix decided that his flight to the Center would indeed have to wait. There was mystery here, and a certain ephemeral beauty, and he decided not to go farther until he watched and understood. So he spread his wings wide, slowed his flight, and finally came to rest on a rounded hilltop a mile or so distant from the crest where the pretty fires were launched. He curled up, making himself comfortable, and continued to scrutinize the display.

"ELVEN riders of Hyac," Janitha declared, standing on the hillside over the mounted band of her companions. "I bring you the Horn of Lath-Anial!"

She held up the curved instrument, hollowed from the spiraling horn of a great ram, inlaid with gold and silver and pearl. The sun, which had just descended to full Lighten, sent dazzling reflections sparkling across the faces of the awestruck elves.

"Khandaughter . . . we followed your path to this place." Falri's normally laughing face was drawn and solemn, tinged with the ashen pale of true awe. "But do you mean that you have entered the tomb and laid claim to the artifact of our forefathers?"

"She means exactly that!" Beval cried, raising her spear and whooping. "Hurray for the khandaughter! Janitha of Shahkamon shall lead us to vengeance against the wyrm!"

Others cheered, perhaps half the band joining in the whoops of exultation, while the rest looked on with solemnity or, in a few cases, outright fear.

"But the curse?" said one, Baridan, the scion of a family of renowned scholars. "Do you not fear that you will doom us all?"

"No, I do not," Janitha replied. "It was a truth that came to me in the night, and when I saw that truth, I mounted Skyrunner and came here with all speed."

"Truer than the words of the prophet?" pressed Baridan.

"The truth is found in those words; *think* of them!" Janitha snapped. "Say them aloud, and when you are finished you . . . all of you . . . must decide if you want to ride with me, or return . . ." She left the sentence hanging, hoping to drive home the point.

"It is written," began the young scribe, frowning in concentration. "The horn of the ancestors is the sacred tool of the Hyac. . . . It cried for the invasion of the world, and it sounded in the faces of our foes . . . driving them away. It lies upon the breast of Lath-Anial, in the barrows of his realm. And there it shall lay, with curses of death upon its trespassers, so long . . ." He faltered, then looked at Janitha with sudden comprehension. Emotion choked his voice as he finished. "So long as Shahkamon shall stand upon the brink of the world. . . ."

"And our city no longer stands," Beval said, her own tone awestruck. "So you came and reclaimed the horn?"

Janitha held up the artifact. "Once before, this was the talisman that broke the enemies of our people, shattered an invasion from beyond our world. I shall use it now and see if it can do the same for the dragon."

"And I shall ride with you!" Baridan cried.

"And I!" the cry was echoed by all of them, ponies prancing, spears and bows waving over their heads.

"Forgive my doubts, Khandaughter!" Baridan said, riding close, looking at her with tears in his eyes. "My life is yours to command."

"I have no commands," Janitha said, descending to the base of the hill where she had left Skyrunner. She laid her hand on the young elf's knee. "Just a request: Please, let us make our people proud. And if this be the last chapter of our history, then let it be written in glory!"

She swung into the saddle, and they were off, a hundred riders galloping across the plain, the land now rising perceptibly as it neared the base of the Ringhills. She was going by reckoning, recalling the last direction she had seen the dragon fly, fairly certain her bearing was right but terribly worried that they must be falling far, far behind the flying serpent. The horn, the ancient artifact, was a solid weight, and she wondered if, somehow, it might contain the power to smite the wyrm.

The night of rest had done wonders for elves and ponies, and the band thundered along at a steady canter throughout the hot and dusty day. They paused only to water their mounts as they crossed shallow streams. Janitha relied upon Falri, who in the past had made hunting journeys into the hills, to select a passable route among the suddenly looming crags and shoulders.

Darken found them ascending a long, grassy slope, and the elven riders pressed forward until they reached the rounded, gentle crest. Here they stopped for a rest, dismounting, sharing a few cakes of hedras, allowing the ponies to graze on the lush meadow. Some of the elves were already asleep when Janitha, who was at last feeling the weariness of her long trek on the previous night, was startled by a sound like sharp thunder.

Beval and Falri had heard it, too, and they looked around, seeing no sign of clouds that might signal a storm. They climbed a little on one of the shoulders looming above the saddle of the pass, and finally the sparks of light caught their eye.

"Fireworks!" exclaimed Falri. "A spectacular display, too. But who would be doing such a thing?"

"I don't know," Janitha said grimly. Her hands clenched about the horn, which she wore at her hip. "But I have a feeling we're not the only watchers."

It was clear to all of them, then, as a winged and serpentine silhouette passed across the face of one of the bright explosions. It quickly vanished into the night, but the chill of its passing was a clear reality to them all.

The dragon was there.

"Jubal!" Juliay gripped his arm, whispering urgently. He blinked, and the instincts of four years of war took over. Instantly he was sitting up, wide awake. "Do you hear it?" she asked.

He nodded, his hand going to the hilt of the sword he had laid beside him when they lay down to sleep. Something large was moving across the ground, cracking twigs and scuffing the grass. It seemed to be very near.

More noises came from the other direction, and he realized that they were virtually surrounded. He flicked his eyes toward the embers of the fire they had burned, dried apple boughs that had crackled merrily through the hours of twilight and early night. Juliay had kindled it with magic, a touch of her finger working faster and more reliably than a sulfur match.

Juliay nodded, one squeeze of her fingers signaling the time to move. She rolled away, grabbing several branches from their pile of wood and throwing them onto the coals.

Jubal, meanwhile, sprang to his feet, lifting the big sword in both hands. With his back to the fire, he waved the blade before him, straining to penetrate the darkness.

Light sprang high from the fire, augmented into a bright flare by a magical word shouted by the druid. In the hot glow, Jubal saw several figures crouched behind the trunks of nearby apple trees. They looked huge and ghastly, more like wooden carvings than living beings—until they moved. When one, followed by several companions, swaggered into view, he gaped dumbstruck at the leering, fanged mouth and the black sockets of its eyes . . . eyes that were utterly devoid of any reflection.

"Trolls!" cried Juliay. "More of them, to the right!"

One of the hulking brutes was rushing forward from that direction. Jubal whirled, swinging the big sword in a controlled strike, chopping the keen blade deeply into the side of the woody head. With a howl, the monster fell back, thrashing on the ground, both hands clasped to its gouged skull. Two of its fellows dashed forward and dragged the whimpering creature back to the shadows around the trees.

The troll directly before Jubal made to lunge forward when the man struck to the side, then recoiled quickly as the blade, now stained with black blood, swiveled to confront him.

"Behind us, toward the river," Juliay whispered. "There are none there. We can try to get away."

Jubal looked around, his heart pounding, the familiar energy of battle thrumming through his veins. He took in the shadowy shapes, more than a dozen of them in view, to left and right and front. How many more lurked in the shadows of the grove? He didn't want to find out.

"Ready?" he asked quietly.

The bowstring twanged, and an arrow shot into the darkness, drawing a surprised shriek of pain and anger. "Now!" cried Juliay.

He gave her a few steps head start, swinging the blade through a dazzling circle. Then he spun around, leaping the fire to race after the druid into the night. They ran with the speed of desperate fear, grateful that the grassy ground was smooth, listening for sounds of pursuit. Nearing the river-bank, Juliay turned right, along the course of the flowage, and Jubal risked a glance backward before he followed.

The trolls were loping past the fire, many of the brutish creatures backlit by the roaring flames. They were following, but not as quickly as the humans were running. For several minutes they hurried along in silence, alternating between watching the ground before them and looking back at the many pursuing shapes that remained visible on the flat, grassy terrain.

"They're still coming," Jubal said finally. "We need to try something else. Let's cross the river and take some high ground."

"Yes—there," Juliay agreed, stopping to catch her breath. Her heart pounded, and she felt full of energy. Her eyes seemed unnaturally keen, penetrating the darkness to pick out dozens of trolls, a long stone's throw away.

They waded into the water, thankful for the smooth, gravel bed, and quickly emerged on the far side. Juliay hoped the fording, by itself, might serve to delay the trolls, but several of the creatures waded in without hesitation. The humans continued at a trot toward the looming slope of the nearest foothill.

Lighten spread through the valley, the initial twilight of the sun beginning to fall, and they looked up at a steep façade of rock, crossed by a series of sloping, grassy strands. "We can find a path there," Jubal said. "And it will be easier to de-fend ourselves when we have to rest. You go first; you can shoot the bow while I use the sword, if it comes to that."

Accepting his practical suggestion, she started upward, slinging the bow over her shoulder and using her hands to balance herself as she ascended the steep incline. He came more slowly, facing backward and moving from one sturdy foothold to another. The trolls gathered at the base of the bluff, showing no immediate inclination to climb.

By the time sunlight washed the whole valley, brightening the meadows and trees, sparkling like diamonds across the rills of the shallow river, the druid and the warrior were some fifty feet above the valley floor. They found a grassy ledge, as wide and long as a spacious hallway, and here they paused to take stock of the situation.

"Look . . . there's many more of them, under the trees," Jubal said.

Juliay stared into the murk for a while until she saw them. "Like a whole army."

The man snorted scornfully, and she looked at him in surprise. "Reckon I don't mean to be disrespectful," he said, "but that's no army. More likely a tribe of some kind, with a few toughs doing the rough work for all of them. Even so, those few can cause us some real problems."

"I packed some apples in my pouch last night," Juliay said. "At least we can eat."

They crunched on the fruit while they studied the trolls, two dozen of them still waiting at the foot of the cliff. The creatures bickered and shoved in a chaotic exchange, looking and gesturing upward. Finally, one of them started to climb but, after a few upward steps, turned and went back down to berate his fellows some more.

Abruptly, a wicked shriek pierced the air, and Juliay felt a stab of fear. "Harpies!" she cried, looking skyward.

A dozen of the ghastly scavengers glided through the air, shadows rippling across the grass of the riverside meadow. The trolls woofed and barked in agitation, several pointing toward the sky while others looked urgently toward the grove of apple trees on the other side of the river.

"Hide!" Jubal declared, pulling Juliay down into a makeshift shelter between a pair of large rocks perched on the brink of their ledge. From here they could still see the trolls, though they were hidden from the harpies' view.

"Here come the trolls," said the soldier of Earth. "Could they be trying to attack us together? No! Look at that; they're trying to find some shelter against the harpies."

Indeed, the trolls formed a knot on a ledge, lower and narrower than the perch where the humans hid, but protected on two sides, at least, by looming shoulders of cliff. Screaming in a series of sharp, staccato shrieks, the harpies swooped in for the attack. Several swept right over the trolls, slashing with claws, or spitting gobbets of flaming bile. The trolls punched and flailed, but all of the flyers swept away unharmed, leaving several of their enemies swatting at painful burns or blotting bloody wounds on forearms and wrists.

The harpies banked through the air, some of them coming to rest on crags of the bluff, others circling and gaining altitude. Jubal and Juliay crouched low as a pair swept past, then gasped in shock as a shriek announced that they had been discovered.

"Shoot!" barked Jubal, and Juliay reacted to the command as if she had trained for this all her life. She stood, drew an arrow to her cheek, made sure to lead her large, slow-flying target, and let fly.

The missile took the creature through the base of its wing, and with a cry of disbelieving fury, it slumped from the air, wheeling crazily, careening down to land in the midst of the astonished trolls. In seconds, they had torn the creature to shreds, even ignoring the burns as they ripped into the foul belly.

Jubal came out from between the rocks, the bright sword held low. One of the harpies shrieked and dove, spitting fire. The warrior ducked, wincing as a spatter of flame smacked into his shoulder. Then he whipped the sword upward, a slashing blow as the grotesque preadator swept past, slicing the monster's belly from gut to neck. The harpy smacked to the ground, twitched once, and lay dead.

All around, the harpies were cawing and keening in agitation and fury, swooping and swerving through the air. Several circled the humans, though the flyers stayed high and away, fearful of that lethal sword. The rest plunged toward the trolls, again slashing the brutes with an attack of talon and flame.

"I have an idea. Shoot those!" Jubal cried, indicating the harpies below. Several had come to rest on rocks above the trolls, where they could spit their oily flame with impunity.

Again Juliay's response was instantaneous. She stepped to the brink of their ledge, drew a bead, and shot one of those harpies right through the back. It toppled forward and lay still. Before the others could react, she felled another one with a silent, deadly arrow.

Emboldened by these blows on their behalf, one of the trolls lunged forward, braving a spatter of fire across his face as he leaped to grab a harpy by the legs. He pulled the feathered killer downward, swinging it into the merciless arms of his fellows. Meanwhile, Juliay shot more arrows into the wheeling flock, several of them striking with enough force to drop a winged monster from the sky. More trolls rushed outward, and the feathered attackers scattered hastily in the face of the sudden assault.

Soon the harpies, the half dozen still aloft, had had enough. They swooped down to the river valley and flew away with all speed. The trolls quickly finished off the last of the wounded attackers, while Juliay looked at Jubal. "What do we do now?" she asked.

He nodded toward the trolls, one of which was looking toward them appraisingly. "I reckon we see if they're willing to talk."

18

Night of Fire, Day of Darkness

Fakir's sun,
Nightfall's cloak;
Murder done,
Fallen oak.
Wreath of laurel,
Twilit skies;
Might makes moral
Weakness dies.

From the First Tapestry
Tales of the Time Before

The druids raised a mighty wind, and the balloon bearing Natac, Sirien, and Roland across the lake raced with the speed of a soaring eagle. Darken found them already over the Ringhills, still riding in the center of the concentrated stream of moving air.

"Funny thing," Roland said, leaning on the rim of the gondola and looking at the lights of the city fading into a blur behind them. "I kind of wish we could get a view of the stars . . . you know, in case we don't get another chance."

Natac nodded solemnly. His mind was far away, in the villa on the hilltop, in Miradel's arms, basking in the warmth of her smile, the loving center of her embrace. He wrestled with a profound sense of melancholy, even found himself wishing that he'd allowed Owen—or anyone—to come in his place. This light airship seemed like a ridiculously frail vehicle to face a monster as great as the wyrm of the Overworld. The dragon had destroyed a much greater ship with scarcely a perceptible effort. But it was that same destructive power that made this mission necessary.

He reminded himself that the confrontation with the dragon was not intended as battle. Indeed, their hope lay in communication, negotiation. He was prepared to offer homage, even bounty, if the creature would spare the elves and other peaceful denizens of Nayve. But he remembered the descriptions of Shahkamon's fall, and he wondered if such peaceful aspirations were nothing more than fancy.

"It's remarkable, when you think about it." His reverie was broken by the sight of Roland, now looking at the small box on the floor of the gondola. Apparently his thoughts were running along the same lines as Natac's. "Such destruction, such power, contained in those little rocks."

"Pray to the goddess that we won't have to find out if they work," the warrior said grimly.

"Aye to that," the druid agreed.

Sirien had been looking forward, and now she turned to her two companions. Her eyes found Natac's, and she stared with a penetrating, understanding look. "You don't really believe that, do you? You think we'll have to use the . . . the rocks."

Pinned by that gaze, he felt like an insect on a collector's board. He could only nod. "Yes . . . yes, I do. I hope that we'll be able to find the creature on land, that I will be able to approach it alone. But, in any event, I expect that it will be looking for a fight."

Roland looked like he was going to argue, but Natac glared at him, and the druid held his tongue. In the warrior's mind, the issue was already decided. If it came to one of them carrying the rocks—the bomb, he corrected himself forcibly—then it would be him, the man who had devoted one lifetime to the practice of war and another to protecting the safety of this halcyon world. Of course he was wracked by regret; this would have been an easy decision if Miradel hadn't so recently returned. He wondered: Would it have been easier if she had been his partner for decades, for centuries, instead of for a few precious days? In his heart, he knew that his anguish would be the same.

"Look there!" cried Sirien suddenly.

She was pointing, but the guidance wasn't necessary, as both men could see the fireworks blossoming in the skies. "That's King Fedlater's realm!" Natac said. "He's launching fireworks, just like he did when *Skyreaver* passed over. But why is he attracting attention? We warned him about the dragon, told him to get his gnomes underground and wait!"

"He's a king," Roland said, logically enough. "Maybe he didn't like you telling him what to do?"

"But the dragon—if it's in the air, surely it will see!"

"I think that's the idea," Sirien said. "It has to be."

Suddenly Natac saw the logic, and his heart swelled with gratitude and admiration for the gnome king's courage. "He's *trying* to attract the serpent. If nothing else, it might delay the creature's approach to the Center for another day or two!"

"And there it is," Sirien said, her keen eyes focused on a hilltop near the source of the pyrotechnic display. "The wyrm has landed, there. Do you know, it seems to be watching the fireworks?"

The two men couldn't see it yet, but they had long learned to trust the elfmaid's keen vision. The windstream continued to carry the balloon at a high rate of speed. The fireworks were dazzling, bright, and lofty, and as they raced closer, the colorful explosions seemed to fill much of the sky. Natac strained, and finally, in the flare of a particularly bright display, spotted the serpentine shape coiled on one of the six hilltops on the ridge surrounding King Fedlater's palace.

"I'm going to lose some altitude, drop us out of the fast air," Natac said, opening the valve that let helium spill from the silken sphere. Slowly, the balloon began to descend. "Can you bring us to the side?" he asked Roland. "No sense letting the beast see us in the light of the show."

"Of course," the druid replied, already spinning his paddle in the windcasting bowl. A side gust pushed at them, and they continued to sink, but it seemed to Natac that their maneuver was painfully slow. He was acutely aware of the clumsy flight of this airship and again prayed that they wouldn't have to confront the dragon in the sky.

They were some five miles away from the source of the fireworks, and a similar distance from the dragon, when they came to rest in still air, gliding just a hundred feet or so over a craggy hilltop. A deep valley yawned beyond, and a broad, placid lake sparkled from the light of reflected stars. Natac continued to release the gas, and the balloon settled farther, the gondola soon sinking below the level of the crest, though the sphere of the flotation bag, of course, would remain in view for a long time.

The bottom of the little valley, except for the lake, was pretty thoroughly forested, so there didn't seem to be any option for setting the balloon down there. Natac cursed to himself, then tried to make a plan.

"The dragon's attention seems fixed on the palace, the fireworks," Sirien said, as if reading his mind. "We could try to come up on it from behind."

Natac couldn't think of any other plan. Besides, he acknowledged, even if they did find a place to land, it would take them the rest of the night to make their way through the rough terrain of the Ringhills to the dragon's position, and it seemed unlikely that the creature would wait around long enough for them to reach it.

So he opened several of the ballast bags, felt the airship lurch upward as two hundred pounds of water spilled away. Soon they crested the hilltops again, and Roland spun a wind that continued to bear them off to the side, perpendicular to their previous bearing. The fireworks boomed and sparked and flared unabated, and though Natac and Roland could rarely catch a glimpse of the dark, coiled shape of their quarry, Sirien assured them that it remained fixed on the aerial display.

During one particularly brilliant series of explosions, lights of yellow and gold and green blossoming into great spheres, then cascading like a series of falling stars, glimmering, trailing smoke as they settled toward the ground, the dragon sat upward. The massive wings spread to the side, catching and reflecting the eerie glow, and the creature stretched its long neck forward, head raised high, eyes glimmering in the light of the dying fires.

As those embers fell to the ground, there was a minute of utter darkness during which the night seemed oppressively cold, unnaturally still. Even Sirien, straining to see, could make out nothing until the next volley of pyrotechnics began. Then, in the new wash of white light, all three of them saw that the dragon's hilltop perch was now vacant.

"It flew!" gasped Roland.

"Where? Find it, quickly!" Natac said, frantically scanning the skies. Still looking outward, he knelt and picked up the box containing the two rocks that would make Socrates's bomb. He didn't open the lid yet, but he was trembling with tension, terribly afraid that he would be too late.

The balloon drifted across another low hilltop, shadowy valleys plunging steeply to all sides, and even Sirien remained unable to spot the flying serpent. "It could be in one of the valleys beyond the king's realm," she said. "None of the light reaches there. It's all shadowed by the hilltops."

"If it goes that way, it won't have any trouble seeing us," Natac speculated, "if we let ourselves get silhouetted. We've got to get lower!"

Again he released gas, opening the valve wide, so that the airship slid down past the hilltop. They could see the shadowy slope passing rapidly, and Roland frantically spun the wind to keep them moving away from the ground. Only when they had dropped hundreds of feet, far enough so that even the crest of the balloon was below the ridgeline, did Natac close the valve and drop more ballast, gradually easing their descent. This valley, at least, seemed to be mostly broad meadow, clear of trees. A narrow creek spilled down the nearest hillside, a foaming cataract plunging to a small pool at the base of the slope.

He was still clutching the box, and his eyes scanned the horizon above the ridges, looking for some sign of the wyrm, when he heard the low growl from underneath the balloon. Sirien started to scream, biting back the sound into a strangled gasp, and then it seemed that the ground rose up toward them.

The dragon was there, right below! Natac fumbled with the latch, almost dropping the box and its lethal contents. The basket lurched sharply as it was struck, then pulled sharply downward. He heard the rending tear of silk as the air bag was nipped, then felt a hard blow as the gondola struck the ground. He fell, rolling across the turf, the box falling from his hands.

When he looked up, he saw the vast serpentine neck arching overhead. The head, with a mouth big enough to swallow him in one gulp, loomed close, and a great, taloned foot came up, spreading wide enough to block out the sky.

"WHAT are they waiting for?" asked Jordon, lying on the rocks beside Karkald, staring at the great formation of Delvers on the valley floor.

"I don't know," the captain replied. "But I think we should stay here until we find out."

An hour earlier he had sent the infantry, under the capable Gaynroc's command, marching along the ridge crest with instructions to seek civilization and potentially advantageous terrain. Half the Rockriders had gone with them as scouts, while the other half remained here, with Karkald, where they could keep an eye on the Delvers and their gigantic allies.

Jordon looked up, then whispered to Karkald. "I've never been to Nayve before, but I've heard about it. I'm guessing that's the sun coming down, Captain. Is that right?"

Karkald didn't need to check the sky to know that the Lighten Hour was approaching. Already he could see details of the surrounding ridges and valleys with much more clarity than a few minutes earlier. As the illumination increased, he could make out the individual ranks and files within the Delver formations. At the same time, he was increasingly surprised by their lack of movement.

"Won't they have to get under cover before daylight?" asked his lieutenant, echoing Karkald's own thoughts. "I thought I remembered learning that they suffered greatly under the sun."

"Yes . . . at least, three hundred years ago, they did. And I don't see them erecting pavilions or screens, as they sometimes did to avoid being caught in the open. In fact, the whole thing is pretty damn mysterious."

In the growing daylight, the great storm rising beyond the valley looked, if anything, darker than ever. The black cloud roiled and seethed, periodic lightning flashing within the lobes of darkness. The murky mass rose into the sky as high as the dwarves could see, and Karkald had a feeling it continued to rise even beyond.

"Look—what's that?" asked Jordon.

They stared at the face of the turgid cloud, and it looked as though tiny flecks of black ash were being cast from the storm, settling almost like snowflakes all across their view. There were hundreds, thousands of these wispy shadows, and though they looked small from here, Karkald knew they must be the size of blankets or large birds. They settled gently, fluttering downward in utter silence, wisping this way and that as the breeze eddied around the mountains.

Eventually, still falling, the black specks assembled into three great clouds, one over each of the Delver armies. They continued to drift downward, and the swirling clouds tightened until the pattern became clear.

"They're like cloaks, falling right onto the Delvers," declared Jordon, shivering.

"Yes . . . but not just cloaks." Karkald stared hard, chilled by the sense of menace he perceived in that deceptively gentle cascade. Concentrating into aerial globes of darkness, they sank onto the Delver armies very gradually, as if they were great spheres slowly deflating, settling to the ground.

But when the last of them had merged with the Delvers, they might as well have disappeared. From this vantage, the Blind Ones looked unchanged, tiny dark specks arrayed with military precision across the valley floor. Under full daylight now, the wicked dwarves showed no sign of suffering.

Instead, they began to march. Their discipline was clear and impressive, as one company after another peeled away from the great army blocks. The Delvers formed into countless march columns, moving quickly along the valley floor. Some of them forded the narrow stream and moved toward a notch in the ridge across the valley. Others started toward the elevation where the Seers were watching, and Karkald knew that his men would have to mount and withdraw very quickly.

For another few minutes, he stayed in place, watching. He wasn't worried about discovery; the wind was blowing into his face, so the Unmirrored would not catch the scent of them or their ferr'ells.

"I've never seen them move so fast," he said to Jordon, whispering because they knew that sound was the Delver's best sense.

"It's like they can perceive the layout of the ground," the lieutenant answered in amazement. "They're picking the best routes toward the heights and along the valley floor."

Finally, the Seers stood and pulled themselves into the saddles of their restive ferr'ells. For a moment, they were silhouetted against the ridge, and it was then that they heard a shout from below. Many Delvers were pointing in their direction, and immediately, a dozen companies were advancing at a trot toward the Seer scouts.

"Let's ride!" Karkald cried, and the small band urged their mounts to speed. The ferr'ells responded with alacrity, and they were soon a mile away, bounding down the far side of the ridge.

But Karkald's mind was deeply disturbed, and his thoughts went over the events of their discovery like a dog worrying a bone. Every way he looked at it, there was only one conclusion, and it was terrifying:

The Delvers, every one of them blind since the creation of their race in ancient times, had *seen* them.

ZYSTYL felt the cool presence on his shoulders, like a protective cloak that had fallen from the Worldfall, a barrier against the hateful sun of the Fourth Circle. He turned to Jarristal, saw her metal jaws gaping in pleasure, and knew that she, too, was protected. Indeed, a look across the ranks of his troops showed that each one of the Delvers was shaded by the silken darkness, fully proof against the cruel daylight.

Only then did the rest of the truth sink in: He was *seeing* the world around him! Though he lacked eyes, had never known this sense before, the pictures of this valley were somehow being carried to his mind.

His Hurtstone flamed upon his breast, and he touched it, looked at it lovingly. It seemed to carry the answer, telling him that these shadow cloaks were a gift from a great, powerful god . . . one who cherished Zystyl, who watched after and protected him, as he protected all the Delvers, all those who hated the sun, hated the vile creatures of light and warmth.

All around the army was surging forward. He looked across the valley, saw dozens of companies swarming up a hill in a clamor of drums and cries, pursuing some foe they had spotted. Zystyl exulted in the charge, and he sent the powerful command to the rest of his troops. They would advance!

He looked back and saw the massive bulk of the Worldfall, the source of the cloaks that had so blessed him and his dwarves. In that murky cloud he saw the will of his master, and again he turned to face the center. There was a secret there, a secret that held the key to this world. It was up to him to seize and hold that treasure. . . .

Until the real army, the teeming legions of the dead, could come and bring about the real triumph of darkness.

"D'YOU reckon they speak our language?" Jubal asked, looking warily down at the trolls. He blinked, startled by a thought. "You know, I didn't speak it myself, until you brought me here."

Juliay smiled gently. "Yes . . . all creatures of Nayve speak the same tongue. I heard the trolls talking when we first encountered them beside *Skyreaver.* It was a crude version of our tongue, but I could understand them."

Jubal nodded and rested the sword upon his shoulder, pointing backward but quickly accessible. The trolls had finished with the carcasses of the slain harpies, and now that same creature that had started toward them earlier, the large one who seemed to be some kind of leader, was looking upward with an implacable expression on his gnarled, woody face.

"You! Troll!" called the man, taking a few steps downward from the ledge. He paused when he was still about thirty feet above the creature.

"What you?" barked the brute, the words harsh but decipherable.

"I am a man," he replied. "A human. But I am not your enemy."

The troll snorted, then opened that fanged maw. But he waited for a moment before speaking. "Shiny claw!" He gestured at the sword. "Cuts!"

"Big teeth!" snapped Jubal. "Bite! But if you won't bite, I won't cut."

The troll looked around at the apple grove across the valley where most of his tribe was gathered, at the mangled corpses, surrounded by dirty gray feathers, where the harpies had fallen. "Why you kill harpies?" he asked.

"We hate harpies," Juliay said, coming to stand beside the man. "We'll kill all the harpies, if we can."

The troll nodded. This seemed to be a goal he could relate to. "I kill harpies, too," he declared.

"Then let us be friends . . . and kill harpies together," Jubal said. "Shall we have peace?"

"Friends? Peace? These strange words," the troll grumbled.

"I am called Juliay, and this is Jubal," the druidess said. "What is your name?"

"I am Awfulbark, King of Udderthud!" proclaimed the creature, pounding his chest with a fist. "Great king!"

"Why did you attack us?" asked Juliay.

The troll scowled, looking down at the ground almost as if he was abashed. Finally, he raised his gnarled face again. "Hungry," he admitted.

"Y'all can't eat us!" Jubal declared, lifting the sword and holding it high. "Not unless you want to face the silver claw!"

"No," Awfulbark said mournfully. "Can't eat you. You like trolls, only small and ugly. Not food."

"Small and ugly?" murmured Juliay, taking Jubal's arm. He chuckled dryly.

"If we come down there, will you attack us?" asked the man.

The troll looked at him with those black, lightless eyes for a very long time. Finally, he shook his head slowly. "No, won't attack. Come, eat apples, and then we kill more harpies. You shoot sticks, knock 'em down. We kill!"

"Can we trust them?" Juliay whispered.

"On the one hand, I think we *have* to trust them," Jubal said. "Unless you want to head back into the mountains and live on black rocks for awhile. But on the other hand, you know, I think he's telling the truth."

"So do I," Juliay agreed.

They didn't lay down their weapons or abandon their caution, but they started down the hill together, toward the trolls, wondering how long their tenuous peace might hold.

THE dragon noticed a stream spilling down the valley nearby, pleased that such splashing, lively water should be in this place. He noticed that the stream curled into a small pool, swirling merrily before spilling over the rim and on its course toward the lowlands. All in all, he was feeling rather smug, content that he had detected danger and acted to remove the threat.

Regillix Avatar inspected his three captives, the creatures he had once thought of as wingless harpies. Once separated from the floating globe, they were rather small and harmless looking. Certainly each was no bigger than a harpy, but he could see that size was where the resemblance ended.

"What are you?" he asked.

One of them, a brownish creature with a shock of black fur atop his head, rose to stand on his hind legs and looked up at the dragon with a level glare. "I am a human, called Natac. This is another human, a druid called Roland, and an elf, named Sirien."

Somewhat impressed by this display of politeness—a harpy would merely have spat in his face—Regillix bobbed his head serenely. "And I am Regillix Avatar."

"We have come here, to the Ringhills, to talk to you," said Natac. His voice was high-pitched, and his words tumbled over themselves with unseemly speed, but the ancient wyrm was not surprised by that. He knew that such speech was typical of short-lived and weak creatures. He was, however, surprised by what the man said.

"Why should I waste words with you?" asked the dragon slowly. He lowered his forepaw to the ground and squatted at rest. All three people were between his forelegs, in easy reach of talon or tooth. The druid and elf were holding each other tightly, looking up with widespread eyes, while Natac still stood with confidence. Regillix was reminded of the proud pegasus, the stallion that had overcome its natural fear to converse with the mighty wyrm.

"You should speak with us because we seek peace," said the man. In the growing illumination of Lighten, he looked earnest and sincere, his dark eyes level on the dragon's face. "Never before has a dragon come to Nayve, and we would willingly greet you, and treat you well, if you would turn from making war upon us."

The wyrm snorted, a blast of wind that caused Natac to stagger backward. "I am not the first dragon to come to Nayve. The first was Plarinal, and he was killed by your weapons. He will be avenged."

"I know of the killing of Plarinal," said Natac. He drew a deep breath and met the dragon's glare. "It was my weapon that slew him. And I swear to you, and the goddess, I only struck him in defense. He was attacking my airship. The same airship, in fact, that you destroyed . . . so perhaps, in that sense, your vengeance is complete."

"Indeed," Regillix declared. "You speak with some wisdom, not unlike the angels. In fact, you seem more like angels than harpies. I understand that there is little to be gained by war, except against harpies, when they must be slain or they will slay instead. But I have been brought here against my will, and this angers me. I seek justice and retribution."

"I can tell that you are very wise," Natac said. "You see this elfmaid, Sirien. Do you know that when you broke the homes of elves on the rim of the great canyon, you slew her father and her sister? All of her people, a homeland destroyed? Can you see, in your wisdom, how your destruction is dangerous to us both?"

"But the Worldfall?" mused the dragon. "Is that not the work of Nayve?"

"No!" cried the man. "It is a Chaos Storm that brings danger to us all. Our druids have studied the Tapestry of the Worldweaver and seen that this storm has a source beyond your world or mine. Do you know of the harpies that have been brought here by that same storm?"

"Indeed, harpies are a pox upon all the circles. Perhaps you speak the truth—" the dragon started to say, when he was assailed by a blast of sound that tumbled him to the side and left him, stunned, upon the valley floor. He kicked and flapped, and tried to rise, but his wings and legs wouldn't move.

At first he thought that the man had attacked him somehow, but from the edge of his eye, he saw Natac and his companions were also sprawled on the ground, staring at something across the hillside. The trio had not been as sorely stunned by the blast as the dragon, however, for they scrambled to their feet and began waving and shouting, while Regillix found himself paralyzed, utterly helpless.

With a massive effort, the great serpent was able to twist his head enough to see. He was lying beside the small pool, where the stream swirled before tumbling away. But his attention extended beyond the water, toward movement he discerned coming over the rim of the hill.

Tiny figures were advancing toward him, a rank of them on horseback. They had spears held like lances, steel tips glittering in the sun. In the lead was a wiry elf, her golden hair trailing in the breeze. And in her hand was a weapon, and when she raised it to her lips and blew again, the dragon's head slammed backward, and darkness closed in.

His last awareness was that he had been felled by a blast from a horn.

VULTARI sat on a charred log that lay flat on the ground. The lord of the harpies held a haunch of deer, the delicacy he had claimed from a troll's larder, in both hands. Blood slicked his jaws, and he groaned with pleasure as he tore off and swallowed another big piece of meat.

All around, his harpies were resting, feasting, or fighting among themselves over such prizes as they could find in the rubble of the burning town. His precious gem sparkled on his feathered breast, and as he ate, the great harpy spread his

wings, then raised his face and uttered an exultant shriek. He
felt the stone, warm and pleasant, and he knew his mastery
over all his kind.

The summons came through space and time, over Worldsea, and under sky. The dazzling stone was the conduit, and
the will of his distant master came into Vultari's cruel mind as
if it was his own thought. Again he shrieked, three shrill caws
that brought the harpies from their perches in a great, shrieking cloud.

Vultari himself led the flight, and his triumphant cry rang
through the air, piercing like a shock, galvanizing the thousands of his creatures that had come to rest in the lofty
branches of the oaken forest.

In places, the wreckage of the houses where the trolls had
lived still smoldered. Every one of the wooded abodes had
been ransacked, anything edible being fought over and de-
voured by the rapacious harpies. Everything else they had set
on fire. Blazes crackled through the trees, wasting the great
trunks, filling the air with clouds of acrid smoke.

For several days, the great flock had stayed here, looting,
burning, and feasting. But now they had a goal. Vultari spread
his great wings, twenty feet across, and scooped the air to
gain altitude. The shrieking numbers of his flock followed,
and the commands of Karlath-Fayd burned in his mind.

It was in his response to that command that Vultari turned,
winging a straight line, setting his course for Riven Deep . . .
and the secret that his master had held for more than four
thousand years.

"Wait! Stop!" cried Natac, rising, shaking off the lingering
confusion from the blast that had knocked him down. He
sprinted as fast as he could to try to hold back the riders as
they charged the helpless dragon. But even as he started running, he could see that he would never make it in time.

"Janitha!" He heard Sirien scream her sister's name, but
even that had no effect on the impetuous charge. Now Natac

recognized the khandaughter, saw her wielding the horn in the midst of the spear-carrying riders.

The dragon kicked once, the large rear foot pawing at the ground. The tail coiled and whipped to the side as the great creature, regaining control of its will with a visible effort, slowly rolled onto its belly. The great head came off the ground as Janitha raised the horn, once more placed the mouthpiece to her lips.

Only then did the charging ponies swerve in their approach, suddenly veering to the right and left. The khandaughter pulled her reins, the horn unblown for the moment, and even the dragon reared back in surprise. Magic crackled in the air, a swirl of sorcery bright beside the little stream.

Natac saw that two figures had materialized, women who were now standing to either side of a small pool at the bottom of the hill. He saw the long black hair blowing and knew this was Miradel; the other he recognized as Belynda.

For a moment, his world seemed to stop, and he felt nothing but terror for the elfwoman and the druid who had suddenly appeared in the midst of imminent violence. It seemed certain that they would be ridden down by the Hyac or swatted away by the dragon, who rose onto his mighty legs, and now appeared to be fully regaining his strength. With a roar, Regillix Avatar reared high, his wings fanning a gale through the small valley in the hills.

But the horses swerved, avoiding the two women, the band splitting apart, each side veering away from the dragon as the ponies bucked and panicked and turned to flee. And the dragon, too, held back his strike, though his slitted eyes followed the shape of the elfwoman who had blown that mighty horn.

"Please . . . wait!" cried the warrior, finally staggering up to Miradel and Belynda. He looked for Janitha, who was bringing her bucking pony under control. Sirien ran to her sister and spoke earnestly, while Natac turned back to the dragon.

"We must not fight!" he declared.

"And why not?" growled the serpent. "I have been sorely pained!"

"We must not fight each other," proclaimed Belynda, her voice as firm and strong as any that had ever resounded through the Senate. "Because we have a greater enemy in common!"

The dragon settled slightly, furling his wings and studying the newcomers and Natac from beneath hooded eyelids. "You people are not lacking in courage, I will admit," he declared, raising his head to observe Janitha and her riders. "But if you blast that noisemaker again, I will kill you." The elfwoman looked back with raw hatred but did not move to raise the horn.

"An invasion has begun," Belynda said. She held her crystal Globe in her hands, raising it so that the dragon could see. "I have seen some of it here. The harpies of the Overworld have come from the Chaos Storm in great numbers, and they flock toward the Center."

Natac was picturing that onslaught, already imagining the deployments of his troops and batteries. Circle at Center could be defended, he felt certain, though not without dire cost. But surely the rapacious flyers could be driven off.

Then he realized that Belynda was still talking. "It is worse than that. A great army of Delvers has marched from the storm as well, at least three times the number that allied with the Crusaders. And they, too, march toward the Center." She still directed her speech to Regillix Avatar, though all in the valley could hear. Sirien and Janitha, dismounted, came closer. "It is my belief, Ancient One, that you are no friend of these harpies, nor of the evil that drives them."

"What drives them?" asked the wyrm in a low growl. "What brings attackers from two circles here, to the Center?"

"It is the Deathlord, who shall not be named," Miradel said quietly. "This I have seen in the Tapestry of the Worldweaver. He who sent the legions of the dead against Nayve in the Time Before . . . now he musters again. The Delvers are his vanguard, and the harpies his eyes and his talons. His dark ships mass across the Worldsea, filled with the shades of warriors, deathless legions already embarked, coming here!"

"But the canyon!" Natac said. "The harpies can take to the air, of course, but the Delvers will never be able to cross Riven Deep."

"That may not be true. . . . Is it?" Belynda said, looking to the khandaughter. "You should know that the harpies have already discovered the secret. And I . . . I followed the image of the harpies in the Globe, and I saw the secret as well."

Natac heard Janitha gasp, saw her exchange a shocked glance with her sister. "What secret?" he demanded.

"Across the gulf . . . it is hidden from view of the rim, but it exists, a hundred miles from Shahkamon."

"What exists?" wondered Natac, fearing the answer.

"There is a bridge," Janitha replied. "A secret bridge known only to a few of the Hyac . . . a bridge that has stood across Riven Deep for five thousand years."

19

Roads to Shamhome

*From deeping dell
And lofty peak,
And wood and mead and swale,
Comes stalking now
The lethal shade,
To terrify the pale.*

From the Tapestry of the Worldweaver
Tales of the Time Before

Despite the verbal treaty with the troll king, Jubal and Juliay weren't prepared to put up their weapons. The man
kept the long sword slung casually across his shoulder, cushioned on a makeshift pad of rope, and the druid held an arrow
in the same hand as her bow, knowing she could draw and
shoot in a split second.

But she prayed to the goddess that the troll would be true to
his word.

"See smoke?" asked Awfulbark, pointing the murky cloud
that lingered over a distant portion of the woods. The humans
nodded, and the troll king explained. "Udderthud. My city.
Harpies burn."

Juliay wondered what kind of city these trolls had dwelled
in, since—before the king's remark—she had assumed they
were a nomadic tribe of forest-dwelling savages. She found

herself feeling surprisingly sympathetic toward the crude, dangerous creatures.

"Come. Tribe under apple trees. We go."

The two humans followed the trolls through the shallow stream, retracing the route of their flight from the grove. They were drawing near to the trees when their attention was distracted by a dull screech of noise, suggesting great volume but originating a long distance away.

"If those are harpies, then I reckon there are a lot more of 'em than I'm anxious to meet," Jubal declared laconically. "Mebbe we should get under some cover."

The trolls were already hurrying, lumbering toward the trees in that gangling gait, and the humans wasted no time in racing along. Soon they were under the shelter of the interlocking branches, hearing the noise swell in volume as the shrieking flyers drew closer. There was no doubt this was the sound of a great band of harpies, keening shrieks piercing the air, originating from all parts of the sky, swelling closer until the nightmare cacophony was directly overhead. The creatures made no move to plunge through the branches, however, and in fact it seemed quite possible that the harpies didn't even know the trolls were there. In any event, the sounds continued on, spreading into the distance even as more of the shrill flyers continued to arrive.

"I'm going to climb one of these trees and have a look," Juliay announced. "It sounds like they're all going the same direction."

"No!" Jubal said. "Too dangerous . . . I reckon I should be the one to have a look."

She smiled at him, but it was stern, not a humorous, expression. "I know how to climb a tree. Besides, it's probably just as dangerous down here. Why don't you keep an eye on Awfulbark and his cronies. I'll be back in a minute."

Before he could object further, she seized an overhead branch and pulled herself up. The trees had many horizontal limbs, and climbing was easy, at least until she had worked her way into the slender branches thirty or forty feet off the ground. There she propped herself between two swaying limbs, and by leaning forward, she caught a glimpse of a sky filled with winged, shrieking creatures. They might have been a huge flock of crows, when viewed from a distance, but several flew close enough that she could see the grotesque faces and the bony arms dangling down from the bodies, jointed to shoulders just below the base of the wings.

She was well hidden, and furthermore, none of the harpies seemed to be looking downward, so she felt safe from detection. In fact, the monsters were all flying on the same bearing, and while she watched, the bulk of the great flock passed her by, until there were only a flew stragglers, cawing vociferously, winging as fast as they could in an effort to catch up.

Swinging downward, she dropped from branch to branch with simian agility, and a few seconds later came to rest on the grassy ground. Awfulbark and Jubal both looked at her expectantly.

"They're flying in the direction of the Center," she reported. "All of them, apparently—though perhaps they've left a few behind in the forest. I couldn't tell."

"What do you think we should do?" asked Jubal.

"We have to follow them," she said. "This is not just a few pesky raiders. It looks like a full-scale invasion."

"Reckon I'm ready for some walkin'," the warrior replied. He looked at the troll. "You comin', too?"

"Leave Udderthud?" Awfulbark slumped, as if a heavy weight had been laid on his shoulders. "Our home!" He looked around stubbornly. "Stay here, instead? Eat apples?"

"How much of a home is it now?" Juliay asked sternly. "If they've burned it, you won't find much there, will you?"

The troll king shook his head lugubriously.

"You wanted to kill harpies, you said?" the druid pressed, not waiting for an answer. "Well, so do I . . . and wherever those harpies are going, we're certain to find others—*lots* of others—who want to kill harpies, too. If you come with us, you can help do that. You'll meet allies . . . more people like us, humans and elves—even gnomes, giants, centaurs. All the peoples of Nayve will welcome you."

Juliay shook her head impatiently. "If you don't want to kill harpies, you can go back to Udderthud and try to rebuild your city. As for us, we've wasted enough time." She turned to Jubal. "Are you ready to go?"

"On the spot," he said, hoisting his sword across his shoulder. He looked at Awfulbark. "Those harpies burned your city," he said. "We're going to teach 'em a lesson. Don't you think you should come along, too?"

Awfulbark's woody lips tightened into a glare that might have been determination. "Up! Up, you trolls!" he shouted. "We go—kill harpies!"

THE Bridge of Sharnhome it was called, and it was a secret span that for centuries has been known only to a few of the Hyaccan elves. It was guarded by a black bluff, Janitha explained, which served to conceal it from those who looked into Riven Deep, except from a few narrow vantages on the rim. She explained that a battle had been fought there, during the Time Before, and that the forces of Nayve had held back an invading tide before it could cross.

For an hour they argued and accused, until at last desires for violence and vengeance were supplanted by the need for cooperation, the importance of standing together against an even greater foe. Natac was conscious of time slipping away, but he, Belynda, and Quilene patiently sought consensus from the two Hyaccan elves, who grieved for their homeland but, at last, began to see the threat to the whole world that was looming, so imminent. The druids Miradel and Roland spoke to the dragon, though without drawing any response so far. But they hammered out the bones of a plan, which was all they had time to do.

"We'll split up, then, and meet at the bridge," Natac concluded. He looked up, to the side of the dragon's great head. "Is that agreeable to you?"

Regillix Avatar had remained aloof from conversation or opinion as the humans and elves had frantically formed their plan. The serpent's crocodilian head, eyes hooded as they had been for the last hour, was ten feet above the ground, just to the side of the little knot of people. The rest of the wyrm's great body, wings furled and tail doubled back along the scaled flank, nearly filled the meadow.

The riders of Shahkamon, except for Janitha, had withdrawn to the rim of the bowl-shaped valley and picketed their ponies on the far side, out of sight of the wyrm. They watched from the ridge in a tense knot, looking down at the urgent conference.

Finally, the dragon exhaled a long puff of air and then spoke. "There is wisdom in your decisions. I see now that your enemy is mine—that is, the Master of the Worldfall. And if this bridge is menaced by harpies, then you speak of my eternal enemies. I shall assist you."

"All right," Natac said brusquely, concealing his great sense of relief. "We don't have any time to waste. Belynda?"

The sage-ambassador was sitting cross-legged on the grass, peering into her crystal Globe. "I've found the dwarves and their golems. Still marching this way, on a course toward the bridge. The Seer dwarves are staying in front of them, not far away. As for Owen, Tamarwind, and Gallupper, they've brought the army out of the city and across the Causeway of Wood. They're already entering the Ringhills."

"All right." He turned to Quilene, who was kneeling by the waters of the little pool. The sage-enchantress rose and nodded. "This will work. . . . I can teleport Belynda back to the army—"

"And I will get to Owen, Tamarwind, and Gallupper, have them march for the bridge immediately, with as much force as they've mustered," Belynda noted. "It will take something like a week to get to Sharnhome. But I know they'll move with all possible haste."

"Sirien, Roland, Janitha?" Natac said next.

"We'll mount as soon as we're finished here and ride for the bridge with the rest of the Hyac," the khandaughter declared. "We might be able to make it in three days, four at the most."

"All right, that should be about the same time as the Delvers get there, by my reckoning," Natac said, his mind whirling. There were many forces in motion, many threats closing in, but the plan was the best they could do under the circumstances. At last he turned to the great dragon, who had finally laid his head on the ground so that he met the warrior's gaze at eye level.

"You will bear Miradel and Quilene on your back, and fly to the bridge immediately, correct?"

The serpentine tongue flicked from between the jaws. "I will do my part." He turned one yellow eye toward the two women. "I have carried angels before, and Gabriel has told me that the best place to sit is right at the base of my neck. You will get some back support from my spine, and there are some horned scales for you to grasp."

"And you are willing to try?" Natac asked again, looking at his druid and the sage-enchantress. Both of them nodded, though their eyes were wide as they studied the rough, craggy outline of the serpent's back.

"Then we go! And may the goddess lend speed and protection to us all," said the warrior. He embraced the two sisters and Roland, and the trio hastened up the hill to rally the elven riders for their desperate journey.

Only then did Natac see the box from Socrates containing the two explosive lumps of metal. He picked it up, and then Quilene took it from him. "I will carry this on dragonback," she said. "That will bring it to the bridge as quickly as anything."

"All right," the warrior agreed, anxious to be rid of the container even as he was reluctant to give it up. Quilene and Belynda went to the whirling pool, where the sage-enchantress would work the first of her teleportation spells.

In the meantime, Natac went to Miradel and took her in his arms. Her eyes, the violet as dark as a purpled sky, swam with tears, but her voice was strong as she wished him luck and speed.

"And you, as well," he said. "I can't think that the goddess brought you back here just to have us torn apart by war. We'll come through this."

She smiled, a bittersweet expression. "I love your idealism," she said, "though I have no trouble believing that the goddess brought me back for just such a parting. But whatever happens, know that my love will go with you."

"And mine with you," he replied. They kissed, their lips and hearts melding, and they stayed together until it was Natac's turn to look into the waters of the swirling pool.

KARKALD and a half dozen Rockriders were bringing up the rear of the Seer formation, but they found they had to move quickly to stay ahead of the marching columns of Delvers. Further observation, watching enemy dwarves step over jutting rocks, or point instructions to each other with gestures of their hands, had confirmed his earlier impression: Something had bestowed upon these eyeless creatures a sense that seemed in every respect like sight.

Even more ominously, the Delvers had been joined by a hundred or so creatures that at first had been taken for great birds of prey. When the Seers got a close look at one of them, however, they were appalled by the sight of the ghastly features, the wickedly sparking eyes, and the gaunt, wiry arms of these flyers. The beast spat a wicked gob of fire toward the dwarves before several well-aimed shots from the crossbows shot it dead. Even so, it was an ominous addition to an already deadly force.

Now the mounted Seers were racing down a path into a river valley, a place that was flat-bottomed, with patches of grass and hardy shrubs visible among the smooth stretches of gravel and bare rock. The first riders sprang across the narrow waterway, near an eddy where the current spun about behind a large rock. Karkald was about to nudge Bloodeater into such a leap when the ferr'ell reared back in surprise.

Karkald shouted in astonishment—suddenly a man was

standing on the domed rock that had been bare an instant before—and reached instinctively for his sword. By the time his
mount had settled again, however, the dwarf recognized the
human.

"Natac!"

"Yes, old friend. And what a pleasure it is to find you
among these doughty warriors."

The other Seers had drawn swords and raised crossbows,
but now they lowered their arms as Karkald held up his
hands. "Fellows, this is the *real* hero of the Nayve War," he
said, then winked at the human. "Though I guess you call it
the Crusader War, don't you?"

"I wish I could be calling it the final war, but you probably
already know that's not the case," Natac said, embarrassed
and warmed by his old companion's praise.

"No. And I don't suppose you got yourself magicked here
just so we could swap stories of old campaigns. What do you
know?"

Stepping off the rock onto the stream's shore, Natac
quickly recounted the situation in brief: The Delver march
toward the all-important bridge, the defenses that were racing
to reach the strategic crossing, with the race going to the
harpies and the Blind Ones, as it now looked.

"And if they hold this bridge, then they have the route to
invade the whole of Nayve?" Karkald guessed.

"Yes . . . and Miradel has seen in the Tapestry, there's a
large army—a much larger army—mustering behind the
dwarves. It has been raised on the Fifth Circle, and already
crosses the Worldsea."

"Miradel?" Karkald's eyes widened, as Natac nodded.
"Well, there's another tale I'd like to hear, when we have a little time. But I have one more piece of news, and not a happy
bit, at that. These Delvers are different. They were altered in
the shadow of that great storm, there in the direction neither
metal nor wood."

"I know the storm," Natac said. "But how are they changed?"

"For one thing, they don't seem bothered in the least by

full daylight. More significant, even—somehow, the eyeless buggers seem to be able to see."

Natac looked stunned by the news, but he quickly shook it off and forged ahead. "Do you think you can do anything to slow them down?" he asked.

"Let's keep moving while we talk," Karkald replied, with a glance at the ridge crest behind them. "Our friends will be coming into view shortly. Do you want to ride?"

Natac looked askance as the ferr'ell turned its reddish eyes toward him, then shook his head. "I'll jog along beside, if it's all the same to you."

"Suit yourself." Bloodeater and the other five mounts of the rear guard started ahead, pacing easily, and the human kept up without difficulty.

"Slow them down, eh?" Karkald wondered. "Hmph . . . I was just starting to think we'd best get out of their way. You've probably seen in the Globe. We're five hundred against, what, fifty or sixty thousand? It's a tall order."

"I know," the man agreed. "But I see you've got yourselves some cavalry. These things look pretty fierce."

Karkald chuckled grimly. "Tell you what . . . I see another hilltop coming up. We'll give you a little demonstration."

An hour later, Karkald had gathered the fifty-odd riders who still remained, concealing them among the rocks at the crest of the low hill. The infantry on foot, under Gaynroc's command, had continued onward at a double march, leading the Delvers on, following the route Natac had indicated led to the Bridge of Sharnhome. It seemed obvious that crucial span was the Delver objective as well.

Natac remained with his old friend, and the two warriors looked through a crack between two large boulders, watching the vast, dusty column of the Delvers pass below them. The metal giants strode in the lead, like black behemoths, each step thumping solidly, the huge bodies rolling only slightly as they steadily advanced. "Those bastards are machines, believe it or not," Karkald muttered. "Full of pipes and steam, but killers."

"Golems?" Natac suggested, and he saw the dwarf's grim nod.

The hidden Seers waited until the golems had passed, and then waited a little longer until the full flank of one Delver column was fully exposed below them.

"From here you can really see how many of them there are," Natac whispered in awe. The army looked like three parallel rivers in flood, dark, wide, unstoppable.

Karkald nodded. "I estimate about three times as many as came up here three hundred years ago."

"Are you sure you want to go ahead?" Natac asked.

The dwarf shrugged. "It'll be a hit and run. We can hurt some of them, but I won't expect it to slow the march much."

"Good luck," Natac replied.

In another minute, the Rockriders were mounted. Karkald gave a hand signal, and the sleek mounts leaped out from the boulder field. They raced down the hill, each bounding faster than a galloping horse. Each Seer rider had a shield on his left arm, a sword or axe in his right hand, as they charged in eerie silence.

Even so, the Delvers immediately saw the danger. Those on the far left flank of the vast column smoothly wheeled, forming a shield wall three ranks deep, while the rest of the dwarves continued their steady march.

"Hit 'em hard, lads!" Karkald cried, knowing their only chance of disrupting the march required them to break through that initial wall and tangle the formation of the bulk of the column.

Bloodeater hurled himself through the air in twenty-foot leaps that brought the ferr'ell full into the face of two Delvers. The armored dwarves went down, cruel claws tearing at their necks. Karkald aimed his sword at a dwarf in the second rank, splitting the blank faceplate with a hard chop. All around him, his riders were smashing into the enemy line, and the shock of the charge sent the sturdy defenders staggering backward.

Ferr'ells leaped here and there, rending, kicking, biting. Seer weapons hacked, and with another surge, the charge carried them into the thick of the marching column. Now Delvers were all around, and the chaos of battle rang out in metallic clangs, shouted commands, and the screams of the wounded. Karkald's sword arm worked like a piston, up and down, splitting armor and faces and skulls. Bloodeater whirled beneath him, a living tornado, ripping apart one Delver after another. Enemy dwarves, layered in black armor, threw themselves fearlessly against the talons and weapons of the riders, and the Seers cut them down in droves.

But a quick glance showed the captain that their initial advantage was already lost. More enemy dwarves, countless thousands of them, were rushing out of the column from before and behind, swinging beyond the original formations. They made a pair of pincers threatening to trap the mounted Seers. Harpies, too, started to dive on them, though their claws couldn't penetrate the steel of caps and breastplates, and in the tangled melee, their flaming spumes were more likely to strike Delvers than Seers. Within another minute the two, enclosing wings would meet, and the Seer riders would be trapped in a lethal ring of black steel.

"Fall back!" Karkald cried. His mount leaped high in the air, a bound that carried him free from the Delver throng. The rest of the Seers did the same thing, their ferr'ells jumping high, leaping over the foe to the open ground beyond. Once free from the enemy column, they raced away, bounding up the hill toward the scant shelter of the rocky summit.

By the time they reached that crest, the enemy army had abandoned its pursuit and re-formed its march columns. Leaving the bodies of the dead and dying behind, the great invasion marched on with no apparent delay.

"THOSE are Seer dwarves," Juliay said. "Though I've never seen anything like the creatures some are riding. . . . They look like giant weasels! These dwarves were a staunch ally of Nayve during the Crusader War."

"Why don't you go talk to them," Jubal replied. "I'll stay

here with Awfulbark. But go quickly. It looks like we've got trouble on two sides now."

The druidess nodded. For hours now they had observed the vast marching columns of black-armored Delvers, with a few harpies wheeling protectively overhead. They had seen the ominous sight of the thirty great giants, iron-plated skin heavy and dark even under the bright sun. The whole army was marching on a bearing toward the Center, along the valley of a wide, shallow river.

The trolls and their two human companions had been following a ridge above that valley, taking a parallel course. They were moving quickly through a relatively open woodland, and by staying under the trees had avoided discovery by the occasional harpies winging overhead. The long-legged brutes were going faster than the Delvers, and now, reaching the front of that great army, had spotted the much smaller force of Seers.

The druid started down the hill at a trot. The sight of the bearded fighters filled her with hope. How well she remembered their staunch courage and inventive genius, both of which had made all the difference the last time war had menaced Nayve. She wondered about the fierce creatures that some of the dwarves were mounted on, realizing that they, too, looked like welcome allies, and were clearly under the control of their riders.

Only when she got closer did she see that there was a man with the dwarves, a dark-haired human who had spotted her approach and now waited with one of the mounted dwarves for her to come closer.

"Natac!" she cried, recognition bringing her into a run.

"Juli? Juliay!" he shouted back, racing out to sweep her into an embrace. "By the goddess, you're alive! We were certain you were lost with *Skyreaver!*"

"And you! I thought you perished with the ship!"

"No—and Owen's alive, too!" the warrior said, his expression joyful. "Sirien and Roland—we were teleported out! But the ship fell too fast. Quilene couldn't get you with her spell. Owen was devastated. Why, he'll be beyond joy to know that—"

"Let's talk about Owen later," she said quickly. Emotions of delight and confusion surged within her, but Juliay knew there was no time for explanations and introspection. She shook her head in an effort to clear it and was somehow not surprised at all to recognize Karkald as one of the Seers. In a burst she told them about the trolls, and their march on the track of the harpies. "But that army marching beyond you . . . Delver, isn't it?"

"Yes. Allied with the harpies, it seems."

"Awfulbark—he's the troll king—saw that, though those you see are only a tiny fraction of the group that burned his city. Still, that's part of what drew us in this direction. And did you know that you, and the Delvers, are marching in the same direction as the rest of the harpies flew?"

"The bridge!" Natac said immediately. "Sure, they're under the same command. They have the same objective! The harpies will get there faster than any of us."

"And what is *our* objective?" Karkald said, leaning over in his saddle. "Do we still need to hold up the Delvers?"

"More than ever," the human warrior declared. He looked at Juliay. "Exactly how friendly are these trolls? And do you think you could persuade them to dislike the Delvers as much as they seem to hate the harpies?"

NATAC was surprised as Juliay introduced him to another warrior from Earth, but he realized this was only one of a growing mound of surprises that would require later explanation.

"I lived in the place called Mexico," the Tlaxcalan said briefly. "But I was summoned to Nayve in the year called 1508 A.D."

Jubal's eyes widened at that, and he cast a glance at Juliay before straightening and bowing formally. "I had the honor to serve as a general in the army of the Confederate States of America."

"I have been studying your war," Natac said. "Later, I hope we have time for conversation."

"It would be my sincere pleasure," replied the former rebel with another bow.

Only then did it occur to Natac to wonder *how* Jubal had been summoned to Nayve. He looked sharply at Juliay, but her freckled skin looked as young, as beautiful as ever. Of course she couldn't have. . . . It was just another question that would have to wait until later.

Next, Natac met the troll king, recognizing the features of the brute he had "slain" in their first encounter. "Natac is Nayve's greatest warrior," Juliay said. "He is wise in the ways of killing harpies."

Though in fact he knew relatively little of harpies, Natac let the exaggeration pass without correction. Awfulbark proved surprisingly enthusiastic to Juliay's request, undoubtedly because he had grouped the harpies and the dark dwarves as a single, hated foe. Perhaps, too, he liked the notion of an enemy that did not fly away nor spit gobs of fire.

Moving quickly, the trolls and the Seer dwarves were deployed as Natac suggested. The Tlaxcalan took his place with the dwarven infantry, while Karkald commanded the Rockriders, and Jubal, Juliay, and the grim Awfulbark would try to rally the trolls. All but the riders were hidden, as Karkald's small force rode out to form a defensive position across the Delver's line of advance.

The enemy saw the deployment, but the great march didn't even hesitate. As Natac suspected, the Delvers sent the metal giants at the forefront of the attack. All thirty of the clunking behemoths formed a line and started forward at a rapid march. The army of Delvers, in three massive columns, each a hundred dwarves wide and more than a mile long, proceeded at a jog behind the golems.

Before them stood a pathetically thin line, for the only defenders in view were the fifty ferr'ells and their riders, arrayed in a line on the forward slope of a gentle incline. The Delvers had watched the rest of the dwarves march over that ridge a few minutes before; no doubt they hoped to swallow all of the Seer survivors in one vigorous attack.

But the plan made by the warrior of Tlaxcala and Nayve was not about to let that happen. Karkald and his riders played their role to perfection. Their mounts snorted and pawed the ground, reared high and paced through anxious circles, clearly spoiling for a fight. The giants moved faster, into a lumbering gait that sent shock waves resonating through the ground with each crushing footstep.

When they were a hundred paces away, the Rockriders slowly began to retreat, allowing the golems to close the distance ever so slightly, moving steadily upward, toward the crest of the ridge. The ferr'ells abruptly wheeled and trotted over the low elevation until they had dropped out of sight of the enemy force. Only Karkald stayed on the summit a little longer, watching.

In the face of this evasion, the golems picked up the pace of their pursuit, trotting along with booming footsteps. Their movements were remarkably manlike, with legs bending at the knees, hips, and ankles. But they held their arms, each with its multiple-weaponed hand, straight down at their sides, and kept those blank faces, each a plate of iron pierced by a single hole, turned resolutely straight ahead.

They came across the crest like a line of implacable monoliths and lumbered down the shallow reverse slope. The Rockriders still fell back, though here and there one or a group of the mounted dwarves would feint a charge. Even when they raced within a dozen paces of the giants, however, they did not provoke even a wavering of that steadily advancing formation. A few harpies cawed and shrieked overhead, but—probably remembering the deadly crossbows—made no move to dive at the dwarves.

The three massive Delver columns next came into sight over the crest, following the golems, still marching at a double-quick pace. The formations were so wide, each with a hundred squat dwarves advancing shoulder to shoulder, that they almost spanned the valley. They kept coming, like three rippling, armored snakes slithering forward across the ground, black and purposeful and very lethal.

When the tail ends of the three columns clumped over the low hilltop, the whole vast army was in view, stretched along a flat, grassy valley with a fringe of forest visible on the ridge to the left, and a rocky spine of ridge demarking the elevation on the right. Natac sprang to the top of a boulder on that ridge, raised a torch in the air, and swirled the burning brand around.

At the signal, the Seer infantry broke over the crest around him, five hundred dwarves in a single line, charging at the right flank of the long column. At the same time, more than a thousand trolls burst from the trees on the opposite side of the enemy army, roaring and barking, to sweep down upon the left of the marching dwarves.

Both attacks closed the short gap to the Delvers in moments, and soon the valley rang with the chaotic noise of combat—not the sharp squawk of a skirmish, but the deep, throaty roar of a real contest of arms. Natac was in the middle of the Seers, and he wielded his sword with the skill born of natural talent and hundreds of years of study. In the first clash, he killed three Delvers with quick stabs, then forged ahead into the enemy's broken ranks, bold Seers striving to either side of him.

Across the valley the trolls, too, attacked with vigor. At the first impact, the much taller minions of Awfulbark simply kicked the dwarves out of their path. They reached down to twist heads and break necks or to pick up squirming Delvers and hurl them into the faces and weapons of their fellows. Roaring and slashing, they turned all the force of their fury, their rage at the loss of their homes, against these diminutive foes.

At the same time, the Rockriders split up and circled around the golems, half of them harassing each of the Delver flank columns. Though the attackers were utterly outnumbered, the surprise of the onslaught and the concentrated force of the double punch was enough to savagely disrupt the once-steady advance.

Natac sensed that the Delvers had been thrown into real

confusion. The middle column came to a halt, still unengaged in the battle, incapable of coming to bear because of the masses of Delvers churning around the flank columns. The trailing troops of each embattled formation tried to advance, but on each side, the attackers detached some of their troops as a blocking force, a thin line of trolls or Seers fighting tenaciously, preventing the superior numbers of the enemy to flank the audacious onslaughts.

The attackers surged forward on every front, trolls rending the Delvers with fist and fang, Seers striking them down with steel, ferr'ells ripping into the enemy with cruel talons. Natac slew another faceless Delver and pressed on. Karkald, relying on the speed of his mount, led his Rockriders on another charge along the enemy line. And still the trolls pressed ahead, the wounded limping back from the fray, replaced by fresh and aggressive attackers.

Until shadows flickered across the field, and Natac looked up to a sky black with the presence of a thousand wicked, winged flyers. His heart sank, and he could only hope that his troops would be able to fall back to safety in time to survive.

"STRIKE them, kill them!" cried Zystyl, standing at the head of the center column. All around him, glorious combat raged, and he didn't even mind that he wasn't directly involved. Instead, he had found a large rock and scrambled onto the perch so that he could get a vantage of the field.

Of course, he knew it was a harassing attack, intended only to delay. There was no way this pathetic force, one or two thousand, could hope to defeat his great juggernaut. He sent his commands, mentally, across the field, urging the columns to try to flank the attackers, and he was frustrated by the enemy's maneuver to defeat those blows. But he exulted in the death, the blood that soaked into the ground in such great quantity, and he whipped his troops with psychic power, urging them to greater heights of violence.

And now the harpies had come, called back from the

bridge by the knowledge of danger, knowledge borne from Zystyl's dakali to the one carried by Vultari himself. The flyers came keening down from the sky, a thousand of them or more, slashing across the heads and upraised arms of the trolls, spitting fire onto the armored shoulders of the Seer dwarves. Several ferr'ells, bristling fur set alight, bounded in panic through the ranks of friend and foe alike.

Zystyl watched the trolls falter and then break for the woods, running helter-skelter, each gangly warrior thinking only to save himself. The harpies harassed them for a short distance, then wheeled back, content with the rout.

The Seer dwarves were made of sterner stuff, but even they couldn't stand against this kind of pressure. Their shields could protect them against the worst of the harpy attacks but could not counter Delver blades at the same time. So the dwarves of Axial, too, fell back, though they faced their enemy and still somehow made the Unmirrored pay for every foot of ground with a dozen lives.

But Zystyl found that he even enjoyed seeing his own men perish. Indeed, he was thrilled at the vista of horizons and landscape, of the terrain beneath his feet and the shifting movements of troops on the battlefield. Never had he understood the real glories of sight, and now, as the blessing of Karlath-Fayd somehow gave him these images within his eyeless head, he could not stop beholding the world.

His enemies were scattered now, and the road to their goal lay open. He saw the bridge clearly in his mind whenever he touched the Hurtstone at his breast. He knew the challenger, and he knew what they had to do to win.

"Onward, my loyal killers! Onward! To Sharnhome, and victory!"

20

The Bridge

Spanning worlds,
Binding lives;
Arching high,
And yawning deep

At Sharnhome stands
The focus
Of history and time.

From the Tapestry of the Worldweaver
Song of Shahkamon

Miradel sat astride the neck of the great dragon, too full of wonder even to notice her fear. Truly, they were very high above the ground, and the wind blew her long hair back in a streaming black pennant, but she could only look around in amazement and awe. The power of this mighty serpent, this magnificent capability of flight—surely Regillix Avatar alone would be enough to defend Nayve from all perils, so long as he shared their cause!

Just in front of her, perched like Miradel between two protrusions of the serpent's knobby spine, Quilene sat as still as a statue. Regillix Avatar's flight was surprisingly gentle, after the first violent leap that had hurled them off a hilltop and into the air. He had warned them of the shock, however, and both women had held tightly while they took off. Miradel's heart had nearly stopped as she watched the ground drop away below, but she never came close to falling off.

Now, in the lofty air, she could look back and see the Ringhills fading into the hazy distance. The serpent was moving terribly fast, covering in an hour spaces that would have taken them a day or more to walk. Looking forward again, she blinked away the wind tears that blurred her eyes and finally saw the shadowy gap in the vast plains.

"It's huge," she murmured.

She was certain her voice had been swept away in the wind, but Quilene turned and nodded in agreement. "A barrier in the world," she said, awestruck.

In a short time, the vast chasm of Riven Deep came fully into view. They saw the neat, fenced pastures of the Hyac, then the gaping lip on the edge where Shahkamon had been ripped away. The dragon lingered over that view, and Miradel could only wonder if he felt regret.

Soon thereafter he turned and, in accordance with the directions from Janitha and Sirien, followed the canyon metalward from the location of the ruined town. For two more hours they flew, at a speed Miradel could only try to imagine. Finally, they saw the blocky wedge of darkness jutting from the canyon's rim into the vastness of yawning space, concealing much of the Deep beyond.

"The black bluff!" she shouted, as the dragon nodded his head.

He dove, and the speed of the wind forced Miradel to lie almost flat against the wyrm's scaly shoulder, making her grateful for the knobby spine plate that kept her from sliding backward. They saw that the rim of the canyon swept outward here, that Riven Deep was narrower than at any place else they had seen. The depths of the chasm were still murky, lost in haze, but the far edge was close enough for individual ravines and gullies to stand out in clear relief.

Close to the ground at last, the serpent swept around the shoulder of the black bluff. They saw the slope, a gentle incline dropping down onto the first terrace inside the canyon.

To their right was that wide bend, concealing this place from observation from most of the rim.

And then they saw the bridge, a great span of natural stone arching from the terraced shelf on the center side of the canyon, across the gorge of the raging river, and merging with an outstretched lobe of rock on the far side. The surface was flat and smooth, as wide as five or six good highways running side by side. On the far side, a gentle slope led upward to the distant plateau. A solitary pillar, like a natural watchtower, stood just beyond the terminus of the bridge.

"What are those things?" shouted Miradel, as a great flock of shrieking creatures took to the air. They were scattered across the whole length of the span, and there looked to be many thousands of them. Then she remembered the harpies Belynda had described and knew that those flying scavengers had reached the bridge first.

Still, when she compared the power of the dragon to those feathered specks, she could only imagine that the harpies were doomed. It seemed clear they would have no more chance than gnats against a human.

"I will have to set you down," said Regillix, banking around, finally coming to rest on a bluff overlooking the near terminus of the natural bridge. "These are the harpies . . . bane of the Sixth Circle. I will see if I can drive them off, but you cannot ride then, or you will likely be burned."

The two women slid down from their scaly perch and found cover beneath an overhanging rock, where they could see the bridge and the approach on the far side of the canyon while remaining concealed from any harpies that might fly their way.

Regillix Avatar took to the air again in a prodigious leap that carried him far from the bluff. He drove his huge wings downward and dove. After a minute he leveled his flight, roared loudly, and flew a course along the top of the bridge, just a little way above the stone surface.

The harpies, in great, shrill clouds, took to the air, scattering out of the dragon's way. Many of them settled back to the bridge when he passed, but others closed around, spitting bits of fire that were visible to the women mainly as tiny threads of smoke. Regillix caught several harpies with sudden snaps of his jaws or swipes of his taloned forefeet, but many more escaped, shrieking insults at the wyrm's tail and insolently swarming after the serpent as he flew past.

Puffs of smoke darkened the air, and smoldering spots appeared on the great wings. The dragon curled about and flew back, but once again, the harpies only scattered out of his immediate path before reclaiming their perches on the span. This time, others pursued him more aggressively, several diving right onto the great pinions, tearing and burning at the leathery membranes. With another roar, the mighty wyrm dove away, flying far down in the canyon to evade his tormentors.

It was an hour later that he flew back to the bluff where Miradel and Quilene waited, approaching from the Center direction after making a circuitous return. Exhausted and scowling, he came to rest near Miradel and Quilene. His scales were marked with sooty spots, and in several places burns had singed holes right through his massive wings.

"Never have I seen them behave with such discipline," he growled. "They would have burned my wings off, had I not fled!" He sounded as if he found the very thought unthinkable and infuriating.

"It's because they are following orders, under the control of one who lies beyond the sea," Miradel said, her eyes narrowed, black hair blowing in the wind, as she stared in the direction that was neither metal nor wood.

"I must get out of sight," Regillix said. "Or I will surely draw them up here. I saw a lake several miles toward the Center. . . . It would do me good to soak my wings."

"Go ahead," Miradel said. "The harpies haven't seen us yet; we'll stay and keep watch."

With a nod and a snort, the dragon took off, diving well away from the bridge before winging over the plateau and out of sight.

Quilene had been sitting quietly, deep in thought. Now she spoke. "I am going to go on a hunt. Can you maintain the watch by yourself?"

"Yes," the druid replied. "But what are you hunting for?"

"For hope," said the sage-enchantress before trotting away along the rocky trail. Soon she disappeared behind a bend of the bluff.

FOR three days, the Seer dwarves and the trolls of Udderthud retreated before the advancing horde of dark dwarves. The golems and most of the harpies had disappeared, but Natac entertained no illusions. If the ragtag group of them tried to make a stand, the Delvers would not hesitate to deliver a lethal punch.

Not that the trolls would even have been capable of much resistance. Thoroughly cowed by the massed attack of the harpies, they trudged grimly along, gnarled faces turned downward. Some had fled back to ruined Udderthud after the first battle. The others looked longingly at the woods that continued to flourish off to the left of their march. Juliay and Jubal had used all of their persuasive powers to keep the king and most of his minions still marching forward.

"What do you know of what awaits us?" asked Jubal, as he and Natac walked side by side near the rear of the fleeing band. Only Karkald and a dozen Rockriders, a quarter mile behind, were between them and the fast-marching Delver army.

Natac described the bridge as best he could from Janitha's description. "It's the only span connecting this part of Nayve with the bulk of the world. You've seen the attacking force, though who knows how many of those harpies will be waiting for us. We'll have the help of a dragon and some elven cavalry, at first, and if we can hold out for a few days, we should get the aid of some batteries and a whole army of elves and gnomes."

"Are there others, like . . . us?" asked Jubal.

"There's Owen . . . He was a Viking, brought here I think

in the tenth or eleventh century of your calendar. Quite handy with a blade . . . as a matter of fact, that's his sword you're carrying."

The Southerner nodded. "Juliay told me . . . but she thought he was dead. I shall have to thank him. As I recall, he was on *Skyreaver,* as well?"

Natac nodded, looking at Juliay, who was walking beside Awfulbark some distance ahead of them. Again he wondered: Could she have cast the spell and somehow avoided the sacrifice, the aging that had claimed Miradel so immediately and inexorably? "Yes. Can I ask you . . . that is, how did *you* come to Nayve?"

Jubal's eyes narrowed. "That, sir, is a question that a gentleman cannot, in good conscience, answer."

"I understand," Natac replied quickly. At the same time, he acknowledged that he actually had more questions than ever. "I apologize. Please know that we are grateful to have you wielding a sword with us."

"No offense taken. And there seem to be plenty of wars to go around, don't there?" Jubal replied with a sigh.

An hour later, they came into view of the last descending slope. There before them was a smooth stretch of ground, leading downward, merging with the end of a long, narrow bridge. They saw the harpies darkening the span, as if it was covered with a layer of dirty feathers. To the left was a jaded pillar of stone, either an ancient and very weatherbeaten watchtower or a natural spire.

Near the tower, and of more immediate importance, they saw that the iron golems of the Delvers had gotten there before them. Now the grim giants blocked the bridge, standing shoulder to shoulder across the entrance to the span. The Delvers still came behind, and the Seers and the trolls were now stuck in the middle.

THE elven riders were weary, barely conscious after three days in the saddle. Yet they had stopped only for a few hours of rest, making the rest of the journey at a gallop. Janitha and Sirien rode in the lead, trailed by their fellow elves, with the herd of extra ponies galloping along in the rear. Most of the elves changed mounts several times during the grueling ride, but Janitha found that Skyrunner never faltered. Indeed, the pony kicked and protested jealously the one time the khandaughter started toward another mount, and so she had returned to the loyal stallion's back.

They were cantering along in file, knowing that they drew near to the black bluff, when the ponies neighed in fear and the elves shouted in alarm as a broad shape rose from a marsh beside them.

"You!" spat the khandaughter, recognizing the great wyrm. Her hand coiled around the comforting shape of the horn.

"Yes, I," replied Regillix Avatar. The great wedge of his head swung grimly back and forth. "Do you plan to smite me again with your horn?"

The elfwoman glared. She had seen this monster wreak terrible havoc, destroy her home, kill her father. Now she found that it took all of her willpower to even begin to think of it as an ally.

"No," she replied. "I have been told that there are other enemies more worthy of my fury. Have you seen them?"

"Yes," the dragon replied. "Harpies have claimed the bridge. The druid Miradel and enchantress Quilene are watching them. I have been waiting here for you. Now that you have come, I will accompany you to the bluff, and we will see what we can do."

Conscious of her elves muttering behind her, seeing Falri finger his spear as he stared at the serpent, Janitha nodded and urged Skyrunner to continue on. The dragon came on foot, staying far enough to the side that the nervous ponies didn't bolt.

Soon they came to the crest of the bluff, where they could see the bridge, and here they met Miradel. "Quilene left three days ago," the druidess said worriedly. "She said she was looking for something, something that would give us hope. But I expected her back long before now."

"What is happening on the bridge?" asked Sirien.

"The Seer dwarves have just come into view," Miradel explained. "There's a lot more of them than I thought. They've been reinforced, somehow. I imagine the Delvers are right behind, however, and the bridge is blocked by those black giants—you can see them from here—as well as the harpies. Still, if you can charge, and Regillix attacks from the air, Natac will no doubt urge the Seers to strike as well, and we'll hope they can win through."

"A simple plan, but sound," Janitha said. "Let's do it."

"Wait a moment, my friends," Quilene said, coming into view along the trail leading around the bluff. She had a bundle in her hands, about the size of a large rabbit. The sage enchantress hurried forward. "I had to search very far to find what I needed, but I think I was successful." Holding the leather-wrapped object in both hands, she raised it toward the dragon. "I have done a bit of studying in ancient texts that include lore of your kind. Perhaps you will do me the honor of swallowing this," she said. "It may burn a bit, but I believe it will help you in your battle."

The dragon's nostrils flared as he inhaled the scent of the thing. "Saltpeter . . . and salmon oil. And a touch of flint? I am surprised to find that one of your world would know of such an ancient compendium of ingredients."

"I will share my books with you, sometime," Quilene said. "These are elements that do not exist in your world, do they?"

"No," the dragon admitted. "Yet I knew them at first scent."

"Perhaps there was more connection between our circles in the past than anyone knows," the enchantress replied. "Would you care to give it a try?"

"Indeed. And thank you, lady elf." The wyrm's forked tongue slipped downward, coiled around the object, and flicked it into his great mouth. His eyes grew bright, and the long jaws curled into a tooth-baring grin.

The elven riders had gathered in a tight column on the path leading toward the bridge. They decided to charge ten abreast down the middle of the span, relying upon speed and shock to carry them through. Each elf carried a long spear, which they would wield lancelike, striking down any harpies that didn't get out of the way. The dragon would fly above, and together, they would strike the giants at the far end of the span.

Janitha raised the Horn of Lath-Anial to her lips, drew a deep breath, and leveled a blast into the canyon, along the length of the bridge that was mottled across its entire surface by the huddled forms of many thousands of harpies. The ponies of the elven riders started forward at a walk, quickly advancing into a trot, then breaking into a headlong gallop.

As the Hyaccan elves drew near to the bridge, she blew the horn again, and the harpies took wing. Some of the flyers, those nearest to the blast, fell stunned, vanishing into the Deep, while the others shrieked and cawed and fled.

Regillix Avatar took to the air again, a great pulse of his wings carrying him from the bluff. He tucked those wings and pointed his neck and tail, a lethal missile flying into battle, just above and behind the thundering band of cavalry.

"WE'VE got to charge—now!" Natac declared, glaring into the scowling face of the woody-skinned troll king.

"He's right," Jubal declared. "Just look. That cavalry is coming toward bridge! Spears glinting in the sun! Tight formation, thunderous speed—it's as magnificent a charge as I've ever seen! We hit those iron bastards in the front while the horses get them from behind, and we'll break through."

"No!" Awfulbark declared. "We stay. Trolls charge before, and we get burned, some even kilt."

"Look," Juliay said. She gestured to the army of Delvers, now arrayed behind them for a full-scale attack. "You can stay here, and you *will* get killed when those dwarves attack, or you can help us charge, and make it to the far side of the canyon."

Stubbornly, Awfulbark shook his head. "Go to woods, there. Find apples. No fight!"

Suddenly the druid was shouting at him. "What kind of a king are you?" she demanded. "Do you care if your people survive, or not? Do you want them to be killed by Delvers, or burned by harpies? Do you want to live on apples for the rest of your life, hiding from anything that flies over your head or walks through your woods?"

"Not want to be kilt by metal giants!" the troll retorted with a growl and a gesture at the golems who still stood, implacably blocking the way. "No. We go home. To Udderthud!"

"You're not a king at all!" the druid spat, as the trolls turned and trudged toward the forest. "You're a craven coward—that's all you are! You're weak and frightened and pathetic!"

Without looking back, the trolls hurried away, loping toward the woods. Awfulbark's head hung low as he led his tribe hurriedly through the narrowing gap between the Delvers and their golems.

"Good riddance," Natac muttered.

"Perhaps . . . still, I would have welcomed their help," Jubal said.

"Looks like it's our turn," Karkald said, riding up to the humans. Bloodeater pranced anxiously as the dwarf gestured to the bridge.

The slope down to the span was smooth, except for that tall pillar of stone just off to the side of the road. A ledge spiraled up the outside of that pillar, almost like the thread of a screw, and Natac wondered if, in fact, the pillar had at one point been some kind of watchtower.

Across Riven Deep, the horn brayed again, driving the harpies back, stunning still more of the creatures as the elven riders raced onto the wide, flat span. Other harpies shrieked in protest and flung themselves into the air, some skidding right down the edges to avoid the racing ponies. Those that were too slow were pierced by elven spears or kicked and trampled by the snorting steeds. And then a great, winged shape came into view.

"By all that's holy—it *is* a dragon!" Jubal said, as Karkald and his dwarves looked on in awe.

The serpent glided along above and behind the riders. Abruptly, Regillix veered to the side, diving past the bridge and approaching a great swarm of harpies wheeling in the air. The dragon turned its jaws upward, and a great burst of flame exploded forth, incinerating harpies by the dozens. The cloud of fire and smoke lingered in the air as Regillix Avatar dove past, and the shrill cries of the harpies reached a new level of intensity.

"I didn't know he could do that," Natac declared, awe-struck.

The riders continued their charge, sweeping the bridge clean of harpies, racing toward the iron golems who stood still, backs to the elves as they continued to face the dwarves. The charge was halfway across by now, and it was time for the dwarves to advance.

"They'll be smashed against that iron," Natac said, picturing Sirien and Janitha bearing frail wooden spears, coming up hard against the golems. "Let's go!"

With the Rockriders in the lead, the Seer dwarves charged down the ramping slope toward the barrier of golems standing shoulder to shoulder across their path. Natac, Jubal, and Juliay charged with the dwarven infantry, a great surge rushing at the implacable wall of iron.

A ferr'ell hurled itself at a golem, clawing up the legs and torso while the howling Seer rider bashed at the thing with a heavy hammer. Sparks flew, and the giant actually staggered a step, until a sweeping punch knocked mount and rider into space, sent them tumbling into Riven Deep.

Dwarves swarmed around the golems, chopping, pounding, hacking. Many fell, crushed or wounded, but the rest didn't falter. With a crashing of spears and hooves, the elven charge smashed into the rear of the line of metal. The ponies pitched and kicked and reared, and even then the metal giants didn't turn, instead standing grim and immobile above the melee.

Regillix Avatar came into view, still flying strongly, climbing from below the bridge, angling to sweep into the golems from the flank. Only then did the metal automatons react. Several spun to face the great wyrm, raising their arms straight forward, as if in some kind of bizarre salute. Natac, falling back with the dwarves for a brief respite, watched and prayed.

The dragon roared, diving closer, and in that instant, the arms exploded off of the four nearest golems' shoulders. Trailing smoke, the limbs sped like rockets, each tipped with a wicked array of blades and spikes. One tumbled away, out of control, and two whipped past the great dragon's wings.

But another smashed into that huge, scaled breast, and several ripped through the membranes of the broad pinions. With a bellow of pain and rage, the great serpent spun away, falling into the chasm, torn wings flailing helplessly as he quickly vanished into the mists that swirled below. With his last glance of the serpentine ally, Natac saw the dragon plummet downward, with little or no control of his flight.

Again the dwarves surged forward, utterly desperate now. Natac and Jubal bashed at the ankles, the hinged knees of the nearest giant. The golem kicked, a glancing blow that sent the Tlaxcalan tumbling. In that instant, a small gap opened in the line, and Jubal took Juliay's hand in a firm grip and hurled her through the opening.

"Run!" he shouted, as she cried out in protest. "Please—get away!"

She hesitated, but it was clear that the golems were steadily, inexorably pushing the Seers back. Finally, she turned and sprinted to the elven riders, where Sirien reached down and pulled her onto the back of a pony. As the Hyaccan elves retreated, the giants advanced, and the Seers were pushed back from the end of the bridge. The way was blocked, and Karkald's dwarves could only retreat, or die.

Natac looked up to see the Delvers sweeping closer, a front

a thousand wide and countless troops deep. They roared and ran, banging weapons and armor, raising a nightmarish din. The very ground shuddered from the force of the massive charge.

"The tower!" cried Natac. "It's our only chance. Up the ledge! Everyone!"

With grim speed but no sign of panic, the Seers broke for the pillar, scrambling up the ramp that sloped up from the ground level. The golems pursued, but only until the mass of Delvers got in the way. The metallic giants halted to avoid crushing their own allies, and the rest of the Seers managed to get up off the ground before their hated enemies cut them off. Led by the infantry, the retreating dwarves followed the curving ledge higher and higher up the tower.

Natac and Jubal, with Karkald on Bloodeater beside them, stood shoulder to shoulder at the lowest terminus of that ramp. Delvers closed in like the storm surge of an angry sea, but the trio of warriors and the savage steed blocked all access up the ledge. They fought like maniacs, swords chopping relentlessly, piling slain Delvers in a heap on the ground, until finally, the enemy fell back. The defenders made their way a little higher and settled down to wait.

"Go!" shrieked Zystyl, sending mental flails across the backs of his charging troops. "Take them! Fight to the bridge! Smash them against the golems!"

The need to attack was a compulsion, a screaming lust within him, and he was merciless in lashing his underlings to the task. Even Jarristal stumbled ahead, the arcane just another foot soldier in the great surge toward the goal.

But finally the killing was just too much, and Zystyl's exhausted minions could no longer continue. The Delvers pressed around the pillar, insuring that there was no escape for the four hundred or so Seers trapped there. Next, Zystyl sent his golems in to attack, but three of them were smashed by great rocks dropped from above, and he called them back.

Harpies wheeled through the sky, screeching around the lofty spire but apparently unwilling to attack. Their leader, Zystyl saw, plunged into the abyss after the falling dragon, accompanied by hundreds of his keening followers. The rest, after many had been slain by Seer crossbows, showed no willingness to press home the attack against the dwarves trapped on the pillar of rock.

"My lord!" It was Jarristal, her steel jaws twisted into a triumphant grin. "What matter if we kill them now? They are trapped. They will soon starve, for they cannot get down, cannot escape."

"True," agreed Zystyl. He had little patience for such a tactic but was forced to acknowledge its efficacy.

"Should we not send the bulk of the army across the bridge?" asked the female arcane. "We could leave troops here, ten thousand or more, to insure that the Seers do not escape. The rest can march toward the center and make a camp on the far side of the bridge. Thus we will hold all the span!"

Zystyl looked across that gulf of space and considered. He saw the elven riders over there, and he didn't know what other surprises his enemies had in store, so he shook his head. "No. The harpies hold the road again, and the golems block the entrance. The bridge is safe. We will stay here until the Seers are dealt with. Then we can cross in all our strength and glory."

He studied Jarristal, sensed that she might want to argue with him, but a wet sniff flared his nostrils in warning, and she bowed humbly.

"As you command, Lord Zystyl," she said quietly. He sent out a mental probe, worried about her sincerity, but in the chaos of the battlefield, he could not discern her thoughts.

REGILLIX Avatar clung to the side of the precipice, the great cliff plummeting into the unimaginable abyss of Riven Deep. His wings were torn, shredded by the missiles of the golems until they were useless for flight, and it had taken all of his strength just to bring himself close enough to the wall to catch hold. Pain tore through his body, and he was bleeding badly where one of the missiles had rent his flank.

He heard a screaming caw and saw a cluster of harpies wheeling down toward him, shrieking in triumph. They were led by the largest of the creatures he had ever seen, a ghastly monster wearing a sparkling gem upon its breast. The dragon snorted, instinctive hatred welling up, augmented by fury at his predicament.

The harpies settled upon rocks and other protrusions above the wyrm and began to spit, sending pellets of fire raining downward to spatter off the rocks, or his wings, or the scales of his skin. Oily gobbets trickled down the cliff, sending clouds of stinking smoke around him, stinging his eyes and nostrils.

Grimly, the ancient wyrm held on. He tasted heat, the magical pellet that Quilene had given him, and he wondered how the elfwoman had known of such an ancient power. He was grateful, in any event. Turning his face upward, he braved the little spats of fire that slapped against his nostrils, even came dangerously close to his eyes. He opened his mouth, felt the pressure well up within, and roared.

The blossom of fire that exploded swelled into a great, hellish cloud, oily flame scouring the cliff, billowing into the air, enclosing nearly all of the harpies in its lethal sphere. Those that survived squawked and dove away, panicked into utter flight. The rest tumbled, charred and lifeless, into the Deep. Among those slain, he saw, was that great leader, the once-sparkling gem now charred and black against its breast.

Finally, Regillix called upon every reserve of his strength. His wings hung limply, too charred and torn for flight. So he used his feet, clutching to a thin ledge with his taloned forepaw, pulling himself up a few feet, then gasping for breath.

In this slow, torturous fashion, he began to climb.

"JULIAY?" She heard her name after she dismounted from the pony, amid the elves who had fallen back from the bridge.

"Miradel?" The two druids stared at each other in wonder, then embraced, a hug of shared joy and grief. "Natac told me that you were alive, in Nayve! Now he's over there! He's trapped," Juliay said with a moan. "He and Jubal pushed me through the line, saved me."

"Jubal . . . who is he?"

That night, around a small fire, Juliay told her old friend about casting the Spell of Summoning. The proof of the result was plain to them both, and she offered her best guess of an explanation.

"Do you think it was the water in that stream?" Miradel asked.

"It's the only thing I can think of. If we get back to the Center and the temple, we'll have to study the Tapestry, see if we can learn more. But I think that was it."

"I agree. If you're right, this might be very important—the key to something the goddess herself wanted to learn."

But for now, they watched and waited. For several days, the two druids remained camped with the elven riders and Quilene. They could see the pillar where their warriors were trapped, with the company of Seers, but with thousands of Delvers now camped around the base of the pillar, there was no way to even begin to effect a rescue. At least the Delvers showed no inclination to march across the bridge, to press the attack into Nayve.

Even when they looked at the two lumpy rocks, the components of Socrates's bomb, the druidesses could think of no tactic that would help. Still, they tried to think and to plan and to hope that the troops from Circle at Center would arrive in time. They were in the midst of such a discussion when they heard the rumbling of wheels and looked up to see that Gallupper and the centaurs were coming up, towing the twelve batteries. Beyond was a column of elves and gnomes, the vanguard of the army of Nayve. A great, bearded warrior strode among them.

"Owen!" Juliay stood and called to him.

"Juli—they told me you were alive! I refused to believe,

but now I see!" his voice cracked with joy, and he swept her into his arms. "The rest of the army is a day or two behind, but I came with the centaurs, as fast as I could."

She returned his embrace, then pulled back. "I need to talk to you."

"What is it?" the Viking asked.

The two went into the darkness and spoke for a long time. They were still talking as the sun began to drop, and Riven Deep again welcomed a new day.

Across the canyon, things began to move.

AWFULBARK munched on an apple, but the fruit was soft and unsatisfying. It looked good but tasted rotten. Angrily, he swatted Rumblegut, who was plucking from the same tree.

"Ow!" whimpered the other troll, falling down and crawling away.

How pathetic, sneered the king . . . to simply crawl away, merely because of a challenge. In that instant, he hated Rumblegut, hated Roodcleaver, and all of these trolls. . . .

Even hated himself.

He thought of the strange humans, of the bold way they had stood against harpies, shooting arrows to aid the trolls, even when all Awfulbark had wanted to do was to kill and eat them. Then, at Riven Deep, he had watched from the safety of the woods as the dwarves made their futile charge against the iron golems, thinking that they were foolish in their bravery. But oh! How brave they had been. He knew they were trapped on that tower, now. He had seen them driven there before he turned to lead his trolls back into the woods. The dwarves were trapped, and they were doomed, and they were fools!

He should have been happy. He was King of Udderthud! And even if the city was gone, he was king of all these trolls, their leader . . . he would show them . . . what? He tried to forget what the woman, the insolent human druid, had said. What kind of king was he, she dared to ask? A bold king! A great king!

"How you think?" asked Roodcleaver. She, too, was ill-tempered, and for two days had done nothing but complain about the fact that apples were inadequate fare.

"I think . . . I think I *great* king!" Most vividly, he remembered Juliay's shouting at him as he led his trolls away. Never would he have thought that mere words could sting so much. Yet now, two days later, they still gnawed at him, churned around in his mind, prevented him from sleeping. In fact, they hurt worse now than they had when she shouted them.

In the end, he could think of only one thing to do. He didn't *want* to do it; in fact, that course of action frightened him almost beyond comprehension. But those words gnawed at him so much that he had to do it.

"Come, you trolls!" he barked suddenly, standing up. "Come with king!"

"Where go?" asked Wartbelly, moping beside a pile of apple cores.

"We go—make war! Kill Delver Dwarves! Kill harpies! Show how trolls can fight!"

FOR three days, the Seers and the two human warriors remained trapped on the tower. There was little room on the ledge, so they were cramped tightly together. Lacking wood, they could build no fires, nor did they have any level ground on which to rest. It seemed clear that the Delvers were going to starve them out, and the poorly provisioned defenders had to acknowledge that it wouldn't take very long to accomplish this. By the Hour of Darken on the third day, they finished the last of their water, and they knew the end was near.

Natac spent much time examining the enemy deployments below. He was grateful that the Delvers hadn't moved to establish a bridgehead on the other side of the Deep, and it was his sincere hope that Gallupper, Tamarwind, Owen, and the army of Nayve would arrive in time to hold the bridge.

But he was far less optimistic about their own chances for survival. Even though there were only half as many golems as before posted across the end of the bridge, there were at least ten thousand Delvers in the immediate vicinity of the base of the tower. As Lighten began to break, he looked toward the other rim of the Deep, seaching for some sign of hope, of the army from the Center, until he was attracted by a shout.

"It's the trolls!" cried a dwarf. "They're attacking the Delver camp!"

Natac watched in disbelief. The gangly creatures had come down from their woods, and now they loped out of the fading darkness, racing through the Delver camp, tearing apart dwarven formations and the dwarves themselves. Howling, barking, and whooping, they pressed onward, swarming toward the base of the tower, making a path toward the end of the bridge

"Let's go!" cried Natac. He and Jubal drew their swords and rushed down the sloping ledge. In seconds, all the Seers were racing to attack, joining the trolls, slaughtering the stunned Delvers in their bivouacs. They spilled off the curving ramp and raced toward the bridge, scattering the startled Unmirrored who could only muster a disorganized response. Ahead, those fifteen golems loomed, and even if they would merely smash themselves against the metal giants, Natac was grateful that he could once again feel the ecstasy of a wild charge before he perished.

The golems stood in a line. The dwarves and trolls rushed closer, breaking from the wreckage of the Delver camp, leaving their enemies cursing and shrieking in rage. Abruptly, a large, crocodilian head rose from the abyss below the span. Regillix Avatar was there, clinging to the cliff. He spread his jaws, and a blossom of flame erupted, engulfing the iron warriors. Half of the golems were blasted right off the bridge, and the others staggered and fell, smoking.

In the next instant, the Seers and trolls swept onto the bridge, with the dragon climbing up behind them. They raced across in a frantic rush, scattering the harpies that had settled all across the span.

A few minutes later, they had reached the safety of the

other side, but already the Delvers were massing, a great river of black armor spilling onto the bridge. They came on in a dark tide, with the surviving iron golems in the lead, marching four abreast.

As the attack drew closer, Gallupper's batteries opened up, casting spheres of metal into the mass of dwarves, balls that exploded into white fire. The missiles bounced off the golems, and killed multitudes of Delvers with their fiery heat. But there were too many dwarves, and they were coming too fast. The artillery would not be enough to stop them. Natac looked for help, but saw that the rest of the army had not arrived yet.

The elven riders moved into position, and the batteries kept up their steady fire, but the black tide drew closer, swelling angrily, unstoppable.

But one man stood at the end of the bridge and strode forward, alone, to face that horde. "For Odin!" he cried, in a voice like the roar of a lion. "And to Valhalla!"

He was Owen Viking, and in his hands were two rocks, like gray lumps of lead.

THE explosion was an instantaneous flare of white light, blinding all who were looking. The noise and heat came next, and then the shock that ripped through the bridge, sending the stone span, the golems, and ten thousand Delvers plunging into Riven Deep. The concussion echoed from the canyon walls, thrumming through the ground, and swelling in a cloud of dust that rose high into the sky.

Miradel found Natac standing with the defenders near the smoldering end of the bridge. Smoke drifted through the canyon, smudging the sky and the landscape as pieces of rock broke away and continued to fall. The Tlaxalan was covered with blood but unwounded. He looked at her with consummate weariness, and just the hint of a smile.

"Owen stopped them," he said quietly.

"And you came back to me," she whispered, taking both of

his hands in hers. They looked into each other's eyes, and neither could find words to say.

"What will we do when the tide of darkness comes, the
shades of the Deathlord land?" she asked finally.

"Then, once again, we'll fight. Owen bought us time to
prepare, and Riven Deep stands as a barrier before the
Center."

Nearby, Juliay sobbed, then said something to Jubal, who
held her tenderly. The man looked into the space where the
bridge had been, and his own eyes were wet with tears.

"That was Owen Viking? I wish I could have met him," he
said.

Book One of the Seven Circles trilogy

CIRCLE AT CENTER
by
Douglas Niles

In the realm of the Seven Circles,
a peaceful era is about to end as members of the
various races ban together to incite war.
To protect the land, the Druids decide to recruit
warriors from a world where war is a way of
life—a world called Earth.

❏ 0-441-00960-3

"Absolutely nobody builds a more convincing
fantasy realm than Doug Niles."
—R.A. Salvatore

Available wherever books are sold or
to order call 1-800-788-6262